London-reared of Irish parents, Kate Kerrigan worked in London before moving to Ireland in 1990. Her books have been widely acclaimed – *Recipes for a Perfect Marriage* was shortlisted for the Romantic Novelist of the Year Award and *Ellis Island* was a TV Book Club Summer Read. She is now a full-time writer and lives in County Mayo with her husband and sons.

Praise for Kate Kerrigan

'This story is written with so much heart . . . ' Cecelia Ahern

'With echoes of *Angela's Ashes* and even *The Notebook* . . . *Ellis Island* is a feel-good story about love, freedom, belonging and the meaning of home' *Stylist*

'An enjoyable romantic tale that you'll want to devour in one sitting' *SHE Magazine*

'A moving portrait of love and marriage through the eyes of two women . . . the author looks closely at love as a romantic ideal and poses the question: Can a woman learn true love?' *Sunday Express S Magazine*

'An intelligent, droll and heart-warming read . . . Kerrigan is a lovely writer and her book breaks from the traditional mould of chick-lit' *Sunday Tribune* (Ireland)

'This book is one to keep. Anyone who reads it will return to it, time and again, either for the story or to seek out one of the many old recipes' *Ireland on Sunday*

'Both wholesome and satisfying' *Heat*

Also by Kate Kerrigan

Recipes for a Perfect Marriage
The Miracle of Grace
Ellis Island
City of Hope

LAND OF DREAMS

KATE KERRIGAN

MACMILLAN

First published 2013 by Macmillan
an imprint of Pan Macmillan, a division of Macmillan Publishers Limited
Pan Macmillan, 20 New Wharf Road, London N1 9RR
Basingstoke and Oxford
Associated companies throughout the world
www.panmacmillan.com

ISBN 978-1-4472-1079-5

Typeset by Ellipsis Digital Limited, Glasgow
Printed and bound by CPI Group (UK) Ltd, Croydon, CR0 4YY

Visit www.panmacmillan.com to read more about all our books
and to buy them. You will also find features, author interviews and
news of any author events, and you can sign up for e-newsletters
so that you're always first to hear about our new releases.

For Leo and Tommo

PROLOGUE

It was a mysterious day on Fire Island.

The visitors of high summer were gone and the beach at the end of the walkway to our cabin was entirely empty. It was hard to believe that this thin strip of barrier land off the Long Island shore was less than two hours' drive from the teeming chaos of New York City, followed by a short ferry ride. Although the air was still warm and the sky a sharp blue, I could sense autumn in the swell of the sea. There was no wind to speak of and the white sand along the edge of the beach was as soft and warm as a wool carpet – yet the waves seemed uncharacteristically high. They lumbered towards the shoreline like an advancing battalion of old, slow soldiers. The grey hills kept coming – bloated by an invisible wind, rising into fat mounds, line after line of them until, with a gasp of shock, they shuddered into pathetic sandy bubbles on the shoreline.

I sat and watched them for a while, contemplating their rhythmic symmetry, trying to picture in my mind's eye how I might paint them, when I was interrupted by Tom, who had been playing in the dunes behind me. A brown bobtail rabbit rushed past my eyeline and in its pursuit was my raven-haired seven-year-old son.

'Damn!' he shouted.

'Don't say "damn",' I said in the admonishing tone I reserved exclusively for him. Tom was so different from his older brother. Leo was serious and beautiful, but remained something of a mystery to me. Tom was an open book – stocky and lively and inquisitive. He looked at me, then pursed his lips and shook his head in frustration as if holding the bad word inside and bouncing it around his head. I struggled to keep myself from laughing. His dark curls were sun-dyed red at their tips after a hot summer at the beach, his cheeky round face littered with freckles. A true child of nature, he was barefoot and dressed in just a pair of torn trousers. *He's entirely unsuited for the civilized world*, I thought, *just like me*! I was flooded with love.

'Gotcha!'

Briefly cornered at the shoreline, the rabbit had stopped for a moment to contemplate its options. Which was the more dangerous: chancing a few hops into the sea and risk drowning, or putting himself in the hands of the raven-haired bounder who had doggedly been pursuing him for weeks? While the rabbit made up its mind, my son suddenly threw himself on the creature in an alarmingly quick and somewhat feral movement.

'Mammy! Help me!' he called as the fluffy bundle flattened itself underneath him, threatening to wriggle out from under his torso.

I ran across to him in three long strides, my feet struggling to grip the sand.

'Don't move Tom,' I said, as I slid my hands under my son's chest. I quickly took the bunny's two ankles in one hand, just as it was burrowing an easy escape route through the soft ground.

'Now get up slowly, *slowly now* . . . ' I told Tom. 'Back there now, easy, easy.'

As my son moved his body aside, lifting each limb individually with comic stealth, I scooped up the bunny with my free hand and held it firmly to my chest. The poor creature was quivering with fear, its ears flattened, playing dead in my arms – as if pretending to be no more than a tan-coloured fur muff that I might forget about and cast aside.

'Come on,' I said, 'let's go back to the house and get some breakfast.'

As we walked towards our cabin, Tom swung his arms like a soldier; he was strutting with pride at having finally caught the rabbit he'd been chasing these past few weeks. He nodded his head up and down the deserted beach, as if acknowledging the cheers of an invisible audience.

When we passed the sand dunes at the back of our house I crouched down so that Tom and I were eye-to-eye. The rabbit was a hot, silent bundle in my lap; a terrified prisoner.

'Do you want to stroke it?' I asked.

Tom put his small, slim fingers into a bunch and stroked the bunny's forehead; its eyes half-opened in an all-forgiving ecstasy.

I looked at my son's face and it was pure joy; untainted with pain, unsullied by corruption – full of childish expectation that this feeling of total happiness was his right and would last forever. He had what he wanted now; had finally captured what he had been chasing.

'Thanks, Mam,' he said, 'for helping me catch it.'

My heart opened up and snatched the compliment. The more he grew away from me, the greedier I became for the affection of my miniature man – my own maneen, as we called such sons back home in Ireland.

'He's so soft, Mammy, I love him. I'm going to love him forever.'

A dark cloud moved over the blue sky ahead, and fat drops of rain fell into the sand beside us. Tom put his hand on the rabbit's head as a makeshift hat, then turned his face skywards in an uncertain grimace, opening his mouth wide to catch the raindrops.

I wanted, in that moment, to indulge him, to give myself over to the mawkish instincts of my love for my baby son, but I knew I had to do the right thing.

I lifted the rabbit from my lap and put it on the sand in front of us. It sat quietly for a moment, unsure that it was really being let go.

'What are you doing?' Tom asked, his hands reaching out for the animal.

I put my arms round his waist and held onto him, saying, 'The rabbit doesn't belong with us, Tom. It's wild – it needs to go home to its own mammy. It needs to be free.'

'But I love him,' he said, his face collapsing.

'I know you do,' I said, 'but the rabbit won't be happy living with us, and you want him to be happy, don't you?'

He looked at me uncertainly, struggling to weigh up the rabbit's well-being against his own desires.

'We have to let him go,' I said, as the animal leapt forward and disappeared into the dunes in one square hop.

Tom broke away and ran towards the house sobbing. 'I hate you! I hate you!' he cried.

I followed behind him, regretting that life lessons were always so hard-learned, and wondering if I should have let him cherish his dream a little longer.

Part One:

Fire Island,
Long Island Shore,
New York
1942

CHAPTER ONE

I stood back and looked at the painting. It was a four-foot by six-foot landscape of the dunes in muted grey colours, a barely discernible figure approaching from the distance – little more than a smear – representing the mereness of humans against the magnitude of nature.

It wasn't my best work. It was a commission from a wealthy industrialist with Irish parentage, who was spending his money for the sentimentality of investing in an Irish artist, more than for loving the art itself, so I wasn't going to agonize over it for days.

I rubbed my hands together, before poking at the left-hand corner to check that it was dry enough to transport. The studio was cold and, despite having run the gas heater for an hour before going in to start work, the air had the bit of ice to it.

It was late October, but already vague icy patterns were forming on the inside of the small glass windows.

'You're crazy staying out there all winter,' Hilla, my art bene-factor, had said, 'you'll freeze. Think of the children,' she went on, as a last desperate attempt to talk me into going back to Manhattan and the round of society functions and art-world parties she was always dragging me along to.

I smiled when she said it. Hilla didn't give a damn about my physical well-being; or, indeed, my children. Hilla just cared about art – Non-Objective Painting, to be exact – but she liked me well enough to make an exception for my Abstract Impressionist landscapes. Mostly she missed me as a friend – and that was one reason why I didn't want to return to the city. I was tired of the endless round of 'doing' and being with other people that, as my benefactor, she dragged me into.

As a young woman I had relished and craved the social buzz of life in Manhattan. The glamour and freedom here had helped me escape the cloying Catholicism of my poor Irish upbringing – I thought of New York as my 'City of Hope'.

At forty-two, and after eight years living back here full-time, the novelty of its social whirl had worn off and I longed only for solitude and quiet in which to paint.

'You'll starve,' she finally conceded, but we both knew that wasn't true. My work was popular enough and I had already been paraded about New York society, had fraternized with her friends the Guggenheims and their like, as 'Hilla's new find, darling: Eileen Hogan – she's Irish.'

'Irish? An Irish artist? How unusual!'

How collectible, it turned out. German Abstract Impressionism was old hat at this stage. Irish Abstract art? As far as I could gather, we were few and far between. I liked to think that my work was popular because it was beautiful, serene and dense with colour and meaning. I had started painting as a hobby to please myself, in an effort to recapture something of what I missed of Ireland. I was happy with my life in New York, the vibrancy, the people, the anonymity – but I missed the beauty of my homeland. Postcards and photographs could not express the mixed emotions I felt in memorizing what I missed of the green fields and the crisp air; the soft mist of an autumn morning as it seemed to seep up from the purple bog. So I spread the images as they appeared in my head onto canvas with a paint-brush, daubing dots and lines of colour, trying to recapture my past. I tried to believe it was the work itself that earned my success, but there was an element of novelty around me too. Collectors coveted the unusual and I was not only an Irish Abstract painter living in New York – but a female to boot. There were one or two notable Irish female artists that I knew of because of Hilla's contacts in Europe, who were constantly on the lookout. The furniture designer Eileen Gray, a woman called Evie who worked in stained glass, and 'Mainie Jellett' – a 'fine painter: an original artist', whom Hilla kept threatening to bring over to New York and give my crown to. While I had no intention of giving in to Hilla, I understood that much of her bullying had to do with fear.

Germans were not popular since the war had broken out in Europe, and although Hilla was an artist and argued her lack of bourgeois values, she was, after all, from German aristocratic stock and was surely frightened of losing both her social standing and the good income that her relationship with Solomon Guggenheim – as his art curator – had afforded her. Her tenuous hold on charm was also, I suspected, due to a poisonous and painful relationship with another German artist – Rudolph Bauer – an egocentric fool (and mediocre artist, in my opinion) who undermined her at every turn. Hilla was one of the most powerful people on the New York art scene, but she was a gruff, opinionated person, and was not always easy to like. She had needed a friend when we met, more than she had needed another artist to 'mind'. It might have seemed to her, and to others, that I had given her my friendship in return for her patronage, but that truly wasn't the case. I had earned my own money through working hard and being wily in business all my life – I became an artist because art fed my soul. I had other means by which

9

to feed my body. I had willingly given Hilla my friendship because I knew what it felt like to be an alien in another country. We Irish had always been underdogs, and I recognized her carefully hidden stance of being both awkward and proud of her background, at a time when it was very uncomfortable to be German in America.

I had a habit of looking beneath the obviously unfavourable in a person to the vulnerable human who lay beneath the skin. I was good with other people, but I had come to realize that was not necessarily an asset when it came to pleasing myself.

However, in one sense Hilla was right: it was too cold out here at this time of the year to work with oils. The paint needed heat to help it dry quickly – but even then, my work had to be handled extremely carefully for up to a year.

Leonardo da Vinci said, 'Art is never finished, only abandoned', and never was this more true than when working with oils, where one could scrape off and start again months after 'finishing' a piece of work. 'Abandoned' was such a cruel word that I preferred to call it 'letting go'.

In any case, I was ready to let go of this landscape.

I took it down from the easel and placed it on the large sheet I had laid out on the floor, so that the painting was facing up towards me. I could not risk letting the fabric touch the canvas as yet, and had devised a way of wrapping my canvases for transportation to avoid damage. I never painted to the edge of the canvas, but always left a two-inch margin, onto which I placed narrow wooden slats that I carefully screwed into place with the narrowest, shortest screws that would hold it. On top of these I glued two more slats diagonally across, then finally a layer of cardboard pinned on with thumbtacks, before wrapping it all in a cotton sheet.

I had been nervous that my opulent wrapping would make

it seem that I was churning my work out with such speed that I didn't allow it time to dry before cashing the cheque. However, my agent assured me that the reverse was true. The bare margins and four pin-marks had become my 'trademark' – as distinctive as a signature – and the theatre of unwrapping my pieces (carefully unpinning the cardboard, unscrewing the pins and, finally, removing the wooden slats) gave a sense of drama and suspense to the proceeding, which was so unique that my clients now enjoyed it as part of the process.

'The unveiling' of an Eileen Hogan was almost as important as the work itself. Such was the nature of the New York art scene that my extensive packing had assumed a deliberate artistic eccentricity more than a practical necessity. I had spent the vast majority of my life working at practical things – farming, housekeeping and business – before entering the whimsical, self-indulgent profession of an artist. Few artists were women at that time, fewer again were mothers like me (none that I knew of, at least), so the idea that I would feign eccentricity amused me greatly, especially when my agent asked me to wrap all my work in this way, regardless of whether it needed it or not. It was to perpetuate the uniqueness of my Irish heritage that Hilla insisted that I continue to work under my first husband's name – Hogan – rather than allow me to adopt Irvington, after I married my second husband, Charles.

I went over to the large wooden cupboard where I kept my supplies and tugged at the swollen drawer. I was out of string. Damn! The shop on the island was poorly stocked at this time of year. Most of the inhabitants of Fire Island were already back in their homes on the mainland, where I knew I should be. Maureen and Bridie, my old friends in Yonkers who ran the homeless community I had helped fund during the Great Depression, wrote every week with news and were, I knew, longing to see me. The apartment in Manhattan, after all the trouble I had gone to, creating an elegant home for me and the boys, lay empty.

Fire Island had been my summer retreat for the past four years, but this year I didn't want to leave it, even though I knew it would be a harsh place to spend the winter. Something inside me had shifted that summer. I was tired. I just wanted to be alone – and Fire Island in winter was as remote as the Himalayas. Unfortunately, it seemed, it was also as cold. Nonetheless, this wooden cabin and studio was my haven; the place where I felt most at ease, where I could be alone with my sons and my art, with nothing to distract or bother me. On Fire Island, life stopped and I didn't feel ready for my life to start up again.

So much had happened to me, so much kept happening, that I could not help but think that I was bringing much of it on myself.

All I wanted now was a simple life that would enable my boys to flourish and me to create meaningful art.

Fire Island was the perfect place for me to hide away, physically and socially, from my hectic life. We were a small community of artists and eccentrics burrowing our simple wooden summerhouses into the dunes. Cherry Grove was the most settled of the Fire Island communities: a tiny village huddled around the dock, with a post office, a hotel and little else. I had bought my tumbledown house and plot for very little and had renovated it more or less myself. My first husband, John, whose death in Ireland had precipitated my move to America, had been a skilled carpenter – and I knew how to cut wood and handle a hammer as well as any man. The village had built up over the years into a network of wooden buildings. Most of us preferred simple two-storey houses behind the sand dunes that ran either side of this long, narrow strip of barrier-island off the Long

Island coast. Although we were less than two hours from the city, Fire Island had the remote air of a forgotten land.

During the summer our beaches were busy with holiday-makers, although the crowd who came here were almost entirely bohemian, mostly artists and writers. We creative types prided ourselves on always finding the most beautiful and interesting places to inhabit. Cherry Grove was also a hub of social activity for homosexuals and lesbians. The bohemian lifestyle provided sanctuary for people who could no longer endure the convention of hiding their preferences. Fire Island allowed them to live an alternative lifestyle – at least during the summer months and weekends. My nearest neighbour was a wealthy socialite who lived here with her much younger female lover during July, August and September each year. Her husband was content to have his wife do as she pleased during her summer vacation, as long as she maintained her loyalty to him in front of their peers, so for the majority of the year they attended functions and smiled for the press cameras and nobody was any the wiser. There was a code of secrecy and a respect for privacy on Fire Island that made it, for me, the perfect place to live. So even though we were, in many ways, a small close-knit village, nobody asked any questions and there was none of the interfering, cloying neighbourliness that I was so familiar with from my rural Irish background.

As I had done before, I stepped off my Manhattan carousel in July and settled into my summer routine of happy solitude on Fire Island. My September deadline came and went; I wanted it to last a bit longer.

I had been stockpiling all summer and had arranged everything I needed to hole up here for the winter: enough food and fuel, books and art supplies to keep us happy through to the spring. I did not want to have to go back onto the mainland in search of something as banal as string!

Against the silence of my studio I suddenly heard a strange noise and, when I turned round, I nearly jumped out of my skin. A huge stag was scraping his horns along the rusted metal side of my studio doors. Behind him was a deer and a baby fawn tucked into her side, its tan ears too large for its delicate, pretty face. The stag lifted his huge head and the three of them stood for a moment and regarded me expectantly. They were a perfect family: father, mother and their child. Although the animals on the island were generally tame, it still wasn't a good idea to shoo away a stag. I knew if I just ignored them they would go of their own volition, but I was anxious to get into the house and search for the string. If it were the deer and fawn alone, I happily would have walked past them – but the stag was a different story. As a male, he commanded respect. I was not in the habit of giving respect to males, especially not strutting stags trespassing on my space.

The mother and her fawn were gazing at me and I became irritated by their calm stare. I was in a hurry.

'Shoo!' I said, not very loudly, waving an oil-stained rag feebly by my side. The stag stopped scratching and looked up. His head was not much bigger than the female's, but his antlers spanned the width of the huge open doorway. He looked at me and, sensing this could go badly wrong, I kept the next 'Shoo' to myself. After just a few seconds he turned and walked away, the deer and fawn following him. I was, he had decided, of no interest to him whatsoever. Strangely, I felt more rejected than relieved.

When they were gone, I walked up the wooden steps and opened the door to the kitchen. A breeze followed me in and sent three hastily pinned watercolours fluttering to the floor.

After four summers here I was still so infatuated with the beauty of Fire Island, in love with its muted sea-soaked palate, so grateful for the peace and solitude it had offered me, that I found myself sketching all the time in a sort of homage to the landscape. My passion for creating art – despite my commercial success – was still very new to me, as was the skill of drawing; the novelty of being able to capture life as it was, with merely a soft pencil and a piece of paper, had not worn off. While my sprawling artist's studio behind our house was packed with canvases of my stylized Impressionistic landscapes, the walls of the narrow two-storey cabin where I lived with my two sons were pinned with small, simple watercolours of the natural landscape and abundant wildlife that surrounded us: sketches of the silvery grasses that looked so delicate, and yet anchored our precarious sand dunes with their network of slim, greenish threads; the ballooning clouds of a summer morning that floated overhead on breezy days like 'angel's ships', as my sons called them.

There were sketches of the boys on every surface of the house. Both my boys were adopted, so they looked very different from each other. Tom was stocky and black-haired. Leo, now sixteen, was blond and lean. There was nothing more beautiful to me than my sons' faces; there was no greater feeling than their soft lips on my cheek. As they grew older they paid less and less attention to me. Their arms were directed now out into the world, and not back towards the comfort of their mother's bosom; yet, as with a bad lover, their sometimes feckless disregard only made me love them more. I craved their affection, but perhaps the fact that I wasn't their natural parent made me more reserved in demanding it. I did not feel that I had the right to cloy, so when they came crying to me with a scuffed knee or a cruel slight, my concern for their troubles was overridden by the joy of being allowed to give them comfort; a pleasure so addictively sweet that every mother hopes her child will need her forever.

Although I was certain I loved them with the same passion that a mother loves her natural child, the act of re-creating them over and over again on paper had become a compulsion for me, as if every sketch was in itself a microcosm of giving birth. Each picture was a homage to their detailed, intricate anatomy: the complex formation of their ears, the perfect rounds of their shoulders, the soft confusion of their eyes, the plump innocence of their lips – hundreds, perhaps thousands, of hastily drawn sketches, not just on the walls, but in the pockets of aprons and handbags and jackets. While the few visitors who called at the house would comment on the abundance of pictures, Tom, Leo and I did not see them any more. My drawings were merely an extension of our lives with each other; another eccentricity of their artist-mother's abounding love.

I opened the bits-and-bobs drawer in the kitchen, but there was no string there, or in any other drawer or cupboard. I now clearly remembered putting a large roll of string in that drawer.

'Did you move the string, Tom?' I called over to my son, who was sitting on the sofa with a blanket over his lap, under which was a bag of expensive biscuits that I had specifically told him not to touch.

There was a pause.

'What string?'

'The string in the top drawer,' I said, pulling aside the blanket and snatching the bag of biscuits from him, 'the string that you obviously took, Tom – where is it?'

His biscuits now confiscated, he had no further fear of punishment and said defiantly, 'I made a kite.'

I groaned as I remembered him chasing down the beach, trying to get two sticks and a hankie to take flight. 'Where is it now, Tom? I need the string.'

He looked at me and shrugged, then his eyes opened and he blinked – fearful that he might have really upset me.

I lifted my eyebrows and reset my expression from frustrated to benign.

'Let's see if Conor has some in the post-office shop,' I said.

'Can we get candy, Mammy, can we?'

'Come on,' I said non-committally as he ran ahead of me down the stairs and, still only half-dressed and barefoot, onto the sand path towards Cherry Grove post office.

I watched Tom skip ahead, a cold, fat sun sitting square in the sky ahead of him, and I felt a shot of gratitude for him, for my health to enjoy him and, briefly, for the symphony of circumstance and coincidence that had been my life thus far and had led me to this peaceful place.

My reverie was broken by the figure of our stout postmaster, Conor, running along the path towards me, a look of panic across his face.

'Ellie,' he gasped with exertion, 'Ellie – it's Leo.' He finally caught his breath. 'The school has telephoned to say you must call them immediately – he's gone missing.'

CHAPTER TWO

Leo was boarding in a good Catholic school upstate. For his first two years he had been attending as a day pupil, and had stayed with my friend Maureen Sweeney and her family in Yonkers during the week, then come home to the city at the weekends. Leo had made the decision to board full-time at the beginning of the last school year, dividing his free weekends between Yonkers and Fire Island. He had made friends with a new boy called Julian Knox – a privileged, sporty and, I thought, rather ill-mannered child from California, but Leo liked him and their friendship made my rather sensitive and introverted son seem keen to be a greater part of school life. Because Tom was a bright and attentive child, his preparatory teachers had agreed to allow me to educate my younger child at home sporadically, until he was ready to follow Leo to St Aloysius. This new routine in my son's education enabled me to spend more time working on Fire Island, which suited me very well.

I missed my eldest son, and of course I worried about him sometimes, but I called him every third day from the post office (which had the only telephone on the island) and Leo always assured me he was happy. I had spoken to him the day before yesterday and he had seemed fine. A little subdued perhaps –

but surely all teenage boys are susceptible to strange moods, and it had been a difficult year for all of us.

As soon as Conor's words were out, I immediately began to run towards the post office. Conor, in his mid-fifties and not the least bit agile, trotted behind me, breathlessly filling me in on the details.

'He didn't turn up for his Latin class, then they arranged a search of the whole school, before making the call. They think he's been missing since last night!'

We ran into the post office. Conor asked for the connection and handed me the earset.

'Conor, can you ask Dan to get the boat ready at the dock for me? I need him to get me a taxi to take me into the city, as well.'

'I'll organize it,' he said. He hopped back along the path at a fat man's trot.

Tom was already in the small wooden building, poking about at the jars of sweets behind the counter. He jumped when I came rushing in and instinctively said, 'Sorry!' My heart cracked at the sight of my youngest child – what had happened to his brother? What had I let happen to Leo? But I had no time for sentiment now – I had to find out what had happened, and get back to the mainland and find Leo.

'You go outside for a few minutes, Tom,' I said, 'and help Conor find Dan.'

I didn't even greet the school secretary when she answered the phone, just said my name.

'Ellie Irvington, Leo's mother . . . ' That's who I was – the bad mother of the bad boy who had run away. She put me straight through to the principal's office.

'Mrs Irvington, I have been trying to reach you . . . '

Bastard man! Don't you dare make me feel guilty! Where is my son? What have you done with my son? You were supposed to be looking after him!

'I'm so sorry. I'm not at home in the city; this is the – a friend's phone. Sorry if that's confusing.'

Jesus, what's the matter with me? Give him a piece of your mind! In truth, I felt so hysterical that I had separated from myself: the furious, terrified mother in me had given way to the calm pragmatist, keeping the terrible confusion of panic at bay.

'There has been a development, I think you had better come in.'

'Have you found him?'

'Erm – no. But one of his friends, Julian Knox, thinks he may know where Leo has gone.'

'And where is that?'

'I would rather you spoke to the boy yourself . . . '

'Could you please give me some idea?'

'Los Angeles. We think Leo may have gone to Los Angeles. Really, Mrs Irvington, if you could just make your way over here and we can—'

Los Angeles. My stomach did a somersault.

This past summer my lean, handsome sixteen-year-old had outgrown the isolated idyll that I had created for us on Fire Island. When he asked to spend the summer of his sixteenth birthday holidaying with Julian Knox and his family at their home in California, it was Maureen (whose own son was not much older than Leo and was already working) who advised me to let him go.

'You have to let Leo have his independence, Ellie,' she said. 'If you try to hold onto him, he'll only rebel.'

The Knoxes were respectable people – the father was a wealthy California-based businessman of some kind, and they were good

Catholics, hence their setting up home in New York so that their son could attend St Aloysius, where his father had been educated. The snobbish, sentimental ideals of Catholic respectability didn't concern me, but I admit that I don't know if I would have let Leo off on his own to stay with a gang of eccentrics like me! Julian's mother had sounded nice enough when I spoke to her on the telephone, so I accepted their invitation that my son spend the summer with them. There was no reason I could find for objecting, except that Leo's rejection, him wanting to be with other people that summer, had stung me dreadfully. Leo was sensitive to my feelings – too much so at times – and I could see he was torn at leaving us, but that he really wanted to go. His worry at upsetting me hurt almost as much as the rejection itself, so I sent him off with a smile and an envelope of money, and a promise to stay in touch throughout the two-month break.

Gloria Knox had picked them both up on the last day of term and they had taken the train from Penn Station. I had not even gone to wave him off. He had sent a postcard shortly after they arrived, detailing their adventures on the seventy-two-hour journey, the excitement of nights spent in the sleeper carriage, seeing real cowboys through the window of the train – and letting me know that he had arrived safely and had his own 'suite' at the Knoxes' house, that they had a pool the size of the entire garden in Yonkers and three servants. He telegrammed just once, to ask for more money, as he had spent much of his allowance on new clothes. My eldest son was peculiarly fashionable about his dress – a habit that he had inherited more from me than from his father.

 'Leo's not coming home this summer?' Conor had asked, when I wired my son money from the post office on Fire Island.

'No,' I answered.

I felt the failure of myself as a mother in his absence almost as keenly as the absence itself.

'You have to let them go eventually, Ellie,' Conor had said, repeating Maureen's sentiment.

'Of course,' I had agreed, but inside I disagreed with them both. Leo was too young for me to let go of. I had felt a hole in my heart all through the season. I rang California a few times from the post office, but Leo was out every time I called. Once or twice I woke up in the night and panicked myself into believing that something was wrong. Then I would calm myself by concentrating on Tom and throwing myself into my work. *Everything is fine; Leo is safe, staying with a good family*, I kept telling myself. When I picked him up at Penn Station a week before school started again, I all but fell on him with relief, but as he stepped off the train my little boy appeared taller and more sophisticated than when he had left. It was too awful to contemplate that he had moved away from me in spirit as well as body, so I spat on my hankie and rubbed an imaginary stain from his tanned cheeks and pretended that no time had passed.

In that last week before he had started school and moved back into his Yonkers weekly routine with the Sweeneys, Leo gave me a simple account of his two months in Los Angeles and assured me that nothing of any particular interest had happened. No special adventures, and certainly nothing untoward – I was assured at least of that.

His insistence that the summer had been entirely without event convinced me that he was holding something back from me. But boys always have secrets from their mothers – that is nature at work. Even so, while common sense told me all was well, my intuition suggested otherwise.

Leo's running away was a disaster, but not a surprise. This was some dark dread come to pass; the fact that I had intuited it made me angrier with myself for not having acted, and more determined to get him back.

I should never have let him go last summer. He was only sixteen and still too precious; I should never have let him out of my sight!

'No, there is no time for me to make it north of the city. I need you to bring the Knox boy over to my apartment in Manhattan, so that I can question him myself. It will take me—' I did a quick calculation – 'less than two hours to get there myself, so you will have plenty of—'

The headmaster let out an officious laugh. 'I'm afraid that is out of the question, Mrs Irvington. I could not possibly leave the school in the middle of a working day to chase into the city!'

'And yet you allowed my son, at sixteen years of age, to walk straight out of your school?'

'Well now, Mrs Irvington, that was hardly my fault . . . '

Now I was mad.

'It most certainly was your fault, as the Police Department will agree when I report you for child negligence – and I am sure the other parents will be most perturbed to hear of the lack of security prevalent in your school, especially given the exorbitant fees you charge, to ensure us of our sons' moral and physical safety. You have a car, I presume?'

'A driver, but . . . '

'Good – then I expect to see you at my apartment, with the boy, in just under two hours. Your secretary has my address.' And I hung up.

I was shaking as I put down the receiver and stood for half a moment taking in the news. I suffered a mother's curse of knowing my children inside-out. There was nothing they could do or say that I did not intuit as soon as it became apparent; everything bad that happened to them was easily foreseen, after the event; everything bad that happened to them I would choose to interpret as my own fault.

The miracle of a mother's devotion is the way that one's heart grows larger to accommodate the enormous emotions children cause. My heart was now beating so fast, and felt so huge, that I feared it would explode in my chest. At the same time I knew that if that happened I would never find my son, so I put the lid on my emotions and concentrated on making haste.

I would have run straight to the dock and Dan's waiting boat, except that when I looked down I realized I wasn't wearing any shoes. So I ran back to the house and straight up the stairs, my heels hardened from a summer spent barefoot, and immune to splinters. I dragged a large carpet bag out from under my bed and started to throw things in haphazardly. What did I need? Clothes – for me and Tom. There was no need for me to take all this. I could pack when I got to Manhattan. I would have to get a train to Los Angeles. A flight would be quicker. Should I go straight to the station? Why was I bothering to pack a bag? Clothes: I needed something for Tom to wear. Shoes: I was still barefoot. Keys: the keys to the house; the keys to the studio. They were always left open. I had better lock up, if I was leaving. Leaving – I should never have come here. I should never have sent Leo back to that school. I was panicking now. All my thoughts came tumbling down on top of each other like the clattering chaos from a dropped kitchen drawer.

I forced myself to stop and take a deep breath, then put a smart coat on over my working clothes, and some city shoes from under my bed; they pinched, as if they didn't belong to me, so I grabbed some thick stockings from a drawer, along with a pair of pants and some boots for Tom, and threw them all in the bag.

I ran down the stairs and grabbed the keys from the hook where they had been hanging, untouched, for the best part of four months – then left.

At the front gate I called, 'Tom!' My words fell flat on the silent dunes, sucked into oblivion by the vast mass of sea and sky. I felt a flicker of rage at my youngest son, already knowing that he was going to hold us up, then remembering that he was with Conor. I had to calm down. I would get nowhere in this flustered state.

Calm . . . I needed to stay calm. Tom was doubtless with Conor and Dan, waiting for me on the dock by now. I had his shoes and a sweater in my bag; I just kept running.

Everything will be fine, I kept repeating in my head, over and over. *Tom and I will find Leo and we'll be back – yes, back, all three of us, together, in a few days, then we can decide what to do next*. St Aloysius was clearly the wrong school for Leo. He had probably just fallen out with his friend and had run back to see Bridie and Maureen in Yonkers. Perhaps he had gone to the apartment in Manhattan? He had a key. He could have gone there. Yes, he was surely in the apartment in Manhattan.

Except in my gut I knew that he wasn't. He was on his way to Los Angeles. On the other side of this vast continent – on his own – for some reason that I knew nothing about.

As I arrived at the dock Dan already had the engine running on the converted clam-boat that acted as the island's only off-season taxi. He was standing, waiting to help me on. Tom was nowhere to be seen.

'Where is that little tinker? I'll skin him!' I shouted, 'TOM! TOM!'

I was beside myself.

'Relax,' Dan said, putting his big hand on my shoulder, 'he's with Conor – I saw them a minute ago.'

Dan was a rugged forty-five, from the Midwest, and younger than his New York lover, Conor. The two of them were Cherry Grove mainstays. Men living openly as lovers was both illegal and dangerous, and when I first moved onto the island I had been somewhat alarmed by them. I had not lived a sheltered life, and as an artist had met people of all predilections and backgrounds. However, homosexual behaviour was never expressed by anything more than subtle implication. So I feared, not for the moral safety of my sons (it was my own belief that people should be allowed to live as they chose, and love whom they chose), but that we might get caught living among people openly engaged in criminal activity. As time went on, however, Conor and Dan seemed to me as settled and respectable as any ordinary married couple; Conor wore an apron and kept house, while Dan fixed the roof slates, and the peculiarity of their both being men had come to seem completely irrelevant to me. They could not bear the pretence of not being together all the time, so they lived on the island twelve months a year, making a good living from the post-office shop and taxi service during the summer, with Dan supplementing their winter income with some taxi work in the city. It was their friendship that had sustained my longer stays, and their practical support that made it possible for me to stay on the island through the winter. My sons adored them and I was grateful, in the absence of their father, for Leo and Tom to enjoy the company of these kind and unusual men. Conor and Dan had built a happy life out of the impossibility of two men being in a marriage, and in doing so had made my own dream of remote, artistic motherhood a possibility. I respected them, and respect was hard come by for men of their type – so they loved me and my sons like family.

Dan pointed. 'There they are.' I looked back up the pier and could see the portly postmaster trying to persuade Tom to come back down from the second-floor decking of the closed hotel, where he was launching leaves through holes in the wood.

Dan waved at him, but Tom would only wave back.

'Ellie, you're in a rush now. What say you leave him here – and we'll take care of him till you get back?'

'It's too much trouble. I'll—'

'We love taking care of him, Ellie. Besides, you'll be back in a day or two – with Leo.'

I was anxious to get going, and Tom was always a demanding distraction in the city. I would travel more quickly alone.

'If you're sure, Dan.'

He waved my assent to his older, stouter lover and I climbed on board the boat.

As we pulled away from the dock I had a moment of panic as the land behind us grew smaller. Would I be back in a few days? Was this the start of another horrendous period of grief in my life? Would I have to endure all the pain and uncertainty of the past ten years, again? I felt a snap of anger at the child – selfish, selfish! – then quickly put Leo to the back of my mind. I had a journey into the city to make before I could do anything, and I needed to stay calm.

'Will Tom and Conor be all right, do you think, Dan?'

'If they're not, sweetie, I'll bring him right over to you. Yonkers – Manhattan – wherever, Ellie, you just call.'

Dan went over to the mainland and back all the time. He did sporadic work with a taxicab firm in the city throughout the winter and would make good on his promise to deliver Tom wherever I needed him to be. That, at least, was settled.

Dan pulled down the accelerator lever with his right hand, and the low thrum of the old fishing-vessel engine turned to a screech as it started to make the short journey towards Sayville. I remembered the first time I had taken this journey, four – nearly five – years ago now.

I had been on my own that day. The boys were in the care of my surrogate Irish family in the rambling house in Yonkers that we had renovated together and run for a while as a home-less shelter at the tail end of the Great Depression. My own parents in Ireland were long since dead, and with them now were Maidy and Paud Hogan – the old couple who had all but reared me and whose son, John, I had married. Maidy had been the last to go, five years ago. She died three years after her son, John, my husband – and it had been my grief over his sudden death that had chased me back to New York. When I received news of Maidy's death I did not return for her burial. Instead I enshrined her in my heart and left her living in the neat, rose-covered cottage where I remembered her. That was where my old beloveds were now: John, Maidy and Paud were tucked away in my heart, still living in that cottage in Kilmoy.

My parents had been products of Ireland's two least-attract-ive institutions – the Church and the privileged middle-class Irish who had survived the famine of 1879. They were not unkind people, but they were cold. Perhaps because of my craving for warmth and love as a child, I had become good at gathering people close to me.

My 'family' now comprised the faithful friends I had made in America. Maureen and Patrick Sweeney and their two chil-dren now lived with Bridie – the fierce old housekeeper I had first encountered as a young woman in domestic service. They all lived in the house in Yonkers that I had bought for a song during the Depression and renovated from a homeless shelter into a family home over the years. In turn, these friends had become a true family to my adopted sons. Leo's father was my second husband, Charles, and his mother was a vain, shallow socialite whose disinterest in Leo had led her to abandon him completely when she met her second husband. Tom's mother was a poor unfortunate young girl who had presented herself, while pregnant with him, at the house in Yonkers that we had run as a homeless shelter during the worst of the Depression. His father was unknown. Both boys belonged to me now – the sons of a single woman artist. They were not mere products of their birth or background, but my cherished children, because they were fortunate enough to have been born in America: the land of reinvention. My own life had changed its course many times. I had worked as a housemaid, typist, farmer's wife, businesswoman and now artist. My family – from the sons whom I had gratefully adopted, to the people I trusted to care for them and love them alongside me – were not of their (or my) birth, but of my own choosing.

The sea journey to my new oasis on that first occasion had taken less than twenty minutes. I had stood at the front of the Fire Island ferry on a bright spring day, facing out to what seemed like open sea. The horizon was blurred – any land made invisible by a gentle mist blending into the grey sky – and there was a moment when I felt as if I were at the stern of the boat that had brought me from Ireland to America as a young girl in 1920. For a moment, with the wind whipping my hair sideways across my face and no children tugging on me, I now allowed myself to remember how innocent and beautiful and brave I had been back then. My beloved husband had been injured in the Irish War of Independence, and I had stayed in New York just long enough to earn money for his operation. I returned to him and lived in blissful contentment until his death

in 1934, when I came back to America in search of solace and, yes, reinvention. From the other side of the world it was easier to imagine that perhaps John was not dead, but still back home in Ireland waiting for me. Being apart from the one you love – separated by miles, or time – is close to death, in any case. John was alive in my heart as the first person who had taught me how to love. The man, and the memory of the man, had long since become one and the same, but John was no less precious to me for that. His death, and all the life that had happened to me since, had deepened the love I had always felt for him. Instead of gaining solace from my grief, the grief itself had become my solace.

That day I had lost myself in a reverie of sweet memories until Fire Island came into view. The low strip of land appeared to bubble into my eyeline from behind the mist, as if it were somehow emerging out of the water. Like some mysterious place in history, an illusion – the straight line of treetops growing taller as we got closer, as if they too were growing out of the water. I began to see a few white buildings emerge, a toy town, and above them grey clouds tinged with slight blue and a shy, hazy sun reaching down to the surface of the water – transforming it from grey to glittering sun. This was, I decided, a magical place. A new land, as America had once been to me; a place where the artist, the mother, the free spirit that I had become could thrive and belong. I was, that day, filled with the same feeling of adventure and excitement that I had felt when first arriving in America.

Fire Island had been all that I had ever hoped for; a place for me to settle and live out my days with my family, in solitude and creative fulfilment.

Now I was leaving and, although I hoped otherwise, I had a premonition that I would not be returning for some time.

Chapter Three

Sayville was asleep today. In high season the port was buzzing with crowds of colourful city people getting on the ferry, piling large bags on the narrow benches and all around their feet, their personal belongings spilling over – groceries, clothes and beach towels. They also carried larger items such as lamps and chairs, decorating their island abodes bit by bit, because the lack of roads (and therefore of wheeled transport) on the island made it impossible to move everything in one go. I once helped a man up the ramp as he struggled with a life-sized glass flamingo. 'It was my mother's' was his only explanation or excuse. There was always something to amuse or entertain me on my journey to and from Fire Island.

However, today there was nothing but a single yellow taxicab waiting for me.

'Chico's a man of few words,' Dan said, opening the door of the taxi and nodding to his friend, 'so he won't bother you with chit-chat. I've given him the address of the apartment and told him to take you straight there.'

'Thanks, Dan,' I said climbing in, 'I don't know what I'd have done—'

'Go!' he said, 'hurry!' Then he shut the door and slammed his hand on the roof to give Chico instructions.

The leather seating was cold underneath me, and my coat was too thin – I was still wearing the clothes I had chased out of the house in. I wished now that I had Tom with me. He could cuddle into me, and he was so full of energy that he was always as warm as a bedpan! He would offer me distraction too, and I suddenly craved an impossible question ('Mam, why do rabbits have such big ears?') to ruminate over and pass the time.

I pulled my cuffs down over my hands and folded my arms. Outside, a slight spatter of rain on the car window interrupted my view of the disappearing sea.

Where had Charles, my second husband, been on that first day I took the trip to Fire Island? I couldn't remember, but I remembered that he wasn't there. Away somewhere chasing his political ideals – but not with me.

Our marriage had been a long time coming. Charles and I had first met when I was an innocent young housemaid and he the wealthy son of a shipbuilder. I was over in America earning money to send home to my first husband, John. Charles had fallen hard for me and, between his looks and his money and his noble ideals on behalf of the 'ordinary working man', he came close to turning my head. However, I returned to Ireland, leaving him heartbroken. In my mid-thirties, after John died, I returned to America again and we met through a series of coincidences that can only be described as 'fate'. Quite by chance, Charles came upon the charitable community that I was running in Yonkers with Bridie and Maureen Sweeney. Once again, he swept me away, but while we consummated our love, we only stayed together for a short while. I was demented with grief for John, and Charles had family problems, as this was the time when his ex-wife unexpectedly abandoned their son, Leo, into his care.

I left the community a few months after that and set up home in an apartment in Manhattan, along with baby Tom, who had been left in my care by his young mother. There had been another man in the community, Matt, who had wanted to marry me – and in a matter of a year after my husband's death everything I thought I knew about love and passion had become so confused, so enmeshed with my grief over losing John, that I decided I needed some time on my own.

It was the right thing to do. Tom thrived under my exclusive parenting. I bought an apartment near Central Park, and every day we adventured in its fields: explored the broad bases of its large gnarled trees, listened to the shouts of its baseball courts, fed ducks in its ponds; through the eyes of my toddling son, I was reborn into a happy world of carousels and zoo animals. I had taken some lessons and started drawing. Tom slept in his perambulator as I walked him through the city's art galleries and drank in every last piece of work on public view. It was the first time in my life that I had done exactly as I pleased. There was nothing expected from me – from family or society. I still had some means from the businesses I had sold in Ireland, and had time to do completely as I pleased. From that place of freedom inside me, and with the passing of time, my terrible grief at losing John began to soften. I also began to imagine I had an artist's eye and harboured an idea, which, with the confidence that age and motherhood gave me, grew into a belief that I could become an artist.

So, just over a year after I had left my life in Yonkers – two years after John died – I was happier and more settled than I had ever been. I had met an influential German artist, Hilla Rebay, who was mentoring me and had arranged a studio for me to work in. Hilla was also the curator of the renowned Solomon Guggenheim Foundation – and her confidence in my potential as an 'important Irish Abstract artist' gave me such huge faith that I had found my path. Not as somebody's daughter, lover or wife, not even as a businesswoman hell-bent on making money for fear of the poverty I had once known, but as an individual. I had found a way of expressing who I was and it felt important and true. I was excited about where this awakened passion for art would lead me, and was filled with the same spirit of adventure and excitement that I had experienced as a young woman in New York. I felt ready to launch myself into whatever came my way.

It just so happened that what came my way was Charles.

I had just put down the phone to Hilla, who had rung to tell me that my first painting had sold to an industrialist friend of Guggenheim. She was quite disgusted because this man seemed flummoxed by most of the work she showed him, so she assumed he was looking for something representative and traditional. Hilla found people with such uninformed tastes exhausting and was quickly walking him through the artists' studios – wealthy art collectors liked to see the chaos where we artists worked – when in mine he spotted a large, vague, but entirely abstract landscape that I had done from memory, of the view from my cottage in Ireland. It stopped him in his tracks, Hilla told me.

'What did he say?' I had asked.

'"Now that I like,"' she had said. '"Now *that* I like" – that's what he said.'

She sold him the work for a vastly inflated sum, then rang to tell me that I was now – officially – a professional artist.

When I put the phone down I was soaring with pleasure. I was longing to share my news with somebody, but Tom was asleep and the family out in Yonkers didn't have a phone.

I was beaming with excitement and could only think of running down to the museum on East 54th Street and making Hilla tell me the whole story over and over again, until I grew tired of it. I would have gone immediately, had Tom not been asleep in his cot. If I had, I would have missed that ring on the door and Charles, standing there, clean-shaven and chiselled as a god. He was holding flowers.

I had not seen Charles since he left me in the house in Yonkers something over a year before, to attend to the family business of his wife and son. In my grief for John I had rejected him for the second time and had believed that I would never see him again. Only a fool would come back for more and, in all honesty, as caught up as I was with my art and being a good mother to Tom, I had barely given him a thought since. Enough time had passed perhaps for me to be pleased, if somewhat surprised, to see him.

'Hello, stranger,' he said. I smiled, but it went so wide that it turned into a small laugh. I knew he thought my shining from the inside out was because of him, so I blurted out, 'I've just sold a painting!'

'Well, congratulations – these are for you,' he said, handing me the flowers.

We celebrated my achievement with a walk in the park with Tom, a glass of champagne in The Plaza, taking the perambulator into the Oak Bar, which was such a gloriously decadent act that even the staff were not sure how to react. By the time they decided children were not appropriate customers, Tom had started crying and we had decided to move on.

Charles came back to the apartment and didn't leave.

That first night we made love as easily and as freely as if the intervening years separating us had never happened. There seemed no reason to question what was happening. Charles loved me still and had come in search of me. (I had not been hard to find – one call to the house in Yonkers and he had my address.) His life was as settled as it would ever be; his ex-wife was remarried, and his son Leo was living with him as much as his erratic life as a union activist (and communist agitator!) allowed – but most of the time Leo resided with Charles' brother and his family upstate. The terrible grief and confusion I had felt after my husband's death had gone and had been replaced by the maturity and certainty of motherhood.

After we made love I lay with my head on Charles' chest and wondered how my life – my simple life as an unmarried mother and professional artist – would accommodate him. Was this a good idea, allowing Charles back into my life? This force-of-nature of a man? Would he take over? However, thinking of such things seemed humdrum after the great celebration we had enjoyed that day.

He kissed the top of my head, gently cupped his hands around my naked breasts and said, 'So, selling paintings to the great industrialist elite, eh? What would my union buddies think of that, eh?' – and I turned to him willingly.

After all, what was the sense in thinking things through, when living in the moment felt so good?

Charles had wanted to get married, but I was uncertain. Firstly because I had already been married. John had only been dead for two years and I still felt as though he was my husband. As a seventeen-year-old girl I had been desperate to marry John, to consummate our love. We had eloped to Dublin on the train and breakfasted in Bewley's afterwards on coffee and sweet cake. That was my wedding day. I had no need or desire for another. Charles and I had consummated our passions already. What was the point of entering into a legal formality, especially for two people – communist and artist – who had little truck with conventional society?

In my heart perhaps, deep in my heart (with hindsight), I had not wanted to tie myself to him in that way. I might never have done so if I had not met Leo.

Charles brought him to tea at the apartment.

Leo was tall for his age, coming up to my shoulder. A slim, elegantly formed child – but no scrawny waif – and as beautiful as a girl from an Irish ballad, with full lips as 'red as a rose' and blue eyes rimmed with lashes 'as black as coal'. He shook my hand and his eyes looked downwards. He sat, only at his father's instruction, on the low settee in my living room. His back was straight and his small, smooth hands were folded tightly on his lap, and his cheeks pinked as I spoke to him.

'Would you like some cake, Leo?'

He looked at his father, uncertain how to answer me, unclear who this strange woman was and what this invitation to tea meant.

Although I had never met the child before that afternoon, Leo's history and mine ran parallel.

I had first met his father in New York as a young woman and, despite the fact that I was already married to John, he had turned my head. A few months after my return to Ireland I read that Charles had married a rich socialite, a woman found for him by his parents – he had been weakened by losing 'his Irish colleen' and had married her, I knew, to get back at me.

She had borne him a son, and shortly afterwards the marriage had broken down and they had divorced. Leo was raised by a series of nannies until the age of seven, when his mother had remarried and finally abandoned him altogether, placing him entirely, and legally, into Charles' care. A man could not raise a child alone, especially not a man with such an erratic and adventurous working life as Charles, so Leo passed from nannies to schools, spending his holidays with grandparents and uncles and – only when it suited his father – with Charles himself.

Those first ten years of Leo's life were the years when John and I had tried, and failed, to start a family. I lost three babies – the first at seven full months. A boy: he had been taken away and buried while I lay howling on the bed. The cure for my grief was to lose another, and another after that, until I knew that God Himself was against me and we gave up trying. I always remembered the first – the day I bore and lost my first son was etched forever into my mind: 15th May 1927.

It was, by coincidence, that same date ten years later when Charles brought Leo to meet me for the first time. Perhaps that had played a part in the softness in my heart that I felt for him. His perfectly shaped eyebrows were furrowed, as if the worries of the world were on his shoulders. I felt such an urge to mother him. I wanted to lie him down on the cushions and run the back of my hands gently down his cheeks, until his eyes closed and I soothed him off to sleep. In an instinct as immediate and as strong as falling in love, I knew that what I wanted – more than anything – was to be this child's mother.

Charles and I got married shortly after that, in City Hall, on 20th June 1937. Leo attended, with Patrick and Maureen Sweeney as witnesses. Bridie walked Tom around the broad blocks outside the large, formal building. She didn't like Charles and was openly disgusted that I was marrying him. 'You know, and I know, you're marrying him simply to give that child a mother, Ellie.'

'That's not true, Bridie, not entirely . . . '

'Pff,' she interrupted, waving her bony hands across her substantial bosom. 'He won't thank you for taking on his son! Men are selfish, Ellie – they want all the love for themselves.'

'That's a terrible thing to say, Bridie. Look at Patrick – he's a wonderful father.'

'Patrick is an exception,' she said, giving me a glowering look that left me in no doubt what she was thinking.

Yet Charles seemed to be the very definition of an exceptional man. He had turned his back on his parents' money to work alongside his father's shipyard labourers; he had eschewed the wealth of his birthright and had worked his way through the Great Depression, negotiating for workers' rights and setting up unions.

Most people – Bridie being a notable exception – loved him. Men admired him, and women coveted his admiration. He was a good catch.

'You'll see,' Bridie had said, quite openly in front of Charles, when we emerged from the short, legal service. 'You mark my words, you'll see.'

Charles had put his arms around the old lady's waist and had given her a squeeze. He loved to tease and charm her – and never took her criticisms of him too seriously.

I had always thought it very good-humoured and generous of Charles not to take Bridie's dislike of him to heart. However, that day, on the steps of City Hall, I felt a snap of irritation for the way he was patronizing my old friend with his unwanted affection, as if being old and Irish made her a figure of ridicule and absented her from a valid opinion. I pushed the thought aside, but part of me must have been wondering if Bridie was right.

CHAPTER FOUR

Chico was silent and efficient, as Dan had promised; the back of his head was as impervious and unfriendly as the cold, utilitarian interior of the yellow taxi he was driving. I wished there was a paper or magazine in its spotless empty interior, something to distract my thoughts from Leo. Although I knew from the concentrated stillness of Chico's posture that he was making as much haste as he could, my heart was pushing itself up into my mouth, urging me to call out at him to go faster – faster! It seemed as if I had entirely lost track of time.

How long had passed after I heard the news before I got on the boat? How long had the boat journey been? I looked at my watch – pointlessly, as it was no more than a piece of plain jewellery to me. It read 'eight'. It might have stopped days, weeks, months ago, and I would not have noticed anyway. The easy pace of life on Fire Island, and my obsession with work, ate all concept of time for me. We ate when we were hungry, slept when we were tired – in between we worked and read and wandered. I gazed out of the cab window, willing myself away from worrying about Leo. The autumn trees were in full fall colour: blazing reds, auburns and golds. These huge displays were undoubtedly New York's most extraordinary landscape feature, and yet I had never felt drawn to painting them. They were striking and yet – like a woman in church at a wedding wearing an extraordinary feathered hat that draws attention away from the bride – they screamed, 'Look at me! Paint me!' and so I decided they were too gaudy and obvious for me to capture on canvas. I was contrary like that. I wouldn't let anybody tell me what to do. Not even nature.

Sayville, Bohemia, Bay Shore, Babylon, Baldwin – Long Island towns with pretty names and organized, tidy streets bridged the gap between the wild solitude of Fire Island and the frenetic crowding of New York City. All the smart wooden houses were set in manicured gardens, and the shop fronts were pristine and painted – goods piled in neat displays on gingham-covered tables outside the grocery stores, polished apples, jars of home-made pickles piled up into symmetrical towers, brooms and brushes lined up, inviting people to be even tidier, to wipe up every last leaf from the ground. Even the residents themselves, springing along the paving, seemed universally cheerful, apparently delighted to be living in this friendly nirvana – to have hit upon the perfect note between smug mediocrity and ideal happiness. Surely there were weeds and unwashed windows and grubby affairs going on behind the main streets, but we were travelling the road where they put their best face forward.

For all their efforts, these small towns – neither suburb, nor wilderness, nor city – seemed like no-man's-lands to me, where the inhabitants surely led such unadventurous lives that they had the time to polish apples. They were too similar to the small Irish town where I had grown up. I had never fitted in there; my mother was a snob and my father a failed priest. The only thing I had ever achieved, in the eyes of the townspeople, was marrying their hero John Hogan. When I returned from America as a young married woman I set up businesses that transformed the town: a typing school, a hair salon, a grocery shop and, latterly, a drapery (the profits from the sale of which I was still enjoying). But I was still, when all was said and done, John Hogan's wife. I was at best respected and at worst tolerated, because of the man I was married to.

Nobody in that small, ordinary town could possibly come close to understanding the voracious, consuming adoration that I had for my husband. We were childhood sweethearts, but more than that, the very foundation of who I was – any compassion or sweetness I had in me – was fashioned by John's kind heart, and I knew that. However, my desire for adventure was my own; and for all that I loved him, I defied him. He would have stayed a cripple all his life rather than lose me for one short year to America to earn the money to save him. In the end I stayed in New York for four years – out of sheer pig-headedness, because he refused to join me there and start a new, better life. I returned to Kilmoy eventually and stayed, for John. We lived, happily enough, until his death from a sudden heart attack parted us in 1934, when I returned to my New York.

I had run away in despair after John's death. It wasn't poverty that chased me out of Ireland that second time – in fact, I found more poverty during the Great Depression in New York than I had ever experienced at home. It was the small-minded, keeping-up-appearances, craw-thumping Catholic neighbours who had chased me away with their judgements on my 'airs and graces' and with their snide remarks and cynicism. Although I had been back in America for eight years now, the memory of them had hardened with time. Perhaps, beneath it all, there was that longing for home, yet what protected me from all that I had lost was a shallow disdain for small-town life. That and the snobbery of the free-thinking artists and radicals, because, for all our liberal ideals, in our own way we were as snobbish about the bourgeoisie as they were about us.

'Most men lead lives of quiet desperation . . . ' was a quote by the philosopher Henry Thoreau that Charles had used to separate 'us and them'.

'Nothing wrong with that,' Bridie had said, the first time I had used it. 'Nothing wrong with keeping your mouth shut and getting on with it.'

' . . . and go to the grave with the song still in them' was the second half of the quote. I was determined to sing my song, and for my life to have meaning – to be the best I could be; and now, with my painting, I had found a way to do that.

After Charles and I got married I was as happy as I had ever been in my life, even with John. We lived in the apartment on West 27th and 10th, near Chelsea Park. The neighbourhood was rich with a mixture of artists and the colourful New York society of hookers and drinkers that Charles, with his working-class aspirations, loved to hang around with.

It seemed that everything had fallen into place in my life; this was my time – I was sure of it. My second chance, after the pain of John's death; my reward for enduring the disappointment of not being able to have children.

Charles was so happy, and that made me happy. He was so in love with me that loving him back was easy.

'Do you remember our first kiss?' he asked me on our wedding night.

'Of course I do,' I said. It had been in the crisp dawn chill of a spring morning in 1924, after a glamorous party on his brother's upstate estate. The air had been laden with the smell of lilac and our bodies heavy with the desire of an illicit, unrequited passion. He had asked me to marry him that night, and a few hours later, before I had the chance to answer him, I was called home to Ireland and to my marriage. That had been fifteen years ago. The intervening years had seen us both married, divorced and widowed – and although we had been lovers for a year, when he kissed me on our wedding night I could see that Charles was carried back to those heady days when we first met. In the sanctity of our married bedroom, with the children asleep in the room next door, he cupped my chin in his hands and said, 'You are the most beautiful girl in the world,' as if we were two young lovers again; as if I looked the same to him now as I did then. Every time he kissed me I could feel that it held the same resonance for him as that first kiss. Charles was a good man, and he was deeply in love with me. I did not imagine anything could ever go wrong between us. Added to this, the marriage had undoubtedly been the right thing to do for the boys.

Tom's birth mother was a young woman whom we had taken into the homeless hostel in Yonkers when she was pregnant, but had run away and left him in my care when he was less than a year old. A year after John died I realized that my greatest sadness had perhaps not been losing him alone, but the fact that we had been unable to have children. When this baby came into my life, he became my life. I had been rearing him as my own, on my own, before Charles found me again. The cruelty of Charles' ex-wife in casting her son aside for the love of a man was so disgusting to me that I wasted no time whatsoever in establishing myself as Leo's mother. The two boys locked in as siblings right away – Leo was so kind and patient with my lively baby and his gentle soul seemed to calm Tom in a way that my admonishments rarely did.

Not a day passed after I adopted both these children that I did not feel gratitude for the gift they were. I had been barren and desperate for a child until these two boys were sent to me. As our paths converged I gathered them both to me with a confidence that was so considerable it surprised me. I knew I had been a headstrong daughter and was a difficult and defiant wife, but I was a born mother. There was no doubt in my mind and my heart about that.

I was so proud of my prowess, my natural feeling for motherhood. Yet it was perhaps the undoing of my marriage.

I can trace the first souring of our relationship back to a small domestic incident.

Our apartment was a simple affair. We ate in the kitchen and, unless we bought food in or Bridie came to stay (as she did from time to time when 'looking after' the Sweeneys got too much for her – and them!), I cooked. My food was as simple as the limited time I was prepared to give it; in the winter mince, gravy and potatoes; in the summer pasta with a salad. I could, and did, prepare sauce for a steak, or bake and ice a cake, but not every day, as I had done when I was living with John. My priorities were different. I had always managed to derive some small pleasure from domestic chores, and I was careful now to keep things as simple as possible so that I didn't come to resent my own home.

Good manners were observed at my table – but I was not fanatical. I was reared in a tradition of priestly politeness that I loathed, so while there were linen napkins, even for the children, with every meal, they were often used twice in one day and seldom starched!

On that evening Charles was in an ill temper as we sat down to our evening meal. We had been making love earlier that day, a delicious illicit tryst while Tom was taking his afternoon nap. At a crucial moment Tom had woken and started screaming for me. I had left Charles where he was and gone to comfort the child, refusing to be lured back. Charles was a bit sharp with me, but I didn't pay much heed. I didn't blame him, for he was frustrated, and anyway sharp words were a feature of marriage from time to time. When you had children, I was quickly learning, there was not so much time for one another.

I put the food on the table – pork chops and potato – and we began eating. Tom was spooning the food as near to his face as he could approximate, with me helping him between my own mouthfuls. Charles, despite having been educated to act like a wealthy gentleman, made a point of eating with his sleeves rolled up like a shipyard navvy. However, his son Leo, who had been reared by nannies and expensive schools, ate in the convoluted manner adopted by upper-class Americans. They cut their meat, then put the knife down, resting the tip of the blade on the side of the plate, transferred their fork to the right hand, took the food up using the fork alone, put it in their mouth, then placed the fork down on the plate until they had finished chewing and started the whole rigmarole of transferring cutlery from one hand to the other all over again. In Ireland even bishops gripped their cutlery – knife in right, fork in left – all the way through a meal, so I had always found this way of eating that Americans had faintly amusing. I found the way Leo ate endearing, although admittedly I should have preferred him to enjoy his food while it was still hot. Charles and I were all but finished, while Leo was still cutting and transferring his food to his fork in this meticulous way.

'Oh, for pity's sake, boy – stop eating like a bloody priss!'

Charles shouted at him so loudly that Leo jumped in his seat, dropping his fork. I picked it up and went to fetch him another from the drawer.

'Let him eat with that one,' Charles said and then, arguing with my silent glower, 'What? It's clean enough – that boy is too fussy, and your molly-coddling is making him worse.'

Leo's lip quivered, his little hands placed neatly in his lap. Even Tom had ceased with his spoon-banging and was watching

Charles and me with an eerily quiet curiosity. I was furious. Charles carried on eating.

'If you're finished,' I said to Leo, 'you go on into the other room, and I'll bring you your pie in there.'

The poor child, blushing wildly, all but ran from the table.

'What the hell was that about?' I confronted Charles when Leo was out of earshot.

'Nothing,' he said, shovelling the last of his steak into his mouth, 'I just don't want him turning into a girl.'

He didn't seem bothered that he had upset Leo – either he hadn't even noticed the boy's distress or he was careless about hurting his feelings.

'He looks up to you, Charles – you're his father, he worships you.'

Charles finished his food, grabbed me around the waist and pulled me into him playfully.

'Aha, but do *you* worship me, Ellie Irvington?'

I played along, but I could feel my smile withering along the edges.

He had been careless with the feelings of his child and, for all that it was petty of me, the incident coloured my view of him for the worse.

CHAPTER FIVE

As we approached the bridge into the city I leaned forward in my seat and allowed the panic to set in. It was mid-morning and the traffic was reasonably light, although when we came to the edge of the bridge it seemed that the road was becoming clogged with cars, and I was just seconds away from getting out of the taxi and running the rest of the way up to the apartment on 27th, before Chico started moving again.

Once we hit Manhattan, Chico showed his skills as a cab-driver, jerking the taxi swiftly between the avenues, darting up and down the side streets as if they were deserted conduits to aid our speed, rather than the busy city roads they were. As we hurtled past delivery trucks and milk vans, earning the abuse and fist-waving of pedestrians and fellow drivers, I didn't know where he was going and a few times doubted his route, until the moment he confidently brought the taxi to a halt and pulled up outside the apartment.

I opened the cab window, but he shook his head, waving me away, refusing my money – still not speaking. As I was closing the door of the taxi, Chico leaned out the window and said in a voice so soft I could barely hear him, 'I hope you find your son, lady.' Dan must have told him; I guessed that Chico was a family man and had felt the pain in my silence.

Hanging on the mirror in front of him was a picture of Our Lady of Guadeloupe. My anxiety halted long enough for me to touch my fingers to my lips, then reach in and touch her.

'Say a prayer, Chico,' I said and he closed his eyes in assertion. Then I threw a wildly generous ten-dollar bill onto his lap and ignored his objections. I always paid my way – even in my prayers.

The moment I set foot in the building I knew that Leo had not been back there, but I ran into his room anyway and checked the wardrobe. His few clothes were still hanging neatly in the closet – his winter coat swung like a cadaver when I wrenched open the door. I immediately went into the bedroom and, unlike my last attempt, packed a large trunk of belongings with great efficiency. The panic was gone and in its place was an assured but nonetheless terrible anxiety that drove me to fold and pack piles of my own and Leo's clothes with a speed and dexterity that was peculiarly disconcerting.

I rang my friend Maureen and barely had the words out before she said, 'Stay where you are, we're on the way in . . . ' And as I hung up I could hear her calling out to her husband Patrick, 'Warm up the truck – I'll explain on the way.'

Like me, Maureen's instinct was to act first and ask questions later. Since we had met some eight years before, Maureen had been more than a sister or friend to me. We both understood what it was to be desperately poor, and we both knew what it was to lose a loved one. Maureen had become separated from her husband when he went in search of work during the Great Depression and she had ended up homeless with two children in New York. I had come upon her sitting on the steps of the Metropolitan Museum on Fifth Avenue, where she had been all night, in a state of such desperation that she had put aside her

Irishwoman's pride (we are no beggars) and accepted my offer to help her.

Together we had started a community to help rehabilitate and rehouse homeless families in Yonkers. Her warmth as a friend and fellow Irishwoman helped me recover my spirits after John's death, so that when her own husband, Patrick, reappeared a year after we had met, I was delighted for her.

I had left the community in Yonkers quickly, and under false pretences. In truth, I had no longer been running from my grief over John, but from the attentions of a man whom I had promised to marry. Matt was a part of the community, a good, kind person who would have made an excellent and attentive husband – but I had not been in love with him. I agreed to marry him because life looked easier with a man in it, and in the wake of losing John I had been grateful to slide into the easy companionship that he offered me. Matt made me feel safe, but deep in my heart I knew that the feelings he instilled in me were more to do with comfort than with real happiness. So, fearful that his love for me and my rawness over John would talk me into a passionless union, I put the infant Tom on my hip and headed off in search of adventure and a whole new life, leaving Matt, Maureen, Bridie and everyone else in the community with the most cursory of goodbyes.

With plenty of money in my pocket from the sale of my businesses in Ireland, and the whole of America unexplored in front of me, I only managed to make it as far as the apartment in Manhattan.

Within months of my grand exit I had realized that learning to be a mother to Tom was all the adventure I needed.

In any case, I found I could not stay away from Maureen and my beloved Bridie. I had relied heavily on John for his friendship as well as his love, but it had been my friends who had held me up after he died. Katherine, my right-hand woman in Ireland, had bought out several of my businesses and continued to manage my remaining affairs there without complaint or comment as to when, or if, I would ever return to claim them; Maureen, my soulmate in experience and age; Bridie, the old housekeeper who, for all her gruff complaining, had been more of a mother to me than my own ever had. How could I rear a child alone, when I had such wonderful people to share him with? Stepping away from them for a few months made me realize the wealth of love and warmth I had discarded along-side my fear of hurting Matt.

So I wrote to Maureen and she contacted me within days, informing me that Matt, broken-hearted, had left to go back to Ireland shortly after I took off.

He had written once to say that he had arrived safely, although to a great fuss, as the young wife he had left behind (whom I knew about) had told the entire town that he had died in America so that she could marry again. It seemed from his letter that he was rather enjoying the drama of being the maligned, returned emigrant – and I had no doubt that, with his fine figure and gentle demeanour, the other women of his village would be throwing themselves at him. Vindicated in my having done the right thing in not marrying him, I continued my close alliance with the Sweeney family and Bridie from my home in Manhattan.

So my journey back then was not by plane or train, as I had imagined it would be, but was the longer and more significant inner journey from mere businesswoman to 'artist' and mother.

Fire Island had been as far as I had felt the need to travel away from New York for a number of years, but now I was being pulled away from my haven, my home.

CHAPTER SIX

The headmaster arrived ten minutes after me and had Leo's friend, Julian Knox, with him. We stood in the hallway of the apartment. I did not offer them a seat.

Mr Cunningham seemed without his usual headmasterly puff – he had undoubtedly spent part of the hour since we had spoken consulting a lawyer: 'First, can I just say how sorry . . . '

I ignored him and addressed the boy.

'Where is Leo?' I asked.

He looked at me with diffident, disinterested eyes. He was a good-looking boy, broad and square-jawed – a sportsman – dripping with the gloss of privilege. So different from my sensitive Leo; I could not imagine why they had chosen each other as friends.

'Well?' I went on.

'Julian,' the headmaster said firmly, 'tell Mrs Irvington what you told me.'

The use of my married surname immediately irked me, and I watched as Julian's lip curled into a small smile.

'Leo met a man,' he said, looking me directly in the eye, full of bravado. I felt sick.

'And . . . ?' the headmaster said, missing the point.

Julian shrugged and looked away. 'There was a man at a pool-party at my parents' house – he said he was an actor's agent, and he offered Leo a screen test.'

He looked away again, bored. So help me God, but his insouciance made me want to lift my hand and strike him hard across the face.

'Julian . . . ' Cunningham reprimanded him.

'Leo thought this was a big deal, and kept on and on at me to help him follow it up, but we didn't go into the city for the rest of the summer, so . . . ' He widened his eyes at me and said, 'I think Leo's gone back to Hollywood to make his fortune.'

'Who is this man – what's his name?'

Julian shrugged again.

'Well then, I will need to speak to your mother,' I said, picking up the telephone.

Julian recited the number with an ease that was obnoxious and suggested that he had no fear of his mother, so I said, 'I should also like your father's place of work and telephone number in California, so that I might contact him when I get there.'

That struck a chord. Cunningham started flapping around like a black crow in his teacher's gown (which he doubtless kept on for the visit for added gravitas – like a priest – to intimidate me, no doubt). 'Now, really, there is no need . . . '

'Mr Cunningham, my son – who was in your care – has gone missing and, as far as I can gather, one or both of this boy's parents could be at least partly responsible. Either you proffer me contact details for Mr Knox, so that I can make my own investigations, or I put this matter immediately into the hands of the New York Police Department – in fact, perhaps I should hand this matter entirely over to them.'

Julian blushed bright red and started talking.

'I think his name was Fred – I'd never seen him before, so he doesn't know my parents, honestly. There's no point in calling my—'

'What was his surname?' I asked.

'I don't know – I can't remember.'

'Go on.'

'He gave Leo his business card, and Leo made a real fuss about it and kept going on about how he was going to be an actor – it was very annoying . . . ' the boy said under his breath, threatening to trail off.

'Continue, Julian,' the headmaster boomed. Julian looked at him with pleading eyes, but knew he had to go on.

'Last week I dared him to call Fred. Leo and I sneaked into the secretary's office and telephoned him – Leo had kept his card.'

'How did you get in?' the headmaster snapped. 'That door is kept locked.'

'The window from the gym,' Julian said, 'everybody knows that.'

The master covered his face with his hands and drew them down slowly in despair as the boy continued.

'Fred said he remembered Leo and that, if he made his way to his office in Hollywood, he'd arrange a screen test for him.'

'For the love of Christ, boy!' the headmaster had lost all semblance of propriety.

'Leo had stolen some money from his family in Yonkers the last time he was there.' I gasped with shock. Leo, steal money? 'He said he had enough for a one-way ticket. He left last night on the train – that's all I know, I swear.'

'Where is this man's office? What is his full name?' I asked.

'I don't kno-ow,' Julian wailed and then started to cry. 'Leo took his card with him. Honest, I don't know who he is. Please don't ring my father, Ma'am? Please, Sir? He'll kill me, he'll . . .'

I picked up the telephone and held it out to the headmaster, but he declined to take it from me.

'Please, Mrs Irvington, allow me to contact Mr Knox myself, on your behalf. I promise I will get onto it directly and contact you immediately after I speak with him.'

My hand tightened around the telephone. Men needed to hold on to their power, especially in front of other men – even boys. I wanted to hit him across the face with it – *You have lost my son! You stupid idiot, you let my vulnerable, sensitive son walk straight out of your charge!* – but instead I put the handset back in its cradle.

'One hour,' I said. 'I expect to hear back from you, one way or the other, in one hour, otherwise I shall be calling the police.'

'Of course,' he said, with the boy snivelling beside him. I stood aside and ushered them out of the door.

I had no intention of contacting the police. Leo, for all that I was petrified of what might have happened to him, was sixteen years of age and therefore old enough to look after himself, in the eyes of the law. Reporting him missing might only result in his arrest for vagrancy and even worse trouble. In any case, I could deal with this myself. I was his mother, and therefore more capable of finding my son than all the cops in America. Wherever he was, whomever he was with, I would find him and make things right.

When the door closed behind them I sat for a moment in the hallway of my empty apartment. What was this place now? I could hardly call it home any more, yet that's what I had intended it to be, for Charles and our two boys. Once it had been a family home: that clean kitchen table had been littered with the day-to-day detritus of family life – bills, invitations, discarded cups, gloves, a drawing from Leo awaiting my approval, a half-eaten sandwich discarded by Tom. The dresser had been neatly stacked with crockery; the small larder packed with dried goods; our outdoor garments and coats hung messily on the backs of chairs. Now it was just the pied-à-terre of a wealthy artist who preferred to live elsewhere. Fire Island felt like my home although I had no history in the place, but perhaps that was the very reason I felt so comfortable there. The simple, barefoot life between beach and studio suspended me in limbo each day: no looking back or forward; no fear of the future, no pain of the past. This apartment had once held the dream of how my life could have been – the vibrant, busy life of a loving couple in the heart of a big city with their two children. Now it was just a holding place for the forgotten accoutrements of a family life once lived: the jigsaw that nobody could be bothered to finish, left behind on the dresser; a bag of rotting flour for cakes that would never get baked; drawers of Charles' starched evening shirts and my fancy silk underwear – clothes for the corpses of our marriage. The family life that I had craved for so long seemed only to exist in these unwanted belongings, abandoned fragments from our life together.

It was late afternoon. I would have to act fast if I was going to get on my way that night. It had taken Leo the guts of three days to get there and back. For him, it had been a great adventure, travelling across America by train. How I wished he had done that journey with me! Perhaps, if I had been a more attentive mother, taken him on more adventures myself, he wouldn't have needed to go chasing off looking for one himself.

The quickest way would be to fly. Some years ago Charles and I had considered a plane ride to Los Angeles on a Douglas Sleeper Transport passenger plane. The trip took seventeen hours and thirty minutes westbound, with stops in Pittsburgh, Kansas City and Albuquerque. The flights were very expensive, but Charles had almost persuaded me, except that in the end I had not wanted to travel without the children, so it had become just another source of friction between us; another unlived dream. I was on the point of scrabbling around his desk to look for the brochure when I remembered that air travel was impossible. There was a war on (even though it didn't really feel like it in New York), and a lot of aircraft had been commandeered by the war effort. With a sudden panic I realized that I had heard on the radio recently that they were following suit with train travel. 'We will all have to make sacrifices,' Roosevelt had said. I had taken no notice whatsoever at the time, but now that bit of unimportant trivia came booming into my head as a glaring headline: 'Restricted train travel as a result of war effort'.

With my hands shaking, I called Grand Central Station and cried, 'Thank God!' with relief, when the man booked me into the last private compartment on the *Broadway Limited*, an express passenger train with limited stops. It left at six that evening and arrived at nine the next morning into LaSalle Street Station in Chicago. 'Just fifteen hours to Chicago,' the ticket seller boasted.

From Chicago the next train to Los Angeles was *The Golden State*, which left at 10.15 that evening and arrived at 5.15 p.m. two days later. At more than forty hours' travel time, it was somewhat slower and slightly less smart than the other trains, but neither of them left Chicago until early the following morning.

Two more days. That was three days' travel in total. It felt like a lifetime.

Maureen arrived as I put the phone down.

'Ellie,' Maureen grabbed my hands, 'this is all my fault!'

She had checked in her bureau drawer before leaving and found that Leo had emptied the envelope of money that I regularly sent her for his keep. Maureen rarely spent the money, so there was a tidy sum piled up – she had no idea how much, but certainly enough to buy him a train ticket.

I waved her guilt aside. There was no time for recriminations. I was still absorbing the fact that Leo had lied, and stolen, as well as run away to Hollywood, of all places! In any case, we had to leave for the station.

As we were going out the door Mr Cunningham, true to his word, called me back.

'The man you are looking for is called Frederick Dubois and, as far as Mr Knox could find out, he can be contacted at the Chateau Marmont – a sort of hotel, it seems, in North Hollywood.'

I wrote it down, my stomach sickened even at the spelling of his name – what did 'sort of hotel' mean, and what kind of person would live in such a place? The kind of man who would lure a young boy away from his family?

'Mr Knox would like to apologize for any inconvenience caused and assure you that Julian will be punished accordingly.'

Cunningham's voice sounded dry – as if he knew the boy's punishment would be greater than the crime. Julian Knox might have been a troublemaking weasel of a child, but I did not want him hurt.

'You can tell Mr Knox there is no need to punish his son. I am sure Leo was just as responsible.'

'I'm afraid it's too late for that,' Cunningham replied, as if this whole thing were my fault, and putting another's child's welfare on my conscience.

Honestly, I thought, not for the first time, *men really are such petty fools – always passing the blame and never taking responsibility for problems they cause.* Men were brave when it came to their rash and usually pointless acts of war, but they were cowards, each and every one, when it came to owning up to their mistakes. If women were running the world, how much smoother and more sensible our lives would be.

I rang the operator and asked to be put through to the hotel that Cunningham had mentioned and asked to speak to Mr Dubois.

'You mean Freddie?' the man asked and then, before waiting for an answer, got off the line and another man came on.

'Mr Dubois?' I asked.

'Yes – this is he.'

He sounded arrogant – young. I tried to keep my voice steady. Although every inch of me was aching to scream hysterically down the phone, I didn't know this man and it was important not to antagonize him.

'My name is Mrs Eileen Irvington – I understand my son, Leo Irvington, is with you?'

'Leo? He's on his way here, he called me last night. Is there a problem?'

How could he ask me such a thing? And yet his voice sounded so calm, with no hint of contrition or fear. For a moment I considered this stranger's question. Leo was sixteen. In less than two years' time he would be eligible for conscription into the US Army. John had joined the Irish Republicans and fought when he was barely a year older than Leo was now. Some might consider Leo already a man. Leo was not my natural son and had only been in my care for six years; it was too short a time, and I was not ready to let him go. Not yet. He was confused, distraught. Despite having run off in this way, Leo was not ready for me to let him go, either. Even if he did not know it yet.

'No problem,' I said. 'I was just concerned about him, and was checking that everything was all right.'

'All tickety-boo,' the idiot man said. He didn't sound dangerous, but then, what does dangerous sound like? I established that he and Leo would be staying at the Chateau Marmont indefinitely, but decided not to tell him that I was on my way to Los Angeles.

Frederick sounded innocent enough, but nonetheless I did not want to give him the opportunity to abscond with my son; nor did I know what hold he had over Leo. I loved Leo as much as if he had been my natural son – at least I believed that to be true. However, at that moment I realized that I was not as certain of his love for me. Leo was doubtless confused, and somewhat lost, after the death of his father. The world was a big place, and I was sharply aware that if this man decided to move them away from the hotel for any reason, they might disappear off into the big wide world and I could lose my son forever. The idea of that was intolerable to me, so I gave no indication that I was coming to get Leo; I merely established his whereabouts, in case I needed to get in touch for any reason.

At least I knew where Leo was. Now all I had to do was find him and bring him back home.

On our drive to the station both Maureen and Patrick offered to come with me to the West Coast, individually and together, until they ended up squabbling over it. I told them I would prefer to travel alone. I would focus my mind on what needed to be done and get through the journey that way. We agreed that they would collect Tom from Fire Island and keep him in Yonkers until I returned, hopefully in a few days' time, and with Leo.

Patrick collected my ticket and loaded my case onto the train, while Maureen took a moment to take my hands and settle me. We had been through a lot together and she never forgot my original act of kindness to her family. I didn't need her thanks. She had more than repaid any debt she thought she owed me, but she was the only person from whom I would take advice.

She squeezed both my hands in hers and said, 'At least you

know where he is now, Ellie. Leo is a sensible boy. He'll be fine. Now, you call me – as soon as you get there.'

I nodded, lost for words. Then she hugged me and, taking my shoulder, said, 'Have you everything you need – enough money? Do you need to get a cardigan out of your bag for the journey?'

'Stop,' I said.

'I will telegram Patrick's cousin Anne, in Chicago, and have her collect you from LaSalle Station. She lives nearby.

'There's no need, Maureen, please . . . '

I did not need, or want, the company of some strange woman.

'Rubbish,' she said insistently. 'It's a long journey, Ellie, and there is a full day to kill before your train leaves for Los Angeles. You'll be glad of some interesting company once you get there and, believe me, Anne will provide quite a distraction.'

'Really, there's no need.'

'It's done,' she said as if doing me a huge favour, and I could not disabuse her of the notion that she was helping.

'Besides, Anne lords it over me something terrible – I swear that is the only reason she is friendly with me, because she can brag about her big life in Chicago. I want you to tell me what you think of her house; whether it's as magnificent as she says it is. For me, Ellie? Meet her for me?'

She was pretending to ask me a favour. It was our currency, our secret Irish way of doing things – the way we looked after each other.

'Oh! I wish I was coming with you,' she suddenly said.

In that moment, so did I. 'Are you sure you'll be all right?' she asked finally.

No, I was not sure. I dreaded having to endure this long journey to find Leo, and was terrified he might be gone when I got there. He was out of my sight, outside of my jurisdiction. I felt completely powerless and out of control.

'Of course,' I said smiling, 'I'll be grand.'

The *Broadway Limited* had been sitting like a giant metal slug on the platform. It was reassuringly large and solid, more like a boat than a train.

Its engines suddenly screamed into life and both Maureen and I jumped, each letting out a half-laugh that ended with a smile. It felt like a relief.

'I'll be fine, Maureen – really. I'll call as soon as I get to Los Angeles.'

I had booked a single sleeper car. Sleeping was unlikely, but I wanted to travel alone. I could not bear the idea of attracting company, no matter how convivial, but the moment I was settled in my seat and the train started moving, I regretted the decision.

The light was gone from the day, but New York City was never dark and, as the train thundered along the tracks above the streets and shops, the sky above me glowed a dull, misty orange. I closed my eyes and finally allowed myself to sink into my thoughts.

Although I had never sought Charles' advice when he was there to give it, now I had an urgent longing for my second husband. He was Leo's father, after all – he would have known what to do. In those early New York days Charles' friendship had given me confidence and comfort. Later, when I started the community in Yonkers, he had protected us from the interests of gangs and criminals. Charles was a man's man, a union man – handsome, self-assured and principled. Most men were happy to let him into their midst and negotiate with their bosses; most women would happily have allowed him to sweep them completely off their feet. Perhaps, if I had been a different sort of woman – the sort of woman who could give herself over entirely to the better capabilities of a man – I would not be alone here in this situation. Perhaps if I had not been so selfish in pursuing my own needs as an artist, perhaps if I had been less pig-headed in my everyday dealings with Charles, if I had been more respectful of his household foibles, had bowed to his wishes more – perhaps if I had been less enthralled with my sons, and more loving towards him – Charles would still be here with me now?

Yet, I reminded myself, while he had been an affectionate beau, and then a persistent and passionate lover, once we were married, I had felt Charles move away from me.

There was no defining moment, no specific incident that made it clear that Charles' love for me was waning, just a gradual ebbing of passion and respect, on both our parts, if truth be told. The love that began our marriage started falling like sand through a sieve; shaken by small cruelties – a sarcastic remark, a turned shoulder, a joke fallen flat – until our marriage was emptied of affection and kindness, but running simply on the mutuality of a shared roof and children.

I believed it was because Charles had craved having me for so long that, once he got me to marry him, I lost the cachet of the unavailable. As his wife, I became humdrum to him, and Charles loved drama; he hated things to be ordinary. That was, I came to believe, where much of his motivation as a political agitator and activist came from – the drama of rhetoric. The plight of the downtrodden. While I became cynical about his activities, he became dismissive of my work as an artist. Our love was not strong enough to humour our differences, although, looking back, it should have been. It certainly should have been. Anger and bitterness and grief – war wounds from our previous marriages – destroyed us. Life and experience are supposed to make you strong, but sometimes life itself can batter and weaken love. Love needs nurturing and protecting, especially marital love, which is so easily muted by disagreement and the dullness of the everyday. We took our love for granted. Perhaps I did more than him.

Charles believed that our marriage had died because I still loved my first husband. 'I can't compete with a dead hero,' he said to me late one night, after he had been drinking and I had refused his attempt to make love.

I had left Charles and returned to Ireland and my husband John. Charles, as dashing and as handsome a charmer as he was to this young, heady housemaid, had not succeeded in keeping me in America. John's love was my life-blood. Charles was a bonus – his attention flattered and pleased me, but he had never held the same claim on my heart.

We spent more and more time apart from one another. At first because we were busy; I worked in the studio during the day, and when I could I attended functions and openings with Hilla in the evenings – leaving the children to stay over with the Sweeneys rather than inconvenience Charles. Charles stopped expecting me to cook him meals in the evening – I did not ask him to help me with the children. By not asking anything of the other, or allowing the other the satisfaction of giving, we were disallowing each other's love.

He began to travel more and more with his union work. The war raging in Europe had brought talk of it to America. That aside, we were in recovery from the Great Depression and every-where there were pockets of political activity brewing – male sap would rise with the promise of empowerment, and Charles Irvington, the great charmer, would be called in to set up a new union or negotiate a failing one into better terms.

The previous November, less than twelve months ago, Charles had announced that he had to go to Hawaii.

'You'll be back for Christmas?' I said – more as an accusation than a question.

In truth, I was growing tired of the coldness between us. I did not ask Charles any details of his business in Hawaii, but some part of me resolved that, when he did return, I would take some time away from my own work and make the effort to be a good wife to him that Christmas.

The evening he left I had planned to cook for us all, but at the last minute Hilla had begged me to join her at dinner with a visiting collector from Los Angeles. 'The Arensbergs are important collectors, Ellie, but Walter can be a frightful bore – he's obsessed with the idea that William Shakespeare was really somebody else and goes on and on about it until I think I'm going to scream – please, Ellie.' So Maureen took the boys out to Yonkers, and I left a note for Charles telling him there was a hot plate of food in the oven and that we looked forward to seeing him again in a couple of weeks' time. When I returned late that night the oven was switched off, but the plate of food was still inside, cold and congealed. The note was where I had left it, with no comment from him. His travel case was gone from above the wardrobe, his shaving kit from the bathroom.

I never saw Charles again.

CHAPTER SEVEN

My friends from Yonkers had shared Thanksgiving with us the weekend after Charles left. There were ten of us sitting around the table in the apartment and, like most homes in America even in the thinnest of times, it was groaning with the best food we could muster. In addition to the turkey, Bridie had roasted a ham and made a corned beef, 'Irish-style'. Despite myself, I had felt Charles' absence. As we sat holding hands to give thanks, I saw how petty and pointless many of our small cruelties were. For my part, at least, it seemed unfair that I would prepare such a lavish feast for friends, yet resent doing the same for him as an act of female servitude. Many of our problems stemmed, I knew, from the fact that I had married Charles despite being uncertain if I wanted to be married at all. He picked up on my reticence and it frightened and hurt him, so he turned against me. Yet with my friends all smiling around the table, the warmth of the fire and the food, the candlelight glow of Maureen's Thanksgiving centrepiece and Patrick carving the turkey, being married didn't seem like such a terrible thing.

During the Depression, Patrick and Maureen had lost each other. He had gone looking for work and she had become evicted from their temporary shack. They were reunited by virtue of their refusal to give up hope of finding each other, and a dose of God's good luck. Fate refused to part them, and they gave thanks for that every day. Fate had played its part with Charles and me, too – reuniting us over oceans and continents and decades – and yet I took his love for me for granted and, at times, reviled it as a curtailment of my freedom. Perhaps a happy marriage was not caused so much by fate, I thought, as by our response to it. I held the hands of both my sons and outwardly gave thanks for them and 'for the love of my absent husband', inwardly making a secret pact with myself to be a better wife on Charles' return.

On Sunday 7th December I had given the boys a pot-roast chicken lunch straight after Mass and told them to occupy themselves, as I was going to get stuck into cleaning the apartment. Leo was reading in the drawing room and Tom was in his room playing with his building blocks, having turned the entire room into a tent using the bed-sheets I had just stripped. Both my sons were happily occupied and I was free to clean.

I had decided to prepare early for Christmas and give the apartment a good clear-out before putting up the decorations. I wanted this Christmas to be a special one. Leo was fifteen and Tom six. Charles had called each Saturday night while he was away and had promised he would be back by mid-December.

'I'm taking the full month of December off from work,' I said.

He paused on the other end and I felt he was happy about my decision, but before he could make a comment to that effect, I could not help but add the proviso: 'Hilla says I have too much work stockpiled, and I should take a break and come back with fresh ideas in the New Year.'

'Well, bully for Hilla!' he said.

'And I want to spend some more time with the boys . . . '

And you. I meant to say it, I should have said it, but I just couldn't.

'I'm almost finished up here anyway,' he said. 'I've done as much as I can for them for the time being, but I'll probably need to spend a good bit more time out here next year.'

Was he tapping another nail into the lid of the coffin of our marriage? Or inviting me to beg him not to go? It was not a conversation to have on the phone, but it was a conversation that I was determined to have. One way or another, I could not continue living in this no-man's-land of a marriage. We would have to move forward or end it. Christmas and the New Year would be time enough to tell what would be for the best.

I was up on a chair, dusting. The ceilings in the apartment were high and their dust-filled edges easy to ignore; dead insects and other debris clumped in the corners, unseen and ignored – I didn't dare think when I had last given the apartment a thorough going-over. I had spent the best part of my youth and my twenties scrubbing and cleaning – for myself, because I had been reared to believe that cleanliness was next to godliness; and then for other people, to earn money, before I was sure that I knew how to do anything else. By the time I was in my late twenties I had enough sense and money to pay other women to do it for me. Yet here I was, in an old dress, with a scarf wrapped around my hair, choosing to dust and quite enjoying myself!

I turned the radio up high on *Sammy Kaye's Sunday Serenade*; Jimmy Durante was singing 'Inka Dinka Doo', and Tom danced into the room so delighted with himself that I was afraid he would knock me off the chair. The song finished and just as Tom was begging for more music there was an announcement: 'From the NBC Newsroom in New York. President Roosevelt has said in a statement today that the Japanese have attacked Pearl Harbor, Hawaii, from the air.'

The statement was repeated twice, to let us know this was not simply devastating news, but had the gravitas and consequence of history.

Charles was in Hawaii. I didn't know anything about why he had gone there or what he was doing. I just knew that he was in Hawaii. Although I could not imagine any reason why he should be near the naval base, I still felt sick.

I immediately switched off the radio so that the boys could not hear the news, then ran to the bureau in the hall where Charles had left his contact details for Hawaii. It was for the offices of the Communist Party of the United States of America in Honolulu. The CPUSA was by no means in charge of all of the unions in America, but was usually involved, officially or unofficially, in much of the work that Charles did, particularly in setting up new unions or agitating workers to rise up against the unjust and exploitative methods of ruthless corporations – many of which, far from merely surviving, had actively used people's desperation to enable their own businesses to thrive during the Depression.

I reached frantically for the phone. It was a Sunday, so of course there was no reply.

I had to wait. He would telephone. Charles would call as soon as he heard the news, to let us know he was all right. He would know I would be worried. As soon as he could get to a phone, he would call. An hour passed. Two hours. I cleaned. What else could I do? The radio was full of news, although I could not leave it on in case the boys heard what had happened, so I just sneaked into the kitchen and put my ear to the wireless while they were occupied. I would not have them see me looking uncertain or frightened. There was no mention of civilian deaths, and it was the naval base that had been attacked. Charles would most certainly have no business with the Navy. Perhaps it was not as bad as it sounded – although one of the bulletins mentioned that Burma had been bombed, and there was quickly talk of America going to war, but I didn't care about any of that. I just wanted my husband to call and let me know he was safe, so that I could reassure myself and, more importantly, the boys. Cars had come to a standstill outside our window – Leo called me over to look at a small gathering of our neighbours on the corner of West 27th and 10th talking excitedly, shaking their heads, a woman crying.

'What has happened – do you suppose someone has died?' he said. 'Shall I call over and see?'

'Don't be such a nosy parker, Leo,' I snapped. 'Get in there and finish all those studies – I'll come in and check on you.'

He made a face, but went back to his books without thinking. I just thanked God that it was winter and our windows were closed. In the summer they were open all day, and Leo loved to gossip with our neighbours across the fire-escape door at the back. His mother had brought him up in the cold privilege of a big, isolated house with servants, and Leo loved the novelty of living somewhere he was surrounded by people. For all that he was sensitive, he was turning into a friendly and outgoing young man, full of charm as well as good looks, although he seemed to relate better to adults than to boys of his own age, and would happily gossip for hours with the mothers of his peers while they played baseball in the alleys below.

The afternoon Pearl Harbor was attacked the whole of the United States was in shock, but I would not breathe a word to my sons of war or bombs, or of any potential danger to their father, until I was certain what was going on. Uncertainty was, quite simply, not on my agenda as a mother. The boys might choose what to have for dinner, but everything important was cut and dried and presented as a neatly wrapped package to them. As much as I loved them as my own, they were, in reality, both waifs abandoned by their mothers. It was my duty to make their lives secure, to make them believe that the world was a safe place.

As two hours turned to four, I kept on telling myself there was nothing wrong. The selfish man had not thought to call and reassure us that he was alive, which he surely must be. The CPUSA office would be open on Monday, and I would keep the boys from school until I had spoken to the office and they had reassured me that Charles was fine. I wanted to know he was safe; but, more than that, I wanted to speak to him myself, so that I could lift the shadow on my conscience that feared Charles did not think I cared for him enough to bother whether he lived or died.

I prepared a meal of ham and mashed potatoes for the boys, although I could not face eating myself.

'Are you all right, Mammy?' Leo asked when he saw that I wasn't joining them.

'I'm fine, love,' I said, 'I just don't feel like eating.'

'Can we go to the park?' Tom asked.

'No, Tom, not today.'

'Pleeease . . . '

The phone rang and I ran to the hall, almost tripping over myself and grabbing the handset.

'Charles?'

There was a pause on the other end of the phone, then a man's voice said, 'Is that Mrs Irvington? Mr Charles Irvington's wife?'

I knew immediately what had happened.

CHAPTER EIGHT

Charles had been driving to the docks with three shipyard workers. It was not a Japanese bomb that hit them, but a misguided anti-aircraft shell. They were all killed. It had taken them some time to identify Charles, and more time again for the CPUSA representative in Hawaii to be contacted.

It was the office manager in New York who called me. He asked me if I was sitting down.

I was shocked, but not as shocked as I might have been, had I received the call before I heard the news about Pearl Harbor on the radio. Bad things happen in life. Losing John had taught me that, and I cannot pretend that the death of my first husband wasn't the first thing that entered my head. This was a terrible thing that had happened, a tragedy, but it could not compare to going out to feed the hens and coming back to find the love of my life dead in the kitchen, from a heart attack in his thirties. So my first reaction was more dismay than despair – followed by a presiding sense of guilt that I was not overcome with a widow's grief.

My main concern was how to tell the boys, how to break it to them that their father was dead.

Charles had an easier relationship with Tom, even though he wasn't his biological son, than he did with Leo. Tom was so young when I married Charles that he always thought of him as his actual father, and Charles adopted the boisterous toddler fully as his own. Leo was the image of his father – and perhaps his well-spoken, gentle teenage son reminded Charles of the life he had hoped to leave behind. Tom was a bawdier child, out-going and affectionate; he demanded Charles' attention in a simpler way. A man likes to mould his sons to his way of thinking, and Tom was younger than Leo. Charles could pick Tom up and throw him over his shoulder and, as the child screamed with delight, he would feel like a king. With Tom there were no lost years to make up for; no disappointments, no judgements, no history. Tom was another man's son for him to impress; he was easy. Leo was a more difficult child for Charles to love, and in matters of love, I had learned, men like things to be as simple as possible.

As I put down the receiver, I took a deep breath in. As I exhaled, it came out in a loud sob and I clasped my hand to my mouth to quell the noise. The tears came automatically; the shock would not let me hold them in, after all. I took a moment to myself and cried some of it out, but I would not let go completely. After John died it had taken me a year before I started to grieve, then it had crippled me to my bed in a dark depression. I was a mother now, and no such indulgences were possible. I would grieve for Charles properly, with dignity and respect – but first I had to look after the children.

I swept the palms of my hands across my face to push back the tears, then went into the living room and gathered Tom and Leo onto the settee.

'I have some sad news,' I said.

'Father is dead,' Leo blurted out.

Tom looked at him, blinking, waiting for an explanation.

'How did you . . . ?'

'I heard the news about Pearl Harbor, and he was in Hawaii, wasn't he? Plus you've been crying.'

I was so taken aback, I didn't know what to say. So I just sat between them and gathered them both by their waists into me.

Tom started to cry. I don't think he was even sure why, but then Leo's beautiful face collapsed in a grimace of grief and, unable to bear their pain, I started too. We sat like that and cried together for ten, maybe fifteen minutes, then they followed me to the kitchen and I made us all hot toast and butter, washed down with sweet milky tea.

That night they both slept in the bed with me.

'Is father in heaven with the angels?' Tom asked.

'He most certainly is,' I assured him.

And Tom seemed pleased 'that was that', replying, 'Good – I don't feel sad any more.'

Leo said nothing more about it, but I knew that, in his private world, he was afraid I might abandon him, as both his birth mother and, in all honesty, his father had done – in his life, and now in his death.

Nothing could have been further from the truth.

Charles' funeral was a nightmare to organize.

I rang his younger brother straight away. The opposite of Charles, Edwin Irvington was a wealthy buffoon, who had to make good – when times got difficult financially – by taking a job in a bank. He turned out to be rather good at it and, although he had sold much of the land, he still lived in a grand family house in upstate New York. I liked Edwin. He was a bit of a posh fool, but he was a decent man and very fond of Charles. Leo had stayed with him and his family for much of his early life.

Edwin cried out in shock and broke down when I told him what had happened. After he had gathered himself, he said he would break the news himself to his parents.

'How's Leo?' he asked.

'He'll be all right,' I said.

'Let us know if we can do anything.' And, while I appreciated that the offer was made in good faith, he added the warning, 'I expect my mother will be in touch with you.'

The following morning I got a call from The Plaza from Minnie Irvington, Charles' mother. She did not bother addressing me by name or offering condolences. As far as Minnie was concerned, I was (and always would be) her errant son's Irish whore – the font of all his socialist aspirations, and therefore all of her family's ills.

'I need to know what time the – corpse – will be arriving, so that we can arrange to have – it – picked up by our family undertaker. We can make arrangements with regard to Leo after the funeral.'

The Irvingtons were an influential family. Although they had lost much of their fortune during the Great Depression, Charles' parents nonetheless saw themselves as being of an elevated social class. While it was Edwin who had worked with his father and salvaged enough of their business to keep them out of the slums, Charles was their golden boy. Although he had turned his back on his parents at a young age (even organizing the shipyard union that his father believed had crippled his business – although good sense suggested the opposite was true), I knew that Charles' death would turn him immediately back into their blond-haired, blue-eyed son.

Leo, in whom they had shown little interest in the five years since I had adopted him, was now their beloved grandson – a miniature Charles – and doubtless they had plans to turn him into some sort of Irvington heir to make up for Charles' undoing of the family name. They were also terrified, I think, that, being Irish, I might give their son a Catholic burial before they had the chance to claim him back. Minnie Irvington may have been Charles' mother and Leo's grandmother, but in my opinion (and that of my late husband and adoptive son) she fell woefully short in both roles.

'I will let you know as soon as I am told myself,' I said, knowing full well that he was arriving on Wednesday morning, 'and I'll leave details of the funeral arrangements for you at The Plaza front desk,' I added.

'He was an *Irvington*,' she said, 'and he will be buried as such.'

'He was my husband,' I said, 'and a great man, and I will give him the funeral he would have wanted – and there will be no arrangements regarding Leo, who is my son by law. You are welcome to come and visit him here at our home in Chelsea, by appointment with me.'

'You'll hear from our lawyers by the end of the day,' she said.

'Crack on ahead and do that, why don't you?' I said in my best Irish drawl. 'I look forward to hearing from them.' And I hung up.

Next on the phone was the CPUSA, which was equally determined to take over. Although the Communist Party had played an important role in setting up unions and starting a labour movement, it had never really succeeded in bringing America's working man round to their political agenda. Men were happy to take support and organizational expertise from the communists, but they drew the line when it came to joining the Communist Party itself.

Charles Irvington was the jewel in their crown. The son of a wealthy industrialist, he eschewed a life of privilege for his beliefs. Charles' death was an opportunity for the failed bureaucrats of this failed party to make a martyr out of their best union negotiator.

Charles was a fully paid-up member of the CPUSA, but while he agreed with the overall principles of equality and justice, I knew he was deeply cynical about what he saw as the petty ideologies that stood in the way of communism becoming a popular belief system. He had started out in the Socialist Party of America and, when he became disillusioned with them, had simply defected to their rivals, the CPUSA. In truth Charles, despite espousing politics as his motivation, was never a party player. His loyalty was always with the people, not the principles. He saw his fellow members as little more than civil servants, but he needed their organizations to employ him to do the work he loved, and he was enough of a politician himself to never let on how little he thought of them. If Charles had been a more ambitious type of man, he would certainly have been party leader. With his good looks and charm, he possibly had what it took to lead the communists into mainstream American politics. The party bosses knew that and, while Charles could not be persuaded to take a public role while he was alive, they were determined to make a communist hero of him in death.

The CPUSA had taken responsibility for Charles' body in Hawaii. Respectfully deferring to me at every turn, they had arranged and paid for him to be embalmed, dressed in a suit and put into an expensive mahogany coffin, and then organized for the body to be transported back to New York.

By all news accounts, the attack had caused the worst kind of carnage.

Body parts around the harbour were being buried in mass graves. Hundreds of people were missing and assumed dead, while badly burned corpses remained unidentifiable. Charles and the shipyard workers were matched to the car they were in, and were quickly missed by the people they were going to meet. Having been hit by falling debris, their car had collided with a wall; but, protected from the worst excesses of fire, their bodies were still intact. It was a small mercy, but a mercy nonetheless.

I was grateful for all that the party had done, but I was not wrong in assuming that there was a proviso attached to their generosity.

'Although Charles had been working with our Hawaiian comrades on the withdrawal of the US armed forces, since Germany attacked Russia, things have changed. Perhaps Charles' untimely death was no coincidence. The Comintern believes . . .'

I wasn't going to listen to this nonsense.

'Frankly, I don't much care what the Comintern believes. Charles was negotiating with plantation owners for better conditions and wages for Hawaiian workers – that is all.'

They weren't going to give up that easily. This was wartime, and dead bodies were valuable political currency.

'The Comintern believes that Comrade Irvington's death offers us an opportunity to show ourselves allied with . . . '

'When the body arrives in New York tomorrow, I would like it brought directly to my undertakers,' I asserted. I would not be bullied by some petty bureaucrat.

'Provision has already been made with an excellent firm, on behalf of the Comin—'

'Well, unmake it,' I snapped. 'Charles will be buried, by me, in a place and with a funeral home of my choosing.'

I thanked the speaker for all his help, and he said he would have to get somebody else to call me to finalize delivery of the body – doubtless a more senior figure, to further try and persuade

me to let them give my husband a 'hero's funeral', which would
have driven his family insane and presented him to the world
as a political zealot, which I knew he was not.

Bridie recommended the funeral director who had buried her
husband of forty years. I was astonished when she produced his
business card from a pocket in her purse the day the Sweeneys
came to console me, as if she had been carrying it about with
her all those years, to use on just such an occasion.

'He was a good friend of Mr Flannery, and he'll be sure to
look after Charles. Everybody deserves a good funeral,' she said,
'and Lord knows your wedding was scant enough.'

It was her way of apologizing for her harsh judgement of
Charles for much of his life.

The night before his funeral I arranged for Charles' body to be
brought down to a public house on the docks that he used to
frequent, to be properly waked. I left him in the care of his first
union cell, the men who had worked for his father in the shipyard – his oldest, closest friends. They drank and sang around
him all night and he would have loved it. His old workmates
and friends, the labouring men, released his spirit across the
bleak grey buildings and warehouses and loading bays that he
loved so much, and out to sea – to freedom. Charles was always
striving to be somebody else, somebody that the privilege of his
birth would never allow him to be. That was my gift to him:
the wake of a working man, a tribute to the life he always
wanted to have.

The funeral itself was a much more muted affair. I loved Leo
too much to cause a ruinous relationship with Charles' family,
so I gave Minnie Irvington her Protestant service and he was
buried alongside all the great political activists and abolitionists

in Green Wood Cemetery, which appeased his CPUSA associates somewhat.

The boys and I followed the coffin. I put my hands firmly on both their shoulders as they cried while walking down the long aisle – Tom in confusion, Leo in shocked disbelief that his father was in the black box with the brass handles. I did not cry. I kept myself strong for them although, in all honesty, I could not cry with so many strangers' eyes on me. I had been here before, when John died. The sea of mourners, their solemn clothes, the expectant pity on their faces; quiet speculations and judgements silently shuddering through them like whispers of warm wind.

I held on to my boys and focused on keeping them safe; moving them through the strangeness of the day as if we were one beast. At the graveside I looked across and saw Minnie for the first time that day, although I assumed she had been sitting behind me in the church, as she would not have shared a pew with me. She had a small, delicate physique and was, as always, immaculately turned out, but her face did not look like the grieving face of a woman who had lost a son. She wore an expression of stoic defensiveness, but for one moment she looked across and held my eye and I saw a look of profound disappointment, deeper and more terrible than any sadness, and one that I recognized in myself.

Charles had let us both down. He had been the measure of our dreams: her for a golden son to carry on the family empire, me for a good man to complete my family idyll.

One way or another we had lost our dreams, and probably not through Charles' misdoing, but through our own expectations of how things should be.

After a few seconds Minnie arched an eyebrow at me and

pointedly pulled the black veil of her broad hat down over her face.

We had wrestled for control of this day, yet neither of us felt the pang of victory.

CHAPTER NINE

My sleeping compartment or 'roomette' on the train was very comfortable, with a broad window and a comfortable divan seat that doubled as a full-length bed. Nonetheless it became claustrophobic after the light outside faded and the rural landscape disappeared into blackness. On such a long journey it was important to relax into the time ahead and enjoy the luxuries on offer. However, I could not settle and the first hour passed like a lifetime, looking out of the window and ruminating on my past, watching ten minutes turn to fifteen. Leo was on his own. Or rather not on his own, but in the company of some stranger – my mind began to wander down dark alleys, and I drew myself back, knowing I would lose my mind if I let myself wonder what was happening to him. My son was outside of my care and this damned train wasn't going to get me there any quicker because of it.

One way or another I had to find a way of occupying myself for the next fifteen hours or so. I checked myself in the vanity unit next to the bed – I looked unkempt and worn. I had not brushed my teeth or eaten since dawn. It seemed longer than a day since I had left Fire Island – what a distance I had travelled since then!

I straightened my hair and applied a little lipstick and rouge, and was pleased to note that I felt hungry. A meal would pass the time and perhaps, with food in my stomach, maybe even a half-bottle of wine, I might sleep.

I walked down the corridor towards the dining car. When I presented myself to the maitre d' at the desk, he informed me that the dining car was full and there were reservations for the next hour at least. By this time I was famished with hunger and desperate to eat. His manner implied incredulity that I expected to get a meal on a train without prior reservation, and I could see behind him that every seat was taken, so there was no sense in arguing or pleading with him.

He took my name and told me he would do his very best to accommodate me, if I would like to wait in the lounge car.

I made a beeline for the one free seat left in the lounge. Next to it was a small table with a bowl of nuts and a folded news-paper on it. I picked up the paper and opened it, grateful for the distraction, and began hungrily popping the nuts into my mouth.

'Ahem.'

I looked up from the paper and there was an elegant, older man standing in front of me. He looked foreign, with olive skin and a distinguished silvery beard that stood out against it, and he was wearing a casually cut linen suit that seemed expensive.

'Do you mind?' he asked.

I thought, there being no seats left, that he intended to perch himself on the table in front of me. The cheek!

'Yes, actually, I do,' I said. It was clearly dog-eat-dog, getting seats and meals on trains these days, and it was his hard luck for not coming down sooner.

Before he could object any further, a steward came over and addressed him: 'Mr Lilius, your table in the dining car is ready.'

I looked at him haughtily – mad that he was getting his dinner and I wasn't – then moved the paper up over my face again. As I did so, the bearded gentleman asked, 'Would you mind if I take my paper? You see, I do hate eating alone.'

Oh God, I was in the poor man's seat! I jumped up, mortified.

'Unless, of course, you'd care to join me?'

Stanislaw ('Stan') Lilius was a successful composer in his native Poland, and he had come here at the beginning of the war three years ago.

'I knew Hitler would get round to us,' he said, 'and I didn't want to be there when he did.'

As far as I could gather, Stan had no family back in Poland and had come to America out of a mixture of curiosity and greed. 'Why does anyone come here from Europe?'

'For a new start?' I said.

'Is that why you came,' he asked, 'from Ireland, yes?'

He obviously didn't want to talk about what was happening in Poland. European refugees, and even ordinary immigrants who had come to America before Hitler's reign, were sensitive about the war. I understood that – the guilt of leaving people you loved and would never see again, of walking away from your history. It was easier to focus on 'the land of opportunity' than face what you had left behind.

'Is my accent that obvious?' I asked.

'I am a musician – I listen to voices, sounds. And Ellie is Eileen, yes? What were you running away from? War as well, perhaps? I know the Irish love to fight with the English . . . '

'And with each other,' I said, 'when we've taken a few drinks.'

He laughed and I felt ridiculously pleased with myself for having made a joke.

I smiled and then, despite myself, raised my eyebrows at him

playfully and took another mouthful of steak to indicate that I
didn't intend to answer any more questions about myself. I didn't
feel like talking, just listening.

'A mystery . . . okay . . . okay.'

Stan didn't push me, but just talked about himself while I ate.
He was travelling back to his home in Hollywood after a one-
month teaching stint at the prestigious Manhattan School of
Music. He lived alone in a house in the hills above Hollywood
– and he lived well, as far as I could gather.

'The movie industry has been very good to me,' he said.

'Would I have seen any of the movies you have written scores
for?' I asked.

'Almost certainly you have,' he said, 'but they are all rubbish,
and my scores for them are contrived – ridiculous! The directors say, "This woman is falling in love – I want it to sound as
if she is being 'kissed by butterflies'" – did you ever hear of
anything so stupid? So I write them some simple melody, a
nonsense for six strings, and they think I am a genius. They
don't know what genius is, these people. They have no intellect.
They have no soul . . . ' He was getting quite heated, then remembered himself.

'But I expect you love the movies. Everybody loves the movies.
Women love to be taken to the pictures, yes?'

I smiled and shrugged.

'I don't go so often any more.'

'Who knows,' he joked, 'what this mysterious woman does,
or does not, like.'

This interlude was nothing if not distracting. My steak was
delicious and very welcome, and as long as I was able to sit
here being enigmatic, flirting vaguely with this foreign stranger,
I was free of worry, and time was passing quickly and pleasantly.

'Every few months I must travel to New York to teach, because I like to do something normal, something worthwhile. In New York I am taken seriously as a great composer – and yet I keep coming back to Hollywood,' he said, raising his hands dramatically. 'There is too much money in movies,' he said. 'We artists are like prostitutes: the Hollywood moguls open their purses and we poor immigrant musicians come running!' And he laughed.

I liked this man. He was entertaining, easy company – and his story was interesting enough to take me completely out of myself.

'What about your family?' I asked. 'Are they still in Poland?'

'My parents died in the last war,' he said. 'I was an only child. My professors at the Kraków Conservatory were my family.'

'Wife?' I asked.

He had a nice smile and was handsome – for his age, which was perhaps sixty.

'So, maybe this mysterious Irishwoman is not so cold after all?'

I found myself blushing, which was annoying.

'I only meant . . . '

'No, no, I am joking,' he said. 'I have never had the honour of being married – although I have been in love many times. To tell you the truth, the women in Los Angeles who work in the movies are full of artifice. They dye their hair and wear too much rouge – or wigs – and they have straight white teeth that they take out at night and put in a glass!'

I let out a loud laugh. Really, this was wrong. I was supposed to be full of anxiety and misery, but here I was, with this strange man making me laugh out loud!

'I am too old to get married now. My work is the great love of my life. Passion, romance – it interferes with my creativity, I don't expect you to understand but . . . '

'I'm an artist,' I said suddenly, 'I do understand.'

Although I was not sure that I did, I wanted to let him know that I was not just an ordinary person.

'Ah,' he said and he nodded, as if he had seen something in me all along.

We ordered a second bottle of wine and talked about art. He knew something about Impressionism, but very little about Non-Objective Painting, and although he had seen some of the Guggenheim Collection, he was fascinated to hear more about the movement itself and the new gallery that Hilla was working on with Frank Lloyd Wright, designed specifically to best display the collection that she had worked on for Guggenheim himself. He was very impressed that I knew Hilla Rebay.

'Is she a Jew?' he asked.

'No,' I said. It was a common misconception that all Germans in America were here to escape the Nazis. 'She came here well before the war.'

'Like me,' he said.

Then he became suddenly melancholy, his expression hardening.

'The Germans have Poland now – they have won. They call it *Intelligenzaktion*,' and he cracked his hands together as if he were snapping a stick. 'This is what they called the murder of our intellectual elite; this is the way they break us: by destroying our music, our art – everything. There is nothing left for me – nothing.'

It was a shocking outburst, and Stan seemed grateful when I picked up the dessert menu and changed the subject. The world was altering, and those of us who had escaped the drudgery and dangers of our old countries for a new life in America had to avoid going back, in our own minds. Falling into sentiment about the places we had come from was unwise and dangerous. It could cause the kind of pointless pain that led to deep and abiding unhappiness. It was important to look forward, to stay grateful for the wealth and security to be found in our new lives. It was important to remember that we were, first and foremost, Americans.

I ordered apple pie and ice-cream, and when it arrived I ate hungrily as if my steak had never existed.

'I like a woman with a good appetite,' Stan said, and I blushed at my obvious greed, before reprimanding his impertinence.

'I've been travelling since early this morning, and have not eaten all day.'

'So sensitive,' he said, 'clearly you have the temperament of a true artist!'

I smiled – I really did like this incorrigible old flirt.

'I should like to see your work sometime,' he said.

Suddenly I felt really, really tired. On top of the wine and the steak, the dessert had finished me off, and I just wanted to lie down and go to sleep. It had been a long day and my tiredness reminded me of why I was here.

I looked up – I am afraid quite rudely – and signalled to the waiter.

'You're tired,' Stan said, and he smiled and studied my face queryingly, but didn't pry. 'I can see you need to retire – let me pay for dinner, please.'

He did not ask how far I was going and, as far as he knew, my journey ended in Chicago.

'Thank you,' and I stood up and shook his hand, 'you have made the evening pass very pleasantly.'

His hand was cold and he held mine to kiss it, barely touching it with his lips.

Then he reached into the pocket of his jacket and produced a crumpled card with his name and address printed on it.

'If you ever find yourself in Los Angeles,' he said, 'for any reason – any reason at all – you can contact me at this address.' I took the card and he added, 'Any time, Eileen. I won't forget you.'

It was a strange declaration, perhaps made from this old man's confidence in his own memory or intellect, certainly not with any romantic sentiment attached. But something about his words reminded me of my first husband, John; never forgotten. The feeling of having been so deeply in love as a young girl had faded with time, but the smell of carbolic soap or lavender or freshly chopped mint would bring me back to the fields that I grew up in and to the strong, beautiful boy that I married. John never kissed my hand like a gentleman; he held me around the waist and drew down on me like a departing soldier. I was tired and, with all that had happened that day, my emotions began to rise.

'Thank you – nor I you.' I said. It was a polite lie. Stan had been a distraction, and a generous host, but I had much more important things on my mind and would surely have forgotten him by the morning. I put his card in my purse, then went back to my small cabin, where I slept until dawn.

CHAPTER TEN

As soon as I stepped off the train in Chicago anxiety hit me again like a blast of cold air. I was less than halfway on my journey to find Leo, and yet when I was trapped on the moving train I knew I was powerless. Somehow, having my feet on solid ground made me feel as if I should be doing something. Modern conveniences being what they were, a part of me was itching simply to telephone the Chateau Marmont hotel and speak to Leo directly and check that he was still all right, but my greater instinct told me it would be a bad idea to notify him that I was on my way. It was best for me to wait until I got to Los Angeles, so that I could deal with it all in person. I wanted to see him and was afraid he might take flight again. In the meantime I would have to bide my time and occupy myself as best I could on this interminable journey.

Maureen's cousin-in-law, Anne, was holding a chalkboard with the LaSalle Street Station logo on it, and EILEEN HOGAN emblazoned across it in the confident hand of a schoolteacher, which I knew her to be.

I was, of course, Eileen Irvington now, but Patrick's school-teacher cousin might not have known that; in any case, the Yonkers gang had never really registered the change. To them, I would always have the name they first knew me under – the name of my first husband. I also painted under the name Eileen Hogan – the only time I used Irvington was as a mother to my sons. Charles had hated me using the name Hogan, and even though he had always disliked his own family name, he always referred to me as 'Mrs Irvington'.

Anne was a tall and substantial woman in her early fifties, wearing a red blazer, her jet-black hair arranged about her face in severe waves and with just that little bit too much make-up, especially a shade of deep-red lipstick that was smeared somewhat haphazardly across her wide mouth. Just from looking at her, I could easily see how my understated friend Maureen might find her a frightful house-guest. A spinster with a big salary and long teachers' holidays, Anne would come and stay with them in New York at least once a year (although the Sweeneys had never been back to Chicago) and Maureen always dreaded her visits.

'She's so bossy . . . ' My friend's complaints about her cousin-in-law came flooding back to me – too late, or I would have objected more heartily to her being contacted.

'I am so pleased to meet you.' Anne grabbed my hand and shook it vigorously, crunching my fingers with her many rings. 'Maureen has told me so much about you!'

'It's very kind of you to meet me like this,' I said.

'Nonsense,' she said, picking up my suitcase as if it were no bigger than an evening purse.

'Had we better put that into Left Luggage for the day?' I suggested.

'No need,' she said, 'I checked and there is a terrible queue – I'll put it straight in my car, it's just outside.' And she marched ahead, indicating with an assertive nod for me to follow. From that first instance I knew I was to be taken hostage, and I was right.

She immediately reminded me of the nuns who had educated me at the Jesus and Mary Convent in Ireland. Well-meaning but bossy. As we walked through the busy station concourse she parted the sea of men in grey suits and hats going to work, with her sure-footed stride, and I followed behind her, like an obedient schoolgirl.

Anne had our day all mapped out with military precision and she was determined to give me a guided tour of Chicago. Breakfast (which I had already eaten on the train) was at Lou Mitchell's, a very nice family bakery on Jackson. The owner flirted a little with Anne – or rather she construed that he was flirting, becoming somewhat girlish and coy as he took our order: coffee for me and flapjacks for my hostess.

I was relieved to see that Anne's desire to impress me with her life in Chicago usurped any interest she might have had in asking about my life. She asked me no questions about myself, as if she had already garnered all the information she needed from Maureen. She knew I was an artist, twice widowed and was travelling to Los Angeles – Maureen, God bless her, had obviously not revealed why, and perhaps it was the misguided belief that I was a tourist that had led to Anne's sightseeing schedule. When we were finished in Lou's she intended to take me on a tour of the city, including a trip to the Art Institute of Chicago, followed by lunch at her house, tea with a neighbour of hers, an early dinner in town, before she dropped me back to the train in time for its 10.15 p.m. departure.

However, for all her frightening bustle, I noticed that my hostess was considerably more groomed than I was. I had bathed on the train, but had not washed my hair, and was badly in need of a trip to the hair salon. Working on Fire Island for the past few months, I had let my hair grow long and never bothered with make-up. Now that I was back in the 'civilized world'

I was self-consciously aware that I needed to smarten myself up, especially if I was going to have to deal with people I didn't know in Los Angeles. I needed to prepare myself.

'That all sounds wonderful,' I said, 'but I wonder if it might be possible to fit in a trip to the hair salon?'

She looked at me, incredulous at my cheek in interfering with her plans.

'Only I didn't have the chance to go before I left New York, and now – well, I feel so unkempt next to you, Anne.'

She patted her waves proudly and pursed her lips.

'I could take you to my hairdresser,' she said. 'Her salon is near my house, but it might mean *not* meeting Mrs Podmore for tea – which would be a terrible, terrible shame, particularly as she is an artist like you.'

'Oh?' I said, vaguely curious.

'Not for *money*, of course – oh no, *no* – she is *married* to a *doctor*.' Anne paused to let me take in the magnitude of this achievement, then continued. 'She works in watercolours mostly – wonderful *wonder-ful* detailed pictures of her garden and her cats, like photographs really.'

'Oh – she sounds very impressive,' I said, imagining just the sort of folksy, flowery fripperies that counted for nothing in the art circles in which I moved. 'Perhaps I could meet Mrs Podmore another time? As you can see, my hair is in need of urgent attention – it's a real mess.'

She nodded sagely in agreement and I felt a snap of anger, quite disproportionate to the veiled insult.

Anne Sweeney, I decided, was the epitome of what could happen to women when they had never known the love of a man. People pitied women like Anne, and because eyes were on them for never having married, sometimes it could turn them into overbearing spinsters who had to pretend to know everything, because they in fact knew nothing about life, or love, or anything else – including, and *especially*, art!

Maureen was a saint to put up with this obnoxious woman in her house every summer – no wonder she had kept the two of us away from each other previously. I would happily have escaped through the bathroom window in the restaurant, if she hadn't had my suitcase locked in the trunk of her car!

For the next hour we drove around Chicago while Anne pointed out this building and that, giving me the history of 'this great city', how the Great Chicago Fire in 1871 had destroyed it and how it was rebuilt into the Second City. As she showed me each building – 'That building was the first skyscraper in America: ten storeys high!' – she would repeat salient points of history that she had already described ('1871? The Great Fire? You remember?'), in her bossy schoolteacher manner. I could tell she was longing to ask me to repeat the facts myself to show her that I was paying attention. As a result, I made a point of barely listening. Instead I gazed out at the towering skyline of downtown Chicago and thought how similar it was to New York – hundreds of thousands of people all packed into tall buildings – and I wondered how I could have travelled for such a long time and be in a place that was so similar to the place I had come from.

Walking around the Art Institute was even more of an ordeal because, actually, Anne Sweeney was very knowledgeable – far more so than me – on the subject of Impressionist and post-Impressionist painting. Had I been in better form and had not decided she was so loathsome, I might have found what she was saying fascinating. Instead my own prejudices meant I found her informed manner so insufferably irritating that it ruined for me some of the most inspiring works by Monet and Van Gogh.

By the time Anne drove me out to her house for lunch I was

paying as little attention to her as possible and, mercifully, she followed my lead and we drove the last part of the journey in silence.

The house was in a quiet neighbourhood on the edges of the city, a small two-storey terrace in red brick with steps up to the front door. Inside it was as tidy and ordered as one would expect from a woman of her type. Anne had prepared us a lunch of cold meats and salads, which was already on the plate and covered in wax paper on a table set with a pretty lace table-cloth, good bone-china and napkins. She bustled about putting the kettle on and fetching milk for the table.

'Do you take sugar?' she asked. 'With your lovely slim frame, I doubt that you do!'

She seemed softer, more self-conscious, now that we were in her home, perhaps believing – correctly – that I would judge her by the environs in which she lived.

When we had eaten, Anne showed me around her neat, overtly feminine home. A pink bedroom with a candlewick bedspread and lacy cushions, neatly stocked with cosmetics and decorative bottles of tinctures, and some of Mrs Podmore's watercolours along the narrow hallway, which were not as terrible as I had imagined. Although every surface was polished to shining, the house was peculiarly still – as if nothing were ever moved around: a spinster's mausoleum. Her home was not nearly as large or as well furnished as the Sweeneys' home in Yonkers, and I made a note to tell Maureen not to be so intimidated by this woman's puff. I thought of Anne coming from this somewhat atrophied environment into the bustling warmth of the Sweeneys' family home and could not help but feel slightly sorry for her.

She dropped me at the hair salon, where I spent the rest of the afternoon being gloriously pampered, having my hair washed, trimmed and set, as I read copies of *Vanity Fair* and *Vogue*. It was a welcome escape from everyone and everything that was troubling me.

Anne collected me, utterly refreshed, in time for supper in a small Italian restaurant near the station, where we had an excellent meal. I was so caught up with my new hair and gleaming nails that Anne's 'expert' blathering about her knowledge of Italy specifically, and Europe in general, hardly bothered me.

She drove me back to the train station, and as we were getting my case out of the trunk she suddenly turned to me and said, 'I hope everything works out in Los Angeles, Ellie. Maureen told me about your son. You must be so worried.' I was completely taken aback, but before I could respond she added, 'I lost a child once. It was a long time ago. I had to give him away. A mistake, you understand? I'm sure – I think – I know something of how you are feeling.'

Her gaudy face was shadowed with pain, and I understood in that moment that she knew something of what I was going through.

'I hope I was able to offer you some . . . distraction from your trouble today.'

I did not know what to say to the woman, so I grabbed both her hands in mine and said, 'Thank you, Anne' as warmly and sincerely as I could, although as I walked away from her I knew it wasn't nearly enough.

How harshly I had judged her, and how wrong I had been.

As I boarded the train I thought how true it was that you could never know a person, and I felt guilty for my own petty judgements and for having let the opportunity for warmth and friendship pass me by when, perhaps, I needed it most.

CHAPTER ELEVEN

I arrived in Los Angeles at five in the afternoon two days later.

It was warmer than New York or Chicago, but not markedly so. Although Union Station was busy, nobody seemed in any particular rush. A porter sauntered over to me and helped lift my case onto a cart, but seemed happy for me to wheel it myself through the concourse. The main entrance to the station was reminiscent of a cathedral, with ornate wooden ceiling panels and a polished tile floor. Either side of its broad walkway were banks of seating, which, given the church-like decor, looked immediately like pews, but on closer inspection were revealed as large, rather comfortable and expensive leather chairs, with people sitting in them reading and chatting as if this were one large living room. I thought the whole set-up very strange.

It was stranger still outside, where the station entrance opened onto a gaping, dusty road. I saw a tram and cars passing, but very few people. It seemed they were all inside the station reading their newspapers! I had been given to understand that the train was arriving in downtown Los Angeles, and so had been expecting a busy urban scene, but there were no taxis, no shops and precious few pedestrians. Desperately I looked around for somebody to ask where the taxi rank was, but there was nobody except for a bum some twenty feet down the road. On his haunches and with his head down, he was doubtless searching for cigarette butts and, given the lack of action here, I was guessing that he wouldn't have much luck. A polite query from an Irishwoman with a kind face and a big bag might encourage him to follow me, and I had enough troubles already. *When I was younger*, I thought, *I would have relished this adventure*, although in reality I was not nearly as adventurous as I gave myself credit for. Otherwise I would have made this journey before now, and not waited until I had to go chasing off after an errant son. I had made the two big journeys in my life, across the Atlantic, out of necessity. There was no point in fooling myself that this trip was any different.

I looked around for a taxi, up and down the road, but there was nothing. Opposite the gaping, dusty road was a large building, maybe a church, with steps leading up to it and a few tall, spindly palm trees around it. Beyond them, as I squinted against the failing light, I could make out one or two tall buildings and signs of civilization. For all that, I felt as if I had landed in some godforsaken no-man's-land. I sighed heavily with irritation and, having left my cart in the station (although, in all likelihood, I thought, nobody would have looked up from their newspaper if I had taken it), hauled my heavy bag across the road towards the church.

Cars appeared without warning and almost ran me over, twice. They didn't honk their horns or holler at you first, like in New York. They just appeared eerily next to me with a sharp stop, and gave me a fright. I did not like this place. This was not like America at all, not the America I knew. My America was full of crowds and smells and traffic, and there was every convenience on your doorstep! This was like another country, and not one that I cared to be in.

On the other side of the road I was barely recovering from my ordeal with the cars when I heard music – a sign of life. It was coming from in front of me, and I followed a brightly dressed family, who had appeared from behind the large building with the steps, into a courtyard. Quite suddenly I was in Mexico; at least, that was how it felt: stalls hung with every kind of religious gewgaw, banks of rosary beads, statue upon statue of Our Lady of Guadeloupe. Children chewed on strange-looking buns, which I later learned were *burritos*, while their mothers knelt keening at an outdoor altar; among the chaos of people wandered little dark-skinned angels – girls dressed as brides in elaborate costumes. This was a First Holy Communion festival. Goodness me! I had not even registered that it was Sunday. Everyone around me seemed excited, arms waving, drunk with the religious fervour that was so very attractive in other cultures, yet had been so sombre and punishing in my own Irish Catholic upbringing. I looked around to see if I could spot a man who might drive a taxi; this was a charming scene indeed, but it was not why I was here.

I went up to a woman of around my own age and said, 'Taxi? I need to find a man who has a taxi?'

She obviously didn't speak English, but shouted in Spanish above the crowd and grabbed my arm, dragging me through a door to our left. There was gold everywhere: a gleaming gold altar, gold panels inset with religious imagery – the whole place glowed. Inside, the church was considerably quieter than outside, but there wasn't a stifling reverential silence. Some people prayed, others talked quietly, some men even looked as if they were there doing business – one person at least was looking for a taxi driver.

I stopped at a side altar where there was a statue of Our Lady and a few people kneeling at her feet, clutching their rosary beads, their mouths moving in prayer. Her shoulders and hands were lavishly draped with gifts of jewellery that people had left as offerings; curious to think that this selfless Virgin would be impressed with such trinkets, but then that contradiction ran deep in the Catholic Church wherever you were in the world. In Ireland our priests ate like kings while the rest of us starved; in Mexico Our Lord's mother wore diamonds and pearls like a wealthy socialite. Yet we kept coming back. The woman who had been guiding me stood back reverentially as I took off the simple gold wedding band from my marriage to Charles and put it in a small, clay pot at the Virgin's feet. I did not kneel and pray. I did not need to; the Virgin mother and I both knew what I wanted.

The woman's husband (or brother, or uncle) spoke a little English and, in any case, knew where Chateau Marmont was. His 'taxi' had no sign on the roof and, as I got into the back, I found that I was sharing the journey with a couple of chickens crammed into a cage.

'Chateau Marmont,' I said to him, repeating myself in case he should be in any doubt as to where I was going. My journey was, hopefully, nearly over, but this drive seemed interminable. My first impression of Los Angeles was of an enormous, ugly suburb – long, wide roads messily lined with low, sprawling buildings. The light was almost gone, and lights began popping into view advertising Coca-Cola and pharmacies. Dim street lamps threw scant light on apartment complexes, but there was no way of seeing what lay behind the security gates. Everywhere there were tall, uniform desert trees in unnaturally symmetrical lines; it seemed as if they had been planted as an afterthought to make the place look less like a desert. There seemed to be no centre, and each road looked the same as the next. From what I could see of it, this was a place lacking in character and heart.

Already Los Angeles was giving me the creeps. I would get Leo and go back to New York as soon as possible. We would have three days on the train to talk everything out. It could work out for the best that he had taken us both on this foolish adventure, because it would offer us an excuse to spend some badly needed time together. I had neglected Leo, left him to his own devices. He was lost, and now I was here to find him again and bring him home.

At last a sign on my right read 'Chateau Marmont' and behind it was a tall white building with turrets. We drove for a few yards up a steep hill, the driver tipped his hat to a security guard at the narrow gateway and we were in a small, cobbled court-yard with a brick wall on either side, topped with high fencing and with a locked gate to my right. In front of us was an open porch leading to the left, with a couple of large palm plants on it that looked as though they belonged to a private villa. It certainly did not have the air of a great hotel like The Plaza or The Waldorf, or one deserving of such a grand French name, but then I was looking for a man who called himself 'Frederick Dubois'. I paid the driver and, carrying my own bag, went into the porch to find there was no reception desk or even names and apartment numbers – this was very annoying. I was in a hurry to find my son. There was a lift, but I opted to drag my heavy bag up a dark, Gothic staircase. I didn't have the time to get stuck in an elevator in a place I did not know.

On the first floor there was a reception desk, and a large lounge area opening onto a terrace. The Gothic theme was continued with monastery-like arches and lots of dark wood. It looked like a decadent cathedral, and was emptier than any hotel lobby had a right to be at this time of evening. There was nobody at the desk, so I rang a bell and eventually a man appeared – a concierge, I supposed.

'I am looking for Frederick Dubois,' I said.

'He's out,' the man said, looking at my case, 'but he should be back soon. You can wait out by the pool, if you like?'

'Fine,' I said, 'he must have forgotten I was coming.' My heart was pounding. Leo was here. The concierge indicated for me to follow him as he reluctantly picked up my case.

'Have you seen a boy with him,' I said, 'Leo Irvington?'

'Fred has a boy hanging around with him all right,' he shrugged.

I wanted to grab the man, shake him urgently and tell him to get my son – NOW! But I held on to myself. I knew it would not be good to let my emotions get the better of me. I had to stay calm, find Leo and bring him home.

We walked down the stairs and back out to the porch, then the concierge used the key to open a door that led into a tropical garden. It was dark now, but balmy, and the narrow path was sprinkled on either side with small lights. There was thick vegetation all around and the heavy scent of tropical flowers everywhere; small chalets nestled amidst the growth, visible only by the occasional window light. I felt as if I was in the midst of a secret, and I did not like the feeling. We walked down some steps as they opened out onto a lit, decked swimming pool – a small and intimate area, pretty and peaceful.

'Dubois is in chalet nine,' the man said, nodding in the direction of another hidden pathway, 'but he'll have to come through here on the way, so you can grab him then. There's a gang in from Paramount, so it looks like things are gonna start getting pretty rowdy around ten. If you want something to eat, you'd better let Fred know – we're closing the kitchen early.'

When he had gone I sat on the edge of a lounge chair and waited. Somewhere behind me I could hear music and, in the distance, talking, muffled by the heavy vegetation all around. This was a strange and eerie place. On the surface of the water

I thought I could see the white globe of a full moon, but when I looked up I saw it was just trickery – a lit window beaming down from the Chateau itself. *Perhaps I should go in search of number nine myself?* I thought. *Perhaps Leo would be there on his own, and I could bustle the child away without even having to meet this Frederick cad* – although now that I was here, it would be a shame not to give him a piece of my mind. The mere thought of him made me feel angry again.

I heard laughter and chatting, as a young couple – the girl in a pretty summer dress and a young man in a light-coloured suit – came down the steps in front of me. Their arrival made the decision for me, so I stood up and decided that I would go and find chalet number nine after all. In any case, I didn't want to interrupt some young lovers' romantic tryst.

I turned quickly to make my getaway before they registered my presence and, in my haste, banged straight into another young man who was coming up the path behind me.

'Mother?' he said.

Chapter Twelve

Leo looked no different from when I had last seen him, not quite three weeks before on Fire Island, yet he did not look like my little boy any more. He was, instead, an elegant young man, perfectly well suited to this environment. He did not seem in the least frightened or overawed or, it had to be said, especially pleased to see me.

'Leo! I have been out of my mind with worry! Leaving me no word of where you were going! Have you any idea what I have been through?'

I could have left it at that, but four days of anger and worry came tumbling out. 'We've all been beside ourselves – Bridie, Maureen . . . all of us!'

Leo pursed his lips and his jaw hardened. I could tell he was shaken to see me, but was more afraid of how I was embarrassing him in front of his friends.

Nonetheless, I was his mother and I had come a long way to have my say.

'And Julian is in the most dreadful trouble for helping you – why, his father will probably beat him to within an inch of his life, and it will have been your fault, Leo. Your fault! What on *earth* did you think you were doing, running away from school like that!'

'School?' the other young man said, his voice sounding genuinely horrified.

'Oh,' I said, turning on him, 'Frederick Dubois, I presume? Well, don't you play the innocent – a man of your age should know better than to snatch a boy from his school, away from his family . . . '

I trailed off, partly because the expression 'a man of your age' barely applied to Frederick, who, while he looked a little older than Leo, was far from the depraved, middle-aged cad I had been expecting, and partly because the young woman in our company had put her arm through Leo's, as if comforting him from my harsh words. She was also a little older than I had first imagined. Not mature exactly, but somewhat worn. A hardened broad – not suitable company for my son.

'Yes, well,' I went on, uncomfortable at the way these strangers were gathered around my son, leaving me out in the cold, 'it's done now.'

'Oh, man,' Frederick said, 'I had no idea he was in school. He said he was nineteen.'

'Well, he's not,' I said. 'He's only sixteen years of age.'

'Oh, right – sixteen.' The young man nodded as if it wasn't so bad after all. 'Am I in trouble then?'

'Can we go and have something to eat now, Freddie?' the girl whined. She hooked her arm into his and slithered into his side, making it clear they were a couple.

'I'm starving,' said Leo suddenly, having recovered from the shock of seeing me. 'Will we go around to Greenblatt's and get corned beef and coleslaw again?' Then, as an afterthought, 'Maybe, Mam, you could come too?'

The girl looked over at me, her pretty, expressive face easily read as she pouted nastily as if she did *not* think that was a good idea.

This encounter was not going at all how I had expected it to. Not at all.

'Shall we start again?' the other young man said. 'Freddie Hickey,' and he held his hand out to me. I took it and he smiled, a lovely broad, innocent smile, full of possibility. 'Hollywood talent scout and impresario – at your service.' Then he added apologetically, 'Dubois was made up. You know how it is in Hollywood.'

Freddie carried my case up to reception, where he arranged a room in the hotel for me for that night. I stood with Leo and the girl, who eventually introduced herself as Crystal.

Another fictional name, but I said nothing.

'She's only eighteen,' Leo said, 'so you see, I am not too young to be an actor.'

There was no way that 'Crystal', with her bleached blonde hair and made-up face, would see twenty-one again – and I could intuit from her maternal manner towards my son that that was a generous assessment. However, I kept my mouth shut for the time being. I had found Leo, he was alive and well, and until we had eaten dinner and I got him on his own, that was enough.

We took a booth in Greenblatt's, a deli-restaurant on Sunset Boulevard, just down the hill outside the hotel – a short walk. It was a relief to be eating good deli-food after three days' travelling, and the busy interior reminded me of New York.

Mostly it was a relief to be with Leo, although he seemed different in a way I could not quite put my finger on. As I watched him nudging and laughing with these two new friends, I realized that – strange though it was, and loath though I was to admit it – I had never seen him so happy before in his short life.

Leo had always been at best a thoughtful child and, at worst, and certainly since his father died, quietly troubled. He adored his baby brother Tom and they had fun fooling around the place together, but sometimes I would catch him when he thought I wasn't looking, and his expression of studious worry would break my heart. I often tried to talk to him, to get him to open up to me, but he never did.

'You can tell me anything,' I would say, 'never carry cares around with you, Leo – you can always come and talk to me.'

'I know,' he said, 'but I'm fine.'

So it came to be that a muted 'fine' was the pinnacle of Leo's emotion as a teenage boy – never too happy or unnaturally sad, but in a constant quietude somewhere in between.

'He's just quiet,' Bridie would say to reassure me, 'he's content enough.'

I never quite believed her.

'I bet you I can eat this sandwich in four clean bites,' he said now to Crystal.

'Bet me what?' she said.

'Bet you'll be fat in a week,' he said, then she pinched him and he raised his eyebrows, his eyes full of laughter and light, and poked her playfully in the arm.

'Children, children . . . ' Freddie said. He lit a cigarette and passed me the packet and I took one. Although I hadn't smoked in a while, I felt as if I needed something.

Over the next hour Freddie filled me in or, rather, sold his story to me.

He was from up the coast in Santa Cruz and his father was a bigshot movie producer, whom he didn't know on account of the fact that he had abandoned Freddie's mother when she was pregnant with him. Freddie had come to search for him when he was eighteen, and 'fell into movies' by getting bit parts and working as crew.

'Then I met this lovely lady – and got into the scouting side of things.'

Crystal looked across at him with adoring eyes.

'Yes, indeed – there is my fortune sitting right there, Mademoiselle Crystal Paris Marseille; the rest is history.'

I could not believe the drivel I was hearing.

'And Leo,' Crystal said, 'he's going to be a star too.'

'Of course,' Freddie said. 'A big star.' Although he did not sound as convinced.

'You must be doing really well,' I said, 'where are your offices?'

'We're between offices right now,' he said, shifting in his seat, 'but everyone knows I'm at the Chateau.'

I wondered who 'everyone' was.

The story, as far as I could gather, underneath the not-very-convincing smokescreen of Hollywood bull, was that the young couple had been one of hundreds of guests at the Knox's party this past summer. Crystal had spotted Leo and persuaded Freddie to give him his card.

'Of course I am Freddie's main star,' Crystal said, 'but he really needs a man on his books too, and as soon as I saw Leo – well – he's got that look.'

Leo gazed out of the window dramatically, playfully arching his eyebrows to show me what she meant. Bizarrely, he did look something like a film actor.

'So when Leo called him up, I said, "Freddie, you have to get him out here. We've already got the chalet, and as long as he can get himself here – well you've got nothing to lose!"'

Freddie smiled over at me to confirm the story, but he did not look as convinced as his girlfriend.

Leo had been sleeping on a settee in their small chalet, but I gathered from Freddie's manner that he was almost relieved that I had turned up.

'Oh sure, this kid's gonna be a great screen actor, then it'll all come good,' which I took to mean that Freddie had been feeding and clothing my son, because he was being bullied by his girlfriend, was too kind to send Leo home or did not have enough money to provide him with the train fare back to New York. Possibly a little of all three.

I called for the bill and paid it. Freddie made a big show of reaching for his wallet, but I could tell he was happy to have 'the kid's' mother foot the bill.

We went back to their chalet to collect Leo's things, although in truth most of the things littered about the living area of their small chalet seemed to be on loan from Freddie.

'Did you even bring a toothbrush with you, Leo?' I asked as he tried to find his schoolbag and half-heartedly checked over various socks and undergarments before deciding if they were his.

I was beginning to feel for this young couple. For all the horrendous worry their foolishness had put me through, they clearly had been acting in some approximation of *loco parentis* with my son. Once we returned to New York I would be sure to send them a cheque.

Crystal went straight into the bedroom while Freddie ran around tidying the place up, hanging ties on the backs of chairs and apologizing for the mess – I think he even claimed something about his secretary being on holiday. Despite all the ridiculous movie-puff and artifice, he was really rather sweet.

He cleared a space on the sofa for me to sit down and offered me coffee, but I declined.

'Leo and I had better get up to our room – we have a lot to

talk about. We'll call again tomorrow, if we have time before our train leaves.'

Crystal ran out of the bedroom.

'Oh no, you can't go tomorrow. Leo has a screen test at Paramount. For the next big movie! – I know he'll get the part. You have to wait until then.'

'Now, baby,' Freddie rowed in, 'you hear what the lady said. The kid's still in school . . . '

'You can't let him go, Freddie, not now – I won't allow it!' she said, standing in front of my son.

My hackles rose, but something prevented me from acting. Some hint of desperation in the pretty young woman's eyes.

Our room in the hotel was actually an apartment much the same size as the chalet. Freddie had explained over dinner that Chateau Marmont had originally been opened as luxury private apartments for the Hollywood set, but the rents were too high and once the Depression came, the owners had to turn it into a hotel to make ends meet. Prices were reasonable, to keep the place ticking over, and it ran on a skeleton staff. Most of the residents were long-term, living there for months – some for years at a time. Freddie looked as if he was struggling with the rent, and I guessed this was the kind of place where you could live on tick until 'the big break' came. That way of carrying on was anathema to me. *But then*, I thought, *I don't have to live here!*

Our apartment had a small kitchenette with an electric stove, a refrigerator and a separate eating area with a jolly red table and shelves above it, stocked with tea and coffee and a generous supply of alcoholic beverages and snacks. I poured myself a gin-and-tonic and opened a bottle of Coca-Cola for Leo.

'Oh, this is charming,' I kept saying, 'isn't it, Leo? Quite lovely. And the bed seems very comfortable.'

It hardly seemed worth unpacking my case for one night, but at the same time I wanted to make the room cosy for us. I had decided that there was no point in reprimanding my son any more than I already had. What was done was done, and there was no damage evident to his character or his body – I would leave it at that, and allow us both to use this whole silly experience as an excuse to simply enjoy the next few days that we would have on our own together.

Leo remained silent. It had been a shock, me turning up like this. I had taken him away from his new friends – it was understandable, but he'd get over it. By morning we'd be back to normal. Friends again.

'I had better go down to reception and ring Bridie and Maureen shortly; they will be so glad I found you. We'll have a few days in Yonkers when we get back – maybe go to your old school up there, or find a new one. But sure, we can talk about that on the way back. We have plenty of time to sort things out, Leo, eh? Plenty of time, don't we?'

'Yes, Mam,' he said.

'I'll organize our tickets in the morning. I've no idea what time the train leaves. I wonder if there even is one tomorrow – the war has disrupted all the services on top of everything . . . '

'If there isn't a train, can I go to the Paramount studios for the screen test?'

It came bursting out of him – a shot of enthusiastic, hopeful energy.

'No, Leo, it is out of the question. You are far, far too young to be carrying on with that sort of thing.'

Leo hung his head in disappointment, although it also looked like shame. He was wearing just a vest and pants. His naked legs were hanging over the side of the bed. He was still tanned from the summer, and the light from the lamp caught the downy blond hair on his forearms and calves. His large feet were set squarely on the floor. My son was a good foot taller than me these days; he did not look like a child any more. However much I did not care to admit it, he could easily pass for twenty.

'You do understand that, Leo, don't you?'

He paused, then looked up at me and said, 'Yes, I understand.'

I could tell from his face that he understood, but did not like it. He was not being petulant, he was just offering me the automatic compliance of an obedient child who doesn't want to upset or anger his parents. At that moment something inside me snapped. An old memory made itself known to me: I had fallen in love and run away to Dublin and got married when I was only one year older than Leo was now. My parents had disowned me for a time, and John's guardians were furious – but, as kind-hearted people, they helped us nonetheless.

Compliance was not in my nature. So now I had this sweet son, who would do as I bid him. Was that such a good thing after all?

'Tell me then,' I said, 'about this audition.'

His face lit up immediately with the possibility that he might persuade me. He became animated and expressive in a way I had never seen in him before. It was for a movie called *Five Graves to Cairo* – a war film, of sorts – and Leo was auditioning to play a young soldier.

'The thing about the movies is it's not just about acting – it's all about having "the look".'

He talked absolute nonsense about wasting long tracts of his school study time reading foolish magazines and gossip columns, which explained why he was so behind academically. While I barely listened to what he was saying, I observed his mannerisms closely and saw, once again, what I hoped I had been mistaken in seeing earlier.

Leo was happy. When he talked about acting and movies, he lit up from the inside. He looked as if he was in love, and I knew that denying him this chance would only crush him.

This was not the life I wanted for my son, not by a long shot, but then . . . my own father had wanted me to be a nun, and I had run away to marry John. Was that the right thing to have done? I still could not tell, but it had happened and my parents' reaction in rejecting me had only caused me, and them, pain. I could make Leo do my bidding, because he was not as headstrong as I was, although in running away he had proved himself determined.

'We'll stay for the audition tomorrow,' I said, 'and a few days besides, until we see if you get it.'

He flung his arms around me, and his joyful kiss on my cheeks was sweeter than that of any lover.

'But no more lying about your age – and straight home if it doesn't come through, Leo. You can take acting lessons in New York and come back when you are twenty-one and have finished college – have we a deal?'

'Of course – thank you, thank you. Can I go and tell Crystal and Freddie – please?'

I smiled and let him go.

As he shut the door behind him I sat on the bed and cried pathetically painful tears for the passing of time and the loss of the darling little boy I had so desperately wanted to mother forever.

Part Two:

Chateau Marmont, Hollywood 1942

Chapter Thirteen

I had no inkling that night that the screen test would be a success, and that I would still be in Chateau Marmont almost a month later.

Leo's first audition was with a casting director from Paramount, and she put him in an item for the factual film series *Popular Science*, which was shooting at a location upstate, about an hour away from Los Angeles, a few days later. *Popular Science* was a series of short films shown in cinemas before the main movie, and featured true-life stories of interesting scientific discoveries and facts. They did not normally use actors, as the items were news-oriented, but they were doing an item on a gym resort that was using state-of-the-art equipment and needed a fit, healthy young man to ride a stationary bicycle. Seemingly the 'real' practitioners were not as fit as they might have been and were a little coy about being filmed in their shorts and vests.

'This is a big opportunity for Leo,' Freddie said, almost exploding with excitement. I was sceptical – it was hardly *Gone with the Wind* – but at least it would be over soon and I would be able to get him back to New York, happy that the trip to Los Angeles had made some small part of his dream a reality.

Leo had one line, which he practised over and over and over again.

'When the presenter comes and asks me how I am getting on, I have to reply, "A little puffed out." Now, Mam – you be the presenter.'

He would kneel up on the desk chair in our room and say his line in a variety of different styles and voices.

Actually, it was great fun. I could feel his excitement and joy and that made me happy.

Freddie asked me if I would like to come along to the studio to see Leo being filmed. I told him I would love to go, but Leo quickly said, 'I'd rather you didn't – it would make me too nervous.'

It hurt to feel that I was an embarrassing hindrance to my teenage son, but it was an inevitable price of motherhood. It only saddened me that my years with Leo had been so short – and I longed for him to like me enough to allow me to extend them by sharing his life with me. This was another step back, but at least I was here.

Freddie seemed slightly relieved also when I bowed out, and I imagined that was because they had both lied about his age, and a mother in tow would give the game away. This would surely be Leo's one and only shot at stardom and so, confident that there would not be a next time, I let it go.

On the day of the filming a car came to collect Leo and Freddie. It was the first day I'd had to myself since leaving Fire Island. The first day, in any case, when I was free from worrying about other people and able to take some time to think about my work. I took my sketchbook down to the pool, although I had learned from doing so beforehand that I would probably not get a chance to use it. The pool was rarely quiet enough for me to work in peace, and there was too much distraction in watching the other guests at the Chateau come and go.

The permanent guests here (of whom I was now counted as

one) were a strange and mixed bunch, and all of them had that affected way of carrying themselves that revealed they were in the film business. Speculating on their comings and goings was every bit as entertaining as watching a movie! The middle-aged man and his younger male friend – they always entered their chalet a few moments apart, even though it was obvious they were together. An improbably glamorous woman whose age was impossible to discern lay on a thick, purple towel on a chaise by the pool; always in dark glasses, her thick red hair cascaded down her shoulders in perfect glossy waves, and when she smiled at the waiter her teeth were so white that one feared if they caught the sun they might blind you. I saw the same woman with a scarf around her bald head, scuttling back to her room after some assignation at reception (probably getting her wig cleaned). Her face, devoid of make-up, seemed strangely drawn – and I remembered my Polish travelling companion and his comments about Hollywood actors and their false teeth.

There were a couple of movie veterans living in the main building, being cared for by the staff. Nobody terribly famous that I could gather, but rather respected casualties of the talking pictures – silent actors whose glory had diminished overnight. Not wealthy enough to be living in mansions with servants, yet with enough of their heyday left to pay for room and board at this strangest of exclusive boarding houses. One very much got the impression that if the money did run out, some mysterious movie mogul would come along and foot the bill. On the one hand, this place seemed to have gone somewhat to seed. A palatial facade of a building – which had failed to live up to the grand expectations of a French chateau, and now ran as a motel for Hollywood has-beens and kids like Freddie, getting their feet on the first rung of the ladder. On the other hand, the Chateau

Marmont ran like a private house for the best of the racy film-industry set.

Studio heads came here to relax and drink beer by the pool; in the few days that I had been here I had already seen several people I recognized as movie stars just milling about, sitting in the lounge smoking. Freddie knew them all. 'There's Bogie,' he said walking through the lobby one evening and signalling to the famous star, who raised a somewhat automatic eyebrow back. 'We're all friends here,' the young scout told me in a conspiratorial tone. 'Bogie, Turner – I know them all; we look out for each other.'

Leo remained resolutely quiet, although I could feel his eyes boring a hole in me, desperate for a reaction.

'Very impressive,' I said, just to keep my son happy, although really I was wondering how much longer poor, broke Freddie was going to be able to blag himself a room here.

The pool area was empty now, and the chalets all around it were quiet. I remembered there had been a party the night before, so it was unlikely there was going to be much activity about the place before noon. Good. I would have the place to myself and a few hours of solitude, to drink in the surroundings and seek inspiration.

I lay back on a lounger and looked up and around me. The sky was a perfect crisp blue, the grand turrets of the Chateau set against it in shimmering white; a couple of palm trees bent themselves symmetrically at the edges of my view. This place was really . . . I looked for the words to describe it. Beautiful? Idyllic? Paradise? And extraordinary. For the visitor I was, it was all of those things, but to the artist in me, who was hoping for something fresh and new to paint, it felt curiously bland. The colours were too perfect, the architecture too tidy, and there seemed to be no centre to this reclaimed desert region. I felt it was a hollow landscape that, while exotic and beautiful, held no particular meaning for me. Perhaps it was my rural Irish upbringing in the rough fields and hedgerows, the black, leathery forests, the purple, heathery bogs; but my passion for landscape was about being able to imagine beyond it. I could sit and look at the same sea, on the same day, in Fire Island, and see a dozen different pictures, conjure up a world of nuance and meaning. Here, every aesthetic seemed set out for me. There was nothing beyond the pretty facade. *That is not to say it isn't there*, I thought, *it's just that I cannot see it.*

However, once this idea became fixed in my head, I knew I would not work that day. I put my notebook aside and picked up an Agatha Christie novel that I had found in the library of the hotel. Although my republican Irish roots discerned that I ought to dislike the quintessentially English style of this crime novelist, it was her very descriptions of quaint villages and people taking afternoon tea (while vicars were being bludgeoned to death in the rectory!) that made me feel strangely as if I were home in Ireland. The English and the Irish, despite our ancient animosity, had lived in close proximity to each other for so long that our cultures were intertwined. My middle-class parents had aspired to be English in their manners and refinements and, despite myself, some of that had rubbed off on me. In any case, there was very little in the way of popular Irish books available to me, so I had to make do with stories set in England. I still, after all these years, thought of Ireland as 'home'. It was a secret failing, and one that I contradicted openly at every opportunity, claiming myself to be a true American.

I had not finished the first page when I heard the by now irri-tatingly familiar clip-clop of Crystal's high-heeled mules on the steps up from their chalet. She hadn't gone with Leo and Freddie.

'We've been abandoned,' she said dramatically, taking off her cardigan and lying down on the striped sun-lounger cushion, before pulling her sunglasses down over her nose, then addressing me again. 'Have you ordered coffee yet? I'm sure the kitchen is open by now.'

Where on earth did this spoiled, stupid girl come from? She really did seem to expect everybody to go round waiting on her hand and foot!

I swung my feet over my lounger and gave the end of hers a good kick.

'Oi,' she said, jumping and removing her glasses. 'What was that for?'

'For being such a lazy strap,' I said. 'Get yourself down to your chalet and make some coffee yourself.'

'I don't know how,' she said, pulling her sunglasses back down over her eyes. 'I am an actress' – she waved her hand around vaguely – 'not a coffee-maker or whatever.'

'How can you *not* know how to make coffee?' I asked.

She let out a sigh, sat up, pulled her cardigan over her shoulders, then turned round to face me, pulling her glasses off and placing the arm of one side coquettishly between her teeth, while she thought about how to explain it to me.

Then she drew her tiny frame up to her full height, her set blonde curls twitching as she straightened herself. 'It is like this, Eileen,' and she jabbed the air with her sunglasses, 'I am an actress – a star in the making, if you will. I am not a *fool* – I know how to make coffee, and if I *was* a complete fool I would be making coffee and mixing drinks and preparing sandwiches for every damned scout and producer in this town, possibly in this very establishment. Instead I am sitting around the pool at the Chateau just being . . . ' She trailed off, her heavily mascaraed eyes flitting about as she searched for the perfect word to round off her profound statement.

'You?' I said.

'Yes,' she said, delighted with herself. 'Just Being Me!'

'So you're not going to go and get us both some coffee?'

'Nope,' she said, lying back down on her lounger, 'I am not.'

I did not know what to make of this young woman. She was certainly incorrigible, spoiled – but not unattractively so. There was warmth and a charm to her certainly, but really – could any human being be that shallow? That deluded? Surely nobody beyond the age of a child, like Leo, could possibly be so ego-centric and vain?

Deciding that there must be more to this young woman than met the eye, I reached for my sketchpad to draw her. Answers – even to the most casual of questions – could usually be found on the page.

'Oh! Are you drawing me?' Crystal bounced up again, instantly aware of my interested eyes on her. 'How thrilling! How would you like me to pose?' She began to twist this way and that in exaggerated poses, until she made me half-shout, half-laugh, 'Sit any way you please, you silly girl – just keep reasonably still!'

I took out my pencils and found a soft brown one, then began mapping out the young woman's features.

'I have a perfect chin, you know – a *top* make-up artist said that to me once,' she wittered on. '"Miss Moody" – (that's my real name) – he said, "never wear your hair too long, or people will be denied the benefit of your perfect chin." I do think it's important to make the best of yourself, don't you? I mean, I know being pretty isn't *important* as such, but all the same if you *are* pretty, I do think it's important to do your bit. I mean, the world can be such an ugly place . . . '

I zoned out on what she was saying as my eye scanned from her face to the page, until my hand and eye were moving in the automatic unison that made me who I was: an artist. Seeking out truth – sometimes finding it and sometimes not, but with the eye looking and the pencil moving – I knew I was at least on the right road.

Then, suddenly, there it was.

'I mean, I never really thought of myself as having the perfect chin. Or the perfect anything. I mean, I know I'm pretty, but . . . you don't want to be *too* perfect, do you?'

Crystal stopped talking for a moment, and while she was drawing breath between the senseless shallow wanderings where her mind and her mouth met, I caught a glimpse of something behind her eyes: a shrewdness. Crystal, I saw, was a good deal more intelligent than she let on, but her canny game did not make her unattractive to me. In fact, the opposite was true. How vulnerable a person must be to want fame, to need to be adored that much, by everyone, to the exclusion of almost everything else.

Yet surely the desire for fame was not so different from the desire to be loved, and everyone in the world wants to be loved. The desire for fame and love is born from a deep human need to be seen, and I felt as if I could really see this young woman now, beyond the mules and the dye and her ridiculous ideas and affectations. So I started to draw her.

My intensity must have rubbed off on my subject because, as the first page began to fill, I noticed that Crystal had stopped talking and was sitting, quite peacefully and thoughtfully, and very, very still like a proper artist's model.

A dozen drawings and perhaps an hour later, we had gathered a small audience.

'I'm being drawn,' Crystal said, quite unnecessarily to the older homosexual actor.

'Excellent,' he said in a marked English accent, looking over my shoulder, 'these really are *very* good.' And his young partner stood behind and watched, politely turning his head to exhale his cigarette smoke.

As they were admiring my work, the glamorous lady with the red wig set herself up on another lounger and pretended to ignore us.

'How much do you charge?' the older man asked.

I bristled, but this was, after all, Hollywood.

'Don't be so cheap, Bertie,' Crystal suddenly piped up, clear and loud. 'This is Eileen Hogan, the famous New York painter – not some sketch artist for hire.'

The girl was smart.

The two men sat and chatted and invited me to a party in their chalet the following evening. '*Everyone* will be there.' People kept saying that.

'The Queen of England?' I asked playfully.

'Certainly,' said Bertie, 'several of them.'

I laughed and said I would 'try', which, I thought, made me sound very enigmatic and important.

When they had gone I could sense the other actress taking surreptitious glances over at us.

'She's jealous,' Crystal whispered, nervous that my attention was waning. 'She's ancient – you know that's a wig?'

I put down my pencil and said, 'That's enough, Crystal – now, what about that coffee you promised me?'

By the time the boys got back that evening they found us still sitting by the pool, surrounded by the debris of a day's eating and drinking and sketches of almost every resident in the Chateau, including Bertie, and Gloria in her magnificent red wig.

The lights around the pool were on and there was a holiday atmosphere. We had argued about what time Cocktail Hour was – Crystal had said four, but Bertie had made us wait until five, then provided us with a staggering array of drinks: Gin Fizzes, Gibsons and Whisky Sours.

I was quite tipsy when Leo and Freddie appeared, like a couple of angels in their white suits, at the steps to the pool.

'I've an announcement,' Freddie said. He was beaming, as was Leo, standing beside him. 'Meet Leo Irvington,' he said, his hands on my son's shoulders, 'the new face of Paramount Pictures. He just got cast in his first big movie role today.'

CHAPTER FOURTEEN

I rang Maureen and asked her to bring Tom to me in Los Angeles. She did not say as much, but I could tell she thought I was crazy for not dragging my son back to New York – kicking and screaming, if necessary. Part of me thought maybe I was making the worst decision of *his* life, but the winning part of me knew it was not my decision to make any more. I had to hold Leo's hand on this part of his journey.

Maureen had collected Tom from Fire Island a few days beforehand and, while she assured me he was fine, I could tell by her tone that he was missing me. Tom and I had not been apart for more than a single night since he was an infant and, from the moment I had located Leo, the ache of my worry had simply transferred itself to missing my baby. Tom was like another limb to me – always within easy reach. It did not feel natural, being apart from him. Maureen was a little taken aback that I was staying in Los Angeles, but said that she would get them both on the first train she could. One hour later she called me back and whispered down the phone, 'Bridie is insisting on coming with me. I can't seem to dissuade her!'

'That's not like her – she hates going anywhere,' I said.

'I *know*,' Maureen spat, still whispering, but her voice was raised. 'She became really peculiar when I said I was going with

Tom, and insisted that I book a ticket for her too – then she went upstairs to her cash box and counted the notes out and wouldn't leave it alone until I took them.'

'Did you tell her it was only a temporary thing?'

'Yes – but she was *adamant*. She says her bones will not endure another New York winter and she wants some West Coast sun.'

'Well, that's a lie – she hates the sun. What's got into her?'

We eventually agreed that, once the old bird got an idea into her head, there was no stopping her, and Maureen would just have to make the cross-continent journey with the old lady in tow.

Maureen groaned. 'She'll hardly make it, Ellie.'

Bridie was getting old – although, to me, she had always been an old woman, but she was nonetheless coy about her age. I had calculated that she must be in her eighties. Maureen and Patrick were looking after her more than she was looking after them, these days. Between running the business and trying to get their children set up, the Sweeneys had busy lives, and Bridie, I feared, was becoming more of a burden than a help to them.

'Bring her here anyway,' I said. 'Sure, it'll be great to see her.'

Three days later I took a taxi to Union Station to collect them. Leo had wanted to stay back at the Chateau with Freddie and Crystal, but I had made him come with me. The movie he had been cast in, *Five Graves to Cairo*, did not start shooting until January, but the studio had set up some more screen tests for him and wanted him on hand for other castings that might be coming up. The director of the film, Billy Wilder, was a young man – not yet forty and an Austro-Hungarian Jew. The fact that he was a foreigner, an outsider, made me trust him somehow, and he had a gentle, likeable demeanour – I could see that he was an intelligent man. Our meeting in the lobby of the Chateau (ordered by me, via Freddie) was brief, but I was satisfied that he was a decent, creative person and not out to exploit my son, so I gave my permission for Leo to be cast as a young soldier in his war film.

'Your son is very talented, Mrs Irvington,' he said as he was leaving for his next meeting.

I sensed that he was just being polite as he walked off towards the courtyard and, doubtless, a much more important person than some young actor's nervous mother. He was barely out of earshot when Freddie almost exploded. 'He's about to become a *very* big director,' he said, 'this could be *it* for Leo, Mrs Irvington.'

Whether or not my son was being groomed for stardom by anyone other than this relentlessly optimistic young scout, I had noticed a change in Leo. After agreeing to stay in Hollywood, and after a few days spent living a relatively ordinary domestic life together in our small hotel apartment, I had felt him returning to me. He slept on a settle bed on the floor next to mine and had taken to preparing coffee for us both in the kitchenette before I woke. Half-asleep, I'd gradually wake up to the muted sounds of small domestic clattering and could almost believe it was Charles or John moving around behind me.

One morning, as Leo was leaving the coffee by my bedside, he leaned down to kiss my cheek. There was nothing sweeter. No matter how old my son (I refused to call him my stepson), no matter how tall or manly he grew, there would never come a time when I would not welcome his innocent kiss. Leo's displays of affection were all the more important to me because, as I was not his natural mother and had come into his life late enough for him to know that, I never fully felt I had a right to expect affection from him.

In the past two days, however, I could feel him pulling back from me. It was natural – I knew that. Being on the other side of the world, after running away so impulsively, he had at first been relieved and glad to see me. Now, like any young man, he didn't want his mother clinging to him. He wanted me there, in the background, doing his bidding and available for support should he need it, but taking a back seat publicly, so that he could be the big actor. I would do that for my son, make myself thanklessly invisible, yet I would never have done it for his father – or indeed any other man, not even John. The idea of them even requesting such a thing was anathema to me, yet I was utterly helpless when faced with my son's desires. Here I was, in Hollywood of all places, following Leo's dreams. My dreams were back in the solitude and the sky of Fire Island – not in this gaudy place with its imported foliage and fake people. Yet I loved him so much, there was nothing to do but fold myself into his dreams.

When Leo ran away from school, I thought I had lost him. Now that I had found him, I knew I could lose him just as easily again.

He didn't want to come to the station.

'Maureen and Bridie are dying to see you.'

'Won't they be angry with me for running away?'

'Don't be silly,' I said. 'Don't you want to see Tom right away?'

'Oh yes,' he said with a sudden burst of enthusiasm, having been reminded that his brother was coming.

As we travelled in the back of the car I reached over and took his hand. Leo's hands were long and elegant and smooth, my own much smaller, the nails dry, the skin lined and roughened with work. These were the hands of an ageing mother. I brushed the thought aside and resolved to get a good cream and a regular manicure, and as I did so, Leo curled his hand up from under mine and gave it a comforting squeeze, as if intuiting my thoughts.

'I can't *wait* to see Tom,' he said. 'Do you think Maureen will have brought us any treats from New York?' His eyes were shining with the same excited anticipation that he had shown before his first audition, and it was all I could do not to laugh.

I realized that, while he looked and behaved (as it suited him) like a young man, Leo was still only a child, excitedly waiting for his next bag of sweets. He needed me there to bridge that gap for him, between childhood and adulthood.

Maureen and Bridie were already walking through the station concourse by the time our tardy taxi driver got us there. Tom ran towards us and I wept as I swept him up in my arms and hugged him all but inside-out, while Leo shuffled impatiently beside me waiting for his turn with his brother. Poor little Tom's lip was quivering and his eyes filled with tears when he saw Leo. He had become lost in this somehow, but at the age of seven he was old enough to intuit what was going on.

'We're all together again now,' I said, stroking his head as he rubbed his eyes with his chubby hands, pretending not to sweep away the tears. 'We'll never be apart like this again, Tom – I promise.'

'What in the name of all God's Good Grace were you doing running away like that, child!'

If I had any worries about being an overprotective mother, Bridie had no such doubts. She was standing square in front of Leo and, for a moment, I thought she was going to raise the large, brown leather handbag she had bought with her from Ireland in the 1890s and clip him round the ear with it.

'You have frightened your mother half to death! You stupid, silly boy – why I've half a mind to . . . '

Then she pulled him into a vice-like grip-hug, from which we all began to worry that she would never let him go.

Maureen and I exchanged a look. This was why Bridie was here.

Finally she let Leo go, turned to me and simply said, 'Dragging me across the country like this – an old woman – you should be ashamed of yourself!'

With more guests arriving at the Chateau, they had moved me to a three-bedroom poolside bungalow. It was more spacious than either our hotel suite or Freddie's tiny cottage, but even at that, the basic kitchen – designed more for mixing cocktails and managing deli-takeouts than for preparing big, hearty dinners – was not up to Bridie's standards.

'Two saucepans! Look at the size of this colander! No loaf tin – for goodness' sake, how am I supposed to bake bread?'

'Bridie, sit down and relax for a few minutes, would you? You've just travelled across the whole—'

'Matter a damn about that,' she said, 'look at the size of this oven. Sure, you'd barely fit an egg in it – never mind a chicken!'

'We get most of the food delivered in,' I said.

'Aayyyyyy – Abbott!'

Tom and Leo were sitting on the floor of the living room listening to *Abbott and Costello* on the radio. Leo had his legs spread out in front of him in a wide V, and Tom was leaning back into his chest. He was holding a large bag of cookies that they had found in a cupboard, which the two of them were dipping into at ferocious speed. Every now and again there would be a shot of laughter from the radio, and Tom would automatically laugh along with it, not understanding the joke, then looking up at his brother for approval.

For a moment I stood and watched them, thinking, *It doesn't matter where we live, as long as we are together.*

Bridie was frantically opening and closing kitchen drawers.

'Where did I put my green apron?'

'Here it is,' Maureen had pre-empted a full attack on the hotel kitchen and had opened the old woman's case, removing her apron, two favourite tea towels and a box of 'good' tea, which she dumped on the kitchen countertop.

Bridie seemed calmed by the sight of her belongings, tied on her apron and set about filling the kettle.

Maureen called me aside into the hallway.

'She's gone stone-mad, Ellie – pure upside-down! She barely slept the full journey to Chicago, but was up trying to make her own tea in the buffet car. Then she was so tired she went out cold, asleep at the lunch table in front of cousin Anne, and we had the devil of a job trying to haul her back onto the train again, with Bridie flustering about opening and closing bags, and up and down to the toilet every five minutes. She wouldn't let anyone touch her bag or carry it for her – not even Patrick – and it seemed to me that it weighed a ton. I know she's old, Ellie, but how in the name of the good Lord Jesus I got us all here, without throwing her off the train, is a miracle. Wee Tom, for all his jumping and excitement, was a pure pleasure next to her!'

'Well, you're here now,' I said. 'Things will calm down.'

'I mean it, Ellie – she's got worse.'

I wasn't sure what she meant. For months now Maureen had been complaining about Bridie's erratic behaviour, but I had put her concerns aside as petty criticisms. Perhaps it was all to the good that Bridie had come to Los Angeles. I could use her help, and the presence of an older woman around the place was good for the boys. Her age brought an authority that was as helpful as, and certainly more consistent than, the male voice we were missing. In any case, this blustery old housekeeper was the closest thing I had to a mother now and, with the loss of Charles, it would be no harm shoring up our small family with another person.

Bridie finally conceded that we could bring in cold meats and salad from the deli, but she simply would not rest until she had the ingredients for making her own bread. Sunset Strip did not have an 'ordinary' neighbourhood corner store to hand, so I had to send Freddie down to the hotel kitchen, to charm flour and milk and baking soda out of the kitchen porter.

'No egg?' she said when he handed her the tray. When her back was turned, Freddie mimicked slapping her on the bottom and I laughed, then briefly thought how like Charles this young, carefree man was, and wondered if that had been why Leo had run off to Freddie as he had.

'Can I go to the pool now, Mam? Can I? Can I?' Tom was chomping at the bit to get outside and cause mischief.

'I'll take him,' Leo said.

As the light faded, our party gathered around the pool. Freddie and Crystal balanced on a lounger, while Maureen and I sat on chairs under a parasol with Bridie. Tom was pounding in and out of the water, his tanned skin goosepimpled as he rubbed his arms, before flinging himself into the pool with such ferocity that I was afraid he would hit the bottom and break his neck. Leo was in the water beside him, his body slimmer and his skin paler than his younger brother's. He was splashing and laughing, grabbing Tom and swinging him in and out of the water, head-locking and play-fighting in a way he had never done with boys of his own age. Their brotherhood was a unique friendship – the delicate older son made more manly by his younger acolyte. They needed each other, and I felt a tinge of regret that I had ever parted them by allowing Leo to go to boarding school.

'To be sitting out under the open sky at this time of night . . . ' Bridie grumbled, as she poured from the full tray of tea things that she had made us bring up from the bungalow, including a plate of her own soda bread, which she continued to munch. 'It's just not right.'

Nonetheless her tone was soft, and she eased her stockinged feet out of her shoes and curled and twisted them delightedly in the warm Californian breeze.

After a pleasant half-hour or so I saw the red-haired actress Gloria pause at the top of the steps, as if trying to find a way past our noisy family gathering without being seen. As I was raising my hand to greet her, from the corner of my eye I noticed Tom at the side of the pool.

'Maaaa-aaam – LOOK!'

He whipped off his soaking pants and waved them in the air, before plunging naked into the water.

Gloria's eyes had followed mine, and I smiled at her weakly and shrugged an apology. As she scuttled past I heard Bridie huff behind me, 'Well – *that*'s a wig,' and I knew that, first thing in the morning, I would have to find us all somewhere more suitable to live.

Chapter Fifteen

I found us a house on Franklin Avenue in the Los Feliz district of Hollywood. Near Paramount Studios, Los Feliz had more character than the sprawling Sunset Boulevard, which, despite its name, I had found strangely cold. Freddie had tried to persuade me to rent a house in the mountains above Sunset, where many of the stars lived in vast balconied haciendas looking down into the valley. Although the properties were spacious and I could afford them, I did not warm to the idea. The hills seemed an impractical place to live – one had to get into a car in order to do everything, even something simple like buying a pint of milk required effort. Even when I had been living in the back-of-beyond in Kilmoy in Ireland, there would always be a cow on hand if you ran out of milk, and eggs in the henhouse if you were stuck for food.

Los Feliz, while certainly Californian in architecture and mood – all skinny palm trees and low houses – was nonetheless the closest thing I could find in scale and convenience to New York, in that it had a 'village' area. Our house was two minutes' walk away from a long strip of shops, including a cinema and several restaurants set along both sides of Vermont Street, which was narrow enough to cross on foot without taking your life entirely in your hands. At the edge of the strip was Hollywood Boulevard and, if you walked down to the right, rising up from the wide, dusty road was Olive Hill, where Hollyhock House – the empty home of the eccentric heiress Aline Barnsdall – was tucked flat into the shallow, sun-scorched grasslands. The peculiarly designed, squat building was just visible from the road and although it was only twenty or so years old, it had been designed by Frank Lloyd Wright and, for that reason, with my foolish New York snobbery, I felt it gave the area some history and gravitas.

Our new home was an airy bungalow with four bedrooms and an open kitchen-living-area opening out onto a large lawn at the back. To the front were two ludicrously grand Roman pillars – a nod to the pretension evident almost everywhere in this crazy town – but there were also ornate filigree screens on every door and window to keep the house cool, and a wide front porch that opened onto another generous lawn at the front. There were enough beds for us all, plus an extra room that I planned to use as a studio. Ironically, the decision to commit to signing a six-month lease had little to do with Leo's movie aspirations, but was based on the needs of the two people who were least involved in our being there: Bridie and Tom. Having survived one long journey, Bridie was not ready to embark on the return one yet; and then Tom announced over dinner in the Chateau one evening, in front of everyone, that he wanted to 'stay here and be with us all in the same place again'. The table was silenced by this awkward pronouncement, so he took that as an invitation to continue, saying that he was 'sick of being with Mammy all the time' and would like to try going to school 'like a normal boy'.

Bridie snapped at him, 'Don't be such a cheeky pup, or there'll be no cake!' but she gave me a look that left me in no doubt that it was something she herself had been thinking for a long time.

The rental came with basic furnishings, including sheets and towels, and I did not send home for any of our belongings. While I agreed to relinquish my artist's isolation by keeping the family together in this one place for a while, I was not looking to create anything fancy from it. We just needed somewhere comfortable to lay our heads while Leo played out this idea of his, which, I hoped, would not last much beyond this first film. We could then return to New York to resume both boys' schooling and my art.

One of the best things about living in Los Feliz was that we were relatively close to the Paramount Lot. There was a good bus service to the studios, although, more often than not, Freddie or I would drive Leo there. The roads here were wide and seldom clogged with traffic, the way New York's streets were, so that the journey – almost an hour on foot – took only a few minutes by car.

In my case the 'car' was a dusty blue pickup truck that I had bought from our Mexican neighbour a few days after we moved in. For no reason that I could logically discern (my farming roots perhaps?), I had always hankered after a pickup truck. I associated them with good weather and sunshine – in truth, they were one of the few things about living outside the city (New York being the only 'real' American city) that appealed to me. However, they were not vehicles suitable for New York, as they required year-round good weather. Actually they were not vehicles for Los Angeles, either – because they were associated with hillbillies. By the time I discovered how deeply unfashionable they were, it was too late, and I was already witnessing the open surprise on the faces of my neighbours at my eccentric choice. Nonetheless, I drove it everywhere and found it to be extremely practical. There was room in the front cab for Bridie and one other, squeezed between us. However, Tom adored sitting in the back on a wooden crate and gripping onto the sides to stop him getting slung around.

Leo, of course, was mortified at being driven around in such a hillbilly vehicle, which made me all the more determined to keep him grounded – and meant that Freddie was a regular visitor with his car.

Leo had signed a standard contract with Paramount. Freddie explained to me that it was unusual for him to have been cast at all, given that he was not attached to any particular studio. He said that young actors were signed up as studio workers before being sent for castings. Leo was in a unique position, he told me, because he had not been found by a studio scout, but by Freddie, 'an outside agent'.

Nonetheless, Leo would have to undergo voice-coaching, grooming and acting lessons in the employ of the studio, before filming started in January. There was no need for me to even see the contract, Freddie assured me – it was a given that Leo would be looked after.

'This is his big break, Mrs H. This film could make Leo into a big star.'

I groaned inside whenever Freddie spoke like that, but the poor young man seemed so enthusiastic, and had looked after Leo so well, that I could not crush his dreams, any more than I would have crushed Leo's.

'What do you get out of this, Freddie?' I asked him one morning when he came to collect Leo to take him across to the studio. I could not see where Freddie was making his money and it made me nervous. All this time and effort he was putting into my son, and for what? How was he paying for the Chateau and the car?

'Oh, don't you worry about that, Mrs H. I've got this whole studio thing all worked out. Things are changing. Things are happening, Mrs. H. Soon the studios won't have the control they have now. I've got the inside track.' He dramatically looked round to check that nobody was listening in – in my empty kitchen. Was there anyone in this town who wasn't an actor at heart?

'Between you and me, all the big actors in the Screen Actors Guild are sick of the studios having complete control of their careers, and they are muscling in with a bunch of big lawyers. We're talking names,' he counted them off on his fingers, 'Olivia de Havilland, Paul Harvey, Jean Hersholt, Gene Lockhart, Bela Lugosi, George Murphy, Gloria Stuart, Irving Pichel, Franchot Tone.' Then he opened his hands to allow me to collapse at his feet, which I didn't, before continuing, 'In a few months, my friend the lawyer says, once this big case goes through, all these stars' contracts can be revoked, and what are the studios going to do without all their big names?'

Find new ones, I thought, but I didn't say it out loud.

'The studios *need* their stars, right? So that's where I come in: *BAM!* I already have a dozen big names, Mrs H., big – and I'm talking *big* – names, ready to sign up as soon as the case comes clear. The old system, it's gone; so now I come in and negotiate on the stars' behalf and then take a percentage. The studios will have to pay me for the talent – it's called "agenting", Mrs H. – and that's the way it's going to be from now on. I'll be the hottest agent in town. Hell, I'll be the *only* agent in town!'

Unions. Big ideas. I'd been there before, with Charles. Except that Charles had been motivated by the morals of social justice, so at least he had right on his side. What poor, optimistic Freddie was hoping for was beyond impossible. The kid was just following another improbable Hollywood dream – with all that greedy talk about paydays, he just wanted to play the bigshot in his own Hollywood fantasy.

'How do you know all this?' I asked.

'I have a friend – a lawyer. Well, he's not exactly a lawyer himself, but he *works* for this lawyer, anyhow. And they have this big case with the Department of Justice – something to do with movie theatres.'

I looked at him blankly.

'It's too complicated to explain,' he said, 'but when it comes off, everything is going to come tumbling down with the studios, and yours truly will be on hand to mop up all that talent!'

He seemed so certain that I was inclined to believe him; or rather I *wanted* to believe him. This madcap scheme was Freddie's dream, and while he was doing his level best to make it sound feasible, it was probably as likely as Crystal being the next Olivia de Havilland, and as grounded in reality as the Chateau guest Gloria's magnificent red wig.

'Well, I hope Paramount will at least pay you a finder's fee for Leo, Freddie?'

'Don't you worry,' he said enigmatically. 'The studio knows me. They're always hassling to take me on as a scout, but I've got it covered, Mrs H. I'm holding out for the big time. Me and Billy Wilder? We're like that . . . ' and he crossed his fingers. 'I know all the big names. It's only a matter of time, Mrs H., before the big time rolls in for Freddie Hickey,' he finished, tapping his nose and winking.

'I thought your name was Dubois,' said Bridie, who has been half-listening while working her way through a pile of ironing.

He smiled a wide, white-toothed grin and said, 'Sure it is, Bridie', and she flicked a creased pillowcase at him disparagingly.

I couldn't help but like the young man – despite all his silly talk and big ideas.

*

One of the things that contributed to the village atmosphere in Los Feliz was that, while Paramount stars and studio heads lived in the hills close to Sunset, the technicians, set designers, electricians, carpenters, cooks, costume-makers, make-up girls, hairdressers – the everyday workers in the movie industry – mostly lived and worked around here. There were a few grand houses and some smart apartment buildings, so every now and again I would pass a face that I recognized on my way into a local restaurant favoured by movie stars and producers, but all in all the atmosphere was that of an ordinary, pleasant neighbourhood.

This was one of the few places in Los Angeles where you could do your everyday business – shopping, posting letters, collecting laundry – without having to get in a car.

One day I decided to clear my head and walk to the studios to collect Leo. His acting class finished at three that afternoon, and I needed to get out of the house. I had started to feel that this new house was becoming a kind of prison. Fixing up houses had always been something of a passion of mine. I liked nice things – good crockery, starched table-linens, polished wood – and it seemed now, looking back, that I had spent a large part of my early life setting up homes, from modernizing our cottage in Ireland with my first husband, John, to the community home I set up in Yonkers, the apartment in Chelsea and finally the cabin in Fire Island. I had always taken pride in my surroundings and was careful and creative in the way I presented everything in my home, from a simple table setting to the way the cushions were set on a chair. Floral arrangements – be they in a cut-glass vase or a jam jar – were always tastefully displayed. I took pleasure in the simple tasks of housewifery. When I made my fortune in business as a young woman, and time for household tasks was scarce, I seemed to enjoy them even more.

Now, however, since I had moved into this rental apartment, that had all changed. I did not feel like fixing it up. The very idea of turning this house into any kind of a home bored me. While Bridie fussed about cleaning, she deferred to me on purchasing new linens, a few pieces of smarter crockery, new table napkins, encouraging me to prettify some corner with shop-bought flowers, but I found myself responding with uncharacteristic indifference.

Bridie had been like a whirlwind since her arrival, and attacked each meal and each pile of washing with a vigour I had not seen in her for years. Los Angeles had given her a new lease of life, which was great, but it made me even more redundant.

Although I could not say so to Bridie, who had given her whole life to the domestic service of both herself and others, I had come to feel that, at forty-two, I had earned the right not to waste another moment of my life on domestic fripperies or chores. I did not include in this feeding my family or spending time with Tom, ministering over baths or doing his lessons, but when it came to arranging his room – painting little sailboats on the wall above his bed, as I had done in the cabin on Fire Island – I had no interest whatsoever.

I was, in truth, preoccupied with the fact that I had not been painting. Aside from that day sketching Crystal, I had not picked up charcoal or a brush since leaving Fire Island. I made excuses, the greatest one being all that I had to do in the house, but the weeks rounded into a month and I began to fear that my art had deserted me. The artist in me – the Ellie who could lose herself in the flurry of paint on canvas, the spirit who existed through the colour and shape she could see in the world – had deserted me already. Perhaps it was because I had allowed her life to take second place, or had ignored her pleas to paint, in deference to the drama of Leo's disappearance. Whatever the reason, I made excuses to myself that I didn't have the right tools, that I had yet to get my bearings and find where to buy canvas and paints, that I was waiting for Conor to box up some essentials from the studio and have them sent over to me; but the truth was that the compulsion to create had left me.

The day was fine, warm enough for a sweater – maybe a light jacket, as I would be walking some distance and it might rain. I had spent all morning with Tom doing his lessons, and he was now working on his 'tunnel': a shallow hole that he had scooped out of the back lawn, as part of a long-term project to dig himself to Australia. Bridie was at the sink washing potatoes for Irish boxty – which is what Bridie, incapable of sitting down for one minute of the day, did when there was nothing else left to be done. She grated the raw potatoes, mixed them in a bowl with salt, flour, milk and eggs, then fried them in a pan. She and Tom would have made history of the boxty, smothered in butter and honey, by the time I got back with Leo.

My sketchpad and charcoals were in the bedroom that I had allocated as my temporary studio, on the stranger's dressing table where I had left them the day we moved in. Before I left the house I opened the bedroom door and considered bringing them with me, in case I saw something en route that inspired me. I closed the door quickly again and, in that same action, fearfully imagined that I felt another door inside me close itself off. I would not think about painting today, I decided. I would not look for inspiration. I would just walk for an hour, collect Leo and maybe get a taxi and be back to catch some of Bridie's boxty.

I walked past the grocery stores, the bank, post office, restaurants and coffee shops of the village and down the empty, wide, dusty sidewalk of Hollywood Boulevard. A few bicycles dashed past me, veering away from the cars that sped up and down the wide roadway. I walked past the bland, low commercial buildings, spread out so that you'd hardly know – or care – what was in them, if not for the gaudy signs 'Car Wash' and 'Dime Store Bargains'. The air was fresh, but I was going at a good pace and it felt warm enough for me to take off my sweater. It was as if the seasons had stopped. It certainly did not feel like mid-November, and my mind wandered to New York. The air would be crisp and the ground covered in leaves now, children gathering them into huge piles along the sidewalks. I thought further back to Ireland, and how wet and dark it was there at this time of year. I had never minded the bad winter weather, although I suppose I had known no better. John and I would light a big turf fire and sit and watch the flames dance as the light outside faded to . . . *WHACK!*

My mind was not on where I was going and I had tripped over the root of a huge carob tree. The wretched things were everywhere, their curling, treacherous roots reaching up from the shallow mud path and all but grabbing at passing ankles. This was certainly *not* a town for pedestrians.

I stood up and put tentative pressure on my foot. No damage had been done. There was nobody around to witness my fall, or help pick me up, or ask after my welfare. The nearest building was half a block away. I was fine, but I told myself I might not have been – and that realization brought up in me a sudden fit of petulance. I *hated* this place with its relentlessly sunny weather, its lack of character and its row after row of palm trees. I had, I told myself, gone for this walk to find some inspiration, something to paint, but instead I had been assaulted by a stupid tree! My petulance turned to fury and, before I knew it, I found myself kicking the carob and hailing a passing taxi to take me to the studio.

Chapter Sixteen

Leo had been going up to the Paramount Lot most days for the past three weeks since his contract started. When he was not at the studio I did lessons with him and Tom, and constructed our time as much like a school day as possible. On these days Leo was just on the polite side of surly, still frightened that I might drag him back to New York if he didn't show some pretence for study. The rest of the time – three, more often four days out of five in the working week – he was at Paramount, being trained in a group of twenty other young actors. Each day they underwent a routine of acting classes, deportment, voice-training and grooming. They were also taken around and introduced to the idea of working among the hustle and bustle of cameras and microphones, lighting and 'sets', and all the other terminology that Leo was full of when he came home after his days at the studio.

'Watch my face,' he said one evening when he came in, then simply gazed at me intently for a few moments and then relaxed. 'Did you see anything?' he said.

'Well, not really,' I admitted. 'You were just sort of – staring?'

His face fell. 'It's a *close-up*, Mam – it's *really* important. If you can master the close-up, then you'll be a star. That's what we learned today.'

I didn't know what to say.

'Show me,' said Bridie, waving me away, 'sure, she doesn't know anything.'

Leo did it again, and this time, with a little more obvious drama, he glared intently at Bridie for a few moments.

She gasped dramatically when he had finished.

'Well, I declare,' she said, 'it was like watching Bela Lugosi in *Dracula*, and I am covered in goosebumps – that was very, *very* dramatic altogether. Oh, we have something on our hands here, surely, Ellie. You'd better pick yourself up, lady – your son is going to be a big, *big* star.'

I was somewhat taken aback. I had no idea Bridie knew who Bela Lugosi was, but my sixteen-year-old son gave her a hug that any eighty-year-old would be proud of, and she ruffled Leo's hair and kissed him repeatedly on the head, until he eventually recoiled with embarrassment, then re-emerged back into the groomed, sophisticated young man he was becoming.

'I had better go and practise my lines for tomorrow.'

He could memorize pages of complicated text when it was in script form, I noted, but not remember two lines from the Shakespeare sonnet that I had taught him the day before. Bridie raised her eyes to heaven at me, to make it clear she was only humouring him, and when he had left the room she said, 'He'll get over all this nonsense, Ellie – you'll see.'

The taxi dropped me off at the tall, opulent entrance arch of the Paramount gates.

'Want me to drive you through, lady?' the driver asked, but I said no. What was the point of that? I had legs.

There was a security guard in a small cabin to my left, and he reluctantly put down his paper and came out. He looked at the taxi driving off and seemed a little surprised that I was on foot.

'I am here to meet Leo Irvington,' I said. 'He's a trainee actor with the studios.'

I had never been through the studio gates before, having always collected Leo at the entrance. And I had planned to do the same today, except that I was now an hour early.

'You got a location for him?' he asked. *Location* – another one of Leo's film terms. What was wrong with 'place', I wondered.

'No,' I said, 'I do not have a "location". Surely there must be some place where the students all . . .'

'Then he could be anywhere,' the guard said, anxious to get back into his hut and finish his coffee and paper. 'Try the back lot – they're shooting a big crowd scene today, they've drafted in loads of extras. If he's training, he'll have been sent down there – they need all the bodies they can get. Sorry, lady, this is the first time I've sat down all day – he might be there with them.'

'Is there anywhere I can wait?'

He shrugged. 'Go on through,' he said, going into his hut and closing the door. 'If he's not on the lot, try Stage 21 – down on Second Street, far left; they use it sometimes in the afternoons.'

Street names? In a film studio? I looked ahead and could not even see a left turn – just what looked like warehouses. I walked and walked until the warehouses were distinguishable only by the numbers above their vast, closed doors: 'Stage One', 'Stage Two', and so on. There was a turn to the right, so I took that, and the numbers on the warehouses increased, then stopped and gave way to flat, box-like buildings with windows, which I assumed must be offices. *Small wonder*, I thought, *the taxi driver was surprised that I chose to walk through – this place is vast!* People passed me here and there, but nobody stopped to ask who I was or what I was doing. There were men with clipboards, girls carrying trays of coffee through mysterious doors, workmen loading shop signs (or slabs of wood painted to look like shop signs) onto wagons, who wheeled them with determined speed off to some other urgent location.

Among the sprawling office buildings there suddenly appeared a pretty, village-like area of houses painted in candy colours – pink and primrose doorways, some with sweet little porches on the front. I had been walking for a while now and still had no idea where I was going, but everybody milling about looked so determined, so resolutely in the middle of doing something, that they seemed beyond interruption. I decided just to knock on a door and was naturally drawn towards the cottage-type buildings – silly though it seemed, I assumed their inhabitants would be more amenable to questions. So I stopped and knocked at a small, white two-storey cottage with brightly coloured bougainvillea creeping up its doorway. There was no reply, so I simply tried the handle and stepped inside. Except that there was no inside – or rather it was not the inside I was expecting, but a dark empty space with no floor and rows of metal rigging instead of a roof.

I stepped back out of the doorway and as I did so I tripped – again – and, trying to catch hold of something to stop me falling, took a handful of the bougainvillea with me, which, as it turned out, was also fake. I was lucky I didn't take the whole facade with me.

After my fight with the carob tree earlier I was really mad now. Mad with myself for opening the door, and for putting myself through the indignity of a public fall for a second time, but mostly with this bloody stupid place. What kind of insanity was it, putting a building like that there, when it wasn't a building at all – some kind of stupid trick! I knew it was a set, a stupid film set, but – well, there should have been a sign.

'Are you okay?' a young man with a visor and clipboard leaned over me.

'Yes, I am perfectly all right!' I snapped at him, starting to stand up and grateful that I was wearing trousers, for the smidgeon of decorum that I had left.

The boy backed off, raising his hands in the air. 'Okay, okay, lady – just trying to help.' And he hurried off.

'That was some fall.'

A man in a panama hat and a smart beige suit wandered over from the building opposite. He did not rush to help me, but rather sauntered into my company in a way that was, frankly, infuriatingly insouciant. His panama was pulled down, obscuring his face, which I found very rude in itself.

'Thanks for the help,' I said, by way of greeting – not that he deserved a greeting at all. '*You're* certainly a real gentleman,' I continued.

'I prefer to let the younger generation do the heavy lifting,' he smiled. 'I just make myself available for consolation and comfort after the event.'

'Well, you're doing a lousy job of it,' I said, 'and I object to being described as "heavy".'

'Object all you like,' he said, 'it wasn't meant to offend. To tell you the truth, I prefer my women with a bit of girth.'

'How dare you – why I have half a mind to . . . ' Then behind my blind fury I noticed something familiar.

'Yes, I prefer a nice, real Irish woman like you – not these Hollywood types, with their silly pointy chests, their false teeth, their wigs . . . '

The man pulled back his hat and it was Stan, the composer I had met on the train. My mood lightened immediately. What a pleasure!

'You are a terrible old rogue and a diabolical trickster.'

'And I have finally seen the lady artist's artistic temperament that I suspected was there.'

'Finally? It didn't take very long,' I demurred.

'Indeed, and I would have been disappointed if it had. I was not sure it was you. What are you doing here?'

'Looking for my son.'

'Still?'

'No, no – I found him, he's fine; he's becoming an actor.'

'And you think that's fine?'

I was so delighted to meet this virtual stranger, who made me laugh and whose vigorous character stimulated a feeling of intelligence and good humour in me.

'Not exactly – to be honest, I don't know.'

'Have you time for coffee,' he said, 'before you go seeking your actor son?'

'If you can help me find the Back Lot or Stage 21? I have no idea where I'm going – this place is such a maze.'

'You get used to it,' he said, as he lifted his elbow for me to take his arm and we started walking deeper into the lot. 'You know, in the first place I *had* to come here to work. I was required by producers, directors – for meetings, rehearsals – and was dragged into this world of pretence and artifice. I thought: "This is such a terrible place, so soulless and silly." Then one day I realized that I was coming in the gates even when I did not have to! I said that it was good for me to find some corner here, where I could compose with no distractions; the studios would provide me with a good piano and a room with no window, where a writer like me can find solitude to create his masterpiece. But there is something else – another thing that I can find here.' Then he paused and, putting his long, thin fingers over my hand, closed his eyes, smiled and said in a breathless, almost ecstatic tone, 'People.'

We had barely walked a hundred yards when suddenly it was as if we were back out on the street. Not a strange, sprawling empty Los Angeles street, but a street in Brooklyn on a busy Saturday afternoon. It was uncannily real. On the corner there was a pizza parlour, with people eating outside under a striped canopy; next to that was a newspaper stand, where a couple of city slickers threw coins at the vendor and got their papers back almost without stopping; a woman rushed to get onto a passing tram; a bunch of kids played hoopla further along the road; and there was a man getting his shoes shined outside a barber's shop. It was such a strange and captivating sight to come upon suddenly that I almost didn't notice the cameramen looming above us on all sides, perched precariously on high rigging. In fact Stan had to hold me back from wandering into the shot and, as he did so, a woman hurtled directly towards us shouting, 'Cab!' before stopping suddenly, then dropping her bag and sauntering towards a long cabin with an open front, laid out with tin mugs and trays of sandwiches and cookies.

'We'll get coffee here,' Stan said, 'if we're not thrown off set for not looking like genuine New Yorkers.'

'I don't think that will happen,' I said, 'although – come to think of it – I'm not sure about that hat!'

'Cut! Break for twenty.'

The catering stand was suddenly deluged with 'New Yorkers' grabbing greedily at the coffee and sandwiches. A man with a megaphone walked past shouting, 'All extras to Stage 31 – ten minutes. All extras to Stage 31 for hair – ten minutes.'

'We'll go to the canteen,' Stan said.

'Mam? What are you doing here?'

It was Leo. He was dressed as a shoeshine, wearing a scruffy waistcoat and hat, his face dramatically blackened with polish.

'You must be Ellie's lost son?' said Stan, holding out his hand.

'Who's *he?*' Leo asked. My cheeks started to burn with embarrassment. I could have slapped him for being so rude.

'My name is Stanislaw Lilius. I am a friend of your mother's.'

Leo ignored his hand and turned to me.

'What are you *doing* here? We arranged to meet at the front gate.'

His eyes were shining. He was all excited – hyped up by the thrill of the camera, no doubt. I wanted to scold him for his rudeness, but at the same time I didn't want to draw attention to it, and I didn't want to look defeated as a mother in front of Stan.

'I was early, so I came through . . . '

'Well, I have to go now to film another scene, so I'll be late. In any case, Crystal is filming here too today – Freddie will be coming to get her, so I'll get a ride back with them.' He gave me a cursory kiss, then threw a filthy glance at Stan before running off.

'He is not normally that rude,' I explained.

Stan was charming. 'He is young and in love . . . '

When I looked puzzled, he added 'with Hollywood. This is a very exciting place, after all.'

'His father died last year,' I said by way of explanation – and only as I said it did I realize that Charles' death was probably the cause of all this upheaval.

'Oh,' Stan said. 'Will we talk about that?'

'I'd sooner not,' I said.

'Dead husbands are for another day then.'

I smiled in agreement.

Stan gave me a tour of the studios, showing me around 'Chicago' and 'Paris' and more, before taking me to pass a pleasant hour in the canteen. We talked about everything and nothing, until he said, 'I must, alas, return to my composing, although you have been such a charming muse that I will work better now – I am sure of it.'

He insisted on having his driver and car take me back to the house.

'The studio must pay, my dear – for everything. That is the first lesson of Hollywood.'

As I was getting into the car I turned to him and said, 'I am so glad we met again – and thank you for coming to my rescue outside the fake house. I know you meant to, really.'

'Ah,' he said, 'actually, I must confess now that I was watching you from the writers' office opposite – I use it sometimes for composing. They have that line of houses set up as a ruse for visitors. You would be amazed how many people are drawn to step inside the charming cottage with the pink flowers climbing up its side . . . '

He had such mischief in his eyes that I felt compelled to kiss him warmly on his cheek, then raise my palm to his face to press it fondly.

As the car drove out through the gates and back onto the wide palm-lined streets, I thought that perhaps I might come to like this foolish place called Hollywood after all – and at least some of the people in it.

CHAPTER SEVENTEEN

I was dreading Hilla coming to town.

She was coming around Thanksgiving to track down and buy up any interesting work by the Los Angeles artist Rolph Scarlett. I had met him a couple of times in the gallery – a rugged handsome man, Rolph had been a successful stage and set designer in Hollywood until the mid-1930s, when he had moved to New York to become a 'real artist'. His work was brightly coloured, chaotic, non-objective – right up Hilla's street – so she made him chief lecturer at the Guggenheim Museum teaching new modernist abstraction – if it were possible to 'teach' such a thing. I had my doubts. Hilla was so enthused by Scarlett's work that she had become his greatest collector. Scarlett had sold some work privately during his time in Los Angeles, and she was coming to see if she could track down any of it for the Guggenheim collection.

I had written to her, eventually, telling her where I was and explaining that I would be in Los Angeles for a while. As I knew she would be, Hilla was horrified and called me immediately to try and persuade me, in her forthright Germanic way, to 'come home'.

'Your career as a painter is finished, Ellie, if you don't come back to New York. Whoever heard of a "real" artist working in Los Angeles? Rolph will never go back there – *never*. Who can take somebody seriously in such a cultural desert? A real desert, perhaps. Mexico I could understand, but Los Angeles? What will you paint?'

'Well, I have to be here at the moment Hilla, for Leo.'

She puffed. Hilla had little to no interest in children generally, and none whatsoever in mine specifically!

Shortly after that conversation I got the call to say that she was coming to LA on her Scarlett expedition just in time for Thanksgiving, although I could not help but feel that the two were connected.

'I will stay with Aline Barnsdall – do you know her? Of course not. She is an ex-employer of Lloyd Wright – they were friends, of course, then he built her a house that she *hated* and they fell out for a while. I need to talk to her and see what happened, as I've just got him on board for the new museum. I like him, but I believe he can be difficult, so I need to be prepared.'

Difficult, eh? *That will be a match made in heaven*, I thought, but said nothing. Despite her abrupt manner, Hilla had a way with artists – and Lloyd Wright was certainly that. We all liked and respected her, both as a painter and as a discerning collector, but more importantly we felt liked and respected by her. She was bossy, sometimes overbearing, but she was always genuine in her best intentions for the art – and the artist.

'You must come and stay with us, Hilla – especially as it's Thanksgiving.' But I knew what was coming next. 'Is that horrible old woman still living with you?'

Bridie and Hilla did not like each other. Both well-built and forthright women, they were actually very similar, which doubtless fuelled their mutual dislike. Hilla, no matter how she dressed, always came across as rather substantial and indelicate, in both appearance and manner. Among the delicate egos and whimsical fashions of the New York art scene, this sturdy, no-nonsense persona gave her a unique, if somewhat intimidating edge. When faced with my housekeeper Bridie, however, it was as if she was looking into a distorted mirror of sorts, and, although Hilla herself could not see why, she just didn't like being around the outspoken old Irishwoman. Bridie's dislike of Hilla was much more straightforward, based entirely as it was on blind prejudice.

'I hope you're not inviting that wretched *German* for Thanksgiving.'

Hilla's plans to stay with Aline Barnsdall fell through, which was a shame, as I would have liked to have met Aline. I had read an interview with the heiress and arts benefactor in the local paper and she was, by all accounts, a woman ahead of her time. A fiercely independent feminist, a bohemian and a devotee of experimental theatre, Miss Barnsdall was also, scandalously, a single mother. Like me – except that she had given birth to her child out of wedlock and, even though both my sons were adopted, I had enjoyed the status of being a married mother of two. Aline now lived in a smaller house than the Lloyd Wright-designed Hollyhock House that she had rejected, and must be in her sixties.

Tom and I walked through Barnsdall Park almost every day, clambering up the steep hills at the side of Hollywood Boulevard – Tom running in and out of the olive trees scattered across the scraggy, sandy lawns – until we would sit on a shallow wall outside the empty Hollyhock House, looking down onto the dusty road below and across at the big movie-star hills. Stan had two friends who were members of the California Art Club, which had been based in Hollyhock House for the past fifteen years, only closing down the year before, partly because their lease ran out, but also because the place was falling in around their ears. The California Art Club focused on figurative painting and landscapes, the kind of traditional work that Hilla had no time at all for, calling it 'too much in the past. I have no interest in the past.' According to Stan's friends, it had been Aline Barnsdall's intention for the land that she had donated to be developed into an 'Art Park' by Los Angeles City Council, with a theatre and gallery – but her ambitious plans seemed to have been thwarted by bitter legal wrangling over some small matter.

Land, I understood from my own background in rural Ireland, was seldom as simple a matter as it seemed. I had known farmers who would chop a neighbour's foot off if he encroached on their property, and elderly brothers fall out – after a lifetime of loyalty – over a square inch of grazing land.

Shortly after reading the interview with Aline I remember sitting on the wall outside the empty building – its fat, sandy walls and decorative turrets were as inviting as its small, dark windows were ominous – and looking down at the city below and, for the first time since I had arrived in California, thinking that perhaps this was not such a bad place to end up after all.

Hilla called the day she arrived and said that she was staying with the Stendhals in their home in Hollywood. Earl Stendhal was a collector of great note, like herself. They had met some years before, and she was anxious to talk to him about Rolph's work – if anyone knew what had changed hands in recent years, it would be him. I invited her for Thanksgiving lunch and she reluctantly accepted.

She arrived on my doorstep on Thanksgiving Day in a taxi, carrying her suitcase.

'Such a bore,' she said, 'we disagreed on everything.'

I was pretty sure the first part wasn't true, but the second part was.

When I had first encountered Hilla, at an exhibition party in Guggenheim's suite in The Plaza Hotel fifteen years beforehand, she had seemed to have something of the charming, if somewhat serious, socialite about her. Now, in her fifties, she was becoming somewhat – although I hated to admit it – charmless. Her relationship with Bauer was souring, and yet she continued to be enthralled by him as a man and an artist. I wondered if that was happening to me as I got older. Was I becoming less tolerant, less charming with time? Kicking trees and fighting change, being less enamoured with adventure – was this the beginning of my slide into old age? Perhaps losing two husbands within ten years had made me bitter? Or, in Hilla and myself, was I simply observing the wisdom that a woman earns with age? Perhaps the more we see of the world, the less we can fathom its trivial cruelties, the more embittered we become, and therefore the less inclined towards pretence and politeness.

Whatever the case, I was not wrong in thinking that Thanksgiving lunch was going to be hard going, with Bridie and Hilla at the same table.

I took charge of the turkey, but Bridie insisted on doing everything else and, in any case, hovered over me, checking I was doing it right.

'It'll never brown with that excuse for a spoonful of butter – put a right lump of it in, for pity's sake – do you know nothing at all!'

'I'm managing fine.' I don't know why Bridie didn't annoy me. When I was younger her manner used to both terrify and upset me, but I had become so used to her, even her criticisms – no, especially her criticisms.

'You'd want to be – that was an expensive bird!'

'Jesus, Bridie! Where did all that sugar come from?'

She was spooning cuploads of it into a large saucepan of mashed pumpkin-pie mixture. Coffee and sugar had been rationed for more than a year now. We had managed fine on a half a pound a week, especially as none of us had a particularly sweet tooth except for Bridie, who had compromised somewhat by using honey in her tea and making cakes using sweet apple purée. Like many Irishwomen of her generation who had barely tasted sugar before she reached America, it was a passionate addiction and she complained bitterly about having to restrict her use of it in her cooking. She had gone down from three spoons of sugar in her tea to one, and barely lifted a cup to her mouth these days without grimacing. So it was therefore note-worthy that she had almost a potato-sack full of her white drug up on the counter.

'Oh, never you mind . . . ' she said, pouring a bottle of black porter into a saucepan full of currants and throwing another generous handful of white sugar on top. She was making her Irish porter cake.

'As well as pumpkin pie?' I asked.

'*And* an apple tart,' she said triumphantly. 'If we're going to give thanks,' she added, 'I might as well give you something to be thankful for!'

The old woman still had the extraordinary energy that she had arrived on the West Coast with, but although she seemed in good health, I worried that she might be overdoing it. She had not sat down for almost two days, cleaning the house in preparation for this one-meal holiday. When I had pleaded with her the night before to go to bed early, she had snapped, 'I'll not have some uppity Kraut cast aspersions on the state of this house – not that you seem bothered, one way or the other.'

'Where is the sugar from, Bridie?' I had a horrible thought.

'You didn't open the door to some dreadful black-marketeer did you?'

She huffed.

'Oh Jesus, Bridie – you know those guys just come back and back; once you buy one thing off them, they—'

'I've been saving it up,' she said, 'there – now you know.'

'What do you mean?' I asked.

'You heard me,' she said, 'I've been putting a bit away every week, stockpiling it for Thanksgiving.'

'But you've only been here for a few weeks,' I said, 'there's a half-ton of it in that bag.'

'I brought it up from New York,' she said more quietly.

'From *New York*?' I said, 'It must have weighed . . . '

'Yes!' she shouted at me, 'it did. But it's a poor house that can't have a proper feast on Thanksgiving. Now, will you get out of this kitchen and let me get on with it in peace!'

How long had Bridie been sacrificing her beloved sugar consumption and stockpiling it for this special day? She had hidden and packed the heavy sack of sundries in her case, refusing to let anyone else carry it, in case they guessed at her contraband.

As I left the kitchen I turned and watched for a moment unseen, as she threw half a pound of her own creamy, salted butter on the mashed potatoes, her worn face set and stern as it always was – except for the rarest occasion when I'd catch her dragging Tom over to her for a quiet cuddle, or when she'd pushed him up the stairs to bed as a toddler; 'Get up those stairs, like a long-dog,' she'd call to him and gently slap his bottom as he crawled up, hands first – doing Bridie's bidding was one of the first things he learned. Like the rest of us, Tom did as Bridie told him, and he didn't mind. As she drew the fork backwards and forwards, fluffing up the spuds as I had seen her do a thousand times before, I realized that it was Bridie, not me, who was the true matriarch of this family. This Thanksgiving meal was hers and – as I did every year – I had set the guest list without even consulting her.

Chapter Eighteen

As soon as the food arrived – before I'd had the chance to blow on my soup – Hilla got straight to work.

'You have not set up a studio here,' she said, nodding disparagingly towards the kitchen, 'so you are painting nothing. When are you coming back to New York?'

Small mercy, perhaps, that she had at least waited until the Thanksgiving formalities were complete. Tom had been thankful for the frog he had found in the garden that morning (which was now residing in a box under his bed); Leo had been thankful that his career as an actor had begun and, after a glower from Bridie, to his mother for moving everybody to Los Angeles. Bridie thanked the Merciful Lord Jesus and His Mother the Blessed Virgin Mary, and several lesser-known saints, for a litany of interventions that they had carried out in the past year – St Anthony for finding her glasses for her, and the like – purely to embarrass me in front of Hilla, who abstained rudely with a wave of her hand.

I was thankful for the family being together, remembered absent friends and loved ones – the Sweeneys, and then Charles and John.

Even Hilla bowed her head at that. Tom got up from the table as soon as I said his father's name, curled himself into my side and rubbed the tears from his eyes on the shoulder of my blouse. He was such a sturdy, playful, outdoor child that it was easy to forget he was still grieving the only father he had known. I tried to create moments like these to let the children's pain out. Tom threw tantrums now, which he had never done before his father died. I had lost so many people – parents, two husbands, countless friends and neighbours in the Irish War of Independence – that grief was a familiar companion. I knew her well. The banshee would settle her black mantle over the bereaved and play out her drama of irrational anger and unreasonable pain. She didn't care if you were a child or a seasoned widow; neither age nor experience could cheat her.

It broke my heart to see Tom's jagged tears, but at least I had the comfort of knowing that his pain was escaping. In any case, although his tears for Charles were real, they were always fleeting; the pain flew out of him suddenly, and would then disappear like breath in a gust of wind with the smallest distraction – *Abbott and Costello* on the radio, or a cookie. My own pain was tightly secured, and when loosened from its moorings hung around me for days: a derelict rowing boat in a swamp, gradually dragging itself down the slow river in its own time.

Leo seemed the least affected, and that was the most worrying thing of all. Grief is poison to the soul, and I worried dreadfully about him holding it all in. There was every chance that this rebellion was a reaction to his father's death, as his insistence on boarding school had been a need to escape my cloying concern for him. It frustrated me that there was nothing I could do to know that for certain or do anything about it.

Earlier that week Leo had come home with his hair greased down into a side parting and sporting a small, fake moustache. 'Do I look like quite the cad?' he said jokingly. I got a fright, because he looked so much like Charles when I had first met him back in the Twenties. Although Leo was naturally blond like his father, the air of maturity that the make-up had given him and the teasing timbre in his voice were pure Charles.

Leo appeared to be getting more self-assured and adult with each passing day. I did not know if that was a good thing or a bad thing, but I did know that I was losing the supremacy a mother enjoys while her children are young and exclusively hers. I felt the pain of no longer being his confidante and best friend. While I knew that Leo's moving away from me was the natural order, every day that he grew closer to manhood, I grieved the passing of my importance in his life. I had to compete with his first friends, and now with Hollywood, for my influence over him. I would hold on tight, but deep down I knew I didn't stand a chance.

'I am doing some drawing,' I said to Hilla, 'and I have a studio set up in one of the rooms.'

'This is not a place for you to work. You need to start exhibiting . . . '

Bridie got up from the table, taking her soup plate with her, and began flustering noisily around in the kitchen. Tom went to follow her, but I gave him a threatening look that said stay-where-you-are.

The most important family meal of the year was dissolving into an awkward mess. God, how I wished I were back in New York, with us all sitting around the house in Yonkers with Maureen and the Sweeneys, like we did every year – they felt too far away. When Maureen had gone back, leaving Bridie behind, neither of us had realized how long I would be staying in LA, and our goodbyes had been all too cursory. I missed my friend on this special day – and as for Hilla, she should be back in her own apartment in Manhattan!

'An artist at the studio sketched me this week,' Leo piped up.

'It was a very good likeness. It's for a poster of the film I'm going to be in. I'm going to be in a film, Hilla.'

Leo always made an effort with Hilla. Her cool manner towards him made him anxious to be liked. Bridie noisily cleared away the soup bowls, snatching Hilla's away while she still had the spoon poised for the last drop of broth.

I didn't mind Leo being exposed to adult indifference, it was good life-training for him, but it drove Bridie half-mad when people did not dote over my boys as she did.

'Those people are not *real* artists,' Hilla said, waving his comment aside.

Leo looked crestfallen.

'They couldn't get a likeness of you, boy, because you are too handsome, and that's the truth,' Bridie said, touching Leo's hair as she passed and glowering her disapproval across at me, as if Hilla herself was so inhumanly beyond the pale that she was choosing to hold me entirely responsible for her unwelcome presence.

Hilla said, 'I am hosting a symposium of Non-Objective and Abstract art for key collectors in January – you will be back for that, I'm sure.'

Leo looked horrified – as if he might crack at any second and run from the room.

'No,' I said, 'Leo is shooting his film in January, Hilla. It's a very big feature film called . . . '

'Oh, but it's important you are back by then. There will be an exhibition and—'

There was an almighty crash in the kitchen. I ran over and found Bridie lying on the floor, with the turkey and its pan still skidding across the linoleum floor.

'Jesus, Bridie!'

'I'm fine – stop fussing.' She tried to get up, but grimaced as she put weight on her foot.

'You're hurt. Don't move,' I said.

'The turkey . . . ' she said, reaching across to it. 'I slipped when I was taking it out – stupid, stupid old woman! I'll be fine, let me up . . . '

'Stay there, woman!'

Hilla, who had followed me in, rolled up her sleeves, then miraculously gathered the turkey up in one piece and put it onto its serving plate on the counter, as if managing hot, fallen fowl was an everyday occurrence for her. She closed the oven door, threw a cloth down on the greasy floor and came over to me.

'She has hurt her ankle,' she said, 'we'll move her to the couch.' Grabbing Bridie under the arm and around her waist, she signalled to me to do the same and we literally dragged the old woman backwards across to the couch.

'On the chair,' Bridie instructed us, and there then ensued a muted disagreement between the adversaries as to whether Bridie should sit on the couch with her foot elevated on cushions (Hilla), or in her armchair with her foot up on a stool (Bridie), which Hilla won.

Once she was ensconced, I checked Bridie's ankle for breaks and decided it was just a bad sprain. I bandaged it tightly and made a cold compress for it, all the while with Bridie objecting and insisting that she should get up and finish preparing the meal. In the meantime, Hilla organized the turkey with a practical aplomb that amazed me, bossily instructing my sons to fetch plates, drain vegetables and, in Tom's case, mash the potatoes. Bridie was bristling with stress, straining her head to watch 'the German' moving around her kitchen, and while she was in too much pain to move, she continuously called out instructions: 'Don't forget to put plenty of butter on those spuds.

167

The cream needs whipping for the pie. Put the pie in the oven!'
Then she huffed under her breath, 'This is impossible', before
shouting again, 'Did you hear me? I said: put the apple pie IN
the oven and take the pumpkin pie OUT of the oven – oh, this
is hopeless.'

Hilla shouted back, 'We are managing fine – this is easy. Stop
shouting at me, you stupid old woman!'

We set a tray for Bridie and laid a picnic cloth on the floor
for the two boys – Hilla and I sat on soft chairs and ate from
our laps.

'Never mind me, you lunatics – sit up at the table like civilized people,' Bridie insisted, but you could see that she was
delighted to be the centre of attention.

'The turkey is delicious,' Hilla said in a matter-of-fact way,
and then, without the hint of a compliment intended, 'the best
I have ever tasted.'

Bridie said nothing, but her lips pursed in a way I recognized
as her determinedly not cracking into a smile.

We drank two bottles of wine with the meal, and ate our food
hungrily and casually, picking lumps of turkey up from a platter
left on the picnic rug, then wiping our hands on tea towels.
Bridie, who was not used to drinking, knocked back three glasses
of wine to ease her foot, and was in a considerably better mood
at the end of the meal than she was at the beginning. When we
had finished I told the boys to put on the radio so that we could
wait for *Lux Radio Theater* – Bridie never missed it. The Glenn
Miller Orchestra was still playing and Bridie said, 'Come on,
Leo – cut the rug there for me.'

Leo bowed and reached for my hand.

'What about our guest?' I said. 'I think *she* should have the
first dance.'

Hilla blushed like a schoolgirl as my handsome sixteen-year-

old swept her around the room in a fast waltz. I was surprised
that Hilla was an elegant dancer, but the greatest surprise was
Leo's confidence. He had been taking classes in dance, of course,
but it was more his sense of aplomb, the extraordinary ease with
which he partnered this older woman, which showed a maturity that shocked me somewhat, but also made me feel very, very
proud.

The programme ended with that dance and Hilla said, 'Show
me these sketches, Ellie.'

What with the drama, the dinner and the dancing, I had gathered that I was off the hook, but my mentor was having none
of it.

We left Bridie and the boys and went into the spare bedroom.
I could not fool Hilla that there was any artistic endeavour going
on; the paints were still in their box, the brushes clean and new
– the room smelt of camphor and house polish, instead of the
usual studio smell of turpentine and sawdust. I quickly picked
up my sketchpad and handed it to her, open at the pages of
Crystal that I had filled in at Chateau Marmont.

'That's it,' I said, 'that's all there is.'

The depth of her disappointment was shown in her not huffing
and throwing the simple drawings aside, but studying them carefully.

'These are good,' she said, 'but then you are a brilliant tech-
nician, Ellie . . . '

'There's nothing in them,' I said defensively, immediately
regretful that I had shown her anything at all. 'The drawings –
they're just fripperies, a habit . . . '

'No, no,' she said, 'she is a beautiful girl, and the drawing is
perfect, but you have captured something else here, something
more than that – her soul.'

I smiled, half-knowing what was coming.

'But it is not your art, Ellie – this is not what you do. Where are you in all this?' She looked around the room. 'Where is *your* soul?'

I shrugged deeply and sighed, although really I wanted to cry and throw my hands in the air in despair. I couldn't paint. I had nothing to say. My art had left me and all I could do was capture the story behind the eyes of a pretty girl. Somehow, in the past few weeks, I had become silenced. My voice was gone and I was becoming ever less certain that it would return.

Part Three:

Los Feliz
1943

Chapter Nineteen

Christmas came and went.

It did not feel like winter in California. Without the routines of bad weather, clearing the snow, unpacking our boots and sweaters, it was as if time had stood still.

Leo started filming *Five Graves to Cairo* at Paramount Studios in early January and they estimated it would take three months to film, maybe longer. It was a war film, set during the ongoing World War Two and starring Franchot Tone, Anne Baxter and Erich von Stroheim. Leo was cast as a young soldier who gets wounded and is tended by a young female nurse who falls in love with him. All through Christmas he had talked of nothing else, reading and rereading the script until he knew the whole thing off by heart.

I was pleased to see him happy, but was starting to find his incessant acting both obsessional and wearing.

Bridie, on the other hand, was a bottomless pit of admiration. 'You'll end up in the lead role yet!'

'I have a speaking part – you know? None of the other boys in my group have a speaking part.'

'That's because you're a special boy,' Bridie said, 'you were born to it. Read me that bit again . . . '

'I don't know why you're indulging him,' I chided her when

Leo was out of the room. 'We'll never get back to New York at this rate.'

'Sure, what does it matter where we are, as long as they're happy,' she said, nodding over to Tom, who was sitting on a stool in the garden doing his school work. 'He wouldn't be doing that in January in New York, and sure, look at him there – sure, he loves being outside – he's in heaven!'

Los Angeles had caused a notable transformation in Bridie. She had not complained once of her usual aches and pains and, while her sharp tongue would never be curbed, she was generally in a better humour than I had ever seen in her before.

The same could not be said for me. Leo was out of the house filming most days, with Freddie and the studio ferrying him back and forth. I had enrolled Tom in the local school, where he had quickly made friends with all the neighbours' children and – charming scallywag that he was – with most of their parents too, which meant that he was freely wandering in and out of gardens all along our street. Tom was thriving so much in his new environment that I felt guilty for the time I had deprived him of the company of other children, by taking him to Fire Island.

This meant that I now had the time and the freedom to paint – but none of the impetus, which was making me cranky and dissatisfied. I looked for distraction around the house, washing windows and polishing floors, and insisting to myself that Bridie was too old to be doing heavy housework (which she was). All the same, I knew I was just making work for myself to keep me from facing the fear that I might never find it in me to paint again. I feared that my time as a serious artist had just been some brief and interesting excursion. I had become wrapped up in the idea that I was an 'artist' and had attached significance to it; it seemed important that I express myself in that way and, in creating my work, I felt as if I were contributing something to the world. I was afraid that this lull in motivation meant that the artist in me had fled; that all the death and family drama had been too much of a diversion, and she had retreated back to whatever place she had inhabited before I started painting.

Perhaps Ellie-the-artist had been a visiting muse and was now gone forever, like the Polish girl I had briefly rented a room from in New York; sharing everything from clothes and food to the intimate joys and heartaches of our young lives, vowing to be friends forever, then losing touch within months of moving out, never to see each other again. Perhaps now I would return to being the muted, ordinary version of myself, the person I was before I had discovered – or rather before Hilla had told me – that I was 'an artist'. The desire to create had been like a little stream running through me, trickling away all the time, whether I was working or not – and when I got the paintbrush in my hand and the canvas in front of me, it could turn into a fast-moving, sometimes raging river. As I built my colours and shapes on the canvas I became utterly lost in my own world; nothing existed but the work in front of me and my desire to keep creating it. If days went by without painting, it felt as if someone had blocked my way with stones and then, when I got my chance in front of the canvas, I'd move the rocks away and let the waters of my imagination free again.

There had been no moment when I had realized that the stream had dried up – I just believed that it had. There was nothing I wanted to paint; that was the only sign that things were awry, except that I would not test myself by unpacking my brushes and paints, setting up my easel, stretching linen across a wooden frame and then allowing myself the terror of the blank canvas. I would have to find something that I wanted to paint. I needed to find a way back in.

*

Stan had telephoned me to arrange to meet, but he had been so busy working to complete a film score that we had not been able to see each other since that day in the studio.

'The producer I am working for is impossible. A lunatic! I spent three months writing him a "Love Theme" for some stupid film. "Go for it, Stan," he said, "I want something big, something magnificent, something *epic* . . . " So I write a big piece, a strong piece – full orchestra and a chorus of one hundred – and do you know what he asks me to do in our last meeting? He asks me to whistle him the tune. Whistle – like a delivery boy. The humiliation!'

I so enjoyed listening to Stan on the telephone.

'What did you say?' I asked, spellbound.

'I told him, "David – this is so embarrassing. I wish I was a better musician for you – I wish I was a world-class composer, but alas, I can't whistle." He told me I should learn, but in the meantime he had to endure the strain of listening to one hundred world-class musicians play my masterpiece for him. He stopped them of course, after six bars, and went for lunch, or to screw some starlet – who knows. The important thing is that I have been paid, and when we musicians get paid (and sometimes when we don't) we have a party.'

'In the studio?' I asked.

'Oh, my goodness, *no*,' he said, 'no more film studios for a while, if I can help it. It will be somewhere – in a friend's house, my house, who knows where it will be? In any case, this Saturday we will sing and drink, and play and drink, and drink and drink . . . '

I laughed.

'Will you come?'

'How could I refuse?' I said.

This was my first social engagement in Hollywood. I did not

know what I would be expected to wear, so I wore the simple navy dress I always wore to openings. It flattered my curves and fell to my calves – it was elegant without being showy. I tied my hair back with a pearl barrette that I had grown fond of over the years and wore simple pearl clip-on earrings. I applied powder and rouge and lipstick, but did not go overboard, reminding myself that I was going to a musicians' party in the house of an older man, and not an Oscar ceremony.

I checked myself in the hall mirror and realized that I was not as glamorous as I might have been, had I been the kind of woman who made more of an effort with her appearance.

At the age of forty-two, I had long since decided that I was just fine as I was. I was neither too fat nor too thin. My face had lost the plumpness of youth, but I had good bones, and the blue of my eyes was still striking enough to draw the warm attention of admirers when needed, but also to chill the hearts of bigots when I wanted them to. Nobody expected a woman of my age to be overly embellished, and to do so just made one look foolish and desperate. Even in Hollywood – or, as I had decided since I got here, *especially* in Hollywood. Back in my mid-thirties, as I had felt I'd hit middle age, I had stopped chasing fashion and glamour. I worked with what God had given me; what he had taken away in the freshness of my youth he had given me back in the wisdom of my rich life experience. At least that was what I told myself when the mirror showed me, as it often did, the furrowed brow of a woman with the world on her shoulders. Although I was not in the full cup of my youth, on the inside I nonetheless felt a good deal younger and happier than I looked. My answer was to look at my reflection as seldom as I could!

When Stan's driver arrived at eight I gave myself a cursory

once-over in the hall mirror. I looked plain. There was no denying it, but I put aside the moment of insecurity and decided that it wasn't so important and that I would just have to do.

The driver took us up above the city into the richest part of the Hollywood Hills. There was a peculiarly remote atmosphere. Narrow, winding roads with beautiful houses in all different shapes and sizes jutted up out of the vertiginous land. No two houses were the same – a black-and-white Tudor-style mansion; a miniature Scottish castle; a round white building with windows reminiscent of a cruise ship – yet each smacked of the two themes around which I had come to believe people here lived their lives: wealth and fantasy.

The car stopped outside a low building that looked like a modest cottage, certainly by the standards here. Stan was waiting for me.

He held out his arms, wide and dramatic.

'Ah, Ellie – you look beautiful.'

He was smiling so broadly that I could see the gold in his teeth at the back of his mouth and, as he held me in his embrace, he was swaying slightly. The party had obviously started early.

'Come in, come in. This is my house, my home – come, come and meet everyone . . . '

He pulled me through the dense foliage of the narrow cottage garden and as soon as we stepped inside I saw that the modest frontage was deceptive. Inside, the building was vast. The front door led us onto a walkway that looked directly across to a huge glass window with a view of what seemed like the whole of Los Angeles. Below the balcony was an open living area (a feature of houses here were these large, airy living spaces – there were no walls!), at the centre of which was a grand piano, which at the moment we walked in was being played wildly and badly by a man who looked awfully like the curly-haired lunatic comedy actor Harpo Marx. Beside him was a smart-looking man with a thin moustache playing the violin with great gusto.

Stan saw me looking at him and said, 'Ben Hecht – he wrote *Gone with the Wind.*'

'The score?' I asked.

Stan laughed. 'God, no – the screenplay. He's not a real musician, although he likes to think he is. Actually started his own little orchestra, the "Ben Hecht Symphonietta" – diabolical, of course, but we professionals indulge them. The best you can call him is a talented amateur, if there is such a thing, like that other fool with him.'

It *was* Harpo Marx – his brother Groucho was standing in front of the screenwriter pretending to conduct him, waving his arms around like a bat.

'Are they . . . ?'

'Yes,' Stan said. 'Chico is the one who can play the piano – a little – but he isn't here tonight. The other two are part of Hecht's wretched "Symphonietta". We can only hope the idiot actors have left their instruments at home, although by the looks of them I don't think we will be that lucky tonight. Harpo plays the harp – but only in A-minor; and as for the other fellow and his mandolin . . . !'

There must have been a hundred people in the room, wandering in and out of the doors that let out to a wide balconied garden area to the front, but while the building was buzzing with a party in full swing, it was not uncomfortably packed. The house was large enough to accommodate twice as many people as were there, but while it was grandly proportioned, it was not ostentatious. The furniture was modern and simple; the art, I was gratified to note, was well chosen – I recognized a large Paul Klee immediately, but you could tell by the slightly austere decor that this was a house where a man lived alone.

I recognized some of the faces, but no other big stars. Most of the guests were male and, by their casual costumes and the number of instruments lying in corners and on tables, were clearly musicians, orchestra members and perhaps composers like Stan. I spotted half a dozen starlets. They looked out of place, these young women dressed to the nines with glossy hair and pristine make-up; yet after only a few weeks here I had already realized that it was impossible to move in Hollywood without encountering their ambition and their youthful dreams.

'Let me get you a drink,' said Stan, 'there should be some food coming. I ordered it – or I think I did! Perhaps I forgot . . . in any case, come, come . . .'

There was something very attractive to me about this man, but I could barely work out what it was. My instincts for love had become tempered by the harsh experience of losing two husbands. This man, I sensed, might perhaps fall in love with me, and the very last thing I needed in my life was a lover. I knew that common sense must prevail, although I decided that Stan seemed a strong enough character to withstand a little light flirting on my part, without losing his head. I never wanted to hold another man's heart in my hands. I had no desire for the power or the responsibility. If there was one thing marriage had taught me, it was that men, for all their pomp, would always remain in the greatest part of them like young boys, and I already had two sons to rear.

Stan led me down the stairs into the fray. From the four corners of the room the discordant cacophony of musicians practising and plucking and tuning met in the middle, in a terrible clash of sounds. I must have grimaced, because Stan put his hand on my shoulder and said, 'I know, it must be terrible – we are used to the noise.'

'I thought musicians made sweet music,' I shouted at him.

'Sometimes we do,' he shouted back, 'and sometimes we just make trouble!'

We walked into the kitchen, where every surface was covered with bottles of alcohol.

Stan looked around for a glass for me and, unable to find one, snatched one from the hands of a fiddle player who was so inebriated that the glass was about to fall from his limp hand to the floor (although the arch of his instrument was tucked safely between his legs).

He rinsed it under the tap, handed it to me and, seeming to sober up and remember himself, he said, 'We musicians like to party, and we are somewhat Slavic in our excesses. Are you shocked?'

'Horrified,' I said, 'as you know, we Irish are very reserved in our tastes. Would there be a drop of whisky left in this den of iniquity?'

'If you're quick,' he said, handing me a bottle.

I don't know what came over me, asking for whisky. I rarely drank alcohol and certainly never spirits. I wanted to show off to my new friend my artistic propensity to party, or perhaps I just wanted to get drunk and forget myself for a few hours. In any case I achieved both.

I had never experienced such a night. Early in the evening Stan gathered the most interesting people he could find in a group around me in the kitchen. He was trying to impress me by being the perfect host, but I also felt he was trying to show me something that I might become a part of. Everyone there seemed to be a musician or a writer or an artist and, as the new girl in town and a friend of Stan, they entertained me with their stories: the rugged, thrice-published New York novelist who had been lured by a huge contract to write screenplays and now found himself wallowing in the sex and the money, and unable to write seriously; the painter who had studied in the school of the famous Russian landscape artist Ivan Aivazovsky and then, escaping the communists, had arrived a penniless immigrant in America. He had got some casual work painting backdrops, and was so talented that he found himself being promoted to set designer for one of the big studios. These were all serious artists with great ambitions, riding the Hollywood gravy train – some were happy with their lot, others disillusioned, but all of them were fascinating.

Each person was more interesting than the next, but by far my favourite was a make-up artist called Suri – she was the wife of one of the musicians and a stunningly beautiful woman of around my age. We bonded instantly, an occurrence I could not remember since my schooldays, and when we began to talk, the rest of the group melted away and we sat sharing our life stories for almost two hours. Despite being from the other side of the world, we had so much in common. Suri's first husband, an American-born architect of Japanese parents, had died of a heart attack when they were both in their thirties. She had no children of her own, but one stepson whom she loved dearly, of around Leo's age, from her second marriage to a much older oboe player who was a close friend of Stan's. She told me about her life. Her father was an American engineer who had met and fallen for her mother while on a work assignment in Japan, where Suri had been born. They returned to California when she was an infant, and shortly afterwards Suri's mother died in a tragic car accident. Her father remarried an American nurse, whom Suri considered her mother – but her half-Japanese heritage explained her striking good looks and her choice of first husband. It also explained her fascination with the internment of the Japanese population of California. The year before, in the wake of Pearl Harbor, President Roosevelt had passed an order to evacuate all of the Japanese population living along the Pacific coast. I had read about it in the papers, of course, and I knew that the Japanese as a race were, unsurprisingly, unpopular in America at the moment. I supposed that was only natural – just as the Germans were *persona non grata* in Europe – for we were at war. Yet here I was, talking to a woman who was half-Japanese, and I became slightly embarrassed by my ignorance of the bad feelings towards American-born Japanese. Only a few days beforehand I had read an article in *Life* magazine showing how one could differentiate a Japanese person from a Chinese, presuming that you suspected they were involved in political subterfuge or a criminal act and wanted to report them for internment. However, it was not until I began to talk to Suri that I realized it was not just suspected spies being interned, but the entire Japanese-American population, including women and children.

'My parents-in-law had to leave their beautiful house – they are both such proud people, the upheaval was terribly traumatic for them. They are both in their seventies and had lived in that same house for fifty years. They were only allowed to take what they could carry to the camp, and do not know when they'll be back, so they tried to sell as much as they could. I was there when a dealer came to the house, interested in some of their Japanese artefacts – they had such beautiful things. He offered my mother-in-law fifteen dollars for a set of dishes she knew was worth a small fortune. "This is worth at least two hundred dollars!" she told him. He thought about it and said, "I will offer you eighteen dollars. No more." She was so disgusted that she unwrapped each valuable plate and smashed it to the floor as the dealer shouted, "No – no. Stop! They are valuable! I'll give you one hundred dollars!" She smashed them all anyway. "What use are they to me now?" she said. "What was the point of all this – they have taken it all away, for nothing."'

Suri went on to horrify me with stories of the camps themselves. Her mother- and father-in-law were the only Japanese people she knew, and they had written to Suri begging her to try and reason with the authorities to get them out. Her father-in-law was in ill health and neither of them could understand what they were doing there. 'We are not Japanese – we are Americans,' they insisted. 'They are wealthy people,' Suri told me, 'private, civilized people – and now they are living communally, with strangers in a slum. It is like they have been put in prison to be punished for the crime of a country they left behind years ago.'

I agreed that it was an unfathomable injustice and was about to tell her of Charles' work with the unions in Hawaii, and how this was the very type of injustice he would have fought against, when Stan and Suri's husband, Jackson, came over and interrupted our conversation. He was a similar age to Stan – a good deal older than Suri, who, I had now decided, was probably only in her early thirties. I could tell from the gentle manner in which her husband treated her that my new friend had this older man spellbound with love. I flinched with envy as the brief memory of being loved like that passed through me, and for an even briefer moment I wondered how it would be to have Stan look at me in that way. I blinked the idea away immediately as being fanciful and foolish.

Jackson tenderly touched his wife's face while addressing me and saying, 'Suri and all her serious talking. Is she boring you?'

I thought it rather a rude thing to say, but before I had the chance to answer Stan grabbed my hand.

'Enough talking – you must drink and dance now.' And the two men dragged us over to the piano, where a rowdy gang of musicians were ferociously attacking their instruments in a vivacious set of swing music.

Stan bowed comically. 'M'lady, I am now drunk enough to dance,' he said and, holding out his hand asked, 'May I?'

I laughed and for a fleeting moment I felt as young and beautiful and free as I had ever felt in my life.

CHAPTER TWENTY

Throughout February and March Leo was filming every day, so we saw very little of him at home. As it was a big film, the studio had laid on trailers with some sleeping accommodation for the young actors, so Leo often chose to stay overnight. He was getting more grown-up and assertive every day and enjoying his independence. He discouraged me strongly from meeting him at the studio. 'It's embarrassing,' he said, 'none of the other mothers come.' I doubted that was true, but I bent to his wishes nonetheless. I did not like it when he was ill-mannered, but at least it reminded me that he was still a child. It was too early for him to be working, walking around in men's clothes, talking about his 'career'.

When he did come home he talked of nothing else but his prospects of becoming a 'star'. Any day now he was going to be plucked out of the crowd of young extras and actors in his group and put on the path to stardom, he was convinced of it. It was tiresome talk, even for his mother, but Leo became irritable if anyone interrupted his flow of self-fascination – even Tom.

'Jesus Christ, child!' he shouted at his boisterous younger brother one day in the kitchen, when Tom knocked over a cup and some milk almost caught the hem of Leo's trousers, 'why are you are *so* clumsy!'

I was shocked – both at his cursing and at his cruelty.

'Leo,' I said firmly, 'don't speak to your brother like that!'

He threw me a mean sideways glance, as if I were something from the bottom of his shoe, and left the room without answering.

Raging, I went to follow him, but Bridie held me back.

'Leave him,' she said, dabbing at the counter with a rag and adding, with rather more humour than I was in the mood for, 'no point crying over . . . '

'. . . spilt milk!' Tom piped in. Neither of them seemed bothered by Leo's behaviour, yet I found it completely unacceptable – on all our behalves.

'I can't let him get away with that,' I said. Then, struggling to pierce Bridie's indifference, I added, 'He used the Lord's name in vain.'

'I'm horrified by that,' she said, 'but don't you pretend to be, you godless hussy – besides, he's only young.'

'That's no excuse for being mean to his brother,' I replied, although Tom had already skipped outside. 'Tom is a good boy.'

Bridie put the rag down and looked at me straight.

'So is Leo. He is just caught up with himself, Ellie – like all young people are.'

'He has to learn it's not all right to talk to people like that.'

'And you're going to teach him that, are you?'

She picked up the knife and carried on with the carrots that she'd been slicing before Tom's accident.

'Leave him be, Ellie. Let him enjoy being the big "I am", for goodness' sake – it'll not be too long before life knocks it out of him. You were the same, when you came to New York, with your lipstick and your dresses and your gallivanting about the place listening to jazz and drinking . . . '

'I had a tough life before I came to America,' I said. 'I had a crippled husband and I knew what it was to be hungry.'

'And he's not had a tough life?' Bridie asked, looking at me.

I felt terrible. Leo had been abandoned by his mother and had lost his father just over a year ago.

'Who else can teach him what he needs to know, Bridie, if it's not me? Who else is going to look after him and make sure he's not steered wrongly in life?'

She shrugged.

'He himself,' she said. 'That'll be the only person he'll listen to, anyway – or maybe that fool Freddie.'

Although neither of us ever said it out loud, I felt that both of us had a sense that perhaps this young man Freddie might fill the gap left by Charles, which we two women were proving ill-equipped for.

Bridie was right: there was no point in me chasing after him trying to lay down the law. In any case, I was expecting Stan to arrive at any moment.

The composer and I had started to spend a lot of time together. We had become good friends. I had been friends with men before, but it had always led to a romantic involvement, and I could sense that Stan was falling for me. When I was younger, I never took men falling in love with me too seriously. Being loved was a selfish benefit of youth and beauty: admiration and the blind, desirous love of men being the fuel that kept one confident and amused. Then, after John died, I had allowed a good man to fall in love with me and had let him down. I gained nothing from the experience, except for the shame of knowing I had deeply hurt another human being. Charles had been a different proposition in his arrogant acquisition of my hand, although, in my own way, I had let him down too. Stan was different from them all: there was no awkwardness, none of the tension that one finds when a man and a woman are left alone together. In fact there seemed to be no element at play, other than a firm liking of one another – and a thorough enjoyment of each other's company.

In the months since the party I had been to his house a few times for social occasions. Stan threw a small party every other week, at which his musician friends would gather, get drunk and – without the restrictions of studio commissions – play their own and each other's compositions for pure recreation. Much of what they played was beyond my understanding.

That was particularly true of the evening when he invited a rather serious old German composer called Arnold Schoenberg and his wife Gertrud over to his house for dinner. I agreed to cook, on the proviso that he also invited Suri and Jackson. There were also twelve musicians whom Stan had invited to play some of the great composer's new work.

Early in the evening Suri and I continued our conversation about the Japanese internment camps. Our last conversation had stayed with me; I had become somewhat haunted by the plight of all those people – a whole community – being rounded up and imprisoned for no reason, under our very noses. Surely there was something to be done about it? Suri's story about the old couple had struck a chord with me, and I was anxious to see if there was anything I could do to help their cause. Jackson rather rudely, I thought, cut off our conversation saying, 'Ladies, don't get all worked up about things that are none of your business – we are here to enjoy ourselves.'

His patronizing tone infuriated me, so I said, 'Surely the plight of American citizens is the business of all of us during a time of war?'

Stan stepped in artfully, asking some trite question of his guest of honour, and I realized this was not the time or the place and backed down. However, it coloured my opinion of Suri's husband

– clearly a weak man who lacked his wife's compassion – and I resolved to pursue our friendship with her as an individual, rather than socialize as a couple again, which was probably sending the wrong message to Stan anyway.

Arnold Schoenberg had a long face, made longer by a prominent nose and a bald head that throbbed at the temples with a moving, wormy vein that only seemed to herald his genius. He was a lovely man and, as he was also a painter and knew a lot about contemporary art, we had much to talk about. He knew Hilla and, in fact, it transpired that his work had been exhibited alongside that of Franz Marc and Wassily Kandinsky.

However, when the musicians started to play his work it was not like anything I had heard before – not one bit melodic or tuneful. I thought it a grim, disjointed racket, an insult to the ears and, I confess, it coloured my view of him. 'He should stick to the painting,' I told Stan after they had gone.

'He is a genius,' Stan said simply, 'and genius is often misunderstood.'

My host picked up glasses from the table and moved to the kitchen with his back still to me. I could tell he was disappointed in me for not appreciating 'The Great' Schoenberg's music. However, I did not baulk at the idea of his disapproval and perhaps that was the greatest testament to our friendship: that I liked and respected him greatly, and yet did not have the compulsion to either attract or impress him.

'You're a better composer,' I said, and I meant it, 'your music has far more . . . ' – I knew 'tune' would be the wrong word – 'soul.'

Stan shrugged. 'Schoenberg is an intellectual, Ellie; his work will change music forever. I am just a hired hand; a tradesman; a prostitute to money – a nobody.'

'No, no Stan,' I said, 'that's not true!'

'It's the case,' he said, his hands sweeping across the grand room. 'All this – it means nothing. You think I make music for films? No, no, I make music for *money*, Ellie. *Money*, that is all. Schoenberg is a penniless teacher now; he will not work for money alone – he cannot, he is not able. Yet his work will change the history of music. I am nothing next to him.'

He looked momentarily so dejected that I walked across to him, grabbed both his hands in mine and, holding them firmly, said, 'I won't have you talk like that, Stan – you are a *marvellous* musician.'

He looked down at my hands holding his, then smiled brightly up at me until I thought he might try to kiss me.

Instead, he raised his brow to let me know that it was not outside the bounds of possibility, then raised both my hands to his lips, kissed them sweetly and said, 'Ellie, I can never feel worried or dejected when I am with you.'

Mostly Stan called over to our house.

His last movie score written, he was now on a break.

'I am supposed to be writing,' he said, 'but who can work when I can come here and eat this delicious bread?'

Bridie could not quite get the measure of Stan, and he was smart enough to let on that her baking was the thing that drew him down from the grand hills to humble Los Feliz.

'We Jews, we make the best bread, but this woman – *this woman* with her Irish bread . . . ' And he clasped his hands dramatically to his chest.

'Why do you keep bringing these bloody foreigners in amongst us?' she said one day after he had left. 'There'll be trouble . . .'

'We were foreigners too once, Bridie,' I reminded her.

'It's not the same,' she said, but I didn't bother arguing with her. I knew her comments were just Bridie's way of marking my card; of warning me not to 'get involved' with Stan because she didn't want to see me getting hurt again. 'You're barely widowed a year – don't go making a show of yourself.'

'We're just friends,' I said, and then, to wind her up, 'the same as you and Frank.' Frank was the man who delivered Bridie's shopping each week. I could just as easily have collected our weekly groceries from the store, but she insisted that we have them delivered. She had taken to dabbing on a bit of my lipstick before answering the door to him (he always knocked at the front – never the back); I had it hidden in a hall drawer and had caught her at it a couple of times, but said nothing. It wasn't fair to tease her.

'Don't be disgusting,' she said. Then, turning away, she added almost to herself, 'anyway, Frank is from Vermont.'

On this particular day Stan arrived earlier than expected, coming straight around to the back door. I was still in my working clothes, having been up since dawn painting.

'You are still working,' he said, looking at my paint-stained apron. 'I'm sorry. I thought I would come early and take you out for lunch – can I take a look?' he said, walking straight through to the makeshift studio in our fourth bedroom.

I had started work on a large portrait of Suri. The piece of my heart that was in it was more about my burgeoning friendship with this interesting woman than it was about any strong desire to explore portraiture.

Two days after the Schoenberg party Suri had telephoned me and we had met up for coffee. I was fascinated with her stories of the Japanese internment camps and the terrible injustices therein. She told me that there were no separate toilet facilities, so that older women had to sit in toilet cubicles with no doors, alongside the men. They had a cardboard box they would pass around and place over their heads to hide their shame.

'That's appalling,' I said, horrified. 'Why is there nothing in the papers to highlight this terrible injustice? Nobody knows this is happening – clearly if they did, something would be done.'

Suri shrugged, a small fast shrug, her lips tight. Her anger was palpable, even though she tried to hide it.

'People hate the Japanese,' she said. 'There is a war on, and people lose sense of reason – that's what happens.'

I understood that irrational hatred for the enemy. How I had once hated the English, for repressing us Irish for hundreds of years. They had destroyed our native language, stolen our land and, on a more personal level, English soldiers had shot my husband. At one time the mere sound of a hee-haw cockney accent would put me into a rage. Yet since the struggle for independence in Ireland had ended, I had met many English people I liked. Individuals should not be judged by their nation's sins. It was not always easy to put one's prejudice to one side, but it was the only way justice could prevail.

'But your in-laws are not even Japanese?'

'Hatred runs deep,' she said.

'There must be something we can do,' I said. 'It's just terrible that your parents-in-law are suffering so greatly.'

Suri gave me a sharp look and for a moment I thought she was going to tell me to mind my own business, but then she artfully changed the subject instead, saying, 'What a bore I am being. That's enough about my troubled life, Ellie – tell me all about yourself. You're an artist . . . how do you find the art world in LA?'

I had given her a brief outline of my life, but as I had grown older I found talking about my experiences boring and uncomfortable. Life was for living, not for recounting, so I took out my sketchpad and began to draw her in order to create a diversion. It was a party trick that seldom failed me and, sure enough, that afternoon of casual sketching had led to my offering to paint her. Before I had really made a proper decision to do so, I found myself back working again – unwrapping my oils and building a canvas in my makeshift bedroom studio. I built the canvas as large as I did (six foot by eight) partly to kill time and defer the actual painting process. However, as the weeks passed I had put paint on the canvas and found myself pottering through the work in a not-entirely-unenjoyable rhythm.

Suri had come and sat for me a few times, but as our friendship developed I found that our conversations were so interesting they inhibited my work. We talked about politics and what was wrong with the world. We were both avid newspaper readers, and the two of us were interested in subjects I had rarely, if ever, discussed with other women friends – politics and human rights, the details of the wars raging at home and in Europe, of which the papers were packed. So as we talked over coffee or lunch I sketched, capturing her expressions, the shadows of her emotions as they crossed over her face – then used these rough pencil drawings to help me work on the painting afterwards, alone, as I always liked to work.

The portrait itself was shaping up to be a tolerable piece of work, Suri's face and character captured with reasonable accuracy. Suri herself had not seen the picture yet, but Stan had been watching me develop it and, of course, thought it a work of genius, which it most certainly was not. However, while I feared I might never again get lost in the abandon and commitment of my landscape work, I had contented myself that I could hold back the wall of creative depression by painting *something*. If I could not satisfy myself with my work, I could at least satisfy others – and make the painting a gift for Suri and her family.

I did not mind Stan looking at my work-in-progress because I did not care about it enough as a piece of work. It did not represent me as an artist; it was more about Suri than it was about me.

'This is wonderful,' he said, 'really wonderful.'

I became irritated. I didn't need his false flattery.

'Let's go for lunch,' I said, pulling at his arm.

'You don't like it?' he asked.

'It's fine,' I said, 'let's go.'

'But I am interested,' he insisted, 'in your work: how you paint, how you arrive at your themes, why you use one colour over . . . '

'This is not representative of my work,' I said. 'It's a simple portrait of a friend – that's all.'

'Oh no,' he wouldn't let it drop, 'it is much more than that . . . '

I felt an irrational anger rise up in me and could not help but snap, 'You don't know *anything* about my work, you don't know *anything* about me – you have *no idea* what you are talking about, so for God's sake will you just leave it!'

I was immediately embarrassed by my insane outburst, but Stan just stood passively as I ranted and then, when I was done, took off his glasses and looked at me with the intense serious-ness of a seasoned intellectual. There was no discussion, no repri-mand, nothing personal. It was the reaction of a fellow artist; of somebody who understood me completely. He looked lean and dark and quite brilliant, and for a moment I wondered what it would be like to belong to such a man. My eyelids flickered and my body weakened in anticipation of being touched, but then my friend shrugged and simply said, 'Okay, let's go for lunch.'

CHAPTER TWENTY-ONE

We lunched at the Hollywood Brown Derby on North Vine, so named because of its domed roof that looked like a man's brown derby hat. It had a number of branches, including one on Wilshire Boulevard that was closer to where I lived. Brown Derby was not a fancy restaurant chain, but the Hollywood branch was fancier than the others because it was frequented by the Hollywood 'set'. A famous gossip columnist called Louella Parsons, whose show *Hollywood Hotel* had everyone in the house (except me) glued to the radio each week, was never out of the place – according to Bridie, at least, who devoured her column in the *Los Angeles Examiner*.

'Have a good look round this time and tell me if you see Hedda,' Bridie had said. Hedda Hopper was Parsons' rival columnist on the *Los Angeles Times*, and Bridie was such an avid fan of both that it was as if she knew them personally. Since I had made the mistake of telling Bridie that I saw the Marx brothers at Stan's party she had harassed me for movie gossip.

I had little or no interest in movie tittle-tattle, but Stan insisted the burgers were better in the North Vine branch.

'You're a fusspot,' I said. 'Why must we always go to the fancy one?'

'I am in a fancy mood today.'

'Well, I'm not dressed fancy.'

I was wearing slacks and the same blouse I had put on that morning. My working apron had no sleeves and there was a smudge of green paint on my cuff. I did not want to change.

'You look wonderful,' he said (my insisting that I was under-dressed and his insisting that I looked 'wonderful' was becoming a habit). 'Besides, I have my reasons.'

Often, when Stan and I went out, we also went through the comic routine of my trying to persuade him into the pickup, and him declining on account of his snappy outfit. I would then insist it was my turn to drive – we were teasing each other – lampooning his aspirations to style, and he lampooning my pref-erence for the 'redneck-Irish' car.

'Please can you please move your truck to the bottom of the hill,' he said the first time I visited him at home. 'Such vehicles are only allowed in this area with a tradesman's licence – you can't leave it outside my door. It's the law.'

I thought he was serious and was very put out as I got back in to move it, until I saw him laughing.

When Stan laughed it was sunshine on a cloudy day. Even though my composer friend loved to laugh, never passing up the opportunity to tease or play a practical joke, he looked like – *was* – such an elegant, erudite man that raucous amusement from him was always an unexpected pleasure.

However, today we were both in a more solemn mood. Perhaps it was my outburst, but I sensed too that Stan had something on his mind, so I got straight into his car without saying anything. I only ever travelled in Stan's cream Chrysler Royal on short journeys like this. However, as soon as I got into the ridged front seat I always felt warm and cosseted. The soft red leather of the interior was plush and, with the heat of the Los Angeles sun, it was like entering a womb. Stan drove in silence and I slid my body down the warm leather, leaned my head back and enjoyed the comfort of the car. I was pleased we were travelling that bit further, so I could enjoy the pleasure of just being driven by good company in a luxurious car.

We parked and went inside. The manager made a small fuss of Stan and it seemed that he had booked us a booth.

As we walked through the restaurant several people stopped Stan to greet him, including one suited fat cat, flanked by two young women, whom I recognized from the paper as a local politician.

'Stan! Come and join us? Who's the doll? Sit down – sit down!'

Stan quipped, 'And have you rob her off me, Harry? Another time.'

'Idiot!' he said as we kept walking.

'You're quite the popular guy,' I said. 'Is there no one in this town you don't know?'

'You have parties – you get popular,' he said. Stan's popularity was an incidental sideline of his job and his gregarious nature; it didn't interest him. What interested Stan was me.

As soon as we sat down I knew that something was up. The waiter took our drink orders and, when he had gone, Stan just sat smiling at me, saying nothing.

'Are you up to something?' I asked.

'You'll see,' he said, still smiling.

The waiter brought us our drinks and handed us our leather-bound menus with more than the usual flourish, and as he and Stan exchanged a glance I opened mine and two tickets fell out.

'What are these?' I said.

'You know George Szell?' he said. 'The German conductor and composer? I introduced you to him at my party.'

'Oh yes,' I said. I had not the faintest idea who he was talking about.

'He is conducting Wagner at the Met in New York next week, and these are two tickets for the opening night.'

He ran his hands across the table with a flourish.

I didn't know how to react, truth be told.

'Okay – and I assume these tickets are for us?'

'Of course,' he said, delighted with himself.

'But the Met is in New York, Stan. How will we get there?'

'It is all arranged,' he said, beaming. 'Eleanor – you remember Eleanor Steber, the soprano who sang at one of my parties, the first one you came to?' I really must have been very drunk that night. 'She is performing, but on loan from her radio commitments, so her sponsor is flying her from Los Angeles to New York the night before, of course with several other musicians. I have secured us two seats on the flight there and on the return.'

I did not want to go. I could not leave my children and go flying off across America. I liked Stan, but . . . this was too much. Yet he had gone to all this trouble. I didn't know what to say, so instead I asked, 'Where will we stay?' As soon as I spoke I knew it was a stupid thing to ask, because we both had apartments in New York – a fact that made the answer all the more shocking.

'The Plaza,' he said. 'I have booked a suite.' I smiled weakly and he hastily added, 'A suite, with separate sleeping quarters.'

Finally he read me.

'You're not pleased,' he said. 'I should have known this. It was presumptuous of me. Stupid, stupid old man. I am sorry, Ellie . . .' He leaned over and took the tickets from where I held them loosely in my hands. 'Forget I ever did this stupid thing, please – forgive an old fool for thinking . . . for trying . . . '

'No,' I said reaching my hands across and taking his, 'no, it was a lovely gesture. Really.'

I felt an urgent compulsion to say that I would go, just to make my good friend happy again. I sensed I had humiliated him terribly and wanted, above all, for him to stop asking for my forgiveness. But before I could find the words to make good, he looked at the window behind my head and said, 'Is that your son's friend Frederick outside? He seems to be in trouble.'

I turned round just in time to see Freddie being manhandled out of his car by two very large, tough-looking police officers. Frantically I banged on the window. Freddie looked initially surprised, then gathered himself and smiled across, waving to me that everything was fine, when it clearly was not. He looked so slim and vulnerable next to the big policemen that I immediately clambered out of the booth and ran outside, with Stan following me.

'What's going on?' I demanded.

'Hey, Ellie – looking good!' Freddie said, trying to maintain his poise as his collar was being fingered by the large, burly, red-haired cop. Irish. All the biggest, meanest-looking cops were. 'I'm fine,' he said, 'just having a chat with my buddies here – go on inside, Ellie, finish your lunch; hey, Stanley!' Freddie hadn't shaved. His collar seemed loose and a little grubby. His face was sunburned. I realized I hadn't seen him for a few weeks. I cast my eye over to his car. There were a bunch of shirts and a suit hanging up in the back seat. On the floor of the front was a carefully folded woollen blanket and on top of it a towel with the Chateau Marmont logo. Freddie was sleeping in his car.

'What seems to be the problem, Officer?' I asked, polite now that I knew what was going on. Despite my addressing him directly, the policeman started to manoeuvre Freddie into a wagon.

'Go back inside, Ma'am. We are arresting this young man for vagrancy.'

'Don't be ridiculous,' I said. 'Freddie, go back to your car.' And I walked over and stepped between him and the wagon.

'Ma'am, could you please step aside,' the red-haired cop said.

'Certainly not,' I replied, 'until you explain to me why you are manhandling my friend.'

I was shocked to see that Freddie had sunk so low in his circumstances, but not entirely surprised. Common sense had long since told me that his sojourn at the Chateau could not have lasted much longer, but while I hadn't seen the kid for a few weeks, I had no idea he was living in his car. He had been continuing to pick up Leo for the studio run most days, but I had been so caught up with my own life that I had not bothered to enquire after Freddie's welfare. Male pride – probably on my son's part as well – would have prevented either of them asking for my help.

'There have been complaints about this man parking his car illegally overnight in various places, and we believe he is living in his car, which is . . . '

'Well, that's impossible,' I said, 'because he lives with me.' And I reached over and grabbed Freddie's hand. 'Kindly let him go,' I said to the cop, who refused. 'Look,' I said, 'this young man no more lives in his car than you or I.'

The cop looked over at the vehicle loaded up with blankets and clothes, then back at me. He had loosened his grip of Freddie, but still had his fingers round the back of his shirt. 'Those clothes in the back of the car belong to my son, who is a friend of this young man, and he was taking them to the laundry for me. I can assure you, he is perfectly respectable.'

The cop looked doubtful, but I wasn't letting this go. Freddie was now shuffling and raising his brows at Stan in an embarrassed, apologetic stance. Neither man said anything. They could see that I had this under control.

'So he had a few drinks and fell asleep in his car one night, Officer. You know how it is yourself, surely?'

He shrugged. With his bit of Irish brogue, I could tell he wanted to help me, but he took me aside and said, 'He's been in the car lot here for nearly a week, lady. The management said he'd been seen rifling through their garbage.'

I was horrified. The poor kid. I couldn't let the cop see that, so I just said, 'Look, I'll be honest with you. The kid – he's a bit wild and I was worried about the influence he was having on my son. I kicked him out, but I regret it now. Let him come home with me.'

'I dunno,' the cop said. 'Vagrancy is a serious offence – and stealing food? Even from garbage bins, lady, that's an offence too. Add littering and . . . '

Jesus, but these people were stupid bureaucrats at heart. People gunning each other down on the streets of LA, and big, strong cops out hunting down homeless souls like young Freddie – there was no way I was going to let it go.

'Look, Officer, the kid had a few too many, and I kicked him out and he slept in his car for a few nights. That's all. But he's learned his lesson now, Officer – no small thanks to you. There's no need to arrest him. I'll take him home and let him stew on it. This has been punishment enough. You can consider you've done your day's work.'

He was shuffling now, baulking, and I realized that he was expecting me to grease his palm. I looked over at Stan and gave him a wink and, cool as a cucumber, my friend wandered over and casually slipped a five-dollar bill into the officer's palm while commenting on the weather.

The cop finally smiled, then wandered over to Freddie.

'You can go, son, but only because this fine lady and gentleman vouch for you. If I ever see you again . . . '

'You won't, Officer,' I assured him.

By this time Freddie's head was bowed. He looked mortified as well as slightly unkempt, which seemed to me a far more pitiful state than if he were completely torn up. He had been trying to put on a show, pretend everything was all right. The poor lad. I walked over to him and put my arm round his shoulder.

'You're coming home with me,' I said. 'No arguments.'

'I'll meet you back at your house,' Stan said.

I wanted to tell him not to bother, but Stan had already gone back inside the restaurant to settle the bill. In any case, I didn't like to be rude, especially since he had paid off the cop.

As soon as we got into the car I said, 'What happened, Freddie? The *real* version, please – not the Hollywood one.'

He was broke and unable to pay any of his Chateau Marmont bill, which amounted, at this stage, to more than he could ever hope to afford. They had kicked him out, and had put out an order against him for the full amount. He had been sleeping in his car and 'eating out' – not very often, and from garbage bins, by the cut of him. He was clean out of cash, and there was just enough gas in the car to get us back to Los Feliz. On the plus side, the bailiffs had not caught up with him yet because they didn't know where he was. As I had given my name and address to the cop, doubtless they'd be calling soon.

'What about Crystal?' I asked.

'Oh, there wasn't room for her in the car, so she went to stay with a friend. A producer she knows. Brad. Nice guy.'

Crystal had not struck me as the type who would stick around when times got tough, but I was nonetheless disappointed on Freddie's behalf that I was right.

'Well, you can stay here as long as you like,' I said, 'you are very welcome, and really you ought to have called me as soon as you got kicked out – I mean, *left* the Chateau.'

'Thanks, Mrs H. I'll stay for a night or two anyhow, but I'll be back on my feet before you know it. There's just been a delay – you know, with the studio sorting me out with my agent's fee for Leo. I made it clear to them that he was signing a contract on the proviso that I get a stipend, but the message doesn't seem to have filtered through to the right department. These studios are big places – lots of departments.'

Freddie was, surely, the most naive young man I had ever met. He was never going to get paid by the studio. There was no such thing as an actor's agent. He needed to go back into the business of selling door-to-door, like he had done before this crazy idea of being in Hollywood took hold of him. Perhaps I would be the one who had to tell him that – but not today.

Bridie didn't bat an eyelid when I told her that we were making up the bed in my studio for Freddie. 'Another stray,' she said, but she was well used to it.

Stan arrived straight after us, and when I explained that our lunch had been cut short, Bridie raised her eyebrows and said, 'Good enough for you – throwing money away on restaurant food. Did you see Louella Parsons?'

'No,' I said. 'We were busy.'

'Useless, the pair of you,' she muttered as she put the brisket of beef and cabbage into the pot, so that it was ready for us all to eat when Tom came in from school.

An hour after we had eaten, Leo came back unexpectedly early in a studio car. They didn't need him for a couple of days, so he was on holiday. Both he and Tom were delighted, and unquestioning, about Freddie's presence.

After all the excitement, Stan and I found ourselves alone on the front porch. Stan poured me a glass of wine from a bottle that he had at his feet, handed it over to me, then lit two cigarettes and handed one across to me, too. The light had faded and, as the neighbour who lived opposite us went inside, he waved across and Stan waved back.

Stan always made a lively contribution to the household when he was around. He was friendly and open, and although he wasn't the kind of man inclined to kick a ball around, the boys liked him. He was a vivacious storyteller and entertained them (and Bridie) with wild tales about Hollywood stars, his meetings with Laurel and Hardy and the Marx brothers, as well as myths and – probably – mostly made-up war stories about Poland. He was interested in the boys, and although Leo was the 'artistic one', Stan saw something in Tom too and bought the delighted child a tin whistle and showed him how to play it. Without my having intended it, or without his having announced it, Stan was becoming a part of our family. This was not something I had noticed before that particular moment when he wished our neighbour goodnight. Perhaps it was the act of inviting young Freddie to live with us that highlighted to me that afternoon the role that Stan was starting to play in my life – in our lives. It was not what I intended. I had been married twice, had loved and lost two good men. I did not want, or need, to love another one.

Stan's lavish invitation to the Met was still hanging over us. While he had apologized for pushing it on me, he had not retracted it entirely; the door was still ajar.

'I won't come to the Met, Stan – you understand, don't you?'

'Of course,' he said, 'I am sorry for imposing my—'

'I don't want us to get close, Stan. While I value your friendship . . .'

' . . . you don't want us to become lovers.'

'Yes,' I said, 'that's right.'

'I don't mind, Ellie, really. You are a beautiful woman – you know I think this – but I am happy for us to stay as we are: to be good friends.'

He picked up the wine and topped his own glass up before offering it to me, then threw his cigarette out on to the lawn and said, 'Really, I prefer a cigar. I must stop smoking these things. Perhaps I shall take up the pipe.'

I don't know why I had not expected this rational, reasonable response from a man who had never shown himself to be anything other; nor did I know why I should be feeling angry and humiliated by his perfectly charming reply to my brush-off. The truth was that I felt suddenly, irrationally angry that Stan was not prostrate on the floor of my porch, begging to be my lover. Not that love was what I wanted, but, even so, it should have been what he wanted.

'I think you should go,' I said.

There must have been a shake in my voice, some evidence of anger or accusation, because Stan immediately turned and looked at me. He put his hand to his mouth in a fist and furrowed his brows, as he always did when he was thinking carefully about something.

'Of course,' he said and stood up.

He did not object, or ask why I wanted him to leave. He simply picked up his jacket from the back of the chair, walked across my front yard to where his car was parked, opened the door and, without turning back, got in and drove away.

CHAPTER TWENTY-TWO

Five Graves to Cairo finished shooting in April, a few weeks behind schedule, and we were all invited to attend the cast and crew wrap-party at the studio.

Bridie took some persuading. Bridie never went anywhere – in all the years I had known her, this was the first big event that she had agreed to come along to. She had been a housekeeper all her life, living behind the scenes in the kitchen – never front-of-house, even in her own life. She was certainly more family member than servant in my life, and yet she was uncomfortable elevating herself beyond the role of minder and cook. She would dress up to go to Mass, and on occasion had entertained ladies from the church – and even once or twice the parish priest – in our 'Good Room' in Yonkers, but this was the first time I had known her go to an event or party outside the house. To be honest, I thought it uncharacteristic that she allowed herself to be persuaded in the first place – by Freddie. Leo and I had not even bothered to ask, because we had been convinced she would say no. However, once she agreed to come I was thrilled, although in the week leading up to the big night Bridie became almost overwhelmed with excitement.

'Anne Baxter – will *she* be there?'

Bridie was completely star-struck; although going to the cinema was a new thing for her, she was an avid reader of the gossip pages.

'Yes, Nan,' Leo said. Both of my boys called Bridie 'Nan', even though she was not officially family. Bridie had been married, but in domestic service, all of her life and had never had children of her own. We all knew how much she relished the status of being a 'nan' to the boys and, as a result, no matter how grown-up Leo got, he would always honour her with that name.

'And Franchot Tone – will *he* be there?'

'I expect so, Nan.'

'Oh, it's nothing to you, boy – you see them all the time – but oh, oh . . . Erich von Stroheim, will *he* be there?'

'They will *all* be there, Nan – it's no big deal.'

'Leo,' I said, 'please don't talk to Bridie like that.'

I had started to reprimand Leo in a more gentle, pleading tone in recognition of his maturity, but it was proving to be just as pointless an exercise as angrily putting my foot down. Not least because, in the few months we had been here, my opinion had become completely inconsequential to him. It hurt me that Leo no longer valued my views on any subject; if I commented on what he wore, or even expressed a view on a certain film, he would look at me as if I knew *nothing* at all. As a result I was afraid to even broach the subject of what was going to happen, now that the film had finished shooting. I still wanted to return to New York when this movie was over so that Leo could complete his education, and return to Hollywood, should he still wish to, when he was twenty-one. I did not like what was happening to my intelligent, sensitive son. He was becoming spoilt, and especially worrying was his increasingly dismissive treatment of poor Freddie.

Freddie had got himself a job in a real-estate office, which it seemed he had a natural talent for. He offered to move out, but

I told him to wait until he had cleared his Chateau Marmont expenses. Touchingly, having a steady income elsewhere seemed to strengthen his commitment to making Leo a star and becoming Hollywood's first film actors' agent.

Since he had moved in with us, I had come to see that Freddie was both a kind and much more sensible young man than his Hollywood aspirations suggested. Especially since my estrangement with Stan, he had adopted something of the role and responsibility of the man of the house – particularly in his protective role towards Bridie.

One day I came into the house and found him standing behind Bridie, who was seated at the kitchen table while he was curling her hair.

'The cheeky pup said I needed a new hairdo,' Bridie muttered, embarrassed by the fuss. 'He said he can make me look like Margaret Rutherford.'

'I think we can do a bit better than that, Bridie,' the young man quipped, 'Rutherford is a fearsome old battleaxe.' Then he looked at me and winked. 'Nothing like you at all.'

'She might not be any great beauty, but her curls are always so *tidy*,' Bridie insisted. 'If I could get mine to sit like that, I'd be happy enough.'

'You're selling yourself short, Bridie,' Freddie said as he expertly slid a long, treacherous-looking pin into a pink roller. 'What is it with you Irish broads – always putting yourselves down. You're a mature, sophisticated woman of the world, Bridie – if people can't handle how much of a woman you are, well then, more fool them!'

'Get away off out of that, you fool,' Bridie said, flicking the compliment away over her shoulder, although she was bristling with sheer joy at the adulation. For all Freddie's teasing, you could hear that he meant it and that he had a genuine admiration and affection for the old woman.

Later that afternoon I overheard a very different exchange between my son and Freddie.

'Why do I even *need* an agent?' I heard Leo whine at Freddie. 'I mean, *nobody* else in the studio has one. What does an agent even *do*?'

Their conversation was taking place in the kitchen, while I was out on the back step cleaning off a pair of Tom's boots. I had been shocked by Leo's hurtful tone towards a man I thought he respected. They did not know I could hear them, so I hung back and listened.

'Well, agents aren't a big thing right now, I gotta admit that. Hey, you're probably the only guy in Hollywood right now who has one, and you know what? That makes *you* a special kid. As for what an agent does, well, they look out for you.'

'I don't need anyone looking out for me,' Leo said.

'Hell, everyone needs someone looking out for them, Leo. What about your mom? You need her, don't you? I tell you something: she looks out for you, boy – she's some great lady . . . '

Leo mumbled something I didn't hear, but I took it as my cue to cough noisily and come back inside.

On the evening of the wrap-party everyone was excited, getting dressed up to go out together. A neighbour was coming in to stay with Tom, whose disappointment at being excluded had been compensated for by being assured that he could sit and listen to the radio until after 9 p.m. and feast on as much popcorn as he could stuff into his mouth before then.

Although it was not a formal affair, Freddie had rented tuxedos for himself and Leo. 'Trust me – it will make us stand out,' he said, as Leo ran his fingers complainingly under the tight, stiff collar. 'There will be a lot of important people there tonight that we need to impress, and we want to make a good impression.' Leo looked uncertain, but Bridie and I made a great fuss of telling him how handsome he looked. Bridie exclaimed loudly when he came into the hallway, 'Errol Flynn is only trotting after you – trotting, do you hear me – like a wee baby lamb!' And, despite himself, my increasingly surly teenage son managed a smile.

I wore my good navy dress, again, and Bridie her good Sunday coat and her mall pillbox hat, neither of which she planned to remove. She had spent almost the full day in the salon having her hair permed and set, and it curved around her ears under the hat with some style, although her face beneath it was an eerie white, due to the unfamiliar addition of face powder and a smear of dark-red lipstick.

As our car pulled up outside, Bridie started to look for her bag.

'I put it here,' she said, looking at the back of a kitchen chair, 'it was here, in the kitchen.'

We all had a look around, but it was nowhere to be seen.

'I don't understand,' she said, and I could see that my poor old friend was getting really distraught. 'Somebody must have moved it. Where did it go?'

'Did you go upstairs with it?' I asked. 'Outside?'

'No, NO!' she shouted loudly, as if I were accusing her of something. 'I haven't been outside all day. Not once. It's here, it must be here, I put it *here*!' She banged her fist hard on the table, then flinched and grabbed it straight back to her chest.

'Here it is.' Tom came in at that moment and handed Bridie her big brown handbag.

'Where did you find it?' she asked.

'When you were walking in the garden you put it on the hedge. I saw you, but you didn't see me.'

If it was true, it was a strange thing for Bridie to have done; and if she hadn't, it was an even stranger thing for Tom to have lied about. In any case, Tom's babysitter Julie was waiting in the hallway and our car was outside.

'Come on, Bridie, you have it now. Let's go.'

But Bridie sat down.

'No,' she said, 'send Julie home, I'm staying here with Tom.'

'Don't be silly, Bridie.' She was being petulant: what was wrong with her? 'Come on, I have your bag, the car is waiting – we're all set . . . '

'NO!' she said, and pulled Tom, a little roughly, into her lap, then cradled him in her bosom and looked away out the window. 'Now go – enjoy yourselves.'

It was over. There was no sense insisting any further that she come. I knew by the look of her that Bridie's mind was made up and there would be no persuading her.

'Come on,' I said to Freddie and Leo and we went out to the car, dismissing Julie on the way.

In the car I sensed an atmosphere brewing between Freddie and Leo.

'This tux is stupid,' Leo started again. 'My friends are dressing up in army costume for the night. I'll look really stupid in this.'

'All the more reason not to,' Freddie said. 'You'll be glad when we get there. Trust me, Leo, a good suit creates a good impression.'

'I don't need to create a "good impression". I'm a *good* actor. That's enough.'

'Maybe,' Freddie said, placating him, 'but I know what I'm doing here. You have to trust me.'

Leo mumbled something that I suspected was quite cruel, and

so I did not ask him to repeat it. Was it possible that my gentle, intelligent son was turning into something of a monster? Was this what Hollywood did to people? Or was it something I had, or had not, done?

The party was in one of the studios that was still set up as a war hospital. To add atmosphere, some of the actors were in costume – a few of them wandering around in pyjamas with fake blood and bandages wrapped around their heads, laughing, with drinks in their hands. To be honest, there was something vaguely distasteful about it. There was, after all, a war on – although it certainly didn't feel like that here. The war seemed to have caused little more than the vaguest of inconveniences, and an aspiration to sell movies. Even though all of the planes and many of the trains in our country had been commandeered for war use, Stan was still able to get his tickets for the Met and get us on a flight to New York. If the call to war was heard across America, then the clamour for the glamour of Hollywood was a louder shout.

Freddie was right about the evening dress. The young actors dressed in costume looked like extras, while Leo stood out, like the older men, as one of the lead actors.

As soon as we got inside, Leo waved over at some of his friends, but as he was making a move towards them, Freddie held onto him and said, 'Work first, Leo.' He looked around the room, his eyes narrowing as they swept across the milling crowd. 'There's half a dozen – ten at most – "players" here, Leo. Not as many as I had hoped, but worth a round of the room anyway. When we've done them all, then you can go and play.' Then he turned to me and said, 'Excuse us, Ellie?' and started to walk my son around the room, steering him away from his buddies and reintroducing them both to the stars of the film, followed by some older, rather reluctant-seeming fat cats, whom I assumed to be studio heads.

One very large man with an enormous cigar actually turned his back when he saw Freddie come towards him, but my son's tenacious young representative all but caught the man by the tail of his jacket and dragged him into their company. The studio head's face was dead with boredom as he chewed impatiently on his cigar, but Freddie continued to talk and laugh as if this dreadful old boy was finding their conversation perfectly delightful, all the while with his arm clamped around Leo's shoulders in a territorial grip. Freddie was, if nothing else, an arch networker. At the end of the conversation he handed the fat old boy his business card and watched carefully as he put it into his jacket pocket, then I saw Freddie write down the man's number on a scrap of paper. They shook hands, so the conversation certainly ended with more conviviality than it had begun.

With that done, Freddie dismissed Leo, who went flying off to his friends, and came back to give his 'report' to me.

'Ellie, the studio is really impressed with Leo's performance in the film. I'm certain they will extend his contract to the end of the year, and I am going to start negotiations with them this week to make sure he is given star status, with the appropriate salary, of course.'

'Freddie, I'm not sure that—'

I was going to say it there and then: that I didn't think Leo was ready to be sucked any further into the Hollywood star-system, and that perhaps it would be better all round if he returned to New York and completed his education, then came back here in a couple of years' time, when he would be that bit older and more mature and better equipped to deal with the lifestyle. The words were forming in my head, but Freddie interrupted me.

'Have some faith, Ellie – Leo is going to make it big, don't worry.'

And in that moment, surrounded by the loud music and the dancing actors, and the milling executives with their outsized cigars and even bigger egos and the general competitive thunder of the Hollywood roar, it felt as if my objections would fall on deaf and disbelieving ears – would appear petty and ridiculous. Hollywood was too huge and important to accommodate the minuscule demands of personal propriety or a mother's simple reason. Education and manners? What need was there for either, in a world like this where the artifice of glamour and the pretence of beauty were everything.

'No need to thank me, Ellie – that's my job,' Freddie said, with a glittering smile as he touched my arm and then excused himself and went back into the fray.

For the next hour or so I wandered about the room on my own, smiling about me, but not engaging with anyone. I was not an actress or a film worker and, as such, I felt invisible. Once I caught sight of a strikingly handsome young man in a tuxedo, his back as straight as a board with one hand in his pocket, standing apart from the other young men with his elegant, confident demeanour, and it was a moment before I recognized him as Leo. Although he was fully occupied he could feel his mother's warm gaze, and he turned and smiled at me across the room. I felt an ember glow in my heart; whoever this young man was to become, however far he moved away from me, I was helpless in my love for him. I would always be on the other side of the room now – grasping for these scraps of approval, grateful for every smile.

'That was smart,' said a woman who suddenly appeared next to me, 'getting him all dressed up like that – really makes him stand out.'

She was about my age and build and was wearing a not dissimilar dress.

'I let my Arnold dress up in costume with the other boys, but he's just one of the crowd tonight,' she added, puffing hard on her cigarette. 'Thanks for the tip,' she added, throwing the bent butt on the floor and stubbing it out with the tip of her scuffed black courts. 'I'll know next time.' And she walked off.

I wanted to chase after her and explain that I was not like her at all. That I did not care for the Hollywood system and that I wanted nothing more than to return with my son to New York. Explain that it was just the case that Leo was so brilliantly brave and clever and resourceful that he had run away across the whole of America on his own to be here, got himself taken on by the only 'actors' agent' in Hollywood and secured himself a lead role in this film – almost without consulting me. Adding that it was not my concern if my son was so dashingly handsome that he made her mediocre child disappear by comparison, and that it would take more than a tuxedo for *any* of the others to compete with Leo's talent and charm.

I was so furious with the woman, but mostly with myself for caring, that I fumbled in my bag for a pack of cigarettes and found that I had left them at home.

Who was I after all? Was I just a pushy mother who wanted her son to 'be somebody'? Was I even an artist any more, or simply the mother of a boy who wanted to be a film star? Perhaps that was a mother's role – to sublimate who she was for the love of her children. That was why that woman had offended me. Not in her competitiveness – that was merely a misguided love for her child – but in the ordinary way she was dressed and the way she had immediately been able to intuit why I was there. I was not a make-up artist, or a set designer, or a musician or, God forbid, an actress. She had recognized in me a fellow ghost of somebody else, made invisible in the light cast by a talented child; a conduit for somebody else's life – nothing in ourselves. Everybody in that room was 'somebody', or wanted to be 'somebody'. That woman and I were the dowdy mothers – rooting for our sons to be somebody because we couldn't ourselves be anything special in the world.

I looked around the room and I realized that I was utterly invisible, a nobody. I had been John's wife – he was gone. Charles' wife – he was gone. Leo's mother – now he was leaving me too. Of all my roles, the one I had come to understand the value of most was Ellie-the-artist – but now, it seemed, she had deserted me too. Perhaps I had never been a true artist, and she had just been an invention of my ego. Perhaps this was my destiny: to hide in the shadows and let my son shine. After all, I loved both my sons more than life – why should I want for any more than their happiness? Why could I not be fulfilled simply with that alone?

A man passed me and I asked him for a cigarette. He handed me one and lit it for me, offering only a cursory smile, before moving on to more glamorous company.

With a suddenness and an urgency that surprised me, I wished that my friend Stan were here.

Chapter Twenty-Three

The rental on the house had been paid until September, and there was no sense in rushing back to New York before Leo was due back in school. Of course I could have packed us all up when the film wrapped, and dragged us all back to Fire Island, which in many ways was what I longed to do, and might very well have done, were it not for the fact that Los Angeles wasn't just about me and Leo any more.

Tom had settled into Los Feliz in a way I had never imagined. I had always thought of my youngest as a happy, carefree child. He had spent his first year living in a commune of women (which is where I had first met his young mother, who had abandoned him into my care when he was only a few months old), and this had doubtless shaped his easy-going, sociable nature. Tom was a happy child and was always able to occupy himself. Content with his own company, he would play for hours on his own along the shores of Fire Island: collecting driftwood, building intricate sandcastles, hiding out in makeshift dens and making friends of the rabbits. Life was so peaceful there – reading contentedly in front of the stove as the sun went down, my little companion and I tucked into the blanket-covered settee, it seemed to me then that I had made the perfect life for us both.

Los Feliz made me see that I was wrong. Whereas Leo was

sensitive and could be awkward with boys of his own age, Tom was in his element with other children. Attending school and living in this sunny, family neighbourhood had been a revelation to both of us. As soon as Tom's school day ended there was a constant stream of kids coming in and out of the front and back door, with Bridie insisting on feeding them all most days, rather than have 'the waif eating in that "other woman's" kitchen – sure, you wouldn't know what she'd be feeding him'. That 'other woman' was our neighbour and the paternal grandmother of Tom's best friend, Angelo Trapani, whom Bridie had got to know over the fence, so to speak, and was in arch-competition with for the title of Best Mama. The two boys played them off against each other brilliantly – often gorging on Bridie's apple tart before hopping over to tell Francesca, who would scoop them up some of her home-made ice-cream, just so as not to be outdone in spoiling them.

The other element in not returning to New York just yet was Bridie. Maureen and I exchanged regular letters, and she and Patrick seemed to be particularly happy of late. Happy and enjoying a spectacular resurgence of love for one another: 'Honestly, Ellie, I cannot remember the last time Patrick and I so enjoyed spending time together! This Thanksgiving/Christmas/Easter was truly wonderful!' The closer it came to my possible return, the stronger the subtext of her pleas came. My friends were enjoying having the house to themselves and were praying that I wouldn't send Bridie back to them.

In Ireland the spinster daughter was the one who stayed at home and looked after the ageing parents and the farm, which the eldest son and his wife would inherit, leaving her to spend the rest of her days as the sister-in-law's skivvy.

I was an only child, both my parents were deceased *and* I had been married twice, yet Bridie was the closest thing I now had to a parent, and I knew the burden of responsibility for her as she got older and frailer would fall on my shoulders. In any case, she was not up to the journey home. Not yet at least. So, in the meantime, I decided that we should all enjoy a blistering summer in Los Angeles and return home in September, the best time of the year in New York.

Of course Hilla had been phoning me, anxious for my return, issuing dark warnings about my career. In any case, every time the phone rang my stomach lurched. If people had something nice to say, they wrote a letter. That was the civilized way to communicate. Telephones were generally used for emergencies and to convey bad news such as a death or a disappearance. Hilla, however, used the telephone as an everyday means of communication, which was wasteful, uncharacteristically frivolous and, frankly, when you were on the receiving end of it, unnerving.

'Bauer is opening in one month's time. I assume you will be back by then?' she'd say or, more directly, 'I am calling to let you know that one of your collectors came into the gallery today and wants to know when more of your work will be ready to view.'

Why she thought these bullying tactics would work, I could not imagine, although in one sense at least she succeeded in getting me back to work on my portrait of Suri.

'Let it ring,' I shouted at Bridie that morning, 'it's only Hilla.' And I went straight into the studio.

I thought I was nearly finished with the portrait. Goodness knows I had been working on it long enough, but there was something about Suri's demeanour that I found fascinating as a subject for painting. She had an impervious beauty that I was anxious to capture, yet it was also important that I break through her physical realm to reveal the warm heart that I knew lay beneath the perfect, angular structure of her face.

Suri had been preoccupied the past few times we had met, and had twice cancelled lunch with me. She was becoming more and more concerned about the plight of her elderly in-laws in the internment camp. Her father-in-law had said that his wife was finding it impossible to adjust. I shuddered when she told me about the cramped conditions and the families sharing makeshift kitchens. 'The worst thing is how isolated they feel,' she said. 'They cannot understand why they are there. They love America.'

I found it difficult to believe that such terrible things were happening here, in America, the land of the free, in this modern day and age; and yet Suri assured me they were. She showed me one of the letters that her mother-in-law had signed off with the words *'shikata ga nai'*.

'It means "it cannot be helped,"' Suri explained.

The fact that the old couple were becoming resigned to their situation, she said, made it all the more painful for her, on the outside, not being able to do a thing for them. When she spoke with such passionate concern, she reminded me of Charles. I realized, by listening to Suri, how little interest I had taken in my husband's work – how I had taken him for granted. He would surely have done something about this, were he here now. He would have fought for the elderly couple and not stood still until they were released. Perhaps I could help, but I sensed that Suri would ask for my help if she needed it.

Although I kept quiet on the subject, part of me wanted to let Suri know that I understood something of the anger and frustration she was feeling, because I had been caught up in situations like this myself – both during Ireland's War of Independence and then in my work helping to salvage the lives and dignity of people during the height of the Great Depression in New York. One day soon, I said to myself, I would find a way to let Suri know that I was willing to help her in any way I could, should the need arise. For the time being, this was her injustice to fight – all I could do was let it be known that I was her friend and would offer my support, if asked.

In any case, the painting was my concern now. I had been fidgeting with it for some time on my own, and it was still lacking some small element that I could not quite put my finger on.

The moment that I looked at it that day, it hit me. I realized that the sketching was not enough any more. I needed the woman herself in the room to sit for me. One sitting would see it complete. I decided to telephone Suri and ask her to come round that instant. I felt full of artistic vigour for some reason that day, and I was sure she too would be excited for me to finish the piece.

'I'm afraid Suri isn't here – is this Ellie? Did Stan not tell you what happened?'

Jackson sounded irritated at my calling.

'No,' I said, 'I haven't seen Stan for – a while.'

It had been more than a month since Stan had left my house that night. I had not expected him to stay away as he had, and I was hurt by the fact that he had not called round or even telephoned me. However, when thoughts of his absence entered my head, I quickly swept them aside, not caring to remember what he had or had not done that had so offended me that night. I did not wish to be pursued by him. Why should I care whether or not Stan called me? I had enough people in my life to care about, without adding another to my list.

'Where is Suri? Has she gone on a trip?' I asked Jackson.

Suri had been talking about travelling down to the internment camp where her in-laws were being held, to see if she could visit them.

'Ellie – Suri has been interned.'

'What?'

I must have shouted out in shock, because Jackson started to mumble apologies to me.

'Ellie, I am sorry. I expected that Stan would have told you, or I would have called you myself.'

The wretched Stan should have called me!

'What do you mean she's been interned?'

I don't know what came over me, but I felt a terrible panic overtake me. My heart was thumping in my chest. It was the same feeling I had encountered when Leo had disappeared, and when I had heard the news about Pearl Harbor. I was experiencing the same sense of helplessness – something dreadful had happened and it was completely outside my control. It was as if a bomb had gone off in my brain – a mushroom cloud of white anger exploded in my head.

I bombarded Jackson with questions. When had this happened? How had it happened? Where had she been taken? What was he doing about it?

Jackson sounded very calm about the whole thing. 'It happened last week, Ellie. They came for her in the morning. Just two men and a woman in a government car. She didn't object; in fact they waited while she went upstairs and packed a bag. To be honest, we were half-expecting this to happen. They are locking up everybody with the slightest hint of Japanese blood in them. It's ridiculous, but at least we managed to get her taken to the same camp as her in-laws. She has been really worried about them.'

I wanted to leap down the phone and wring his neck. How could he be so laissez-faire about all this? His wife – the woman he loved – had been locked up in an internment camp! A prison! For doing nothing but being born half-Japanese. It was an outrageous turn of events, and Jackson was being so . . . so *calm* about it.

'What can I do?' I asked, trying to keep my cool. 'Should we call the mayor, head down there? You know where she's being kept, right?'

There was a pause.

'She's in a place called Manzanar, across state,' he eventually said, adding, 'but, Ellie, I don't think there is anything we can do. I've contacted everyone I can think of, but there really are no strings to be pulled. It's wartime, and people lose their reason. I know it's terrible, but I think now the only thing to do – the best thing, the safest thing we can do – is just wait it out. The war won't go on forever.'

Best? Safest? What was the idiot talking about? Of course there was something we could do; there was always something to be done – an objection to be made, a door to be stormed. When terrible things like this happened you didn't just leave them be – you had to get out there and try to change things, to fight for what was right.

I wanted to say all of this to Jackson, but finding that I was near-speechless with rage towards the man, I simply excused myself and hung up.

I went straight into the studio and looked at my picture of Suri again. It was unfinished. I would get her – and her in-laws – out of that terrible place and finish the portrait. I did not know how I was going to do it, but I was determined. Let Suri's wimp of a husband put that in his pipe and smoke it!

I began by looking to see where on the map the camp was. I spread out Tom's large school map of America on the floor of the kitchen. Manzanar, Jackson had said, north-east of Los Angeles. It was not easy to find, but I located it eventually. It was no more than a dot, a tiny ranch town between Lone Pine and Independence, about two hundred and thirty miles away. If I packed up the truck tomorrow and started early – before Tom left for school – I could be there before lunchtime. I was not stupid enough to imagine that I could walk away with Suri and the old Japanese couple, but I could at least find my friend and talk to her about what could be done to help them. Except, of course, there was no guarantee that I would even be allowed to see her. This was not, I suspected, like an ordinary prison, with regular visiting hours. I needed help if I was even going to get in through the door. I needed some strings pulled.

The thought of calling Stan was just forming in my head when, in a coincidence that I could not decide if it was wonderful or terrible, he suddenly appeared at my back door.

CHAPTER TWENTY-FOUR

We both acted as if there had been no absence in our friend-ship. I greeted him cheerily, and he wandered in and made himself at home at my kitchen table, as if he had never been away.

Inside, my heart was thumping in my chest, as I imagined his must be as well, although he gave no sign of it.

I had missed him. Not just his friendship and his company, but the idea that he found me enthralling. In his absence I had come to realize how important it was for me to be admired by Stan. I had come to not just enjoy but crave the attention of this interesting man. Despite myself, if I was utterly truthful, deep down I wanted him to love me. I had loved and lost so many men, and I was not a greedy woman, but there was some-thing about the quality of this man that made me want more. Although I was careful to remain casual in my greeting of him, I was secretly thrilled that he had come back for me.

'Where is the delightful Bridie?' he enquired as I poured his tea and gave him a piece of apple tart. 'I sincerely hope this is one of hers. You are a better painter than a maker of apple pies, I suspect.'

'Well, you suspect wrong,' I said. 'I made this tart, and further-more I seem to have given up painting altogether – especially now that my only subject has been interned.'

As soon as I mentioned Suri the flirtation stopped. We had been dancing around each other so nicely, but the playing stopped abruptly as I realized, to my horror, why it was that he had turned up so suddenly and with such perfect timing.

He laid down his teacup.

'Jackson was worried about how you reacted to the news about Suri,' he said. 'He's worried that you are a hothead – like Suri herself – and are going to do something stupid.'

Stan was looking at me in a way that I found so infuriatingly patronizing that I felt like kicking him out. I felt humiliated that I thought he had come here to win me back, when in fact he was here to warn me off! I would have started the fight to end all fights, except that I had already gone one step ahead of him and had decided I was in need of his help.

'Like try and get her out of a prison where she is being unjustly held, for no reason?'

'It's not as simple as that.'

'Oh, really? It seems simple enough to me,' I said, trying not to lace my voice with too much sarcasm. 'Injustice is usually a fairly straightforward thing, based on simple prejudice and hatred – nothing complicated about it at all. *Fighting* injustice, on the other hand, can be complicated, because it requires courage and resourcefulness.'

'I can see you have both, Ellie,' Stan said, without a hint of sarcasm, 'but perhaps you do not fully understand the circumstances.'

I was starting to get angry with these men. John had fought in the War of Independence in Ireland; Charles spent his life fighting for the cause of the working man. What kind of men were these?

'Yes, there's a war on. How *awfully* unsettling for everybody.

That doesn't make it right, Stan. That doesn't make it right to lock people up for no reason and—'

Stan stood up suddenly and shouted over me, 'Do you think I don't know that?'

My turnaround was immediate; this was his war too. 'I'm sorry, Stan, I shouldn't have . . . '

He wasn't listening. 'I have friends in Poland, musicians, composers like me – better, finer, more talented men than me – and Hitler has locked them up, tortured them, for little more than having the wrong name, for being a Jew. Their women, their children too – nobody knows what has happened to them; many of them have disappeared. Every day I am more alone here in this stupid town: the "Polish Jew", the "American Jew". I don't even know who I am any more, but I am alive and I am free. So don't talk to *me* about the injustice of war. The injustice is that I am alive and many of the people I have loved are dead – disappeared – because they stayed, they did not run away, they were not cowards like me; they loved Poland and they suffered for her. What have I done? I came to America to write vacuous music for vacuous people, and so every day inside I suffer. I suffer for what I have done in running away – for what I have *not* done for my country!'

I had never seen Stan so agitated, so emotionally het-up.

I reached for the teapot and calmly poured a refill into his cup. Then, from where I was sitting, I reached to the kitchen countertop, took a cigarette out of the packet I always kept there, lit it and handed it over to him.

'You're no coward, Stan,' I said.

He was not. I knew enough about men to be able to see it, even in his fearful expression of his own cowardice. Brave men always experienced such doubts about themselves; cowards were always full of their own courage, boasting about their acts of bravery until it came to actually displaying them, when they would make an excuse and scuttle off into a corner to hide.

'You can't say that, Ellie,' he said, 'you don't know me.'

He said it in a way that made it clear he wished I did 'know' him. There was no resentment in his voice, more the white flag of defeat, and for a moment I was afraid he might leave. I found I did not want him to go and quickly said, 'I've been married twice, first to a solider – perhaps the bravest and most foolish man in Ireland – and second to a union activist, a man who died in service to the working man. I know a brave man when I see one and, while I don't know how you'd fare in a fist fight, I can tell that you're no coward, Stan.'

His demeanour changed utterly and, finally, he sat down.

He reached to put his cigarette in the ashtray, and looked me directly in the eye. His face, which had been hardened with rage against himself a moment ago, was now warm and soft. He was in love with me. I had suspected Stan's feelings, but now I could see it as clearly as if he had said the words out loud.

I identified the fact, but did not feel the need or desire, at that moment, to consider the fact one way or the other, because Suri's situation was at the front of my mind.

Suri was a strong-minded woman like me, with a keen sense of injustice. I knew that of her. I had no interest in Jackson's concerns as Suri's husband, or in what Stan thought was the right or wrong thing to do. I knew I was right.

Perhaps Jackson was not aware how concerned Suri had been about the welfare of the old couple. Possibly she had not confided in him her plans to help them, because they were her late husband's family; or perhaps, like me, she had found that sometimes we women inhibit the open expression of our determination, afraid that it might throw a cowardly light on our men. At the very least I wanted to see Suri face-to-face to discuss what could be done.

'And you love your country, you old idiot – sure, you never stop talking about the damned place.'

'That's true,' Stan nodded. He was smiling too broadly, weak with love for me.

Although I brushed that thought aside, I could not help but seize the moment. I took a deep breath and said, 'Surely that is all the more reason for you to help me talk to Suri.'

As if conscious that I may have seen the foolish, lovelorn way in which he had been gazing at me, Stan looked down at his feet before replying, 'Of course – of course I'll help you, Ellie.'

I headed off the following morning at first light. The journey, I calculated, would take me about four hours. I'd be there and back in a day.

The night before, Bridie had set about filling dozens of empty bottles with water for my journey, topping each of them with a cotton stop and holding them steady in a wide bucket in the back of the pickup, covered with a sheet.

'God knows what might happen to you, out there in the desert – wild animals and the like, you could get eaten alive. In any case, you'll surely not get a drop of water or a bite to eat for days. It'll be a miracle if you get back alive.'

'I will be back in time for dinner, Bridie. Will you quit panicking – it's only a few miles up the road.'

'It's the desert. Like Africa – or *worse*. Oh, I don't like you heading off up there on your own. Would your foreign boyfriend not go with you? Not that he looks like he'd be much use . . .'

'Bridie, stop fussing! You'll be all right here on your own for the day?'

'Sure, what could happen to me?'

With my family and the rest of Los Angeles sleeping, I headed out of the city as dawn was barely breaking. It was a straight run, and as the empty city streets gave way to the dusty highway, I began to wonder if I was doing the right thing.

Stan had also thought it foolish for me to leave so soon. What was the rush? Surely I could wait a few more days and give us both the chance to explore the official channels, before he had to resort to pulling his social strings at the studio.

'Hollywood is a strange place, Ellie. People who you think are your friends can turn on you when they think politics is involved. Everything is all about money here, and money is power.'

'You're an important guy, Stan,' I reassured him. 'You must know somebody in the studio who can talk to the mayor?'

'Of course,' he said, 'but in one day? I'm not sure.'

'You'll think of something, Stan – for me? I know you won't let me down.'

He knew I was playing him, but he didn't seem to mind and, if he did, I'm not sure I would have noticed. I had been so full of anxious energy yesterday, all het-up with what I had to do – there was no way I could have stood still and waited for a few days for things to be made 'official'. I had to keep moving. I knew I would not settle until I had seen my friend. This was my mission now: to rescue Suri, and her family, and bring them all back to Los Angeles, so that I could finish my portrait of her; the very thought of it made me feel like a hero.

Now, though, driving in the silence of the early morning, with the endless flat line of the highway in front of me, the expanse of sky lifting from muted grey to blue and soon to the harsh white light of the blistering Californian sun, overwhelming in its vastness, I wondered if perhaps I should have waited for a few days and made the journey having already investigated the bureaucratic ramifications (there were sure to be some), with all the correct paperwork and Stan travelling with me. Then again, I had always been impulsive – and look at all I had achieved because of it! Would I ever have come to America in the first place, had I waited for my first husband's approval? I had rushed here again after his death – and started a homeless shelter and then a women's cooperative charity foundation, purely to distract myself from my overwhelming grief at losing him. That was an act of impulsiveness and, although it had helped many other people, all it had done for me was delay the intensity and enormity of my sadness for another year.

Indeed, what was I doing now, in chasing off to rescue Suri? Perhaps rescuing Suri and her family was a homage to my second husband – to the work Charles had done all his life in fighting injustice. Here I was, standing up for something I believed was right – and perhaps it was all because of him? Perhaps this mission was in his name, not mine. My extraordinary husband who, although he had died at Pearl Harbor, would have been horrified for ordinary Japanese people to suffer in his name. It suddenly became clear to me that my second husband was the real driving force behind my wanting to take on this slightly crazy mission. I was carrying out Charles' legacy. It was clear to me now, and I felt happier for it.

I looked at my watch and saw that I had been driving for an hour and a half. I had been so lost in my thoughts that I had not noticed the time passing. The straight dusty line of the roads, the flat scrub of the desert on either side of it, had given me no cause to concentrate on either my driving or the landscape, and I had nodded asleep for a moment. However, I had noticed a sign for a gas station some way back, and I needed to wake myself up, to make sure I didn't miss it. Running out of gas in the desert was not on my agenda for the day!

I had long since finished the bottle of water propped on my dashboard and I decided to pull over to the side of the road, to look in the back for another. As I did so, I noticed something up ahead, rising out of the flat expanse of desert. As I drove towards it, I saw it was a huge rock with deep, wrinkled, creamy folds, like rolls of fatty skin on an enormous animal; on top of it was another flat rock, the colour of blood.

I pulled the car over and stood in this extraordinary landscape. All around me were these bizarre red rock formations: one like the craggy face of an old man, eyes hollowed into deep crevices, with a shock of dry, red hair; another looked like the wet jaws of some crazed monster, foaming at the mouth, stopped mid-bite and turned to stone. I had never seen such shapes and colours – naked hills with not a scrap of life on them, yet their wrinkled shapes seemed to tell the story of age itself; volcanic shapes showing life halted mid-action. And these red rocks were everywhere, as if animals had been slaughtered all about and their blood had been absorbed and had stained the salted rock; the sky behind them screamed a clashing blue. The expanse reminded me of the ocean off Fire Island except that, despite its tides and the way it absorbed the weather, the water was strangely consistent. This landscape changed utterly with every turn of the head, yet it was as mysterious and endless as the ocean.

I might have stood and stared all day, had I not more important business to attend to.

Chapter Twenty-Five

MANZANAR WAR RELOCATION CENTER. The wooden sign was attached at its four corners to two stakes, like some medieval torture victim. It was pathetically small, given the vastness of the landscape it was in. All around was barren scrubland, and in front of me was a range of forbidding purple mountains. The road I was on had long since become dusty and potholed, as if indicating that there was no point in going any further.

The sign for Manzanar might easily have been missed, if it weren't in the middle of such nothingness. A dirt track rutted out by the wide wheels of army tanks veered off to the right. I got out of the car, put on my sunhat and started walking towards this place, as it gradually emerged from the haze like a mirage. As I got closer I saw long wooden huts, lined up in neat rows that seemed to go on forever. It seemed inconceivable somehow that such a place could exist in a civilized world; strange to think that beyond the fence were thousands of people living, sleeping and eating in wooden huts – in the middle of a desert. John and I had lived in a remote spot in Ireland, miles from the nearest town; but there was shelter, and trees, and water, and land to graze animals and grow things. That people would be made to live in such a bleak, barren place was beyond me.

As I was walking towards the place, it seemed to move further away, and I realized that I ought to have followed the tyre tracks and driven in. However, as I walked, my instincts were urging me to keep moving forward – I did not want to turn my back on the place. I had a strange feeling of foreboding, as if I was being watched. I did not see the barbed-wire fence until it stopped me in my tracks and I was nearly on top of it. Rising above it, on either side of me, were two security lookout towers. Inside one was a solider with his gun trained on me.

I had reached Independence, the last town before Manzanar, around midday and had stopped for gas and a large breakfast of bacon, eggs, coffee and toasted muffins. I had been surprised by how hungry I was, although it was now almost lunchtime and I had been driving, more or less solidly, for four hours in the increasingly searing heat. The diner had a phone booth and so I had tried to telephone Stan, but was unable to get hold of him. Now that I was here I realized how ridiculous it had been to expect him to contact anyone about getting me into Manzanar at such short notice.

'Do you have a phone book?' I had asked the woman at the counter.

'Who you looking for?' she said. 'Only five folk or so got a phone round here, and I got everyone's number in my head.'

Small towns are the same the world over, I thought. Always some nosy woman wanting to stick her nose into your business, although by the look of this dusty little outpost, I'd say they had precious little entertainment other than strangers hooking into town.

To hell with it, I thought.

'I am heading for Manzanar,' I said, 'and I wanted to call ahead to let them know I am coming.'

Her eyes widened, then narrowed in an instant. Shock and suspicion: I had made her day.

'You work there?' she asked, bold as brass. 'You don't *look* like you work there.'

'I am visiting a friend,' I said, 'who is staying there.'

Her eyes flashed wide again.

'Ain't no friend of yours or mine up there, girl,' an old man further along the bar called out. 'Full of wicked Japs – *spies* all of them. The kids too; I seen them pass by in trucks. Slanty-eyed gremlins sure put a curse on this town. You wanna be careful going up there . . . '

'Shut it, Bill,' the woman snapped.

She wrote a number on a piece of paper and, before handing it to me, said by way of explanation, 'My cousin Marlene works out in the canteen. She says the Japs are all right in the main – they keep themselves quiet.' Then, as I took it, she held onto it and tugged slightly, adding, 'Although *I* say quiet's not always a good thing – quiet can mean crafty.'

I snatched the scrap of paper from her hand and smiled a sarcastic smile, gratefully noting that I had enough coins in my hand not to have to ask her for change.

Her eyes followed me across the room and I knew she was listening to every word I said. I got through to the Manzanar exchange and, when I told the young woman that I wanted to speak to the person in charge, she put me through to a man who was very taken aback when I explained that I wanted access to visit a friend.

'Are you of Japanese origin?' he asked straight out.

'No,' I said, trying to hold on to my patience, 'actually I'm Irish.'

'Are you a Japanese sympathizer?'

Oh God! What was *that* supposed to mean?

I decided just to bite my tongue and appeal to his sense of decency.

'I am just worried about my friend and want to see that she is all right.'

'I can assure you, Ma'am, that the conditions at Manzanar are perfectly—'

'Nonetheless,' I asserted, 'I would prefer to see for myself.' Then I spelt out Suri's full name and told him that I would be there in less than an hour to see her.

'I am afraid that won't be possible, Miss . . . '

'Hogan.'

'Miss Hogan – you see, this is a military facility and there is a protocol that we must follow. If you would like to write to—'

'Nonetheless . . . ' I said again. My heart was thumping. I knew this was completely outside the normal run of things and I was playing with fire, but I was going to Manzanar anyway. I was going to see Suri, and that was that. ' . . . I shall be there in less than one hour, which should be time enough for you to tell my friend to expect me. Thank you.' And I hung up the phone, paid my bill, thanked the woman for her help, got in the truck and drove off.

Now I was here, standing on the wrong side of a barbed-wire fence, with a young man pointing his gun in my direction. I should have been terrified, but I wasn't. I was angry. At pointless wars; at stupidity; at the suffering of innocent people.

So I shouted up at the security tower, 'You can put that thing down, for a start!'

He shouted something back. I couldn't hear what it was, so I moved forward, but as I did so he hoisted the rifle and pointed it directly at my head. Instinctively I raised my hands as I had seen people do in the movies. I suddenly felt very frightened. The boy holding it was probably no more than a child; the gun could go off by accident and I was out here in the middle of nowhere, on my own. Anything could happen.

I stood still like that for a moment, with my hands raised, until I saw two uniformed guards walk towards me. They signalled for me to follow them to a door in the fence, then as I reached it they asked, 'Are you Eileen Hogan?'

'Yes,' I said. I didn't remember giving the man on the phone my full name. 'I am here to see Suri Cohen? My friend. I called earlier and—'

'Come with us, please, Ma'am,' he cut me off.

At last, I thought. *They are taking me to see Suri.*

'Are you taking me to see my friend?'

'Just come with us, Ma'am,' the taller one repeated. The two of them were flanking me tightly on either side. Both guards were carrying guns, which hung loosely at their sides, although I could see that they had tight hold of them, nonetheless.

We walked past dozens of identical, basic, long wooden huts until we came to one with two American flags hanging ostentatiously from its small doorway.

'Please step inside, Ma'am.'

I didn't like the bossy, slightly officious tone in this man's voice.

'Would you please tell me when I am going to see my friend?'

'Please step inside the building, Ma'am.'

'There is no need to be so rude,' I asserted, 'if you would just tell me . . . '

The other, younger guard tapped the small of my back with the butt of his rifle. Could he really have done that? Taken such an outrageous liberty with my person?

I was about to lambast him when I heard Suri's voice from inside the hut.

'Ellie?'

At last – mission accomplished. The sound of her voice gave me such a sense of relief; this was certainly a frightening and daunting place, but now that I had come here and seen for myself, at least I could offer my friend some comfort in knowing that there was someone here to help fight her cause.

I ran up the steps and into the hut. Suri was standing at the centre of it, red-faced with tears. She had obviously been through some terrible ordeal. There were two female guards in there – severe, stone-faced women, one in each corner of the room. The male guards followed me in and flanked the open door behind me. That was four people 'guarding' two innocent women. Ridiculous!

'Could we have some privacy, please?' I told them more than asked. Somebody around here had to stand up to these bullying bureaucrats!

Not one of them either moved or made a reply. I would have made my point more strongly except that Suri looked fit to collapse with emotion.

'Suri, what have they done to you?' I asked, reaching my arms out to comfort her.

All four guards moved in to stop me, but I would have carried on towards my friend if Suri had not screamed at me, 'They haven't done anything, you stupid bitch – it's *you!*'

Her face was contorted with rage.

'Have you any idea what it took for me to get into the same camp, the same quarters, as my in-laws? Have you any idea how much time and begging and grovelling I had to do, to persuade the authorities to let me come here and look after an old couple who are not considered my blood? Almost a year, including the time it took to persuade Jackson that it was the right time to let me come – almost one year of them in here on their own, and now they have separated us again, and all because of you. *You* come in and screw it all up for me. In one day? What the *hell* were you thinking, Ellie – you stupid, *stupid* woman. I can't even say your name. Get her out of here . . . '

The older guard said, 'We just need to ask you both a few questions about your association.'

This time it was Suri who flew at him.

'Can't you see what's going on here? There are no questions to answer. This woman has *nothing* to do with me – I know her vaguely through my husband's work and, as far as I am aware, she is not a spy, but she is certainly no friend or "associate" of mine. She is just some stupid do-gooder, with nothing better to do than come out here and make trouble – certainly *not* at my invitation, or at the invitation of any member of my family. Now please, please, can we just forget this ever happened and let me go back to my family?'

'I'm afraid we still have to question you separately.'

'Please,' she said, 'really this has nothing to do with me . . .'

Suri was taken from the room by the two female guards, sobbing with genuine distress and screaming profanities at me on the way out.

I was so shocked that I barely knew what to say to the two guards as they sat me on a chair in the centre of the room in front of the simple wooden desk and began to question me about Suri. I just answered them accurately. There was nothing to hide. She was adopted, of Japanese descent; widowed, and the old couple were her in-laws. Her husband was an American-Jewish musician, whom I knew vaguely through another friend – and they took down Stan's name. Suri was not, as far as I was aware, connected to any Japanese organization, nor had she ever travelled to Japan in her adult life, not that I was aware; although, I asserted, I did not know her that well. I had no Japanese blood in me whatsoever and had neither proper reason nor motivation for being here, aside from an overwhelming desire to 'help' Suri, who neither needed nor wanted my help.

By the end of their half-hour interrogation it was clear to them – and to me – that I was exactly what Suri had said I was: a stupid, interfering woman who could not mind her own business.

Chapter Twenty-Six

I cried a lot on the way home, stopping the truck and howling into the darkening day. I was glad of the wilderness and for the fact that I was, for these few hours at least, utterly alone. I could barely face myself, let alone another human being. I felt so stupid; so utterly humiliated by my own foolishness. I had destroyed Suri's well-laid plan – and the welfare of those two old people – by being rash and wilful and inconceivably stupid, not to mention arrogant and ignorant. What had I been thinking?

I briefly tried to pass the blame by wondering *why* nobody had stopped me, but then – everyone had tried. Stan had told me not to go, and so had Bridie. Both had failed because of who I was: a pig-headed do-gooder who refused to mind her own business and determinedly bulldozed every bit of common sense that tried to stand in my way.

The rising sense of my own stupid failure kept overwhelming me. I would drive a few miles, then have to stop the truck and weep away the frustration of what I had done.

On one such stop I got out of the truck to get some water from the back. As I stood drinking from the warm glass bottle, the sun – already low in the sky – disappeared from my view behind a large rock in the middle distance. The perfect pink globe appeared to be eerily nearby, almost close enough for me to reach out and touch it. It was impossible to guess at distances here; a tree that appeared to be only a few yards away might be a mile's walk. Context was everything – a vast mysterious trick of light and dust. Los Angeles had been built on land like this. They had come to make movies here, building fake cities because they were cheaper than real cities and because the light was good. Then the fake city became a real city; they put up tall buildings, defied the relentless sun with their irrigation engineering and built dams as high as mountains. They transplanted fancy trees and fancy people out here, and made things that didn't belong in the desert, like lawns and movies and money. These invaders filled the barren desert with life, defying nature, defying God. The dry, red domain in front of me was the land they could not tame. Mighty rocks driven up from the Earth's core seemed to have been stopped in their tracks by the heat of this unmerciful sun. This was an empty landscape of dry scrub, the scenery shifting with the wind, creating an ever-changing hilly landscape and bringing dead sand to peculiar life. Miraculous trees and strange, deadly cacti peppered the landscape – greenery out of dust, at God's mighty whim.

Standing by my truck, waiting for the sun to reappear from behind its rock, I realized that, for all my problems and whether I liked it or not, I was in the presence of God. Not the religious rule-maker I had obeyed as a child, or the betraying joker who had taken the men I loved, twice abandoning me to fate before I realized I had to take charge of my own life; but God the Creator – for the landscape here was beyond human imagining. On Fire Island I had loved the sea, its hushed musings whispering on the shoreline, the soft white sand between my toes comforting me – the silence made me feel at one with myself. The solitude that I felt here in this landscape held no comfort or peace. The silence out here was suffocating and seemed to have the numb throb of death about it. The sun pulled around the side of the rock, rolling low and slow across the horizon, until it disappeared completely and all but plunged me suddenly into darkness. I felt cold and alone. I suddenly had only an urgent need to be back home with Bridie and my boys.

'The telephone's been hopping all afternoon,' Bridie said, the moment I walked in the door. Tom wheeled a truck past my feet – 'Varoooom!' – followed by one of the neighbour's children chasing after him with a wooden aeroplane.

As Tom turned and careered past me again, I grabbed him by the waist and tackled him into a hug. For a moment I forgot I was having a bad day. 'Who was it?' I asked, kissing my big baby's cheek as he pulled away, embarrassed in front of his friend.

'Damned if I know,' Bridie said. 'I'd never touch one of those wretched things. Dangerous, full of electric – sure, you wouldn't know what'd happen to you.'

'It was Jackson,' Leo said, poking his head around the door. 'He rang four times this afternoon, looking for you – dashed inconvenient if you ask me' – (my eldest son's latest fad was talking like the English actor Trevor Howard) – as I'd been waiting for a call from Freddie. He was talking to the studio about my contract today. Where've you been?'

The phone rang and my stomach tightened. I picked up the receiver quickly, before I had the chance to think. Leo stood glaring at me for a moment, until I dismissed him with a shake of my head. It was Jackson.

'What the hell did you think you were doing?' he shouted down the line.

'I'm sorry,' I said, 'I am *so* sorry. I know I did the wrong thing, but believe me, Jackson, I never meant to cause any—'

'Don't you try to justify what you have done . . . ' I let him go on without interruption. There was no point interspersing his anger with empty apologies. It's the rare person, I realized as he was talking, who sets out to cause harm. Noble intentions are easy; it is having the intelligence to carry them through with thoughtfulness and due consideration that ultimately sets an act out as good or bad. My actions had disastrous consequences, so however good my intentions were, I had done a bad, bad thing. After all, most wars are fought in the name of God, or with the weight of good intention behind them, and what do the good intentions of the politicians mean for the dead soldiers, the wounded men, the widowed wives, the orphaned children? Fighting on principle only works when your sword is weighted with wisdom. I had not acted wisely in chasing off to Manzanar. I could say I was sorry – argue my good intentions – but what would be the point of that? Suri and her family, including Jackson, had suffered because of my rash decision to 'rescue' them.

I wondered, as he was ranting, how many of the good things in my life that I had done – starting up the cooperative in Yonkers, adopting two other women's children – had been done from purely altruistic motives. None. I had long since known that. Others might disagree (Maureen often described me as a 'saint'), but my actions in helping others were almost always born of my need to be needed. I did not delude myself in believing that I was a truly 'good' person; while I had seen that the world was full of do-gooders, very few people I had ever met were truly unselfish. Where I had acted out of turn with Suri was not in trying to do the right thing by her, but in the overwhelming and arrogant conviction that I was 'right'. When had I become this strident woman who had to be 'right' all the time? That was my downfall; I had made an error of judgement by following the assumption that I was right.

As I had grown older I had also come to believe that my life experience – living through two depressions, one in Ireland and one in America, losing two husbands, then mothering two sons – had qualified me with some great insight. This belief in my own absolute wisdom had become stronger and stronger of late, until I had somehow come to believe that I was right about everything! People challenged me – Leo, Bridie, Hilla – but their objections were easily rebuffed by my unshakable self-conviction. Remarkably, it now seemed to me, in the face of my appalling mistake, this was the first occasion in my life when I had displayed a severe error of judgement to such an extreme degree.

'I suppose you know that they interrogated Stanislaw about all this?'

The words shocked me out of my humbling thoughts and caused me to blurt out, unintentionally rudely, '*What?*'

'Oh yes. Some heavy-looking guys in smart suits called by to see me earlier, with Stan in the back of their shiny black car. He looked pretty shook up, as you can imagine. They wouldn't even let him out to talk to me, just asked if I knew him. They picked him up this afternoon, after your little show out in Manzanar. Seems he had gone to the mayor's office and made a fuss for you early this morning – and somebody made a call to some-body else and they made a connection. There's quite a network of spies in the government; there is nothing these guys don't know – and they call *us* spies. They didn't bother bringing me in, because they had already checked me out before they interned Suri – but they're *very* interested in Stan, by the look of them. They'll have him pegged as a Nazi spy is my guess; these dimwit amateur cops can't tell Jews and Nazis apart – we're all just foreigners to them. So congratulations: you got my wife and my best friend in serious trouble, all in one day!'

I could not believe this. How could I have caused such carnage? I had been feckless with Stan's feelings for me. I had done the one thing I had never wanted to do – manipulated a man's soft feelings for me and caused him harm as a result. Jackson was angry. I didn't blame him.

'Who were they?' I asked. 'The police? The army? Where did they take him?'

He let out a dry laugh.

'You've gotta be kidding – you think I'm gonna let you near this?'

'You've got to let me help him . . . '

'Like you "helped" my wife?'

'This is *my* mess, Jackson – not yours. Let me clean it up. Please.'

He paused. Seeming to calm down, he came back with a better story.

'They weren't in uniform, so I reckon it was the OSS – Office of Strategic Services. They were the people who came to see us after Suri declared herself for internment at Manzanar. She should have volunteered herself at the army centre months earlier, but,' he swallowed to stop his voice breaking, 'I wouldn't let her.'

There was another pause. I said nothing. How could I have been so stupid to think Jackson didn't care? He was mad about Suri, and must have tried for months to stop her from going. I had never bothered asking her how she had evaded internment. They were taking in people, she told me herself, 'with a drop of Japanese blood'. Jackson had doubtless pleaded with her not to go – but she had finally given in. He cared that she was there, and would give anything to get her out. If only I had listened to him – stupid, stupid!

'When the army found out she had evaded them, they were worried and arranged to send her to a centre in Arkansas. Suri put in a request with the mayor that she be sent to Manzanar. The army got suspicious about her motivations and sent their "intelligence" wing to question us both. They were okay, actually – two guys and a woman. They were civilians, but working for the government. It seems the world is full of spies these days. They took some convincing that Suri just wanted to help her in-laws and wasn't part of an elaborate plan to overthrow the United States government.'

The sarcastic edge in his voice was no longer directed towards me. Perhaps he was just glad to be talking to somebody about it.

'You miss her,' I said. As soon as my words were spoken I realized how trite and insincere they sounded – after all I had put him through, now I was patronizing him.

He paused, perhaps in acknowledgement of my concern, and said, 'I think the OSS is probably holding Stanislaw. I have the address and phone number of their office here, somewhere on a card. In the end they were quite helpful and said I could call them if there were any problems.'

'I guess this was not the kind of problem you were banking on,' I said, then added, 'I'm sorry Jackson.'

And I meant it. I was sorry.

'Stuff happens,' he said. 'It's a stupid world, and this is a stupid, stupid war.'

This was my fourth war. I was born in 1900 in an Ireland under British rule. My father was a civil servant and loyal to the British government – an unpopular stance. As a child I remember him commending the young men in our local village who joined the British Army to fight in World War One. They were driven to sign up by poverty more than loyalty – and if it was otherwise, they could never let on because their neighbours and friends were part of the Irish Republican Brotherhood, freedom-fighters who opportunely took on our oppressors while their armies were occupied elsewhere. My third war was the worst war of them all: our Irish Civil War, when neighbours, friends and former comrades fought and killed each other on points of principle and policy. Although that is the case in all wars. My husband was a captain – a hero – but heroism is small comfort to those left behind at home. I knew how Jackson was feeling. His wife was away fighting her corner, but this was not his war, any more than it was mine.

'All war is stupid,' I said.

'Yeah, I guess it makes people do stupid things,' he said, and then added, 'they wouldn't be making such a fuss if I had let Suri volunteer herself when she was supposed to. This is partly my fault.'

He was probably right, but it didn't make me feel any better.

'You know what, Jackson?' I said. 'Don't blame yourself. Blame this *all* on me. It's the least I can do – I can take it.'

'Thanks,' he said, 'I appreciate that.' Then he let out a little laugh and paused again as if he didn't want to come off the phone.

'I miss her,' he said. 'I hate being alone.'

My heart broke for him.

CHAPTER TWENTY-SEVEN

It was too late to do anything about Stan that night.

Bridie had cooked a stew, but it didn't look great. The edges of the pot were burned, and I noticed there was a substantial lump of it in the trash. Tom's bowl was still on the table.

'Did you not eat your dinner, Tom?'

The child was a hog – it wasn't like him to leave food un-eaten.

'It's rotten,' he said, 'there's sugar in it!'

'There is not!' the old woman exclaimed.

'How dare you speak about Bridie's cooking like that,' I said, automatically tasting a spoonful from the pot. It *was* vile and sugary.

'Come along now, Tom, send your friend home – it's time for bed.'

I clapped them both into action and said to Bridie, 'It's an easy mistake, Bridie – sure, I'm always putting salt in my tea. We need to get a proper sugar canister and not be using these glasses.' As I said it I noticed that the jar had the word SUGAR emblazoned across the front of it.

'I did not put sugar in that stew,' Bridie said. Her face was red and she looked furious, 'and how *dare* you accuse me of such a thing.' Her lip was trembling. She was genuinely distraught.

'If there is any sugar in that stew, well then, the little bastard must have put it there himself!'

The outburst was so unlike Bridie that I did not know what to make of it. I certainly could not be offended. The woman had a sharp tongue, but she had never, *ever* used language like that before – and against Tom? Whom she adored? There must be something else wrong.

'Is everything all right, Bridie? Is there something wrong?'

She looked at me for a moment, her eyes moist and blinking. Such vulnerability suddenly, all anger and feistiness gone – it wasn't like her at all. Goodness me, she looked so old. Then suddenly she was back.

'I'm going to bed, and to hell with the lot of you.'

She'd be grand, I decided. It had been a long day for all of us. I gathered up the boys and made them put their pyjamas on, even Freddie and Leo, then made them all bowls of hot milk with sugar sandwiches melted into them. As they ate, I watched them and allowed myself to feel warm and motherly after my cruel day.

Despite the sweet interlude and pulling Tom into the bed beside me for comfort, I did not sleep a wink. Every time I closed my eyes I would see the anger and disgust in Suri's eyes, and think of my poor friend Stan imprisoned in some cold army barracks overnight.

The following morning I rang the Office of Strategic Services right away and got through to the contact that Jackson had given me.

'We let him go last night,' he said. 'Matter of fact, the operatives who drove him home came in with bad heads this morning. Seems they went out for dinner first and got caught up with

251

some Hollywood types. Gotta say, your friend knows some goo
people.'

Clearly I wasn't one of them.

I telephoned Stan's house and, when I didn't get a reply, g
straight in the car and drove up there, briefly shouting at Brid
through her bedroom door to let her know that I was goi
out. I was surprised to find that she wasn't already in the kitche
but then I thought, as last night had proven, Bridie was getti
old and sometimes forgetful, and in fairness I was glad to I
her rest.

I pulled up the truck outside Stan's house and banged on tl
door. I was relieved that he had been released, and it certain
didn't sound as if he had come to any harm, but all the same
wouldn't be happy until I had seen with my own eyes that I
was all right.

I banged and called through the door, 'Stan, are you okay?
everything all right? It's me . . . '

The door opened abruptly and Stan was standing there, dresse
if unshaven and a little tired-looking.

'Oh, thank God! Thank God you're all right.'

I fell on him and wrapped my arms around him.

He didn't respond, but stiffened and said, 'I was about
make coffee.' Then he moved away and gestured to me to follo
him to the kitchen. Gentle, polite – but cold.

I was embarrassed by my sudden and, as it seemed, ina
propriate show of affection.

'How did you get out?' I asked, following him into the kitche

'I have a friend, Seymour, he's a writer who, believe it or nc
is in the OSS. In Europe. His father, Schulberg, is head
Paramount; he had a novel out last year – I was at the party
New York – nice guy. Anyway, he told me he was going
Europe and I gave him a few people to look up. Turns out I

252

was going over there to make movies for the government, documentary films and suchlike. He was going to work on a unit with John Ford. I know him – and they asked me to compose some music for the films, something sympathetic to the scenes they were filming. I told the guys who picked me up that it had been my pleasure to work on their department's films – and they checked me out, then let me go. That's Hollywood. Nothing bad can happen when you work in the movies. If I had been just a Jew with a foreign accent teaching music, who knows?'

I knew there was a quip to be made, but could not think of one, as the estrangement of his pulling away was still fresh in my mind.

'I am so sorry, Stan,' I said. 'I never meant for any of this to happen.'

'Neither did I,' he said. I was shocked – and a little put out. He had more or less told me that the experience had not been so bad.

'Well, they let you go and . . . '

'Not that,' he said waving his hands irritably. Then he opened his long-fingered musician's hands and, in the kind of expressive gesture I had come to recognize as his alone, curved them into two wide bowls pointing skywards and said – shouted almost, 'This, Ellie – THIS!'

He meant 'us'.

'I thought we had agreed to be friends, Stan.'

Even as I said it I heard how small and curt and meaningless it was.

'Oh, Ellie,' he said. He put his hands down by his sides and shook his head. 'I have enough friends.'

Just as I had begun to realize how hurt I was, I felt a wild sob drawing up from my stomach.

'I thought you liked me,' I said.

I had not realized how much I wanted this man in my lif
Now he was rejecting me.

'Can you really be that blind, Ellie Hogan? Can you honestl
tell me you cannot see that I am hopelessly, stupidly, in lov
with you?'

It was less a declaration of love and more an accusation.

In that spirit, he waved me aside and turned his face from
me, as if afraid to look at me.

'Of course you are playing with me.' He was getting angr
his temper was rising and he faced me full-on. 'This is the gam
– this is an entertainment for women like you . . . '

'Women like me?' I was getting angry now. What on eart
was he accusing me of? 'Just what do you mean by that?'

'Oh, you – you seductress types, mesmerizing us poor, haples
males with your acumen, your art, your exceptional beauty. Yo
think you can snap your fingers and we are there to do you
bidding!'

Seductress? Exceptional beauty? Was he talking about me
Yes, of course I had known that Stan was a little bit in lov
with me. Perhaps I had manipulated that, but I had no idea h
feelings ran so deep.

'You have made me weak,' he said, 'and I am *not* a weak man

I could see that. Stan was perhaps ten, maybe fifteen year
older than me, his hair was white and, while his elegar
demeanour favoured intellect over brawn, it made his strengt
all the more prevalent and interesting to a woman like me.

'Get out of my house,' he finished as he turned his back t
me.

I should have bowed my head and scuttled out of the doc
after such a pasting, but instead I felt myself becoming fille
with rage. How dare he turn his back to me! All I could fe
was the blood pumping through my whole body as I blurte

out, without giving the slightest thought to dignity or consequence, 'You think you're such a brave man – yet you turn your back on a woman. You don't have the *courage* to seduce me.'

He turned quickly and his eyes were sharp as he regarded me for a moment, perhaps searching my face to see if I was mocking him. I wasn't. Stan had called me a beautiful seductress. I may have been satisfied with his friendship, but I had known from the moment I met him that this accomplished man desired me. In the heat emanating from my body I realized now that I didn't want to lose his regard. He was right – I had wielded my power over him and now I was going to do it again, but in the way that he wanted. I would show him what a beautiful seductress could do.

I walked, quite deliberately, across the room and placed my sharp pickup keys down hard on the polished surface of his precious Steinway. Then, scraping the clawed feet of the piano stool across the delicate parquet floor so that it squeaked in pain, I perched myself on the edge of it and, supporting myself on either side, I leaned slightly backwards, arching my back, and said, 'A strong man doesn't merely talk about love, Stanislaw.'

He did not hesitate.

Stan's kiss was a revelation: assertive and hard. It was also short-lived because it brought about in me such a craving that I cut him short, clawing at his shirt and tearing at my own. My body was starving for love and I strained to his every touch, calling out for more. Writhing on the polished wooden floor, naked and exposed in the huge room, he ministered to me with a masterful strength and a deliberate calm that let me know he had had many, many women in his life. Neither of us were inexperienced; our lovemaking was seasoned with demands and certainties; different from the confused, needy passions of young love, but no less sweet nonetheless.

When I was satisfied, Stan turned me and I bent naked across his beloved piano. Holding my breasts in his warm hands, he rocked me in the soft breeze coming in from the open balcony doors. I looked out at Hollywood and its heroes sleeping beneath us, while my composer made love to me like god to goddess looking down on our kingdom. When he finally dropped his face into the nape of my neck, I turned and held his face in my hands and laughed with sheer delight.

'Who would have thought it?' I said.

'You don't believe my prowess?' he said. 'Will I prove myself to you again?'

'I was promised coffee,' I said.

Stan kissed me sweetly on the forehead before going to the kitchen.

As I started to gather up my clothes, he called, 'You can use my robe, if you like – it's on the back of the bedroom door.'

As I reached for the blue cotton robe, I had a flashback. I had worn John's woollen shirts around the cottage house in Ireland; Charles used to wear my old silk robe with the embroidered peonies, when coming out of the shower, and sometimes kept it on all morning just to amuse me.

Borrowing Stan's robe would indicate a moment of domesticity. This was not what I wanted.

I got fully dressed and presented myself for coffee.

Stan was wearing his shorts and shirt. (His legs, I noted, were surprisingly athletic.) He seemed disappointed that I was already dressed.

'I have no food in – of course, I will call Greenblatt's and ask them to deliver . . . '

'No, Stan – coffee is fine. I have to get back home anyway. The boys, you know?'

'Of course, of course . . .' he said.

We both took a mouthful of coffee.

'So this is it,' he said, 'we make love – you leave.'

'I thought it was what you wanted?'

'The making love? Of course. The leaving afterwards? Not so much.'

'I have to get back to . . . '

' . . . the family – of course, of course. To Bridie and the boys. Not to me; not to Stan.'

'They are my sons; you can't expect me to—'

'I expect nothing, Ellie, but I have a problem. You see, I love you. There. But you cannot love me back.'

'How can you say that after . . . '

' . . . after what, Ellie. After we made love?'

I felt somewhat exasperated, but also strangely frightened.

'Again, I thought that was what you wanted.'

'To make love? That's it? Ellie, I am a rich man, a clever man. You think there is a shortage of women I can make love to, huh? In this town? You are crazy – I can have any woman I want.'

'I thought I was special.'

'Don't shirk me, Ellie – you are smarter than that.'

I was. I knew exactly what he was driving at, but it was sending such a wave of panic through me.

'I can make love with any woman, but can I laugh with her? Can she understand me? Can I admire and respect her, and be happy to spend every waking moment of each day and every dreaming hour of the night with her? Can I love her children because she loves them? Can I eat the lumpy Irish bread of her adoptive mother because I am so hopelessly in love that I have lost myself . . . ?'

I laughed despite myself when he said that about Bridie's bread, then I thought, *Please – please, let this not be happening.*

*Just when I thought everything was going to work out just fine;
just when I was starting to feel in charge of things again.*

'I have fallen in love with you, Ellie. From the moment we
met, I wanted to be with you. I had heard it would happen once
in my life, but I got to this age and I thought it had eluded me.
On the train, I saw you sitting there in my seat and straight
away I thought, "This is my woman." We talked, and oh, I was
so certain then, but I was afraid – you know? I have been alone
all my life, so I thought, "Let her go, and put it in the lap of
the gods. I have met my woman – now she is gone. But at least
I can say she is out there somewhere." Then, when I saw you
at the studio, I thought then, "This was meant to be."'

'Why didn't you say anything?' I asked.

'What would you have thought of me – stupid old man to
mock? You made it clear you did not want us to be lovers.'

'Things have changed now, Stan . . . '

'Because we have made love, Ellie? I am not a boy; my desire
does not define me. You may challenge my desires, Ellie, but I
am a man – and I am defined by higher passions than my body
alone. Making love to you was wonderful – how could it have
been any other way? To give love to you, it's all I want; but I
want to make love to you – not just with my hands and with
my body, but with my mind, my heart, in everything I say and
do. Every moment we are apart it hurts, you know? I thought
we had something special between us.'

'We do,' I said.

'But not love,' he interjected.

I did not know what to say. I could not say, 'I love you.' Not
in the same way that I had said it to John – or even Charles,
although I was less certain in my love for him. Stanislaw was
not like any man I had ever met. He was extraordinary, and his
friendship enriched and enlightened me. It made me happy to

be in his company – and making love, I had recently discovered, was not a problem! However, the certainty was not there; and love without certainty was useless. I had to love him back with the same degree of passion that he felt for me. In my marriage to Charles the love had been unequal, and the marriage was a disaster. I would not have that happen again. Even if I had room in my life for another relationship, which I most certainly did not.

'No,' I said, 'I can't love you like you want.'

'All I want is to be allowed to love you, Ellie. You are the great love of my life.'

'I can't let you do that, Stan,' I said.

'Why not?' he asked.

I didn't answer him, because I did not know why. All I knew was that the idea of it sent me into such a panic that I simply grabbed my truck keys off the top of the piano and ran out of the door.

CHAPTER TWENTY-EIGHT

It was barely lunchtime when I got back. Freddie would be working and he had arranged to drop Leo off at the studio, where he was attending a song-and-dance class. Although his contract was yet to be renewed, Leo was still in the care of the studio and attending classes there. I was happy enough that he had some structure to his days until I decided what was to be done with regard to us returning to New York in September. I would, in all likelihood, have to find a new school for him, and he would probably have to be held back a year, due to all this movie palaver. I already had Maureen investigating day schools in the city that might cater for both boys.

I was expecting to find Bridie alone in the house, so I entered with some trepidation, fearing the old woman might intuit what I had been 'up to'. She had a sixth sense for immoral behaviour, especially from me.

Instead of Bridie, Tom was sitting on the sofa in his pyjamas, lifting spoonfuls of jam with his fingers directly from the jar onto slices of bread.

'What on earth are you doing, Tom?'

'Eating breakfast,' he said, as if this were an everyday occurrence.

'Why aren't you in school?'

'Bridie said I didn't have to go today.'

'What do you mean?'

'She said it was Mr Flannery's birthday – and we were having a party.'

Oh Jesus! Mr Flannery had been dead for fifteen years.

'Where is she?' I said, rushing from the kitchen to her bedroom. She was gone.

'She said Mr Flannery was coming on the train and she was going to meet him. She said to wait here, like a good boy, until they got back and then we'd have cake.'

Oh, good God in heaven, how had I not seen this coming?

'She didn't make a cake. She usually makes a cake when it's somebody's birthday. I asked if she'd made a cake and she said she had . . . '

My head was fit to explode. Where the hell had Bridie gone? What was going on?

' . . . but I looked everywhere and I couldn't find one, so I don't think—'

'SHUT UP!' I shouted at him. Tom immediately started to cry.

'Oh, I'm sorry, Tom, I'm sorry.' I grabbed him and put his head to my chest. The poor child wasn't even dressed. He knew something was wrong. 'I just need to think.'

This was as bad as when Leo disappeared – maybe worse, because Bridie was old. I tapped my forehead with my fist: how had I not seen this coming?

'How long ago did Bridie leave?' I asked Tom.

He shrugged and wriggled out of my hold.

'Okay. Now, you go and get dressed, there's a good boy, then we'll go and find Bridie.'

Tom was mad at me, for shouting at him, and probably for leaving him alone with Bridie that morning, having abandoned him the day before as well. I kept trying to do the right thing, yet I kept upsetting everyone around me.

I guessed that Bridie might have been gone for two hours, three at the most. How far could she have got? She wasn't fast on her feet, she certainly didn't drive and I was not sure she would even know how to hail a taxi in Los Angeles. The roads were wide and long and the pavements narrow. This was not a city with complicated street networks; she could only have gone in one direction or the other, and Hollywood was not a walker's town – it was a driver's town. I was sure to find her in a car. I decided to get out and look for her straight away. I could stop into a cop-shop and report her missing if I had no luck driving around, looking for her myself. I was reluctant to call on our neighbours, because I did not want to invade Bridie's privacy by letting them know she had gone 'wandering'. She was a proud woman – and I was proud on her behalf. I had known Bridie since I was little more than a child myself and I had yet to meet a stronger, more reliable, more steadfast person. If her mind had weakened with age, along with her body, that was nobody's business but her own – and now mine; the least I could do was keep it that way. I was terrified, but I knew I had to stay calm.

As soon as Tom was dressed, I put him into the front seat of the truck.

'Keep an eye out now for Bridie,' I said.

'Is she lost?' he asked.

'Yes,' I said. 'A little lost.'

I realized that was exactly how I felt myself – a little lost. I wished to hell that Freddie and Leo were here to help me, or Stan (although as soon as his name entered my head I pushed it away). Searching for Bridie with a seven-year-old child was not exactly ideal. I made a quick decision to turn left, toward Los Feliz village – that would be Bridie's first instinct. As reached the turn for the shops I stopped to let a streetcar past. A tram! It was as if I had never seen one before. Bridie could have hopped on a tram and be on the other side of the city by now. She could have gone to Union Station looking for her dead husband. On the other hand, she could have got on *any* tram, believing it was going to Union Station, and ended up anywhere.

A bus pulled up beside me and the driver signalled wildly for me to make up my mind which way I was turning. I was signalling right, but what was the point now? I turned left and the traffic beeped loudly. As I turned, all I could see were street turnings off the main road, and down them more street turnings, and dozens more leading off them. Street after street, buses and trams; I imagined going up and down each and every one. This city was a lot more complex than I had realized, and Bridie was infinitely more lost than I had first thought. I could sense my whole body swell with panic. What was I going to do? Who was going to find her, if not me? Even the police wouldn't have the first idea where to look. People got lost and died on the streets in cities like this. Why had I not seen this coming? How could I have been so . . .

'Hey, Mrs Hogan! Look who I just found wandering up St George Street!'

It was Freddie. Sitting next to him in his car was Bridie, her face pure stone beneath her good Sunday hat, her two hands gripped round the handles of her handbag, which sat firmly on her lap.

'I was not wandering, I was shopping,' she said. 'This vagabond wrestled me into his car against my will. Let me out at once.'

'Of course,' Freddie said. As he helped her into the truck, Tom hopped down and Freddie lifted him into the back. I got out for a moment on the pretence of helping him.

'I was showing a house,' Freddie said, once he was out of

Bridie's earshot, 'and I'm out on the front lawn showing th
prospective buyers the front aspect, when I see Bridie comin
up to my left – walking down the middle of the road! Thr
cars veered around her just while I was looking. She was luck
she didn't get killed, or get somebody else killed. She gave m
an awful time getting her into the car. Oh, and even though
told the buyers she was my dear old grandma, I lost the sal
Actually, I think that was *why* I lost the sale. I'll tell ya – fo
an old lady, Bridie sure has got some fruity language. Coupl
things I never heard before – and I've been around.'

I was so relieved to have Bridie back that I didn't questio
him further.

We travelled the few hundred yards or so back to the hou
in silence, went inside and Bridie took her coat off and set abo
making Tom the cake she had promised him earlier.

There was no mention of Mr Flannery or birthdays or Unic
Station. I did not question or chide her, but pretended ever
thing was as it had always been. She was in the devil of a moc
for the rest of that afternoon until she realized that I was goir
to go along with her.

There was no sense in humiliating her with questions or procl.
mations that she was sick. I knew what was happening to n
old friend, and I could see by the defensive stance she was takir
that she knew it too.

All the time I had known her, Bridie and I had been brutal
honest with each other in our daily dealings, but the most impo
tant truths were always left unspoken. That was our way. Brid
would criticize my cooking and my choice of lovers. She nev
made a secret of her dislike of Charles, or the bad decision
made in marrying him. Often, she was right. Then there we:
the things we had never spoken of: my depression after the dea
of my first husband; the way we were both barren and chil

less; the state of poverty that I had rescued her from after her own husband died. These were the unmentionable truths; the sorrows and shame too deep for words.

If the woman who was the closest thing I had to a mother was losing her mind, well then, she deserved to be protected from that fact. I would shield her from the truth and make her life as comfortable as I could. It was my duty now to look after her. Did I relish the thought? No. I was not a saint. I was an ordinary woman who had struggled with authority in my life, but never with my conscience. Sometimes my conscience steered me in the wrong direction, as it had done with Suri, but in this instance I knew I was right. I would look after Bridie now for the rest of her life, whatever it took; she was as much my responsibility as my sons were. I would have to manage my own life and the children's lives around her. We might have to stay in Los Angeles instead of returning to New York, as I still wished. I would have to make some sacrifices. This might go on for as long a time as I could imagine – Bridie could even outlive me.

This relatively harmless domestic incident, which had taken place over less than an hour of my life one afternoon, had nonetheless signalled a change in my life that was so huge I could barely contemplate it.

That morning I had made love to a man for the first time since my husband died. That had seemed important, and yet – Stan had been right. Lovemaking was unimportant; it is what we are prepared to give of our time and our heart and our mind that is important. That afternoon, as I praised Bridie's cake and wrote 'SALT' on the jar next to the stove, I pledged to give all of that to her.

Late that night Tom crawled into the bed next to me. He curled his legs across mine and snuggled into me, by way of letting me know that all was forgiven for shouting at him earlier. 'Mr Flannery's dead, isn't he?' Tom said.

'Yes, love,' I replied, 'he is, but Bridie forgets that sometimes and thinks he's alive. That's what happens when you love people.'

'My daddy's dead and I don't think he's alive. Not even in heaven.'

He said it really quietly, like he didn't want me to hear it. What could I say to him? Tom was a child who believed that heaven was here on Earth. He was visceral, pragmatic. He got an impossible joy from flowers and animals, and the miraculous boundings of his own small body and the adventures it took him on. I talked about God and angels and heaven, but he had always struggled with the concept. I had always believed in God, but I had come to see my faith, such as it was, less as a conviction that He existed, and more as a piece of good luck that I had been born more guileless than my poor grieving son.

'I know, my love,' I said. I held him close and stroked his forehead, as I had done since he was an infant, and soothed him.

When he was asleep I looked down at him. I loved my sons more than anything in the world, and I remembered what Stan had said: 'All I want is to be allowed to love you.' For a moment I allowed myself the idea that it might be wonderful to have somebody love me as much as I loved them. Then I realized that I had to get up and lock the front door, so that Bridie could not 'escape' in the night, and the thought was gone.

CHAPTER TWENTY-NINE

Our family fell into a routine over the coming months. Tom went to school, Leo carried on going to the studio (despite waiting for his contract to be renewed, his tutors were happy for him to continue attending general classes) and I started painting again.

Things carried on much as normal, except that Bridie became increasingly absent-minded and, sometimes, confused. Her lapses could be as small as putting a saucepan of water on to boil when none was needed, or as heartbreaking as pouring an extra cup of tea and saying it was for her mother. Bridie had left Ireland when she was sixteen and had never returned. Over the years I had known her, she had rarely talked about her childhood, but now she seemed eager to share stories from her past with me.

My favourite was the story of the bold donkey, and she told it to Tom and me over and over again.

'My aunt, my mother's sister, lived next door to us and she made the best butter in Cork. She supplied half the county, and had a big butter churn . . . '

'How big was it?' Tom asked.

'Huge,' she'd say.

'Bigger than a big bucket?'

'A bucket? Whisht, child – as big as this room it was!'

'How did she churn it?'

'Ah, now then, here it is,' Bridie would say. Tom knew what was coming and he'd shrug his shoulders and settle into the corner of the chair, thrilled to be hearing it again. 'With a donkey!'

'A donkey?' Tom would say, and would sometimes wink at me. He thought this was all a game; and sometimes, I'm sure, Bridie knew she had told the story a dozen times already, and sometimes I could tell that she thought she was telling it for the first time. Either way, it didn't matter – it was a wonderful story.

'The churn was so big that the donkey would be yoked up to it and would walk round and round and turn the handle. If he stopped, my aunt would whack him on his rump with a big stick.'

'On his *what*?'

'Tom! Stop that!'

(My son was trying to lure Bridie into saying 'arse', which she had done once before when telling the story. Bridie's language was slipping south, and while my sons found it amusing and would try and goad her into using bad language, I found it impossibly sad, given the sort of respectable woman she was. However, occasionally, when I saw the joy she got from making Tom laugh, I wondered if the childlike, fun-loving figure that was increasingly emerging from my fierce old friend wasn't as much Bridie as the old harridan I had come to love.)

'That donkey hated churning that churn, and when he was done he would run straight down to the bottom field, as far away as he could from the farm buildings, where he could stand and chew on grass and brambles for as long as he liked. Until a few days later, when he'd have to turn the churn again.'

That was the difficulty of living with Bridie in those first few months after her disappearance: not knowing which way she would go. I did not want to get a doctor in to see her. I did not want to frighten her. In those early stages I did not even want her to know there was anything wrong. There was no need. This was old age, and Bridie's mind was giving up on her before her body. I don't know what trade-off she would have chosen to make; we never discussed such things. I only knew that I would have sacrificed every physical facility I had, if I could go to the grave with a sharp brain.

Leaving Bridie alone in the house after that incident was not an option, and there was a great deal of juggling between Freddie and me (he was the only other 'adult' in the house I could confide in), with regard to keeping the house running smoothly. Bridie cooked, and hung washing, and went about as many of her chores as she normally did – but she needed a constant eye kept on her. The occasional hanging up of wet washing in the wardrobe, or forgetting to put the heat on under a pot of spuds, was easily managed; but if she were to wander out onto the road again, or scald herself by pouring boiling water on the floor instead of down the sink, that would be on my head.

Before I realized that the lock on the side gate was not fully secured, the doorbell rang unexpectedly and I answered it to find a neighbour, Susan, from a few doors down, standing there with her arm firmly hooked through Bridie's.

'I think Mrs Flannery forgot her key,' she said.

Susan was a trained nurse who had given up work to stay at home and look after her mother-in-law, who had recently passed away.

'You'd think I'd be glad she was gone,' she confided in me over coffee, 'she gave us an awful time in the end – but I miss her. Miss the work, to be honest with you. I'd go back to the hospital, but Dan's old-fashioned like that. Doesn't like me working outside the home.'

'Would he let you come here for a few hours? I could use a hand, and I'll pay you well,' I said.

'Pay me anything and I'd be happy, Ellie. I'd love that,' she said. 'And him? He won't mind – as long as he doesn't know I'm earning money outside the home, and as long as he thinks I'm suffering looking after other folks, he's happy!'

So Susan came round whenever I needed her. It was easy to make the excuse to Bridie that Susan was simply calling in to keep her company while I ran an errand.

At other times I would ask her to sit with Bridie so that I could lose myself in my painting for a few hours, without worrying if there was anything going on in the other room. Susan came those days on the pretence that she wanted Bridie to help her improve her knitting, although she was already competent. As a result, Bridie took up the pins herself and showed a remarkable level of concentration – knitting for hours on end; although she rarely produced anything more complex than a long scarf, it was a relief for her to find a pastime that involved mostly sitting down in the one place, where she was at no risk of any harm.

My painting had started to take off again. Perhaps it was the concentration of being in the house most of the time, and the lack of anything else to do, but I just stopped worrying about what I was producing, if it was any good and whether my muse had left me, and started simply putting paint on canvas. It was not my best work and there was certainly nothing I felt happy about sending to Hilla (if she hadn't written me off entirely by now), but I experimented with some ideas around my views of the desert, and even tried to capture some images of Ireland from memory. On a whim I painted a small canvas with a traditional scene of Ireland: rolling green hills, separated by stone walls, and a small white cottage. It was a close depiction of the

house I had shared with my first husband, John; his family home-
stead. It was the very type of representative picture that I normally
despised, but I indulged myself nonetheless and gave it as a gift
to Bridie, who was thrilled and declared that, at last, I was
producing some 'proper' art that she could appreciate. She got
Freddie to hang it in a prominent position above the mantel-
piece and showed it to everyone who came into the house, to
'prove' what a great artist I was.

I also, finally, finished my painting of Suri.

I had covered it up after our terrible scene and put it in a
corner of the room. One morning I just decided to face her
again.

I had a nasty *Dorian Gray* moment of fear, but when I pulled
back the cloth and saw Suri's face, I was surprised only by how
beautiful and serene she looked. It was a risk calling on Jackson
after our last conversation, but I knew that this painting belonged
to him – not to me. I made a few small adjustments and left it
to dry for two days, before leaving Susan in charge of Bridie
and packing the picture carefully in the back of the truck.

As I knocked on the door, the canvas propped at my side with
a loose cloth hanging from it, barely touching the paint, I had
a moment of dread. Suppose Jackson got angry with me again
and turned me away. Then I pulled myself together and thought,
What if he does? Looking after Bridie had given me a strange
confidence in myself. I was a good person, and I knew that now.
I may have acted stupidly in the past, but it was always with
the best of intentions. This painting was a gift to Jackson and,
if he didn't like it, well then, he could do what he liked with it.

However, he was delighted to see me and gratifyingly moved
by the painting.

'It's still a bit wet,' I said as I carefully picked off the sheet,
'but ready to hang, if you're happy with it unframed.'

'I'll get it framed,' he said straight away. He was gazing at his wife's face. 'It's beautiful,' he said.

'Well,' I was uncomfortable when people admired my work in front of me. I liked a detached, professional opinion, but awe and appreciative emotion around my work made me squirm, for some reason. 'Suri is a very beautiful woman,' I said. 'I'm glad you like it.'

Thankfully he didn't wax lyrical, but simply asked, 'Have you time for tea?'

We sat and talked as if nothing unpleasant had ever happened between us. He gave me news of Suri and her in-laws. They were all living together in a small, one-room house and, by the sounds of it, had fixed it up into some kind of a home.

'Suri is very creative,' he said, 'she can make a home anywhere, out of anything.'

When he spoke of her, he nodded at the picture as if it was her, and I found myself doing the same.

When the subject of Suri was exhausted and there was still tea left in my cup, I found myself asking, 'How's Stan?'

As soon as I asked I wished I hadn't.

Stan had not called me since the day we had made love, nor I him. Enough weeks had passed to call it an estrangement, but I had decided that it was up to him to call me – although obviously he thought it was the other way round. He didn't know about Bridie, or that I was painting again. I missed him, but if he cared, he would call.

'Oh, he's *gre-eat*,' Jackson said, 'he met this *gre-eat* woman.'

Not simply great, but *gre-eat*. Two of them – and a 'woman'.

'How great . . .' I said.

Except, of course, I couldn't leave it at that. Although, as it turned out, there was no need. Clearly this woman was so *gre-eat* that Jackson was happy to volunteer information all about her.

'Not his usual type at all – you know how Stan has this extraordinary reputation for bedding all those beautiful young blonde actresses?'

No, I did not know that; but I just nodded and smiled, trying to keep my teeth nicely apart. *No wonder he's so popular*, I thought, *if he's servicing half the starlets in Hollywood!*

'Well, this woman – Marjorie – is not his usual type at all. She's not so young (around your age, I guess), but really elegant and beautiful, plus she's smart, and funny. She's a screenwriter, not an actress. Beauty and brains: I think he might actually settle down. He seems pretty serious about her.'

'Well, that's just *gre-eat* to hear,' I said, '*do* be sure to send him my best.' And I got up to leave.

Jackson walked me to the door and waved me off, as I got into my truck and drove round the corner. There, as soon as I was out of sight, I pulled over, turned off the engine and started to shake with anger.

I did not even know where to begin being offended. Every word Jackson had said about Stan had seared itself into my brain as clearly as if he had written it into my flesh.

First, Stan had deliberately hidden from me his reputation as a womanizer. Second, he had given me to believe that I was a special woman – an exception to his rule, a one-off; yet here he was, dating a woman who did not sound so very unlike me at all. Except for the offensive way that Jackson had implied that *she* was elegant, and smart and funny; even though she had the crippling misfortune of being the same age as me, she was no drudge.

I was beyond furious. What a vile, deceiving little man he was! I was well shot of him.

I took a deep breath and started the pickup again. I had a family to look after, I had people relying on me – I did not have time for all this nonsense and I was better than all this; I was better than *him*.

At the same time as my anger was pumping through me, I could not help but feel a deep sadness at the back of it – a dream fading; the scent of perfume snatched by a desert wind.

CHAPTER THIRTY

We read about the red-carpet opening for *Five Graves to Cairo* in the paper, but were not invited. Leo was upset, but optimistic. Freddie assured us there was nothing to worry about and that it was no big thing.

'Nah! Those events are all for show. They make the stars go – it's written into their contracts that they have to go. It's a tacky business. Who wants to walk down a red carpet with all those photographers and press hanging off you – all that fuss?'

I certainly don't, I thought, *but I'm pretty sure the rest of you would give your eye teeth for the chance.* I had a bad feeling about it, but Freddie's story worked for Leo, which was the main thing, and so, with great excitement, we left Bridie at home with Susan and headed off as a family to watch Leo's big-screen performance.

Freddie made us get all dressed up, as if it were a real event, and we filled our laps with popcorn and candy. Leo was like a child again, giggling and wondering out loud how far along in the film his scene would be. As the lights went down and the titles flashed up in front of us, I squeezed my son's arm and had to admit that, despite my trepidation about his film career, I was beyond excited at the prospect of seeing him on the cinema screen.

After the first twenty minutes Leo touched my arm and said, 'I think my bit is on soon.' Ten minutes later I felt my son shift in his seat, his mood tightening. 'I should have been on now,' he said. 'Freddie, I think that was my scene – where am I? Freddie, where am I?' he repeated.

Freddie was uncharacteristically silent.

'I'm sure you'll be on in a minute,' I said.

'Shhhh,' a man behind us muttered.

I knew Leo wouldn't be on now, and that the moment in the movie had passed without him, because he had spent months telling us all about the scene he was in, in minute detail. A terrible dread passed over me for every further minute that my son did not appear onscreen.

The film was exactly ninety-six minutes long and we watched it to the bitter end. Freddie's face was like a stone; he was afraid to look at me, and just chewed on cigarette after cigarette. Even Tom picked up on the dreadful atmosphere. After I whispered furiously at him to stop asking when Leo would be on, he got up from his seat, bought some more popcorn and moved to another empty seat, away from his weird, cringing family. We might have walked out, but all of us were paralysed with disappointment, and sitting there watching the whole film was at least a way to delay facing the terrible truth; in any case, as long as the images flickered on the screen there was a chance that Leo could suddenly appear before us. He didn't. I spent the last ten minutes of the film girding myself for the onslaught, and thinking of how to put a positive spin on it for both the boys, hoping that Leo might, at least, appear in the credits. We sat through the speedy scroll of a thousand names, searching for Leo Irvington – but even then there was nothing.

All that time and energy wasted. My son's dream shattered.

As soon as we got outside, Freddie threw down his cigarette

and immediately lit another. 'I can't believe they cut Leo. I can't believe it!'

Leo, however, was amazingly calm.

'I'm disappointed – I really thought I gave a good perform-ance – but you know what? That's the film business; it's tough, and I had better get used to it.'

His mature attitude frightened me more than any tantrum, because it indicated to me, again, that Leo was deadly serious about becoming an actor – a decision that my months living here had done nothing to suggest would lead to a wholesome or fulfilling career path.

In any case his philosophical stance was soon shot when, less than a week later, he got official word that his contract was not going to be renewed.

Leo was beside himself – and screamed out as if in actual physical pain when he tore open the letter and read its contents. (A reaction far more immediate, I guiltily noted, than when his father had died, although, as his mother, I could not help but believe that one thing had led to the other.)

He rushed around the house, screaming and banging surfaces, until I was afraid for all of us. Unable to soothe him, I rang Freddie, who rushed home from work to be with him.

'My life is over,' Leo wailed, 'I will never work again.'

'There are other studios,' Freddie reassured him – but Leo was bereft.

Until now he had believed that the only thing standing between him and a future as a 'Hollywood movie star' was his mother. I was easily pushed aside, but now he had been rejected by the very people that he was counting on to believe in him.

'I'm going to call Universal,' Freddie said. 'They'll love you – of course they will. I know one of the guys in the editing suite at Paramount. We'll get your scenes from him. I'll get a show-reel cut. Never say never, Leo – this show ain't over yet.'

I could tell from the clip in Freddie's voice that he was not entirely certain that was true.

As I watched my distraught son pace the room, then collapse with dramatic anguish, I realized something. It was my prerogative as Leo's mother to pour cold water on his dreams, as I had attempted to do, in the name of common sense and out of my duty to secure him a good future. But – and the three-letter word began to ring as loudly in my head as a fire alarm – BUT no *other* force was going to stand in the way of my son's dream. Cut him out of their film? How dare they! Refuse to renew his contract? By letter? Who the hell did these people think they were?

'I'm going in to see them,' I said, grabbing the letter from the kitchen table and checking the name of the snivelling little bureaucrat who had sent it. 'This is ridiculous – they can't do this to you, Leo. You are too talented and you have worked too hard. I am going up there now to sort this out . . . '

I went out to the hall and pulled a tailored jacket on over my shoulders to smarten myself up, then hurriedly grabbed my lipstick from the hall stand.

'Leo, you go and get Susan – *now*! Tell her it's an emergency and ask if she can come in right away. Freddie? You stay here until she arrives.'

'Mrs Hogan . . . '

'Susan won't be long, Freddie, she only lives a few doors down, and then you'll be able to get back to work . . . '

'Mrs Hogan – Ellie!'

His voice was so sharp that it stopped me, and I turned back to see what the fuss was about.

Freddie moved forward and gently took my arm; both he and Leo were looking at me as if I were quite mad.

'I don't think you should go to the studio, Mrs H. What's the point?'

'Well, to get them to renew Leo's contract.'

'And how are you going to do that?'

His tone wasn't accusatory or even sarcastic, and I realized that the young man was simply trying to reason with me.

This was the same impulsive line as my going to 'rescue' Suri – and it would surely have the same disastrous result.

'Well, what *can* we do, Freddie? This is not fair. We have to do something.'

Freddie shrugged. 'Hollywood is all about who you know, Mrs Hogan – and I know a lot of people, but to be honest, I'm all out of love right now. I've played every card at Paramount and, to tell you the truth, I can't think what we can do now. I've played all my cards . . . ' Then, looking at Leo's crestfallen expression, he added, 'We can try Universal – and I think we *should* – but . . . '

I didn't like the 'but'.

'You've got to have an "in", a name. You've got to know one of the big boys – and I don't mean know them like I know them, a handshake at a party. You've got to know them personally, know them like *friends.*'

Freddie looked at me and I knew what he was thinking, and he knew that I knew what he was thinking, but he was smart enough to leave it at that.

I hated Stan. I thought he was a deceitful, disgusting weasel of a man. For all I knew, he was having sex with pneumatic blondes, then coming straight over to eat food at my table and play nice-guy with my sons. Over the next day and night I could see

Freddie looking at me, wondering, willing me to contact him. Leo, thank goodness, never made the connection. As his mother, my role was always going to be one of a useless nag. I could not possibly do anything, or know anyone, who could actually help him. Except for Stan.

I did not want to telephone Stan, I did not want to call at his house. But as much as I didn't want to do those things, I wanted to help my son more.

'I'm going to ask Stan if he can help get another contract for Leo,' I said to Freddie when we were on our own.

'You're making the right decision,' he said, before I had barely got the sentence out. 'You wanna call him now?'

If I was going to humiliate myself in this way, throw myself on Stan's mercy, beg for his help, then I had to give myself the best possible chance of it working, and it was too easy for him to say 'no' over the telephone.

'I'll call up to the house,' I said.

'I'll drive you,' Freddie said, already reaching for his keys.

'Give me half an hour,' I replied.

There was no harm in getting all dressed up and letting Stan have one last look at what he was missing out on. In any case, I was curious about this woman of his; maybe she would be there for me to cast my eye over. I wanted to satisfy myself that I had made the right decision in turning down Stan's – cheap and insincere – offer of love. As I pulled out a suitably elegant outfit, I reminded myself that I was going to ask him to help my son, and that was the only – the *only* – reason for seeing him.

Freddie was waiting to drive me up, hopping from side to side at the front door, dangling his keys nervously. He was too anxious for my success; his presence would put too much pressure on me.

'Freddie,' I said, 'you need to leave this to me now.'

'I'm only driving you up there, Mrs H.'

'No, Freddie,' I said, putting my foot down, in my best assertive-mammy voice. 'I want you to go off about your ordinary work now, and carry on as if none of this is happening. You've too much invested in this, and you're putting us all on edge. Nerves will do none of us any favours. Leave this matter to me. It's delicate, and I promise I will let you know how I get on, and if – and I do say *if* – Stan can help us. Freddie opened his mouth to object, but I said, 'I am not going anywhere or doing anything while you are standing in front of me looking angsty. Go. To. Work.'

As soon as Freddie left, I called a cab.

I decided that I didn't want Stan's girlfriend to see me arrive in the pickup. The journey was short, but as we pulled up outside the house I realized that taking a cab had been a stupid thing to do, because it meant I was stuck there and would not be able to get back.

'Come back in half an hour?' I asked the driver as I was paying.

'Dream on, lady,' he said, taking off.

Stan must have heard the car because he was waiting at the door. He looked sheepish, as if he didn't want to ask me in. After what Jackson had told me, I assumed he had a woman in the house, and immediately formed a barbed comment in my head. Before I let it out I made myself remember that I was *not* here to make barbed comments, but to help my son get another contract with Paramount.

'I've come to ask for your help, Stan,' I said.

'Would you like to come in?' he said, but did not move his body to one side or simply go in and let me follow, as he normally did. There was someone in there.

'No,' I said. Although I was *longing* to get a look, I didn't want anything to distract me from the business in hand. 'I can't stay – there is just some matter I was hoping you could help me with.'

'Anything, Ellie,' he said, 'you know I'll help you any way I can.'

It was gone: the way a man who loves you pledges himself with every small request. The words were similar, but the meaning was so very, very different – 'I would do anything for you' had become 'I'll help you any way I can'.

Words of friendship and patronage, rather than those of love and passion. I took a deep breath, ready to make my case.

'Paramount have not renewed Leo's contract and . . . '

' . . . you want me to have a word in somebody's ear?'

I had not thought it would be that easy, or rather I had forgotten that this would be the easy part of seeing Stan again.

'Yes, if you don't—'

'Sure. No problem,' he said. 'I know the head of casting – he's a good friend. I'll have a word. Anything else?'

He was dismissing me! Going back inside to his elegant-not-frumpy writer friend, or maybe one of his many young blonde lovers.

'No, thank you Stan, although . . . ?' I needed a lift back to my house.

'Stanislaw?'

I gasped inwardly. The idea that he had a woman in there, and was possibly making love to a woman when I called at the door, had been an indignant suspicion of mine, more than an actual belief.

'Are you coming back in?' the woman called.

'I have company,' he said apologetically.

'So I see,' I answered, trying to keep the prim, horrified tone out of my voice.

'Well, if there's nothing else, Ellie?'

'No,' I said, 'there's nothing else,' then added, 'thank you again, Stan. For helping Leo.'

I wanted to spit in his face, scream at him and give him a good, hard kick in the shins. I felt so humiliated, so hurt. He had been playing me all along, pretending to love me when he was sleeping with all these other women. Amusing himself with the respectable Irishwoman until it was time to have his way with the others.

I walked and walked, down the Hollywood Hills, past the vast mansions perched in this cruel, vertiginous landscape. The roads were narrow and so steep that my legs took on a life of their own, staggering down them. How did people even get the trucks with building materials up here? It seemed impossible, but nothing was impossible here. Money could buy you anything, and it had bought my friend Stan love.

Stan said that he was in love with me, yet he was with other women now – so quickly – and probably had been the whole time I knew him. Why did I care? I was not in love with him; I had too many other responsibilities. In any case, I had loved and lost twice (to death, no less) and had neither the time nor the inclination to love again.

Yes, I felt bereft at his rejection of me. Gradually, as I tripped down the narrow hills, my anger turned to hurt. Although I knew there was no logical reason for it, I felt betrayed, and by the time I reached Sunset and called for a cab, a sadness as deep as loss had settled into me.

Chapter Thirty-One

Bridie's condition was deteriorating. I took over all of the house-keeping, much of which meant undoing perceived chores that Bridie had done, such as clearing items from every surface in the house and putting them into the trash-can, or festooning the bathroom with toilet paper before calling me in to admire the decorations.

It was hard, but Freddie helped me to shield the kids from the full extent of what was happening to their dear nan, and having Susan close by was a godsend.

It was only after Bridie tripped on the back step and cut her hand quite badly that I called in a doctor. He diagnosed her with dementia and said she would only get worse. He recommended that I send her to a home nearby – 'a kind of hospital for people in her state' was the way he described it, but, although he assured me it was a very good place 'of its type', there was no way I was sending my Bridie away.

'In Ireland we look after our own,' I told Susan when she gave me the despairing look of a nurse worried that I would not be able to cope. What I didn't tell her was that my beloved mother-in-law in Ireland, Maidy, had died without me, her only surviving relative. I was assured that the woman who had been more or less a mother to me since childhood had died peacefully, in the care of kind neighbours and friends. Nonetheless I still experienced residual guilt, and had long since vowed that I would never leave anyone belonging to me behind again, to die without me. Bridie had looked after me, one way or another, since I was a young emigrant ingénue from rural Ireland to Jazz Age New York. A dignified old age was her due, and there was no place to die with more dignity than at home with the people who love you. If only I could keep her in the house, and operating within the bounds of human dignity, which, with every passing week, was becoming harder.

It seemed that, for the time being at least, I was resigned to staying in Los Angeles. Conor and Dan had been looking after my cabin on Fire Island and calling regularly, to keep me updated and check when I planned to return to them.

The last time they called was late spring, when the season had been just coming into full swing.

'If you like, Ellie, we can find tenants for the cabin for the season?'

The Island was becoming more and more popular with each passing year, and Conor and Dan found their small home crammed with guests every weekend from May to October. They could, I knew, fill my cabin ten times over, with friends from the mainland. I had been reluctant to tell them to go ahead until now. I did not want to close off the option of going back there – even temporarily.

'Sure,' I said, 'just until October, right?'

There was no way I could get back before then, but even so it hurt to say it out loud. To admit to myself that my Fire Island days were, for the time being at least, all but over.

'All back to normal – it'll be ready for you and the boys again this time next year.'

Even as they said it, in some little part of me I knew it wasn't true. My life of art and solitude seemed a million miles away from the bustling chaos that I now found myself living in.

Crystal's producer 'friend' had kicked her out and she had ended up moving in with us, as well as Freddie – the two of them sharing the 'studio' bedroom, thereby putting a final end to any hopes that I had of painting.

She arrived on my doorstep while Freddie was at work, flinging herself at my chest and all but engulfing me with her sobbing and drama. She insisted that she had left the producer of her own volition because he had 'passed me over for so many parts. And, Ellie,' she said, breathless with the injustice of it, 'he said I couldn't *act*. Can you imagine? That he had only taken me in because I had a pretty face!'

I immediately thought, *I doubt it was your face he was interested in*, but then I reprimanded myself. *Don't be a cynical cow, Ellie, she's obviously in some kind of trouble – even if it is of her own making. Let her stay for a couple of nights.*

So I took Crystal in – for pity's sake, but mostly for Freddie who, for reasons best known to himself, still adored her.

A few days after she had arrived, the house being as crowded as it was, I walked in on Crystal as she was getting dressed in my bedroom. She was applying make-up to her arms, which seemed a strange thing to do. She didn't see me and, as I moved closer to the bed, I saw that her forearm was covered in really nasty-looking welts.

'Jesus Christ, Crystal, what happened?'

'Nothing.' She flinched when she noticed me, as if she had been hit, then blushed and looked immediately as if she might cry. 'An . . . an insect bit me. It's nothing.'

'Let me have a look.'

Reluctantly she gave me her arm. Those marks were from no

insect, of that I was certain. They were man-made, although I had no idea how such angry-looking contusions could have been caused, and neither did I have any desire to know. Some men were cruel and did strange things, I knew that much just from my time on this Earth. Thankfully, that was as much as I knew; Crystal had not been so lucky.

'Make-up is one of the worst things you can put on that,' I said, 'you need to clean up those wounds first, in case they become infected.'

She looked down when I said the word 'wound'.

'It's nothing, don't fuss,' she said, but I went to the bathroom anyway and got some cotton wool and a small bowl with anti-septic lotion diluted in warm water. 'It's an allergy,' she called out to me.

As I walked back in, I could see her face tightening as she gathered together a new story. As I dabbed at the sickeningly uniform welts, I felt myself baulking at the thought of how this might have happened. Crystal's pride told me this was probably the tip of the iceberg, and it felt wrong even to be forming a thought or speculating on the kind of abhorrent behaviour that this was the result of.

'I have *very* sensitive skin, you see,' she said, her voice shaking and high-pitched with the effort of keeping it steady. 'The curse of being beautiful, my mother said.'

If her mother had actually known what had happened to her . . . if, indeed, the waif even had a mother, which I doubted. Otherwise, how the hell did Crystal get into this mess?

'Are there any more?' I asked. She shook her head. 'Are you sure, Crystal?'

And very quietly, barely audibly, she whispered, 'No.' Her eyes were bulging with tears. She'd said that word before I noticed that she was sitting at a strange angle, as if she might be in pain.

As I gently lifted the back of her blouse she did not move away, but released a silent sob of shame. I felt sick. Her back was a mass of the same strange welts and uniform circles. Cigarette burns. I had never seen skin singed with a cigarette burn before – why would I? Yet they were immediately recognizable. Some of them had scabbed; others were weeping and in the early stages of infection.

'Bastard!'

I said it as quietly as her 'No', and with as much reserve as I could muster. My anger and indignation would only add to the poor girl's pain.

However, I could not help but shake my head and say, 'He should be in jail – you should go to the cops.'

Even as I said it, I knew how ridiculous it sounded: a blonde starlet bringing charges against a movie producer in Hollywood? The very idea was ridiculous. Crystal wanted a part in his films, and this abuse was the payoff. She could have got lucky and found herself under the wing of a charming lover with simple tastes; as it was, she had hooked up with a vile sadist. Both men would be as influential as the other, and as respectable in the eyes of the outside world. Their differing sexual predilections were a matter for nobody but themselves.

'He said he'd get me a part; he said . . . ' Crystal was getting distressed.

'Shhhh,' I said, 'no need to explain yourself.'

I tidied away my TCP and reached for some cold cream to soothe the sores, gently smoothing it over her mottled, ruined skin.

'We'll put this on for a few days, and they'll be gone in no time and you can forget all about it.'

'You won't tell Freddie?' she said.

'Of course not, but has he not seen them already?' I asked.

'Not on my back,' she said, 'and I told him they were insect bites on my arm, and he believed me.'

Poor dear Freddie, I thought, although maybe the innocent were those best equipped to survive in this desperate place, after all.

On the day Freddie left there were two large suitcases in the hall, the back seat of his small car was piled with clothes, and another battered old case was tied to the back of the car.

'I don't know how you managed to acquire so much *stuff*,' I exclaimed. *Because you had nothing when you arrived* was on the tip of my tongue, although I didn't say it out loud.

He laughed. 'Most of it belongs to the lady,' he said. By 'lady' he meant Crystal. I bit my tongue.

The letter about Leo's contract being renewed had come through from Paramount less than a week after I had been to see Stan. It was addressed to Mr Leo Irvington, and said there had been a mistake and that they would be delighted to offer him another contract. Leo was thrilled, and I was surprised at how relieved I felt, not just at his joy, but at the contract itself. While he strutted around the house, vindicated by the mistake – 'I thought you were mean, not going to see Stan, Mammy, but look! You were right! There was no need to pull strings, the studio had just made a mistake all along!' – I realized that what I had thought was vanity and childish foolishness was, in fact, my son's heart's desire. When I was his age I had no idea who I was or what I was to become. I knew what I *didn't* want – and that was to take Holy Orders, as my father had assumed I would. I also knew that I loved John Hogan, and I was barely more than Leo's age when I married him. John was my heart's desire – my whole world – but I wondered now whether, had I discovered the artist in me as a young woman, I would have bothered getting married at all?

I realized that Leo was lucky to have discovered his passion for acting so young. It was not what I had pictured for him. Leo was a highly intelligent child – he could have been a doctor or a lawyer and have had an easy, comfortable middle-class life. He was also such a sensitive child, innocent, trusting and easily hurt, that it frightened me to think of him wrestling his way through the tough, competitive world of the movies. I had believed he was carving out a life of hardship for himself, and merely wanted to protect him from it. One evening, after he was happily settled back in the studio, chattering about being cast as the next-big-thing, I said as much to him.

'I worry about you,' I told him. 'I just want you to be happy. Are you happy, Leo?'

'Yes, I am happy, Mam,' he said, 'this is what I want.'

I saw such clarity in Leo's eyes – a certainness that I remembered seeing in his own father, who had also defied his parents as a young man. Charles had worked on the docks, where his father's shipbuilding empire was. His father had wanted him to run the business, and at Leo's age (or maybe younger) had thrown his spoiled, wayward teenager in with the working serfs, to 'harden him up' and teach him the value of an 'honest day's work'. The plan backfired when Charles discovered that he preferred the life of a dockworker to that of a privileged shipping heir, and ended up siding with the men and leading them in the unionization of his family business – all but causing its downfall, in the eyes of his stubborn father.

Everyone – even I – had thought that Charles, for all his good intentions, had caused the split in his family. Looking now at his son, I realized that my own impulses to protect Leo were the same as old man Irvington's; if I were to stand between this young man and his dreams, all I would do was cause the same rift.

Knowing what you want in life – a conviction to do the right thing by yourself, or indeed others – is a gift. I had spent most of my life grabbing opportunities and fighting disasters as they presented themselves to me, without giving any true thought to what I wanted myself. I married John at seventeen because I was in love with him; I rushed to America to earn money when the marriage was not even four years old; became a typist; returned home to Ireland, then stayed; started my businesses, then rushed off to America for a second time as a reaction to my grief over John's sudden death. I started the homeless shelter and the women's cooperative shop not out of any deep conviction, but from a need to escape the pain in my own life by throwing myself into other people's. For all that I loved John, I never relished the role of being his wife, and the one thing I valued in our marriage was the one thing he struggled with – my independence.

The only role I felt certain I was put on Earth to achieve was that of a mother, and God cruelly denied me that gift. When Tom was abandoned into my lap by his own young mother, it seemed a miracle to everyone else, but it did not feel like a miracle to me. Possibly this was another of God's cruel tricks and, any day, his real mother might return to reclaim him. Tom was my sunshine, pure joy and light, but one day the dream might pop and, if it did, the pain would be unbearable, so that the fear of losing him both intensified my love for him and tarnished the freedom of loving him that I should have felt.

Leo was more of a certainty. In marrying his father, I had claimed ownership of this shining young man and of his future. Legally, he was my son and my charge. I had known I was meant to be his mother. I had relished every moment, not just of seeing and helping him reach maturity, but of the certainty of my status as his 'mother'. I was reluctant to let him go, because I loved him, but also because I liked being in charge. I liked being in charge of other people because – and Leo's unerring conviction to be an actor showed me how much this was true – I did not feel entirely in charge of myself.

Leo was an actor like I was an artist. It was who he was. Yet, since the move to LA at least, his conviction to follow his dream had proved stronger than mine. So I realized, eventually, that by standing in the way of Leo and his heart's desire, I had stood in the way of my own dream as well. In order for my son to be free, I had to let him go – but I came to realize that, as his mother, I also had to let him go to achieve the level of freedom that I needed to live my own life.

Crystal gave me a cursory peck on the cheek now, before rushing out and ensconcing herself in the front seat of Freddie's car, beeping the horn at her beau to hurry up. We had undergone a small routine for a few days after I discovered the injuries on her back resulting from the abuse, but I ministered to her silently, as she obviously did not want to discuss the matter further with me. In the past few days Crystal had barely spoken to me, and I guessed it was because she was afraid of my disapproval, or that I might try to interfere with her moving into a house with Freddie. It was as if she believed she had brought the whole thing down on herself, and that her presence in his home might drive this sweet young man to the same kind of cruel behaviour. Or perhaps it was because she was afraid that I would warn Freddie off her. Whatever the case, there was nothing to be achieved by picking over what had happened, so I let her be.

'My baby ain't much of a cook . . . ' Freddie said at the door.

'That's an understatement,' I interjected.

' . . . so I guess I'll be back scrounging for a dinner before too long.'

Freddie had filled out and grown up – with a 'real' job, money in his pocket and his Hollywood-agent plans put away in a file marked 'Dreams'.

So much had changed for him in the few, short months I had known him, and yet how much had changed for me? I would not be here, were it not for Freddie, and the strange set of circumstances that had led him to encourage my son to chase off to Hollywood to become a movie star, and which had me following Leo with such panicky determination. Yet when I looked back at all that had happened in my life, how strange were these circumstances really? Perhaps they were just life happening: sucking you along its path, winding and straight, until you reached some satisfactory destination, settling there for a while. And just when you thought it was safe to relax – *whoosh!* – life's strange circumstances came and grabbed you again.

Freddie had been the cause of my LA movie odyssey, and yet – while it seemed to be over for him – for Leo it was still going on. Freddie leaving us felt like the end of something for us all. For me, it was another person I didn't have to be responsible for any longer. As I stood at the door, straightening his collar and patting his suit jacket and telling him to mind himself, I was not sure if that was a good or a bad thing.

Bridie wandered in from the porch, and Freddie stopped at the door and gave her a cuddle. I watched as the old woman's eyes closed in a reverie of affection, her mouth stretching back into the smile of a delighted child, and I wondered at the mysterious and immense nature of ordinary love.

Chapter Thirty-Two

Leo and I grew close again after Freddie moved out.

Perhaps it was because he no longer had Freddie as his 'minder', or perhaps it was because I had let go of trying to get him back to New York. I also believed that our closeness grew out of Leo beginning to come to terms with his father's death.

One evening my eldest son asked me to help him read a scene from *Henry V*. I thought they were just teaching him rubbish at the studio, how to dress and walk correctly and address people in a fake English accent, like Leslie Howard, so I was delighted that he had come home with something educational. I sat in the chair with Tom at my feet, as Bridie gazed out the window in some distant reverie.

I read Sir Richard Talbot, and he was John Talbot, my son – the scene was a war scene.

'If we both stay, we both are sure to *die*,' I read, smiling down at Tom and raising my eyebrows in mock-fright.

Leo answered me:

> *Then let me stay; and, father, do you fly:*
> *Your loss is great, so your regard should be;*
> *My worth unknown, no loss is known in me.*
> *Upon my death the French can little boast;*
> *In yours they will, in you all hopes are lost.*

Tom was mesmerized by his brother's change in stance, and I had felt a lump gather in my throat from the first line.

> *Flight cannot stain the honour you have won;*
> *But mine it will, that no exploit have done:*
> *You fled for vantage, everyone will swear;*
> *But, if I bow, they'll say it was for fear.*

Every line was drenched with meaning and emotion. Goodness me, but my son could act – and I felt terrible that I had not taken his aspirations more seriously before now – but as I listened, as his insistent, passionate tone demanded that I listen, I heard only the anguish he felt for his lost father:

> *There is no hope that ever I will stay,*
> *If the first hour I shrink and run away.*
> *Here on my knee I beg mortality,*
> *Rather than life preserved with infamy.*

Leo's relationship with Charles had never been an easy one. Charles' biggest fault as a father was giving Leo the impression that he was disappointed in him. Or, rather, leading Leo to believe he was not the son Charles had hoped for. Charles seemed closer to sturdy, playful Tom, even though Tom was not of Irvington blood. That in itself, I believed, was the problem. Leo was too like the gentle, cosseted soul Charles had been, before his father sent him to work at the docks and turned him into a 'real' man. Blond and delicate, his son was a living reminder to Charles of the vulnerable soul that lay beneath his male bravado. Charles was ashamed of his blood, ashamed of his background, and he saw both things reflected in the face and the gentle manners of his son. Like all sons, Leo longed only for his father to be proud of him.

These are by no means unusual feelings that can stand between a father and a son's love for each other, and they may take a lifetime to express and resolve. Charles and Leo were not given a lifetime. I had betrayed Leo by discouraging his dream, but there was no time for the indulgence of self-recrimination and guilt. I had to make things right at once.

'That was wonderful.' I clapped with such vigour that Tom whooped alongside me (although doubtless not entirely sure why). 'Your father would have been so proud of you.'

'Really?' Leo said. 'Do you *really* think he would?'

'Oh,' I said, 'for certain. You may have not known this about your father, Leo, but he had a *deep* admiration for actors. He thought it was a fine profession. He would have been thrilled to see how well you are doing.'

Leo looked at me with the slightest hint of scepticism. 'I never knew that,' he said queryingly.

'Why would you? He was always too busy to go to the theatre or movies, but when we were younger . . . '

I was, of course, lying through my teeth, Charles loathed all forms of entertainment except drinking and carousing with his fellow men – he thought going to the pictures was a terrible waste of time.

'You could not keep him out of the movie theatres. Want to know a secret?'

Leo and Tom, almost ten years apart, nodded in exactly the same childish way.

'I think he would have become an actor himself, if he'd had his own way.'

'Really?' Leo's eyes were shining with delight.

'Oh, most definitely,' I said. 'The problem was that your father was not talented, like you. He would have been so proud to see you perform, Leo.'

'He can see everything – he's up in heaven watching you,' said Bridie in a precious lucid moment, a gift, 'and I mean *every-thing*,' she finished, directing emphasis at my big fat lie.

From that moment on, everything changed.

I did not care that Leo's new-found happiness was based on a lie. What harm did it do? Charles *should* have been more proud of his son, his beautiful, adventurous son, when he was alive. And now that he was dead? Who was to say that he hadn't had a change of heart and wasn't looking down, bursting with pride, at his son reciting Shakespeare? The important thing now was that I was proud – and I showered Leo with my admiration and respect at every opportunity. As a result, the insufferable arrogance that he (and the rest of us) had been struggling with was transformed into the strong, quiet confidence of the lovely young man I had always known Leo would grow up to be.

As our friendship flourished once again, I regretted that I had not told Leo sooner how much his father loved him and was proud of him, and I felt grateful that I had been given the opportunity to make things right, albeit by random intuition rather than by design. There is no rule book – I knew that now; no right or wrong way to be a mother and protect your child from the slings and arrows of life. Even if you tried to shield them, they would get hit, and diligence was no protector. I was right to follow Leo to Hollywood, but I must have been doing something wrong for him to have run away in the way he did. Perhaps if I had done things differently: been more sympathetic, more alert to Leo's needs after Charles died . . . But then, as Bridie occasionally said in crude moments when Maureen and I would drive her mad with our endless analysing and regrets, 'For God's sake, if my aunt had balls, she'd be my uncle!'

*

At the beginning of the summer we were invited to another big party at the studios.

This time, it was I who didn't want to go.

I had barely been outside the door for months. Unable to get to my painting, my life had become a routine of grocery-shopping, housekeeping, cooking for the family, nursing and negotiating with Bridie.

I was content, in the sense that this was how my life had panned out. One day I would get back to my work, and I was anxious that it would happen at some point. Bridie was not a chore, as long as I didn't wish for things to be different – and so I didn't. Susan's support ensured that I never became overwhelmed with looking after her, and as for life beyond that? I had little interest in it. My boys were living with me; we ate and listened to the radio together. I was content.

However, the prospect of getting dressed up to go out to a function, especially one where I might run into Stan? The very idea horrified me. I could not remember the last time I had looked in a mirror, or had any reason to.

In that spirit I was amazed, but flattered, that Leo had even asked me to go.

'I can't leave Bridie,' I told him, 'you'll be grand on your own. Bring that nice girl you're always telling me about – the make-up girl . . . '

'Collette,' he said, 'ah, yes, I have some plans for her that night.'

So that was that, until the afternoon of the night of the party, when Susan came to look after Bridie – at Leo's invitation.

Unbeknown to me, Leo had gone to our neighbour, behind my back, and booked her for an overnight stint. Shortly after Susan arrived and grabbed the dinner things off me, Leo's young friend Collette – a hair and make-up girl he had become friendly with – arrived at the door and announced that she would be attending to me.

'The car arrives at seven,' she said, looking me up and down, 'so we don't have much time.' It was barely 4 p.m.

Collette was a pretty young girl, a year or two older than Leo, and from the way she was looking at my dashing son, I could tell she was madly in love with him. I felt bad for her, because I could tell equally that Leo had no real interest in her whatsoever, beyond her friendship and her skill in bringing his frumpy old mother up to scratch for this big event.

'Collette is a miracle-worker, Mam.'

'I wasn't aware that I needed a miracle,' I bristled, 'and I'm not going, Leo, no matter what you've arranged.'

I could not have objected more heartily, especially when I saw that Collette was carrying bags full of evening wear. 'I hope they fit you,' she said, then called across me, 'Leo, you were right, she looks about the same size as Barbara Stanwyck!'

Susan nearly fainted. 'Barbara Stanwyck! They're her clothes?'

'Well, the wardrobe-department clothes, but technically . . . ' the girl said.

Susan already had me by the arm and was dragging me into the bedroom.

'Ellie, you *have* to go. She's going to make you look like a movie star! For goodness' sake, sit down there and let the girl get on with her job. You've got less than three hours.'

'I don't know what's the matter with the lot of you,' I said, but inwardly I was pleased with the fuss; that my son had thought enough of his mother to set this up for me, and that I had made a friend of Susan, so that she was pushing me to get out and enjoy myself.

As I sat down at Collette's make-up table and she told me to 'relax', I had a moment of déjà vu. The last time somebody had applied make-up to my face had been when I first arrived in America, back in 1920, and was working for the socialite Isobel Adams, under Bridie's watchful eye. One weekend, left to our own devices in the apartment, my fellow maid, Sheila, and I had raided Isobel's wardrobe and gone to The Plaza masquerading as a couple of fine ladies. Sheila had cut my long hair into a bob that day, and I had worn it in that style for the past twenty years, until recently, when I had become tardy with myself and let it grow out. I remembered the sense of revelation as I was transformed from Irish country girl to glamorous city woman. It had seemed like such a significant journey back then: appearing more elegant, more sophisticated than I felt; being admired as I walked down the street gave me a sense of pride, of belonging.

How different the experience was now. Had life itself changed me, or simply the passing of time? I had believed myself plain as a girl, yet it seemed to me now, looking back, that I had been quite beautiful. Although time had taken its toll, I thought more of myself now than I did then. I had taken the abundance of youth for granted – as all young women do – but for all that, I did not miss it now that it had passed. I would not trade fresh, plump skin for the richness that my life experience had given me. I was lucky, in that I had no craving for my past. Whether that meant my life had been a success or a failure thus far, I could not say.

Collette pinned my hair back into fat curls and I closed my eyes as she administered her powder and paint, leaning back into the kind touch of her young, soft hands on my face. I didn't care so much how I looked at the end of it (there would be an improvement anyway), for the journey itself was the gift. As the young girl chattered to Leo about what colours she might use, and what would go with this dress and that, I could only think of what a pleasure it was to be sitting down, feeling the soft brush sweeping across my cheek, and the unusual circumstance of being ministered to – instead of the other way round. Susan came and put a cup of coffee in front of me, placing her hand on my shoulder as she left, in a signal of camaraderie. Another sister who had been sent to me, on my walk through life. I felt lucky. Really, despite everything, I had a lot to be grateful for.

'There,' Collette announced, 'ready to go.'

I opened my eyes and saw: myself. The myself I had forgotten, the elegant, ladylike Ellie who had cared about fashion, and style; the meticulous young woman who had applied powder and lipstick and rouge to her face every morning as a matter of course. With the miracle of make-up and Collette's magic touch, I looked the same as I had done ten years ago; I smiled at myself in the mirror and it was like saying 'hello' to an old friend.

Collette and Leo had picked out an outfit that would have looked at home on Ginger Rogers in a big dance number. It was a calf-length, emerald-green cocktail dress, low-cut but fashioned from a heavy duchesse satin that clung to my curves a little too tightly, but its pleated folds made it reasonably forgiving nonetheless.

Collette dusted my décolletage as I tried to arrange the satin neckline somewhat more modestly around my bosom.

'Pearls,' Leo said, standing back and observing me with the sharp eye of a wardrobe mistress, 'she needs her pearls.'

I wondered at my son's interest in fashion, but then men in the film world were different. More sensitive, artistic – with their talk of 'hair' and 'make-up' and 'wardrobe'; the constant focus on their appearance and image gave them an almost feminine air sometimes. I thought of my friends Conor and Dan on Fire Island and of their struggle to fit into society and wondered, briefly, if my own son was going to experience the same problems, and how my own liberal ideals would stand up, if that were the case. I pushed the thought aside, and filed it away in the already overflowing drawer of things I must worry about as the boys got older.

The party was in full swing by the time we arrived. 'Fashionably late,' Leo said. He was wearing full top hat and tails, with Collette (in the full-length frothy feathered costume I had refused earlier) on one arm and me on the other. The studio had been decorated in zebra-print wall hangings, mimicking the famous New York nightclub El Morocco, which I had been to in my younger days with my wild friend Sheila. That fact alone made me feel instantly sophisticated, and I sashayed across to the mirrored bar (doubtless also erected specifically for that evening), ordered a Martini, then reached into my handbag for the long cigarette holder that Collette had insisted I carry. I filled it from a box that was sitting on the countertop and allowed my delighted son to light my cigarette using the smart, slimline lighter he had recently acquired specifically for the purpose. I had fought with Leo about it, but he had easily won me over, arguing, 'I may not have learned to smoke properly yet, Mam, but I should at least be able to light a lady's cigarette with style.'

This, I decided, looking around the room, was a good idea after all. I had not been out to a party for a long time. Not on my own terms. The last time I had accompanied Leo and Freddie on an occasion like this I had been here for their sake alone, but on this night, with my dress and the cigarette holder, and my clever, marvellous son at my side, I felt as if I could truly take the room. As I finished my Martini and ordered another, I thought, *I might well do just that*, when I looked across the room and saw him.

CHAPTER THIRTY-THREE

Stan was surrounded, but not so much that I could not see the woman standing next to him. She was around my age and elegant, as described to me by Jackson, with shoulder-length, naturally sandy-coloured hair set into thick waves. She flicked the edges back on one side, so that I saw her profile: a long aquiline nose, sharp cheekbones and bright, intelligent eyes. She was drawing on a cigarette and blowing the smoke upwards as she listened intently to Stanislaw. As he reached his punchline she threw her head back. She had magnificent Hollywood teeth, I could see that from the other side of the room. Aside from that, she was understated, in a simple navy day-dress and medium courts. She was dressed like a writer, an intellectual – above all this actors' frippery; like me, before my son and his cohort had lured me into this ridiculous charade of an outfit.

'Look, there's Stan over there.'

Leo was bored already. The novelty of our grand entrance had worn off and he wanted to be off, mixing with his friends. Before I could fully take it in, my son had decided that he could palm me off on Stanislaw.

'Stan! Stan!' he called across.

He looked up and saw us. I raised my glass to him and smiled, as brightly as I could possibly manage. I must have drawn a line under the communication, because he made no attempt to come over, merely raised his glass back and smiled briefly at me. His girlfriend looked vaguely over, to see whom Stan had raised his glass to, but failed to identify me. She asked him something then. 'Who was that, Stanislaw?'

'Nobody.'

I could not hear either of them, but I knew what they had said. I also 'knew' that she called him Stanislaw, and not Stan. She had that formal, intellectual look about her that did not go in for shortening names, or for Americanizing European ones. She had the look of educated money. *She will have been to university*, I thought, *probably in Europe; possibly in England*. I hated her.

As for him. A 'nobody', was I?

'You go and play with your friends, Leo – I'll be fine here on my own.'

'Are you sure, Mam?'

It was a far cry from his abandonment of me at the last party we'd been to here. He was getting so grown-up, so mature, my son.

'Go,' I said, and shooed Collette to follow him. 'I'll be grand. So,' I called over to the barman, 'do you work all these parties?'

'Sure do, lady,' he said.

'I bet they get pretty wild sometimes?'

'Sometimes,' he said coyly. He was an actor, for sure. Would this be what Leo would end up doing, in a few years' time when the next contract didn't get renewed? Or the one after that? Tending the bar at studio parties, still hoping to score a big break?

'Do me a favour,' I said to the barman, throwing back my second Martini. 'I'm in the mood for a party tonight, so mix me up another one of these, and tell me, who is the wildest cad in this room?'

'You're sitting right next to him, lady,' said a man who had slid smoothly into the seat next to me, as if on cue. 'You gotta be Irish in a dress that colour?'

Either this guy was in fancy dress or he was a ladies' man all right. Thin moustache, chiselled face, tuxedo jacket and tie slightly askew. He was straight off the set of *Casablanca* – in fact he looked a bit like Errol Flynn.

'Matter of fact I am,' I said. 'Eileen Hogan – pleased to meet you.'

I didn't relish the thought of trawling around the room, so it was convenient that this Unsuitable Suitor was close at hand.

'I like Irish girls – you Catholic?'

'Is there any other religion?'

'Not that I know of,' he said. 'Catholic girls are great; experts on sin, every last one of them! Lovemaking is no fun if there isn't a bit of sin involved – whaddya say?'

He was a regular sleazeball and rather drunk. In fact, I wasn't entirely sure that this wasn't Errol Flynn himself. Either way, it didn't matter to me. I just wanted a good time. Or rather I just wanted to be seen having a good time, to get one up on Stan.

We drank some more, and I noted Stan looking across once or twice. My cohort, who had yet to introduce himself properly (giving me all the more reason to believe he *was* the notorious Flynn), dragged me over to the dance floor and, despite the state of him, turned out to be a very masterful dancer. He led me in a Lindy Hop and I amazed myself by keeping up with him. Fuelled with drink and the heat of the dance, and with anger towards my ex-beau, a strange alchemy occurred in me, whereby I was able to do dance steps that I had never done before, and before long it seemed that the whole room was gathered around us, clapping us on.

I had not felt so alive for years – so reckless and free. I was, in reality, far from either of those things, but I was drunk and I was dancing, so it felt the same, and in the moment that this lunatic man was spinning me round and round, it seemed that was all that mattered.

During my final wild turn I spotted Leo watching me and, unsure whether it was horror or admiration on his face (and deciding that he was probably uncertain himself), I wrenched myself away from my partner and walked over to him. As I did so, I noticed Stan moving in my direction, on his own. He caught my eye before I could turn, by which time Leo had already disappeared back into the crowd.

I was flushed and still a little heady from the dancing. I did not want to talk to Stanislaw Lilius.

'Ellie?'

'Hello, *Stan*,' I said. Oh God, I sounded drunk. Was I drunk?

'You look well,' he said. He wanted to be talking to me just as much as I wanted to be talking to him. In that spirit I decided to keep him there, talking.

'I like your new girlfriend, Stan. She has lovely *teeth*.'

He knew what I meant.

'They're her own,' he assured me. He could take a joke, I'd say that for him.

'Are you sure?' I said. 'All of them? Have you checked?'

The girlfriend was following behind him with two drinks. Actually, this could be fun.

'Who's your friend, Eileen?' Mr Lookalike-Errol-the-Peril arrived at the same time as Marjorie (now that I was drunk I could remember her name), the not-his-usual-type screenwriter.

I was about to address her and comment on her teeth when my erstwhile dance partner grabbed the two drinks from her hands, downed them one after the other and yanked her by the waist onto the dance floor into a dramatic tango. I was enraged!

The bitch had taken my composer, and now she was taking my dance partner. And while I'd been making a pure show of myself trying to jitterbug, they were doing a tango. I wanted to tango!

'Come on, Stan,' I said, grabbing him by the hand, 'let's show them how it's done.'

'I think it's time for you to go home,' he said.

Now that was *not* very nice. I did *not* like the way he said that.

'You're not being very nice,' I said, then I leaned back and, pointing at his girlfriend and my moustachioed suitor, shouted, 'Someone get that woman a rose, but tell her not to bite down too hard or her teeth might fall out!'

I remembered laughing, and then there was a gap when I don't remember anything at all.

I woke up in the front seat of Stan's car, which was parked outside my house and my friend was beside me.

My head hurt. He passed me his cigarette, then reached into the glove compartment, took out a big fat cigar and lit it, covering his face in a cloud of white, opulent, satiny smoke.

'Really, I must stop smoking those spindly little sticks. I hate them.'

'How long was I asleep?' I asked.

'About an hour,' he said. 'It's not very late, so I decided to let you sleep it off for a while, rather than drag you into the house, with Bridie in there. I thought . . . '

'Thank you,' I said. 'Sorry for ruining your party,' I added after a moment or two, 'and I'm sorry for insulting your girl-friend.' I picked up my bag from the floor. 'I had better go inside.'

'Marjorie is a great woman . . . '

I didn't want to have this conversation, so I opened the door and said, 'I'm sure she is, and I am sorry for insulting her.'

' . . . but she's not you.'

I closed the door again, a little too firmly.

'I am sick of all this, Stan. First, I discover that you are a womanizer, that you have slept with half of the starlets in Hollywood.'

'Maybe more than half,' he said, smirking.

'It's not funny, Stan! Then, it seems, you have this nice woman, whom you are supposed to be taking seriously, but have left standing at a party, to come here with me . . . '

'You are more important to me than all of these women, Ellie.'

'Again this stupid stuff about me being "the great love of your life". I don't believe you, Stan. You're playing me. If you are so in love with me, what are you doing with her? With the peroxide blonde in your house?'

Now it was his turn to speak his mind. Any hint of softness was gone from his voice.

'Life is not a movie, Ellie. I have written enough romantic scores – it's my speciality, actually – to know that. When I fell in love with you, I thought, "This is going to happen now for sure. I have met my great love. We will be together always. This is *meant* to happen" – just like in the stupid movies I have written. What a fool I was! So then, it didn't happen, so what should I do now? Put my life on hold? Never sleep with another woman, while I wait and hope for you?'

'Yes!' I shouted. 'That's exactly what you should do!'

He let out a laugh.

'I can't do that,' he said.

'Well then, Stanislaw Lilius, you don't really love me.'

'You are a practical woman, Ellie, you have to be realistic,' he said. 'How can you say this ridiculous thing? How can you say I don't love you, when I have opened my heart to you?'

'Because I have loved,' I said, 'and been loved. When you love somebody, you will wait forever for them.' Then I opened the car door and, before stepping outside, said, 'Women like me don't just fall into your lap, old man. You have to work for us. You have to be prepared to go to the ends of the Earth and back again.'

It was an arrogant thing to say, but Stan deserved it, and I left before he could make another trite comment. I knew he was watching me walk into the house, and was glad the emerald satin was wrapped so tightly around my curves. He didn't drive away until I was inside the house and out of sight.

Susan was in the hallway putting her coat on.

'I thought you'd be later,' she said. 'Good night?'

'Great,' I said, 'but it's good to be home. All in bed?'

'Bridie wouldn't go to bed. She said she wanted to see you when you got in – see how the party went. She was in a great mood tonight, Ellie; she and Tom were dancing to the radio earlier! She was very lucid too, chatting about the film stars you might meet – we had quite a conversation about Carole Lombard.'

'She does *not* approve!'

'So I gather! Anyway, she's having a bit of a snooze now. I'd say she's pretty exhausted, so she should go down easy. There's the remains of a macaroni cheese, if you like. Tom ate a pile of it before he went to bed. He should sleep late in the morning. Where's Leo?'

'I left him to it. I had too much to drink – Stan dropped me back.'

'Well, good for you,' she said, laughing. 'Ellie, you certainly deserve a good night out!'

She stood at the door to leave, and as she was about to go I had a sudden urge to embrace her. I put my arms around her and said, 'Thank you, Susan – for everything. I don't know what I would do without you.'

She patted my back and said, 'It's my pleasure, Ellie. Any time.'

'Maybe sooner than you think. Tomorrow, if this head gets any worse . . . '

'I'll call by in the morning.'

I felt good walking in through the hallway and into the living room. I had friends; life was good. To hell with Stan – I didn't need a man any more.

Bridie was snoozing in her chair. I put a pan of milk on the gas. The pair of us would have a nice hot drink and a chat, before I persuaded her into bed. I hoped she wouldn't give me too much trouble tonight; my head was starting to pound and I wasn't sure I had the energy for a fight – another one!

I broke some bread into two tin mugs and threw a spoonful of sugar in before pouring the warm milk in on top. The concoction was called 'goodie'. Maidy used to make it for us as children in Ireland – the ultimate warming bedtime snack – and I had carried on the habit with my own children. Some days, it was all Bridie would eat for me.

I laid the two mugs down on the table. 'There you are now, Bridie.'

When she didn't wake up I reached over and touched her hand. She seemed chilly, so I put my hand on her shoulder and, as I did so, her head lolled forward and to one side.

A noise came out of me – a short, sharp shout of sudden, involuntary grief.

Bridie was gone.

CHAPTER THIRTY-FOUR

I was not ready for Bridie to die, but as soon as I realized she was gone, I knew that it was her time.

She would have liked to hold on until I got home, perhaps, but she didn't. Even Bridie wasn't so organized that she could time her death down to the last minute.

Perhaps, after another few months of her health declining, I might have grown intolerant and waited for this moment. Bridie had known that, and would not have wanted to make a drudge or a nag out of me. Her pride would not allow her to decline any further than she did. She was old, and her time was now. It was for the best.

I knew all of those things and yet I was completely distraught. Even when you know it is coming, even when you expect or even wish for it, death is always a cruel and unexpected joker.

For a moment I sat tapping her hand, trying to wake her, refusing to believe the obvious truth of her passing. Then, afraid that Tom would wake up, or that Leo would come in from the party, I ran out of the house and got Susan.

Susan was shocked, certain that Bridie had been alive when she left. 'I am sure of it, Ellie – I am so sorry . . . '

'Never mind, Susan.' And I found myself saying, 'These things happen', as if death were some unhappy domestic accident, like an overturned saucepan or laundry dropped in a muddy puddle. *Bridie would have enjoyed her death to be seen in such terms,* I thought.

Between us, we carried Bridie into her bedroom and laid her out on the bed, as if she were asleep.

'Will you be all right,' Susan asked. 'Is there anything you need me to do?'

'No, you go home,' I said. 'I'll call the funeral home in the morning.'

I sat with her then, my surrogate mother, my old friend.

In Ireland we waked our dead. Sat with their bodies overnight until their spirit was gone, talked to them, celebrated their life.

I was not yet ready to send my Bridie out of the world. So I held her hand as it stiffened, and tried to rub some of my own warmth into it. I kissed her cheeks, splashing them with my hot tears. I combed her wispy hair and tidied it back from her face. I summoned her back by telling her how much she had meant to me in my life, and I joked that if she didn't return to me this instant I would bury her in nail varnish and lipstick and a gaudy blouse! When I was satisfied that she was gone, I placed her arms in a cross on her chest, took her rosary beads from her apron pocket, where she always kept them, and arranged them in her old, bony fingers. I closed the door to her room and went down to the kitchen, and cried and cried and cried myself out. Leo came in and found me.

'What's the matter?' he asked, full of concern. He looked round, perhaps expecting to see Stan. 'You ran off from the party, and Stan said . . . '

'Bridie's dead.'

I blurted it out. I don't know why. Perhaps to remind myself, more than to tell him, or perhaps because I was afraid that if I left it, I might find it hard to tell him at all.

'Oh.'

'She's in the bedroom – do you want to see her?'

'No,' he said, 'no.'

He sat down on a kitchen chair and bowed his head into his chest. Suddenly my son looked very small, and very young to me. The man, the movie actor, was gone and Leo was the shy, vulnerable ten-year-old boy whom Charles had brought to me all those years ago.

I walked over and, standing next to the chair, buried his head in my bosom. 'I'm sorry,' I said, 'I'm sorry, I'm sorry, I'm sorry . . . ' And the two of us wept together. Leo wept for Bridie and for Charles; I wept for them, but also for all the others I had lost: my parents, Maidy and Paud, John. I wept for the children I had carried and lost, and for the two adopted sons I had, and for the fact that they would grow up and leave me. I wept for the knowledge I now had that life itself was simply a process of loss after loss. As soon as you tried to hold anything good in life, to hold it close, to own it, it would fly away. Jealousy, anger, fear – those things you could hold forever and nobody would take them from you; but love, joy, the unspeakable bliss of a baby's breath on your face, the passionate first kiss from a beloved . . . Blink and they were gone. When you love something or someone, you want to hold onto them tight and never let them go, but life doesn't work like that. You had to take the things you loved and scatter them about you like petals, throw them to the wind as if they meant nothing to you. Then God might send you something else to love; someone new to care for. Then again, He might not. Life was, with or without God, a chancy business. The only hope was to let go. Of everything.

The funeral director came the following morning and took Bridie's body away. I called Freddie and he came straight round.

313

'Will you be okay?' he asked. 'You must be pretty shook up?'

'Sure,' I said, 'I'll be fine. I've got my boys.'

In truth, I felt as if my world had collapsed. I was there for my boys to lean on – not the other way round. If I leaned back now, there was no one to catch me. Bridie had been sick and I had been looking after her, but – she had still been there. Maureen had her own family to look after and, in any case, she was so far away.

As I said the words out loud, 'I've got my boys', I realized: that is *all* I had. Two young dependants; no husband, no parents, no family. A handful of friends, who were busy with their own lives.

I was on my own.

We took Bridie back to New York to bury her with Mr Flannery. It cost a fortune, shipping her back. Funeral costs and travel costs were at a premium, with a war on, but it was what Bridie deserved. In any case I was blessed in that money was still not an issue for me. I had grown up poor, but with my art selling well and the businesses I had sold in Ireland, it would be a long time before I could not afford to bury my loved ones in style.

Bridie would not have seen it that way, and I could almost hear her huffing and puffing after me, as her ornate mahogany coffin was loaded onto the train at Union Station: 'All this fuss and expense – burn me and pour the ashes down the sink with the tea leaves; sure, I'm dead now, so what difference does it make?'

'You'll get the full bell, book and candle Catholic High Service, Bridie Flannery, like it or not,' I replied in my head, 'for all the Masses you made me go to over the years. I'll not bury you a pagan and have the curse of you on my head forever!'

Bridie's voice was so ingrained in me that I knew she would

be talking to me, and I to her, for the rest of my life. Her over-powering personality, her practical goodness and her sense of right and wrong were her legacy. In that sense, Bridie could never die. Perhaps that is where people truly go when they die: into the hearts of the people who love them.

Where Bridie truly belonged was back in Ireland, buried with her people. However, she had never been back there – not once, in all the years I had known her. In fact, not since she had come to America as a young girl of sixteen. I had offered to pay her passage, more than once offered to take her home myself, but she always declined.

Bridie's life was in America – Ireland was her fantasy, her Hollywood dream. Had she returned, she once told me, she would have found her family home empty and derelict, her parents dead and their graves overgrown.

'Sometimes it's best just to leave things as you remember them,' she said.

I had packed up a lot of the house before I came east, but I had left Leo behind. It hurt to leave him there – for both of us – but we had decided that he did not need to attend Bridie's funeral. He had loved her, and now she was gone. It was enough that he had lost his father and barely grieved for him before his nan died. His life in Hollywood would keep him distracted and busy, and keep the grief at bay.

I arranged for Freddie to move back into my house in Los Feliz to look after Leo. The house was paid for until the end of the summer and, as Freddie was still pursuing his idea of being an actor's agent, it suited him to free up some cash to continue paying his debts and save for a new office. In any case, Leo had already begun rehearsals for another movie, to start shooting in a few weeks' time – another reason for him not coming to New York, and another reason to support Freddie in his endeavours.

Bridie was old and, while all death is shocking, sometimes it is more expected than others. She would have wanted Leo to be in the movie, more than to have him weeping at her graveside. For all that Bridie spoke her mind, she lived her life in the shadow of other people. Her joy was in accommodating their success. It would have killed her all over again to think that her death had stood in the way of Leo's career.

I was not entirely happy that Crystal was part of the package, but then you can't have everything, and Freddie was trustworthy enough to counteract her craziness. Leaving Leo behind was hard, but I had to let him go. Perhaps Bridie moving on at the time she did had helped me to see that. People are temporary gifts, not permanent structures. Even – especially – your children.

I stood at the door of the house and held his face in my hands and told him I loved him.

His beautiful eyes filled with tears and I said, 'Don't cry, Leo.'

I don't know why I said it. I always encouraged my sons' tears. Perhaps I was afraid that I would not be strong enough to leave him.

He smiled and swallowed, and held me for a long time as we hugged. He was a young man now, but he was still as slim and delicate as he had been as a boy.

'Go in,' I said, 'I don't want you waving at the door.'

As our car drove off I didn't look back, but pulled Tom into my side and clutched tightly at my purse. I had not booked return tickets because I was uncertain when, or indeed, whether we would return to Los Angeles.

We had a full service out in Yonkers. The church was packed. Maureen and her family and Tom and I occupied the front pews, and every shopkeeper and supplier in the area came. Even Hilla showed her face, and Conor and Dan came in from Fire Island.

Afterwards we went back to the house, where Maureen and all our local friends from the women's cooperative had laid on a fantastic spread. The place was packed, with people milling in and out of each room, old friends and new. There was a warm party atmosphere: a home where Bridie had lived could not have been any other way. She might have been there at the stove, scalding the pot for more tea, rolling pastry as she talked, refusing to sit down and be attended to, even at her own funeral.

The table in the dining room was groaning with food like you might see at a Tudor banquet. Everyone coming in the door had an offering: brown bread, lasagne, corned beef, honey-roasted ham, a smoked salmon – the final feast for a woman who had put so much food in our bellies over the years.

'When are you coming back to us on Fire Island?' Conor and Dan asked. 'We assume you're in New York for good now?'

Hilla was hovering nearby and her ears pricked up.

'I'm not sure,' I said, only realizing then that I wasn't certain if I truly wanted to come back. My friends were here, but my eldest son was in Los Angeles. For the first time since I had come to New York, and had fallen instantly and madly in love with the city, it did not feel entirely like home. Nowhere did any more. Bridie, it seemed, was my home.

I left early with Tom and went back to the apartment. I was less in a mood for revelling than I had thought I would be. It had been a long week since Bridie had passed, and I was exhausted from all the emotion and the travelling.

Tom fell dramatically and instantly asleep as soon as his head hit the pillow. I crawled in beside him and lay down for a while, but I could not sleep; I had a chill and couldn't get warm.

So I got up and went out to the kitchen and put the kettle on to fill a hot-water bottle.

While I was in the kitchen there was a gentle tap on the door.

One of the neighbours come to sympathize over my loss, perhap
I did not feel I could endure another minute of sympathy, b
nonetheless something compelled me to open it.

Standing in front of me was the last person I expected to se

'Would this – by any chance – be the ends of the Earth?' Sta
said, smiling.

EPILOGUE

The year is 1950 – and I am fifty years of age. I have lived
through two world wars and the death of two husbands, and I
am happy to have survived both.

I have realized that it is better not to simply dream of a good
life, but to live life as if it were the one you had always hoped
for. I never thought I would end up living in Hollywood – the
land of other people's dreams – yet here I am, existing contentedly in circumstances I had neither decided upon nor dreamed
of. I am living with a man who is too old to marry, on the opposite side of the world to where I came from, and the other side
of the continent to New York, the place I had believed I would
never tire of.

We live in Stan's house in the hills, and we winter in New
Mexico, where we built a cabin so that I could work, and live
sometimes, in the company of other artists. In the desert, which
I have come to love as much as I once loved the sea.

I am here because of the three men in my life.

Stan did not leave my side after that day he turned up at my
apartment in Manhattan seven years ago. We fought many times
after that, and we still do – but never again over his loyalty or
his love for me. Those two things are beyond issue now, for
both of us. As soon as I saw him standing in my doorway like

that, something in me was able to let go. I threw my petals to the wind, then I fell back and he caught me. Stan does what no man has ever truly done for me: not John and not Charles. Stan holds me up.

Tom is nearly the age that Leo was when he ran away to become a movie actor. He is so different from his sensitive older brother, still a ball of powerful physical energy – I am assured that he will get a sports scholarship to compensate for his lack of interest in academia or art. Tom is a complete mystery to me; his sporting prowess is an exoticism beyond my comprehension, but I adore him all the more for it.

Leo is directing, which is a relief. The acting never really took off, but he didn't let go of his love for films, and his time at the studio gave him a good grounding to find himself another career in the movies. He has not married, and shown no signs of doing so yet. I don't know what that means, and I have no intention of asking. Some things are best left unsaid. He knows I judge nobody, and will always love him, and the gift of his confidence is his alone to give.

Parenting is a pleasure surely, but it seems that every ounce of joy it gave me was offset by the pain I felt on watching my sons grow away from me. I discovered, late, that there was no magic trick to keeping them close. The harder I held them, the more they bucked to escape me.

Each day, as I have watched my boys grow from small children into strong, confident boys and then into handsome young men, I wonder why God gave me such luck by bringing them into my life as He did. I still believe God is a cruel trickster, but I no longer worry what He has in store for me. I realize that I am utterly in His command now – or, rather, in the command of whatever force He empowers, if 'He' in fact exists at all. Stan says he is my Irish Catholic fantasy – it is one of the things we fight about. Sometimes I think I might have lost my faith entirely, if I were not living with an atheist and wanted to annoy him. Instead I pray every day (and I try to keep the tone of warning out of my voice as I ask Him to keep my sons safe) because life – all it has given me, and all it has taken away, its gifts and thefts – has finally humbled me.

Stan chooses to write film scores for big movies, rather than the teaching and the more academic composing that I know are his passion. When I confront him on the matter he merely tells me again that his passions have changed; that his art has taken second place to loving me – 'an artist who has enough integrity for us both. In any case, what use would a woman like you have for a penniless professor?'

However plainly I dress, however simple my cooking or small my daily desires for a piece of nice chocolate or a smile from one of my sons, Stan will always see me as the glamorous goddess of his dreams. Perhaps that is what Hollywood does to you after all – you live out your dreams, or life itself becomes a dream.

Stan showers me with love, with gifts and compliments that I have no need or desire for. In my younger years such overt vulnerability in a man, such a desire to please, such frantic proclamations of love would have irritated me. While they frightened me at first, now I relish them, possibly because I have no need of them any more. I am learning to receive love with grace, and have found it to be a harder thing – tenfold harder – than giving love.

Manzanar closed in 1945 when the war ended, and Suri returned to her life with Jackson. Her parents-in-law moved to Florida and never returned, but Suri did not regret the three years she spent with them in the camp. When she got home she was moved to see the painting that I had done of her given pride of place; she approached me and we resumed our friendship, which turned out to be all the richer for my recklessness in trying to rescue her, and her passionate rebuff. As time passed, we came to understand, I think, that we were both simply women who cared.

Freddie is an actor's agent, a very successful one – things worked out exactly as he predicted they would. The studio system fell apart in the mid-1940s and he was there to swoop up the stars. Who would have thought it, but Freddie is now one of the most powerful men in Hollywood. It was he who found Stan and sent him to me after Bridie died, but he was less lucky in love. Crystal fell in with another bad man, found solace in drugs and drink, and nobody knows where she has ended up. Freddie spends his one-week vacation every year searching for her in the bars and whorehouses in downtown LA. I am certain she is dead, but Freddie still goes out there and looks for her. He has had a string of girlfriends, and is sure to marry one of them soon enough. But Crystal was his first love.

As John was mine, and as I am Stan's – and true love never lets you go. It grips you and carries you to the ends of the Earth – and back again if you're lucky, as Stan has been with me, and as I was with John Hogan, all those years ago.

ACKNOWLEDGEMENTS

I would like to thank the following people for their contribution to the researching and writing of this novel:

In Los Angeles, musicians Songa Lee and Jeff Babko, old friend and fellow writer Sophie Ulliano and artist Charlene Gawa. In New York, the fantastic team at HarperCollins US, and Irish-American authors Peter Quinn and Honor Molloy for their endless help and literary cheerleading. Also a big thanks to good friends Jimmy Kelly and Lisa Ferguson and their sons Silus and Marcus for putting me up *and* putting up with me in their beautiful Yonkers home.

Garry King and Gunnar Senum for their invaluable introduction to Fire Island, and my trusty intern and research assistant Lily Stoicheff for her great work.

Fellow writer Helen Falconer for her generous and invaluable first-draft notes, and Martin Smith for his fact-checking, proofreading and being my 'film-buff nerd'.

Special thanks to the UK Pan Macmillan team, especially my editor Trish Jackson for her support, and the talented Natasha Harding for her detailed and invaluable appraisal. Publicists Kate James and Chloe Healy, publisher Jeremy Trevathan and the talented marketing team, cover designers and proofreaders who always put so much effort into my books – thanks to you all.

Agents Marianne Gunn O'Connor, Pat Lynch and Vicki Satlow for managing me and keeping the faith and the money flowing.

My husband Niall Kerrigan for letting me go to the US on those extended trips, and my mother-in-law Renee Kerrigan for looking after my three boys when I am gone.

My beautiful sons Leo and Tom for their constant inspiration (and temporary use of their names.)

Lastly, my mother Moira, for letting me read aloud my work to her every day and providing me with a seemingly endless supply of love and encouragement.

ELLIS ISLAND
by
KATE KERRIGAN

ISBN: 978-0-230-74214-7

**She was living the American dream in the 1920s
but her heart was still at home . . .**

Ellie and John are childhood sweethearts. Marrying young, against their families' wishes, the couple barely survive the poverty of rural Ireland. When John is injured in the War of Independence, Ellie emigrates 'for one short year' to earn the money for the operation which will allow him to walk again.

Arriving in Jazz Age New York, Ellie is seduced by the energy and promise of America. When the year is up Ellie chooses to stay, returning to Ireland only when her father dies. A trunk full of treasures helps fuel Ellie's American dream, but as the power of home and blood and old love takes hold she realizes that freedom isn't the gift of another country, it comes from within.

Praise for Kate Kerrigan

'Kerrigan is a lovely writer and her book breaks
from the traditional mould'
Sunday Tribune

'Wholesome and satisfying'
Heat

CITY OF HOPE

by

KATE KERRIGAN

ISBN: 978-0-230-74771-5

**An uplifting, inspiring and heart-warming story
of a woman truly ahead of her time.**

It is the 1930s and when her beloved husband, John, suddenly
dies, young Ellie Hogan decides to leave Ireland and return to
New York. She hopes that the city's vibrancy will distract her
from her grief. But the Depression has rendered the city unrec-
ognizable – gone is the energy and party atmosphere that Ellie
once fell in love with, ten years before. And while she is used
to rural poverty back home in Ireland, the suffering she sees in
New York is an entirely different proposition.

Walking around the neighbourhood, Ellie sees destitute families and hungry children on every street corner. The horror of
it all jolts Ellie out of her own private depression. Pushing thoughts
of her homeland and her dead husband firmly out of her mind,
she plunges headfirst into her new life to try and escape her
grief. All her passion and energy is poured into running a home
and refuge for the homeless. Until, one day, someone she thought
she'd never see again steps through her door.

'I devoured this book in one sitting – I LOVED IT!'
MARIAN KEYES